Also by Shana Galen

NOV - - 2017

THIRD SON'S a Charm

SHANA GALEN

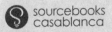

sourcebooks
casablanca

Published by Sourcebooks Casablanca, an imprint of Sourcebooks, Inc.
P.O. Box 4410, Naperville, Illinois 60567-4410
(630) 961-3900
Fax: (630) 961-2168
sourcebooks.com

Printed and bound in Canada.
MBP 10 9 8 7 6 5 4 3 2 1

For Sophie Jordan, who is one of the finest writers I know and a genius at brainstorming. Thank you for giving me the idea for this series. I'm so honored to call you friend.

One

EWAN MOSTYN, THIRD SON OF THE EARL OF PEMBROKE, prowled the main room of Langley's gaming hell like a golden-maned lion stalked the savannah. Ewan moved through the ornate room with its red and black damask walls, gilded moldings, and glittering chandeliers as though he owned it. He had a share in the club, so his proprietary air was not wholly without merit. The illusion that he belonged among such opulence and fragility was somewhat less warranted.

As his feet sank into the scarlet rugs, his gaze passed over the club's dealers, men who straightened at his mere glance. Then he nodded to the courtesans—bold women whose eyes dipped, nevertheless, when they met his. Finally, he studied the patrons. Even these wealthy, powerful men studiously avoided garnering his attention.

Unless they were idiots, like the two men Ewan approached now.

Charles Langley had politely ordered the anemic son

of the Duke of Suffolk out of the club. The pup's debts were mounting, and his frequent bouts of inebriation were becoming tiresome. But since the lad had not taken his leave, he had become Ewan's problem.

Ewan did not like problems.

"She's mine for the night," Suffolk's son said loudly, poking another man in the chest and hauling a painted tart to his side.

The other man was somewhat older than the duke's son and rather more sober. "And I told you, sir, that I have already paid for the lady's charms. Kindly unhand her and scamper home to your father."

Ewan planted his long, muscled legs beside the two gentlemen and crossed his arms over his chest. The older man widened his eyes until his eyebrows all but reached his graying sandy brown hair. "Sir," he said with a quick bow. "I-I-I'm terribly sorry for the disruption. Lord Pincoch and I were having a slight disagreement."

Ewan looked past the older gentleman and fixed his eyes on the duke's son. All around them, conversation ceased or dimmed to mere whispers.

"Get out," Ewan said. He was a man of few words, which meant those he spoke now carried even more weight.

Pincoch was too deep in his cups to realize the danger he faced. "I'll leave when I damn well please, and no half-wit with more brawn than brains will give me orders."

Ewan felt a muscle in his jaw tense. Not personal, he told himself. But it was too late. The old fury bubbled inside him, and he struggled to contain it. His face betrayed none of the struggle, which must have been why the pup swaggered forward, pulling the tart with him.

Ewan took quick stock of the situation. The lad's friends stood behind him, uncertain what to do. The older man had his allies as well. And the tart was gasping for breath beneath Pincoch's tight hold. Ewan's course of action was clear, though Langley would undoubtedly complain about the damage later. Hell would freeze over before Ewan allowed a man to call him a half-wit and walk away in one piece.

With a speed that belied his size, Ewan grasped Pincoch's free hand and wrenched it behind his back. Pincoch immediately released the whore, who sank to her knees and gulped in a breath. Pincoch screeched for help, and that was the signal for his friends, similarly inebriated, to jump into the fray. The four men charged Ewan, who rammed Pincoch up against a gilded mirror with one hand and tossed a man back by the throat with another.

The older man grabbed the woman and pulled her under a green baize table, where several other patrons had taken refuge. Those still out in the open regretted their decision when one of Pincoch's friends heaved a chair at Ewan. It crashed into his back, and he growled with annoyance. Still holding the lad in place, he turned to see another chair sailing toward him. Ewan reached up, caught the furnishing in midair, and thrust it back. It crashed into a faro table, overturning table, chairs, and chips.

Bereft of chairs, Pincoch's friends manned a frontal assault. Ewan finally released Pincoch, and when the boy sank to the ground, Ewan shoved a booted foot against his chest to hold him in place. Both hands free now, he threw a punch with his right and slammed one of his attackers back with his left. Something crashed, but Ewan didn't have time to note what it was before the next man hurtled into him. He struck Ewan in the jaw, and the offense landed the man a blow to the breadbasket and an elbow to the throat. When he was on the ground, wheezing for air, another man took advantage of the lull to dance before Ewan.

Ewan almost rolled his eyes. This one thought he was Gentleman Jackson or another renowned pugilist. If there was somewhere Ewan felt at home, it was in the boxing ring. This man danced more than he fought, and while he did his fancy footwork, Ewan slammed a left hook into his jaw.

Heaving for breath but not willing to show weakness, Ewan turned his head to take in the room. "Anyone else?"

No one moved.

With a nod, Ewan lifted Pincoch's limp body by the arms and dragged him past the broken tables and chairs, the shattered mirror, and the cracked marble statue. Ewan winced. That statue was new, and he fully expected Langley to opine about it for hours. A footman opened the door of the club, and Ewan tossed Pincoch out onto the street.

He turned and saw several other patrons donning coats and wraps, preparing to depart as well.

That was just what Ewan needed—for Langley and the club to lose blunt because Ewan had scared the patrons away. Goddamn it. Ewan couldn't do anything right. He tried to do his job as the muscle of the club, but it seemed he was always making some misstep or other. He'd already broken the statue. He couldn't be responsible for a mass exodus as well. Ewan positioned himself in front of the door and pointed back to the gaming tables. "Inside."

"But I…" A man who had just donned his beaver hat tried to move toward the exit.

Ewan pointed to him, then at the main room, and the man put a hand to his throat. "Very well. If you insist, I could play a game or two."

He turned back to the main room, followed by the rest of the crowd.

One man, however, stood his ground. He looked as though he had recently arrived and seemed in no hurry either to step inside or flee back out the door. Instead, he leaned on his walking stick and cocked his head. He was a tall man—not as tall as Ewan but taller than average—and he had a thin form and dark hair under a beaver hat. His great coat was fine quality, as was the ebony walking stick with a silver handle and tip.

"You are one of the Earl of Pembroke's, are you not?" the man asked.

Resigned, Ewan leaned against the doorjamb, where the footmen welcomed patrons and took their coats. Some of the patrons liked to talk. Ewan had found he was not required to answer.

"Not his heir or even the spare. I know those two well. You are the soldier. The third born—or is it the fourth? I know you have a sister."

Ewan cut his eyes to the man, and then disguised his

interest by focusing on one of the flickering candles in a chandelier over a table where a group played piquet.

"Well, no matter. I had heard you were strong. You fought with Lieutenant Colonel Draven in the war."

Ewan kept his eyes on the candle. It was an ordinary candle, sputtering and fighting to stay lit. In this world, even a candle fought for light, resisted being snuffed out.

"Now that I see you, I'm not surprised you survived," the man said, continuing as though the two were having a conversation. "You are uncommonly strong. And you do not like to be called stupid."

Ewan turned his head sharply toward the gentleman, who held up his hands. "For what it is worth, I do not think you stupid. No man with less than all his wits about him survived the war against Napoleon. In fact, I would like to hire you."

Ewan narrowed his gaze, almost disappointed. It was not the first time he'd been propositioned. Men had tried to hire him to perform in entertainments or to box for them. Women wanted him for bedsport. Ewan liked his place at Langley's just fine. He enjoyed the modest income his portion of the club afforded him and parted with very little of it to rent a room on the second floor. As his father would not deign to step foot in a gaming hell, Ewan need not trouble with unwanted visits from the earl or any other member of his family.

"I suppose this is not the place to discuss such matters," the man said. "Would you come to my residence?" He removed a card from a silver case and passed it to Ewan.

Ewan barely glanced at it. The light in the vestibule was too dark to read anything anyway. He put the card in his pocket.

"Right. The day after tomorrow at ten in the morning then, if you are interested. It is honest work, and I will reward you handsomely. I will give you more details when you call."

Ewan moved aside and the gentleman passed. A footman opened the door so the yellow lights and bright sounds of the gambling hell spilled into the dark street. When he was alone again, Ewan withdrew the card and moved into a rectangle of light.

"Rrr…iii…D," he said slowly, staring at one of the words on the card. "Rid." His head hurt as the letters moved and jumped. He stuffed the card back into his pocket and crossed his arms again.

When the last patron had left the tables and the sun was peeking over the horizon, Ewan did one last turn about the club. Maids swept and dusted. Sweet girls, most of them smiled at him when he passed. Ewan headed to the kitchen. Another perquisite of living here was the food. For as long as he could remember, he'd always had a voracious appetite.

In the kitchen, Mrs. Watkins had a plate ready for him, the mountain of food buried under a thick slab of buttered bread. "Now, Mr. Mostyn," she said, wiping her red hands on her apron. "You sit down right here. I have some nice potatoes and a stew."

The kitchen was comfortable and inviting, and Ewan sat, feeling the chair creak under his weight. He drank deeply from the ale in the glass before him, but he did not shovel food into his mouth as he usually did. Instead, he reached into his pocket and laid the card on the table. He hadn't been able to stop thinking about it.

The cook frowned at it and picked it up. Her kitchen maid, a mousy girl who couldn't have been more than fourteen, glanced his way timidly, then continued scrubbing the pots. The cook held the card close to her round face, red and glistening from the heat. "It's the card of the Duke of Ridlington." She put a hand to her heart. Then she laid the card on the table again and pointed to the words. "See, it says 'His Grace, the Duke of Ridlington.'"

Ewan nodded slowly. He was surprised a duke wanted his services. This was no mere request for an exhibition of strength then. It might be legitimate work. Ewan pointed to the other words on the card.

The cook turned the card and peered at it. "That's his house: 2 Berkeley Square."

"Thank you." Mildly intrigued, Ewan lifted the card and stuffed it back in his pocket. Now he dug into his dinner. His mother would have fainted if she had seen him eating thus. But his mother was dead, and Mrs. Watkins only cared if he enjoyed her food, not if he used the correct fork or a napkin to dab his mouth.

"I wonder why the Duke of Ridlington gave you that card," the cook said, wiping the table where he sat, although it was already clean. "I think he hopes to steal you away."

Ewan wondered the same, but he didn't want to show his interest. He lifted one shoulder, then ate another helping of potatoes.

"Seems like you could do better than this." She gestured to the kitchens, which were as nice as any Ewan had seen. "Surely your own father could find a place for you."

And this was why Ewan hadn't wanted to show interest. He didn't always like where such conversations led. Talk of Ewan's father soured his stomach. As the third-born son, he was expected either to become a soldier or enter the clergy. Ewan had done his part for his country. After Napoleon was defeated, Ewan had sold his captain's commission and left without a backward glance. His father had probably wished he'd died in the war, but Ewan had lived. Now, no one and nothing could ever force him to join the army again.

As for the clergy, that prospect was laughable. Ewan couldn't even read the Bible, much less stand up every Sunday and drone on about it. If God had wanted Ewan to enter the church, He shouldn't have made him such a lackwit.

No, Ewan liked working at Langley's just fine. Ewan had the money he had made from his days in the army and the sale of his commission, but a little more never hurt and it gave him something to do. He didn't exactly belong, but then he'd always been a misfit. He didn't belong anywhere—anywhere but the Draven Club.

Ewan shoved the last bite into his mouth, nodded at Mrs. Watkins, and carried the plate to the kitchen maid so she could wash it. Then, ducking his head so he wouldn't bang it on the low lintel, he left the kitchen and made his way through the club's back rooms, with their gilded mirrors, mahogany tables, and red velvet chairs and couches. His mother would have called it garish, but Ewan rather liked it. After ensuring all was as it should be, Ewan climbed the stairs to his room. Using the small key, he opened the door and stepped inside, locking the door after him.

He sat on the bed, removed his boots and coat, set Ridlington's card on the floor, and flopped down on the bed. In addition to the bed, the room held a wardrobe and a table with a basin for washing. The room had one small window, which Ewan had covered with black cloth to block the sun. The room held nothing else—no books, no papers, no personal mementos. The walls were white and unadorned with paintings.

The room, simple in purpose, was just as he liked it. Nothing to confuse or distract him. He closed his eyes and slept.

When he awoke several hours later, it was to the rumbling of his belly. He might have gone down to the kitchens and found bread and cold stew, but when he sat up and dropped his feet onto the floor, they landed on Ridlington's card. He still did not know what to do about it, but he knew who could tell him. Neil Wraxall would know what to do. Neil always knew.

And Neil would be at their club.

Ewan stripped, washed, and dressed again in one of his finer coats. He didn't don a cravat. He didn't like anything tight on his neck. The club didn't require a cravat. The club didn't require anything except that the members had served in Lieutenant Colonel Draven's special unit.

The suicide unit, as Neil called it.

The survivors called themselves the Survivors. They called Ewan the Protector.

Ewan might have taken a hack to the Draven Club, but it was a sunny, though unseasonably cool, spring afternoon and the walk from Langley's on Piccadilly and St. James's to King Street was short. Besides, he liked to pass Boodles. The ancient lords hobbling inside always hobbled a bit faster when they caught sight of him.

He hadn't walked very far when he was surprised by a streak of brown and white bounding past him and into St. James's, which was crowded with carts and carriages at this time of day. The creature barely avoided being trampled by a horse pulling a cart filled with produce. It scurried away from the large hooves and wheels and then huddled, frozen, in the center of the street.

"Watch out!" a woman's voice called right before she barreled into him. But as he was large and she was much smaller, the impact sent her reeling. He might have caught her and set her on her feet if she hadn't scrambled away, heading directly into the street.

Ewan watched in disbelief as she stumbled directly in the path of a coach and four, whose driver had obviously given his horses free rein. She looked up, saw the approaching conveyance, but instead of jumping back onto the curb, she ran into the coach's path and scooped up the little brown and white scrap of fur. Now both she and the furry creature would be trampled and run down.

Ewan didn't think. He acted. Heart pounding in his suddenly tight chest, he jumped into the street, crossing to the woman in two huge strides. He yanked her out of the path of the coach and four, feeling the breath of the horses on his neck as he shoved her to safety on the other side of St. James's. His heart thudded painfully against his ribs with what he recognized as fear and panic. They'd almost died. For a moment, St. James's became a blood-soaked field, and the clatter of hooves was the sound of rifles. Ewan closed his eyes and drew a slow breath. And then he shook the memory off and came back to the present.

But his hands were still shaking.

Ewan had shoved the woman a bit hard, and she'd fallen to her knees. He would have to beg her forgiveness, though she should really be the one groveling at his feet with gratitude. But instead of looking up at him with appreciation in her eyes, she scowled. "I almost crushed Wellington."

Ewan looked right then left for the duke. Not seeing the general, Ewan glanced in confusion back down at the woman. She pointed to the fur ball. "My dog. You pushed me so hard I almost crushed him."

So the dog was named Wellington, and she blamed Ewan for the danger to the animal. Ewan frowned at her. Was he supposed to apologize for saving her life and that of the beast? Perhaps she had become momentarily disoriented by the tumult. "You ran into the street," he pointed out. Anyone could see the street was busy and dangerous.

She waved a hand dismissively, as though the fact that she had almost been flattened under the hooves and wheels flying past them was but a small matter.

"Wellington escaped his collar and leash at Green Park. I have been chasing him all this way."

That explained why she had been on St. James's Street, which was typically the domain of men, and why the dog was running. It did not explain why she did not thank him, but he'd come to expect women to be difficult. Ewan grasped her arm and pulled her to her feet. Belatedly, he realized he should have offered her his arm, but now it was too late. "Where do you live?"

Now it was her turn to frown. She had light green eyes framed by delicate brows, which slanted inward in confusion. Then she blinked. "Oh dear, no. You must not escort me home. You look like some sort of Viking warrior or Norse god. My mother would… Well, best not to discuss what my mother might do."

Ewan crossed his arms and stared down at her. This pose usually elicited tears from those of the fairer sex. But this one shook her head again in defiance. "My maid is probably wringing her hands at the park. I must return."

He hadn't looked very closely at the woman, but now he noted her fine-quality dress and spencer. Both were soiled with dirt and animal hair. She was a lady. Now the lack of gratitude made sense. He'd known many such ladies. They looked down their nose at everyone. This time Ewan made certain to offer his arm. She looked at it in horror. "Do you want my mother to confine me to my room?" she asked.

Ewan did not know the answer to this inquiry, so he merely continued to stand with his arm crooked. She pushed it down—or rather he allowed her to push it down. "No, thank you, sir. I am perfectly capable of returning to the park on my own. If I encounter any difficulty, Wellington will protect me."

Ewan glanced at the fur ball. The dog wouldn't have scared a flea.

"Good day." She hoisted the wriggling creature in her arms, cradling it like an infant. She must have been completely daft. That was the only explanation for her delusions.

Or perhaps she was just a woman. He did not claim to understand women. He left that to Rafe. The daft woman marched off, thankfully looking both ways before crossing St. James's, and disappeared into the hawkers and vendors on the other side. He could have gone after her, but if he did, it would only be to protect anyone else who happened to fall into her path.

Ewan stared after her for a long moment before being jostled back into motion. The remainder of the journey was uneventful, and Ewan arrived at the club just as Jasper, the best tracker Ewan had ever known, was leaving. Porter, the club's Master of the House, stood in the doorway, silver head held high.

The two former soldiers paused on the steps and nodded to each other. Jasper's face had been horribly scarred during an ambush that cost Draven two men, and he wore a length of black silk tied about his hair and a mask that hid most of one side of his face, including the scarred flesh. "You looking for Wraxall?" Jasper asked.

Ewan nodded.

"He just finished yaffling."

Jasper worked as a bounty hunter and spent time

with the thieves and rogues. He often lapsed into their cant, speaking it as fluently as if he'd been born in the rookeries rather than to one of the oldest noble families in England. At the mention of yaffling—the cant for eating—Ewan felt a pang of hunger in his belly. Was the club still serving or had he missed the meal and would now have to wait until supper?

Jasper slapped Ewan on the shoulder. "You always did have a wolf in the stomach, Protector. If the soup is gone, the cook will always serve you gallimaufry."

Ewan pulled a face. He didn't particularly want scraps and leftovers. The tracker patted his arm, then started back down the steps. "If I didn't know better, I'd think you only came here to grub."

It wasn't far from the truth. If the club hadn't served meals, Ewan would have attended far less frequently.

He entered and Porter closed the door behind him. "Good to see you again, Mr. Mostyn," the distinguished older gentleman said. "The dining room, sir?"

Ewan cocked his head in that direction.

"Very well. This way."

Although he could have found the way with his eyes closed, Ewan followed Porter through the wood paneled vestibule lit with a large chandelier. A suit of armor stood on one wall and two Scottish broadswords on that opposite. The place looked like the sort of establishment Henry VIII would have frequented. But the object that always drew his attention also made him more than a little melancholy. It was a large shield mounted on the wall opposite the door. A big medieval sword cut the shield in half. The pommel of the sword had been fashioned into what Neil had once

told him were fleur-de-lis. A skeleton stared at him
from the cross guard. Around the shield were small
fleur-de-lis that marked the fallen members of the
Survivors—those who hadn't made it back from the
war. The shield reminded Ewan that his lost friends
were here in spirit.

Still following Porter, who only had one leg,
Ewan was forced to move slowly. Porter's wooden
peg thumped on the polished wood floors as he led
Ewan past the winding staircase carpeted in royal
blue and into a well-appointed dining room. Like the
entryway, the dining room was paneled in wood. The
ceiling was low and whitewashed, crossed by thick
wooden beams. Sconces lined two walls and a fire
burned in the mammoth hearth. Four round tables
covered with white linen and set with silver had been
placed throughout the room. At a fifth table, Neil
Wraxall, a.k.a. the Warrior, sat with a glass of red wine
centered before him. Neil liked order. He liked both
giving orders and order in his life. He dined at the
club four days a week precisely at noon. He always sat
at the same table and in the same chair. No one else
ever dared sit in that chair if there was a remote possibility Neil might drop by the club. And if he came
unexpectedly, the man in the chair vacated it without
being asked. They'd all served under Major Wraxall
long enough to know that while he could be flexible
when the situation called for it, he preferred routine
and predictability.

Neil looked up when Ewan entered. Porter paused,
waiting for a sign from the de facto leader of Draven's
troop. When Wraxall flicked his gaze to the empty

chair at his right, Porter led Ewan to it and pulled it out. He sat.

"Wine, sir?" Porter asked.

Ewan nodded.

"And would you like dinner, Mr. Mostyn?"

He looked at the man as though he'd asked if Ewan wanted to be run through with a bayonet.

"Very good then. I will bring the first course. Mr. Wraxall, more wine?" Porter inquired.

The Warrior looked at Ewan. "Will I need it?"

Ewan shrugged. Neil shook his head. "No, thank you, Porter."

Ewan wasn't certain how much Neil drank away from the club, but he was always moderate in his consumption at their club. Once, Neil had told him he always kept a bottle of gin beside his bed to calm the tremors when he woke fighting a battle. Ewan had known what he meant. They all had nightmares about the terrors they'd seen during the war. It was the horrors they'd committed themselves that woke them up at night, a scream lodged in the throat.

For Ewan, life in London had gradually begun to seem more real than the memories of the violence and battle. But he suspected it was different for Neil. He suspected Neil was still fighting the battles nightly, hoping to change the outcomes.

For a long while, he and Neil sat with only the crackling of the fire to break the companionable silence. They'd spent many nights thus on the Continent during the war against Napoleon—a dozen or more men huddled around a campfire, knowing death would probably come in the morning and willing to make that sacrifice for king and country. If Ewan had to die, he'd wanted to die with Neil at his side. He trusted the man implicitly, and he respected him as much as he respected Draven. When they'd been in the army, they could always count on Rafe Beaumont to break long silences or tension with frivolous chatter. Now, Ewan wished he knew what to say to his friend to ease the pain, but Ewan was not good with words. At the moment, it seemed Neil could not find words either.

"Knocked any heads together lately?" the Warrior asked at last. It was more of a command than a question. The Warrior almost always spoke in commands and orders.

Ewan smiled, thinking of the pup last night.

"Good," Wraxall said. "Keep in practice. Give me a report on Langley. I should pay him a visit."

"He'd like that," Ewan said.

Neil gave him a wry look. "I'm sure he would. I always lose at the tables. I'll order Stratford to accompany me. Then I'll have a chance."

Stratford was another of Draven's men and known for his skill with strategy. Ewan frowned, thinking of Langley's losses. But Neil wouldn't go to Langley's. Neil didn't want light and laughter.

Porter returned with a white soup for Ewan and refilled his glass of wine. Ewan's belly rumbled again, but he remembered the card. He'd trusted Neil with his life on the Continent. He could trust Neil with whether or not to pay a call on Ridlington. Ewan slapped it on the table before lifting his spoon.

Wraxall picked the card up and turned it in his fingers. "The Duke of Ridlington? What does he want?"

Ewan sipped his wine and met Neil's gaze. Why did anyone seek out the Protector?

Neil drummed his fingers on the table, probably forming a report in his head. "He's a good man. I don't know him well, but I've not heard anything said against him. Do you want me to ask the others to report what they know of him?"

Ewan held the spoon midway between bowl and mouth. Was that what he wanted? A sense of the man before he decided to hear the duke's proposition? Ewan nodded.

"I have other business tonight, but I'll send Beaumont to Langley's with my findings. I doubt he has anything better to do, and an assignment might keep him out of trouble."

Ewan raised a brow. There was plenty of trouble to be had at Langley's, and Rafe Beaumont was a lodestone for mischief. Still, Ewan appreciated his friend's thoughtfulness. Most men would have sent a note, but Wraxall knew how arduous reading was for Ewan, though the two men had never discussed it. Besides, it would give Neil the chance to order Rafe about, and Neil did like giving orders.

Ewan spent the rest of the afternoon in the dining room, then followed Neil to the card room and watched a game of piquet between Neil and another member of Draven's men. Neil lost, of course. The man was too predictable. It was an enjoyable day, and it took Ewan's mind off Ridlington and the mad female he'd encountered earlier.

Finally, Ewan made his way back to Langley's, the return trip uninterrupted by daft women or racing fur balls, and instructed the footmen to fetch him if Beaumont arrived. Of the eleven other surviving members of the troop, Neil Wraxall and Rafe Beaumont were the men Ewan felt closest to. He saw the other men at the club, and he drank or played the odd game of dice with them, but none knew him like Neil and Rafe. He considered them more than friends. They were brothers.

About half past eleven, a footman fetched him, and Ewan stepped outside the club where Beaumont had struck a pose. Ewan was not in the habit of thinking men pretty, but there was no other way to describe Rafe Beaumont, also known as the Seducer. He wasn't feminine in appearance, but he had a perfect face and enough charm for two men. His dark hair and bronze complexion made him the opposite of Ewan, with his white-blond hair and fair skin.

As usual, Beaumont had a woman on his arm. Ewan's only surprise was that there was but one. "Mr. Mostyn." Rafe bowed with a flourish. Ewan was used to his friend's courtly behavior and ignored it.

"My dear, this fearsome man before you is Mr. Mostyn. He is undoubtedly one of the best men I know. He saved me in the war more times than I can count. Don't let his glare scare you off. He doesn't bite." Then to Ewan, he said, "You don't bite, do you?"

Ewan tried to decide if he was required to answer. Rafe often spoke to hear his own voice.

The woman fluttered her lashes at Ewan. She had reddish hair, freckles, and pretty brown eyes. Her lips smiled broadly. "I could just eat you up, Mr. Mostyn." She winked at him.

Ewan gave Beaumont a look of concern. Unlike Beaumont, Ewan never knew what to say to women. He knew what to *do* with them, but he preferred not to speak while doing it.

"Save your appetite for later, my dear. Would you give Mr. Mostyn and me a moment alone?"

"Of course. I'll wait inside." She looked up at Ewan as though for approval. He moved aside to allow her to enter through the door a footman held open. The gambling hell permitted women, but most were courtesans or women who thrived on scandal. Clearly, this woman did not concern herself with her reputation.

When she'd gone inside, Beaumont sighed. "Hell's teeth! I thought I'd never be rid of her."

Ewan gave his friend a look of incomprehension. If Rafe didn't want her company, why not just tell her so? But then Beaumont seemed to attract women whether he wanted to or not. That was one skill they'd found invaluable in the war.

"Let me think now. If I mess this up, Wraxall will have my head. I'm to tell you Ridlington is an oak. Those are Neil's words, not mine. I don't describe men in terms of foliage, you know. In any case, Wraxall says, no one has a word to say against the duke. Apparently the man does not overindulge in drink, cards, or women. I can't think why Neil should call this a recommendation. The duke sounds like a bore to me, but there you are. Why does he want to hire you?"

Ewan lifted a shoulder.

"Well, don't agree unless he pays you at least double what you make at this club each week. You are worth it, Ewan."

Ewan couldn't have said why, but at the compliment, his throat constricted.

"Now I must be off. I haven't slept in two days, and if I'm forced to drink even one more glass of champagne, I'll cast up my accounts. Good night." He slapped Ewan on the shoulder.

"What about...?" Ewan motioned to the hell behind him.

"Good God. Don't tell her where I've gone. I doubt she'll come looking for me. She'll find other amusements." He doffed his beaver hat and strolled off, turning heads as he walked.

Ewan pulled the card from his pocket and read it slowly. Berkley Street at ten in the morning. He'd go, but he wouldn't wear a cravat.

Two

LADY LORRAINE CALDWELL, ONLY DAUGHTER OF THE Duke and Duchess of Ridlington, crumpled another sheet of foolscap and tapped her brow with the feather of her quill. Francis had sent her a love letter two days ago, and she'd been endeavoring to reply since then. She simply couldn't find the words. His letter had been full of flowery phrases and descriptions of his abject misery without her by his side.

Lorrie was not one for pretty words, but she could not possibly reply as she had on the crumpled letter: *Dear Francis, Let's elope*. That one had been better than the previous one: *Dearest Francis, I want you to kiss me*.

Ladies simply did not propose elopements or ask for kisses. It was unseemly, even if that was what she wanted. Lorrie was tired of begging for her father's blessing, tired of meeting Francis in secret, tired of chaste kisses that fired her blood but left her frustrated. She had persuaded Francis to elope once before. She'd convinced him that once they were wed, her father would relent, give his blessing, and bestow her dowry.

Lorrie had left a note and sneaked out of the house,

but Francis had never arrived at the tavern from which they'd planned to depart. She'd been forced to return home to an irate father and an annoyed mother. Francis had sent a letter of apology. He had reconsidered, worried her father would do as he'd threatened and cut his daughter off. What would they live on?

Francis was such a thoughtful man. He did not want Lorrie to ever suffer from poverty. But what he did not understand was she did not care about money or dresses or jewels. She wanted to be with the man she loved.

She'd cried for a week, and to cheer her up, her eldest brother had given her Wellington as a gift. Lorrie suspected the puppy was meant to distract her from making more plans to elope. Welly was certainly a distraction, but the puppy napped at her feet now, which had given Lorrie plenty of time to reread all of Francis's letters.

She pulled another sheet of foolscap from her drawer, dipped the pen in ink, and began again.

My Dearest Francis—

That was a good start.

Words cannot express my longing ~~for you~~ to see you again. I cannot cease picturing your hands ~~on me~~ writing the beautiful words on the papers I hold so close to ~~my breast~~ my heart. I long to ~~run away with you~~ see you, hear your voice, and so on and so on—

Lorrie tossed the quill down, then started when

Welly jumped to his feet, ran to the window, and began to bark. The little dog bounced up and down, his tail wagging so hard his whole body shook. Lorrie parted the curtains and peered out. This small parlor on the main floor faced the street, and as she peered down, she spotted a man exiting a hackney.

Not just any man. The Nordic giant from the day before.

No!

With Welly right on her heels, Lorrie lifted her skirts and ran from the room. She'd long ago perfected the art of running silently, and she made no sound as she scampered down the hall and all but flew down the staircase. Thankfully neither Bellweather nor any of the footmen had heard the carriage arrive, and Lorrie pulled open the door and jumped outside before the Viking could knock.

He paused at the bottom of the steps when he saw her, and she shut the door behind her to keep Welly from escaping. "What are you…doing here?" she panted.

The Viking stared at her as though she had escaped from an asylum. She supposed she probably did look rather wild and out of breath, but she was dressed and her hair had been coiffed…hadn't it?

"Have you come to see my father?"

The Viking looked at the house and then at her, clearly trying to decide if she could be the daughter of a duke.

"The duke. My father. Have you come to tell him about yesterday? Because you can't, you know."

The Viking raised a brow.

"Very well, you could. I mean, I can't stop you. I could try, but, well"—she looked him up and down—"you're much stronger than I am and certainly bigger."

Which was, of course, a gross understatement. She was not a petite woman, and this man still towered over her. He was easily two or three inches over six feet. He had blond hair, cut unfashionably short, and pale blue eyes. His features were as dramatic as his height. His face was all broad planes and jagged cuts of cheekbone and jaw. His clothes fit him well enough that she could see his frame was honed and muscled. What was more, his clothing was of good quality. He did not wear a cravat or a hat, though, and she found that rather odd, considering that his other garments were fashionable, clean, and polished.

She cleared her throat. "What I mean to say is that you *shouldn't* tell him."

The Viking crossed his arms, the stance of a man waiting patiently for explanation. "Why not? You were almost killed."

"What? No! That's an exaggeration."

"I never exaggerate."

No, he probably didn't. He probably always said exactly what he meant and no more or less. Lorrie sighed, knowing she'd have to explain. Oh, but she dreaded *explaining*. "You see, my father and I are not on the best terms at the moment. I may or may not be at fault, depending on which point of view you take. If you tell him you saw me running down St. James's Street, he'll probably banish me to the country to live with Aunt Prudence, who we all call Aunt Pruneface because her face looks like a prune and she has the personality of one as well."

The Viking did not even smile. *Everyone* smiled at that little anecdote!

"*Please.*" Lorrie put her hands together as though in prayer. "Do not send me to Aunt Pruneface." The Viking looked unconvinced, and a phrase from one of Francis's letters arose in her mind. "My soul will die a slow death."

The Viking's eyes narrowed.

"You don't want to be responsible for the death of my soul, do you?"

In answer, the Viking took a card from the pocket of his coat and handed it to her. It was her father's calling card. She knew it immediately. And that meant her father had summoned the Viking. He had not come to report on her behavior, after all.

Not that she could trust he wouldn't, but perhaps he would take pity on her.

"I suppose you want to knock on the door now, don't you?"

"If it won't endanger your soul."

Was that supposed to be amusing? She would have been amused if she wasn't so mortified. As though to spur her to action, he stepped onto the first step, and though he was still two steps below her, they were now equal in height. She swallowed and reached behind her for the door handle. "You go ahead. And if you—ahem—*forget* to mention you saw me yesterday and, um, today, that small kindness would be most sincerely appreciated."

Lorrie pushed the door open, bent to retrieve Welly, and closed the door again. Then she lifted her skirts and ran back up the stairs just as the knocker banged ominously. She ducked around the corner, then peeked out to watch Bellweather enter the vestibule and open the door.

"May I help you?" Bellweather asked in his nasal voice, as though Nordic giants called at her father's London town house every day.

The Viking handed Bellweather her father's card. Clearly, the visitor was a man of few words. He had quite a nice voice though, low and rich.

"Ah, I see now," Bellweather was saying as he opened the door to admit the Viking. "Come in, sir. His Grace is expecting you in the library."

The library! Drat! She'd hoped the men would meet in the drawing room, making it possible for her to eavesdrop. But this was not a social call. Lorrie could not imagine the Viking ever made social calls. He was not the sort of man to discuss banal topics like the weather.

He followed Bellweather toward the duke's library, looking up at the stairs as he passed. Lorrie ducked back behind the wall. Did he know she watched him? Probably. Those ice blue eyes seemed to miss very little.

She had two options now. One, she could return to her room and sit on pins and needles, waiting to see if her father summoned her to chastise her for her—as he would say—*inappropriate and reckless behavior.* Two, she could try to watch the meeting from the library window to gauge her father's behavior and discover whether or not the Viking betrayed her.

As she had no wish to sit in her chamber and wait, she deposited Wellington on her bed, closed the bedchamber door, and took the servants' stairs to the ground floor and into the garden. Her father's library had several windows, but all had been set rather high off the ground. She crept to the first window and peered inside, but she was too short and could only see the tops of the bookshelves lining the far wall. Nearby, a forgotten flowerpot had rolled on its side behind the shrubbery. Lorrie dragged it out and set it upside down under the window. Her white dress was now streaked with dirt and her slippers ruined, but that was a problem for later.

Cautiously, Lorrie stepped onto the pot and peeked over the edge of the windowsill. She ducked down just as quickly. The dratted Viking faced the window. She peeked up again and then cursed under her breath. The Viking stared at her with a look of disapproval. So much for not being seen. Still, her father's back was to the window, and he was the one she did not want to catch her.

She gave the Viking a little wave, and the line between his brows deepened. Then his gaze went to her father's face and he nodded as though listening to something the duke was saying. When the Viking glanced back at her, Lorrie put a finger to her lips, reminding him not to say anything about the day before.

He made no sign he understood, so Lorrie jumped up and down to catch his attention again. Unfortunately, her father must have sensed the movement because he turned to look over his shoulder, and Lorrie had to duck so quickly she stumbled off the flowerpot and fell on her bottom in the shrubbery.

By the time she freed herself, her arms were scratched, leaves were in her hair, and her dress was torn. At this point, she hardly cared whether the Viking reported her misbehavior to her father or not. Under the window, she dusted herself off just as the Viking peered out and down at her.

His expression was one of concern, and she gave him a little wave to let him know she was uninjured. His serious expression seemed carved in granite. Did the man ever smile? Even though she knew she must look a fright, she blew him a kiss before skipping away. Unfortunately, she hadn't remembered the shrubbery, and she tripped over a trunk and stumbled forward most ungracefully.

Cheeks burning with embarrassment, she didn't turn back.

◦◦◦

Had Lady Lorraine looked over her shoulder at that precise moment, she might have seen the ghost of a smile—or what passed for a smile—on Ewan's lips. She was quite the most ridiculous person he had ever encountered. When her face had popped into the window behind the duke he'd wondered what the hell she was about. And then when she'd seemed to tumble out of sight, he worried she'd broken her neck. He'd almost craned his neck out of concern, but then she was back again.

She reappeared in the window, her hair tumbling around her shoulders in wild disarray and a smudge of dirt on her cheek that made her look...he did not know the word. He tried to think how Beaumont might describe her.

Adorable. That was what Rafe would have called

her. Ewan would have called her fortunate to still be alive, since she seemed to court trouble at every turn.

Ridlington had been droning on whilst the charade outside continued. He seemed quite at home in the large room full of bookshelves and paneled in dark wood. Ewan couldn't have said what the duke spoke of. The duke said whatever men did when they didn't want to state their business outright. Ewan found it much more interesting to watch the duke's daughter make her way back inside via the servants' entrance.

"You must be wondering why I asked you here," Ridlington said.

Ewan turned to face him. Finally, the man would state his business.

"I know something about your background."

Or not. Ewan recognized the signs of more meaningless chatter. Ewan didn't need to be told about his own background. He knew it already, but perhaps the duke felt reassured recounting it.

"I know you served in the Peninsular War. You were in a special unit under the command of Lieutenant Colonel Draven."

Special. Yes, that was one way to describe it.

The duke, who had stood to offer tea to Ewan and then remained standing when Ewan went to the window, sipped his tea. "My understanding is your group was given assignments other units rejected. There were thirty of you, all sons of nobility. The best and the brightest."

"The expendable," Ewan added.

The duke nodded. "Yes, none of you were heirs to

the title. Only younger sons. Twelve of you returned, and you in particular distinguished yourself."

"I did my duty. Nothing more."

"The stories I heard were they called you the Protector because of the risks you took to keep the other men safe. Stories about you running back into a burning building to save—"

Ewan raised a hand. His belly tightened at the mention of that day. The duke spoke of it, his voice flat and even, but to Ewan the memory was filled with panic and anguish. He could still see the face of the man he'd had to leave. Peter had been trapped behind a wall of fire, and Ewan's strength hadn't given him the ability to walk through fire. He'd left Peter to burn to death, left him as the heat seared his flesh and the screams began. Ewan would never forget those screams or how weak and paltry they'd made him feel. A man like Ridlington would never understand. With a wave of his hand, Ewan pretended to dismiss the retelling out of modesty. "We all have our talents. Mine is my strength."

"And that, my good sir, is exactly why I have come to you—or rather, asked you to come to me. I am in need of a bodyguard."

When Ewan didn't speak, the duke swallowed more tea.

"Not for me. For my daughter."

Ewan gritted his teeth. If the duke had said this from the start, it would have saved them both time. Ewan was no nursemaid. The duke's request made perfect sense. It was quite obvious to Ewan that the lady needed a bodyguard, possibly three or four bodyguards. It was also clear that Ewan was not the man for the position. He had no intention of playing chaperone to a spoiled debutante of the *ton*.

His thoughts might have shown on his face as the duke spoke quickly. "I do not want *any* bodyguard. I want a man who knows Society. The Season has begun, and Lady Lorraine will be attending balls, the theater, dinner parties, and whatnot. A man like you, the son of the Earl of Pembroke, can not only protect her but fit in at these affairs." At this last statement, the duke gave Ewan a rather dubious look. Ewan was certain the words had sounded quite pleasing in Ridlington's mind, but saying them to Ewan, who was over six feet tall and built of muscle, was a bit ridiculous. If there was anywhere Ewan did not belong, it was in a Society drawing room.

"I will pay you extremely well." The duke slid a folded sheet of paper across the desk. Ewan imagined if he opened it, a rather large number with several zeroes behind it would be written there.

Without touching the paper, Ewan shook his head. "This is not for me." He gave the duke a curt bow and started for the door.

"Wait!" the duke ordered. "I haven't told you all of it."

"I've heard enough." Ewan lifted the latch.

"Please," the duke said from behind him, his voice quiet as though he was unaccustomed to pleading. "I need your help."

Ewan couldn't walk away from a man who sounded that desperate. He lowered the latch and stood facing the door.

"Lorrie has it in her head that she is in love with a gentleman I find unacceptable."

This was the story of a hundred fathers. Ewan reached for the latch again.

"She tried to elope," the duke said quickly, "but the man backed out at the last minute. He knows I will not give her a shilling if she elopes with him, and he wants the blunt. Her dowry is quite large, you see. She is headstrong and willful, and her mother and I indulged her too much. We see that now. We allowed her to run amok in the country, and we're finding it difficult to rein her in now that we are in Town. I worry she will be easy prey for the fortune hunters."

Ewan looked back at the duke who had taken a seat behind his desk again and who raked his hands through his hair.

"There are as many fortune hunters as there are heiresses. You don't need me."

"But I do. This man—I fail to understand why Lorrie cannot see that his charm is but an act and beneath the handsome face is a snake. But she fancies herself in love. I ordered her to search among the list of eligible gentlemen her mother and I have drafted, and she agreed reluctantly. But I do not think this man will allow her the opportunity to fall in love with another. I fear he will try to monopolize her at events or convince her to pretend she has a megrim and stay home. I need you to keep Mostyn away from Lorrie."

Ewan's focus suddenly sharpened, and a chill ran down his arms. "Mostyn?"

"Yes… Oh, I meant to tell you. I feared you might

not accept because he is your cousin, but I hoped you might look beyond that to come to my aid."

"Francis Mostyn." Ewan had several cousins, but he could see Francis's fingerprints all over this. A cold ball formed in the pit of Ewan's belly, the seed of an emotion Ewan knew well—hate.

"That is he. My information is that you two are not close, but I understand if you feel compelled to reject my offer because of your relation—"

"I accept."

"—but I hoped to convince… You accept?"

"This position, what you want me to do? It prevents Francis Mostyn from taking what he wants?"

"Assuming he wants my daughter and her fortune, yes, I would rely on you to prevent them from eloping and to keep him from her as much as possible. As to whether she meets another man she might consider marrying, I do not know. But I have every hope that given time, Francis Mostyn will show his true colors."

Ewan nodded. He hardly heard the duke. Hate and the desire for vengeance clouded his every sense. "I need a tour of the house and to meet every servant you employ." His voice sounded far away and strangely calm, though fury and rage churned in him.

The duke raised his tea, then set it down again. "You mean you intend to begin now?"

"Now." Ewan nodded.

"I… But you have not even looked at my offer."

If that was what the duke needed to call the housekeeper to show Ewan the house, he'd do it. But the money no longer mattered. Revenge on Francis Mostyn was payment enough. Ewan crossed to the desk and unfolded the paper. It was a number with several zeroes after it, as he'd anticipated.

He raised his gaze to the duke's. "I looked. Where's the housekeeper?"

"Ah, I will ring for her. You could start tomorrow, you know."

Ewan stared at the duke, who finally raised his hands in surrender and pulled the bell cord. "I had thought to prepare the staff and my duchess for your—er, arrival. Please do not be offended if some of the staff is taken by surprise."

What the duke really meant was that the staff and the family might be intimidated by him. Ewan was used to the reaction, and it would not be a problem. The only problem Ewan foresaw was with the Lady Lorraine. She was not intimidated by him.

That would have to change.

Three

LORRIE HAD BARELY HAD TIME TO CHANGE HER DRESS and brush all of the twigs from her hair when the summons came. Both Lorrie and Nell, her maid, looked up in surprise when the housekeeper knocked and then burst into Lorrie's bedchamber.

"Forgive me, my lady," Mrs. Davies said with a quick curtsy. Her pale brow wrinkled to see Nell styling Lorrie's hair, as that was usually a task reserved for first thing in the morning and then again before dinner, but the housekeeper did not comment. She had served the family since before Lorrie had been born, and the older woman claimed more than one of her gray hairs came from Lady Lorraine. "Your father wishes to see you, my lady. In the library. Immediately."

Lorrie sighed. "Of course. I will be there directly." Dratted Viking. She should have known she could not trust him to help her. Now she would have to sit through another lecture about staying close to her chaperone. She would be fortunate if her father did not forbid her to take Welly on walks.

Mrs. Davies curtsied again and rushed back out of

the chamber. Nell hurried to pin Lorrie's hair into place. When she'd finished, Lorrie rose. "Nell, would you please bring Wellington to one of the footmen? He'd better go out before we have a mess to clean up."

The two women glanced at the rug beside Lorrie's bed, where the puppy was asleep on his back with his brown and white paws in the air.

"Yes, my lady." Nell, who was young and pretty with round cheeks and bright red hair, put her hands on her hips and gave the dog a stern look.

Lorrie took a fortifying breath, then marched to the ground floor and tapped on the dark wooden library door.

"Come." Her father's voice was deep and brusque.

Lorrie opened the door enough to peek inside. Her father sat behind his desk, hands folded in front of him as though waiting for her. "Lorraine, please come inside."

She slipped in and clasped her hands behind her back, every inch the dutiful daughter. She'd stood before him in this room many times. When she'd been young, she'd had to stand on tiptoe to see over his desk. She rather missed being able to use the large desk as protection from her father's frosty stares. "Hello, Father. How are you?" she asked, hoping to disarm him.

"There is something we need to discuss."

"I know, Father. And I am so, so very sorry. It won't ever happen again."

Her father's dark eyes narrowed. "It won't?"

"No. I have learned my lesson." She nodded vigorously.

"What lesson is that?"

That was a good question. What lesson *had* she learned? Never trust a Viking? "I learned…the lesson you would have wanted me to learn. And in any case, it's very possible that Viking was exaggerating. I really was not in any danger."

Now her father rose to his feet. "Danger? What danger?"

Something was not quite right here. Lorrie began to explain, but closed her mouth when she heard the sound of a man clearing his throat behind her. She swung around and almost screamed in surprise.

The Viking stood in the back of the room, arms crossed. She had assumed he was gone and her father was alone. She hadn't even checked to be certain her father was alone.

"Lorraine, what danger?" her father demanded.

She gave the Viking a glare as though to say *this is your fault*. But instead of looking smug or impassive, he merely shook his head slightly.

Oh, good Lord. He *hadn't* told her father about their meeting the day before, and now she'd made her own noose. "The danger…of neglecting my…" She had to think of something. The Viking merely raised one brow. How did he do that? Lorrie spun around. "Neglecting my correspondence. I was just about to write to Aunt Agatha. I feel horrible that I haven't replied to her letter from Christmas." She curtsied. "Pray, excuse me."

She started for the door, but her father was having none of it. "I do believe replying to a letter received almost six months ago can wait another few moments.

There is someone I want you to meet, although I have the feeling you have already met."

"Who?" Lorrie looked over her shoulder at the blond man. "The Viking? I've never seen him before in my life."

Her father looked as though he was barely managing to keep a leash on his temper. "His name is Mr. Ewan Mostyn. That is correct," he said with a nod when her brows rose. "Francis Mostyn's cousin."

Lorrie gaped at the Viking with new curiosity. How was it Francis had never mentioned having such a cousin? Of course, now that she looked, she could detect some slight resemblances. Francis, like his cousin, had blond hair, although Francis's was more gilded. Francis was also handsome, but his face was soft and boyish, whereas the Viking's was chiseled from an unforgiving stone. The eyes were different. Francis had soft brown eyes—doe eyes, as she thought of them—and the Viking had those piercing light blue eyes.

And their size. Francis was not but an inch or two taller than she, whereas the Viking was one of the taller men she had ever known.

"Mr. Mostyn, my daughter, Lady Lorraine."

The Viking lowered his arms to his sides and gave her a curt bow.

Finally, remembering her manners, she curtsied. "How lovely to meet you for the first time, Mr. Mostyn."

He issued her a flat look, but as he didn't speak, she supposed she could at least count on him not to contradict her.

"You will be seeing Mr. Mostyn often, my dear,"

her father was saying. He gestured to a chair near his desk, and Lorrie took it gratefully. Being offered a seat indicated her father did not intend to lecture her. And for some strange reason, her legs had begun to wobble.

"Mr. Mostyn?" The duke pointed to a chair near her. The Viking shook his head and stayed where he was, like some sort of frozen sentinel.

"What do you mean, Father?" Lorrie could think of no reason she should ever see Ewan Mostyn again. She couldn't imagine her father had any use for a man like that. He looked as though he should be in the gladiator ring, not a duke's library.

"I have hired Mr. Mostyn to serve as your bodyguard."

Lorrie would have objected if her voice had not abandoned her.

"He is amply qualified. He served under Lieutenant Colonel Draven in the war. Special Forces. I've already introduced him to some of the staff, and he's had a cursory tour of the town house. I wanted you to meet him before I gave him access to the private family chambers."

"The private areas? Will he be allowed in my bedchamber?"

"I must be familiar with every room in the house, my lady," the Viking answered, speaking slowly in that deep voice that seemed to make her skin tingle every time she heard it.

"Why?" She looked from him to her father.

"To keep you safe," her father answered.

"Safe?" she all but screamed. "This is not about keeping me safe. You want to prevent me from marrying Francis."

Her father merely looked down his nose at her. "I would like to prevent another elopement attempt, yes."

"So you do not trust me? You asked me to look over the eligible bachelors this Season, and I agreed."

"You never agreed," the duke said evenly. "You said you would take it under advisement."

"I said *serious* advisement." She pointed a finger at him. "I don't need some brute following me around."

Behind her she heard a low growl.

"He is not a brute. Mr. Mostyn is the son of the Earl of Pembroke."

Lorraine felt the blood drain from her face. Francis had told her many times of the abuses he'd suffered at the hands of the sons of the earl. He'd grown up with them and shared a tutor. The boys were always blaming him for their own misdeeds and seemed to enjoy seeing him punished.

Slowly, Lorrie turned and glared at the Viking. So this was one of the boys who had tormented Francis as a child. Did he think to torment his cousin further by keeping him from the woman who loved him?

"As the son of a peer," her father continued, "Mr. Mostyn may accompany you to various functions where your attendance is required. His role is not to hamper your enjoyment or prevent you from meeting eligible suitors—"

"Only to keep me from seeing Francis."

"—but to protect you from fortune hunters' schemes and anyone who might attempt to possess you in order to gain access to my wealth," her father continued as though she had never interrupted.

"This won't work, you know," she said. "In a year

I will reach my majority, and I may marry whomever I please. You can surround me with a hundred bodyguards, but true love will overcome all adversity."

"True love." Her father gave her a thin smile. "You, dear daughter, do not know the first thing about it." He walked out of the room, leaving her alone with the Viking.

"Your father is a patient man," the Viking said.

"He's a tyrant."

"Then a benevolent tyrant. If you were my daughter, I would have taken you over my knee and spanked you until your bottom was red."

Lorrie's mouth dropped open. It was a scandalous thing to say, and it probably should have scared her. Instead, her face felt hot and flushed as the image of him tossing her skirts up and putting a hand on her bare bottom flashed in her mind. "I...think that is the longest sentence you have ever spoken to me," she stammered, desperate to say something—anything—that would turn the conversation away from his hand on her bottom.

The corners of his mouth turned up in a slow grin. She caught her breath and fought her reaction by notching her head higher. "I know who you are now. Francis told me all about you."

The Viking raised one brow. How *did* he manage to lift only one?

"Isn't it bad enough that you tormented him as a child? Now you mean to ruin his—and my—chance at happiness?"

"No and yes," he answered.

Lorrie had to think back to her questions, which

she had intended rhetorically, and supply his answers. No, it was not bad enough to torment Francis as a child. Yes, the Viking did intend to ruin their chance at happiness.

"If you think I will merely stand by and allow you to wreck my life—"

"Take me to your bedchamber," he said.

"What?" she spluttered. There was the image of his hand on her bottom again. "Absolutely not!"

"Now." Obviously he would brook no argument. When she didn't move to lead him toward it, he started on his own. Lorrie was forced to follow on his heels. It was her bedchamber, wasn't it? She had a right to say who could and could not enter. And finally she resorted to running as his legs were longer than hers.

On the first floor, he opened the drawing room doors, surveyed it, then looked right and left. Finally, his gaze landed on hers—a clear question in his eyes. Which direction to her chamber?

She could refuse to lead him. He might take the left and find her brothers' chambers first. But eventually he would find hers. There was no stopping him. Lorrie sighed. "This way."

Her room was close to the servants' stairs, and when she indicated the closed door, he made a sound of disapproval. Then he gestured for her to open the door. Gritting her teeth, she did so.

Welly didn't bark or run toward her, so he must be out with a footman. Lorrie wished she had the dog so she would have something to do other than watch the Viking survey her chamber. She hadn't really paid much attention to it in the past few years. Whereas her room at the duke's country estate had been refurbished three years before, this one had not. It was done in powder blue and white. The dolls she had played with as a child still sat at a small table adorned with pretty blue-and-white china from her tea set. The lacy curtains, which she did like, had been tied back with large blue sashes, making them look like a child's flounces.

But whatever the Viking thought of her chamber, he didn't voice it. Instead, he walked straight to the window and looked out. Whatever he saw there did not please him. He frowned and shook his head slightly. Then he walked the perimeter of the room, seeming to study the walls. "Secret passages?" he asked curtly.

She almost laughed, until she realized he was serious. "No."

Beside her bed—which looked quite small to her now, especially with Ewan Mostyn next to it—he lay on the rug and peered underneath.

"What are you doing?" she asked.

Not surprisingly, he didn't answer before he stood again. Lorrie prayed she didn't have dirty chemises and stockings under her bed. How mortifying if he should see her underclothing.

"How did you get out?" he asked.

"I use the door, of course."

"Your father mentioned an attempted elopement. How did you get out?"

"Oh." That. She was not inclined to answer that question.

"The door or the window?" he prompted.

"It won't happen again," she said, "so there is no

need to worry over it. Francis is too much of a gentleman to marry me without my father's blessing."

At that, the Viking laughed. It was such an unexpected thing for him to do—she hadn't even seen him smile—that she gasped in surprise. And then she had to take a very deep breath to calm the fluttering in her belly because, when the Viking smiled, he was easily the most intriguing man she had ever seen. Lorrie had the strangest urge to kiss his lips, which looked soft and quite inviting when not set firmly in a frown.

But the laughter died away and the frown returned. "Door or window?" he asked again.

She didn't answer, and he took a step toward her. "Door or window?"

"I don't have to tell you." She took a step back, though she knew he would not hurt her. Her father would never allow it. But he had a way of looking at her that made her shiver—and not in a good way. Oh, very well. Some of the shivering was the good kind.

He stepped closer, the unanswered question still hanging between them. Lorrie stepped back again and abruptly collided with her bed. She sat down hard, and he towered over her. Since she couldn't move any further away, she leaned back until she was flat on the bed. The Viking put his hands on either side of her and leaned over her. "One last chance—door or window?"

He smelled surprisingly pleasant for a man she was coming to consider an uncouth ogre. There was nothing civilized in his scent—no bergamot or hint of citrus—but there was a feral quality to it that spoke of wood fires and the Christmas greenery that overflowed at the house during the Yuletide.

"You can torture me all you want," she whispered, a little unnerved at the breathless quality of her voice. "But I will not tell you."

He stared at her, their gazes locked in battle. Lorrie could hardly breathe. Her chest rose and fell rapidly, and all she could think was that the Viking was close enough to kiss. She could reach up, twine her arms around his neck, and press her lips to his. But her body was rigid with fear, and the Viking made no move to take advantage of his position.

Finally, she closed her eyes, pressing them tightly together. That small capitulation was enough, apparently, because he straightened and moved away from her. When she opened her eyes again, he was walking toward the door.

"I will have words with my father about this!" she called out.

He looked over his shoulder and captured her gaze, held it. "Too late. You are mine."

❧

As Ewan assessed the rest of the town house, he admitted to himself he'd developed a grudging admiration for the lady. It wasn't the caliber of admiration he had for Neil Wraxall or Lieutenant Colonel Draven. He admired no man as much as he admired those two, but considering Ewan had never before admired any sort of female, the fact that he had even the remotest esteem for a silly chit like Ridlington's daughter came as something of a surprise.

First of all, she was no great judge of character if she thought Francis Mostyn a desirable mate. Of course,

Francis could be charming—very charming—and she was young and naive. One look at her bedchamber told him just what an innocent she was. He might have walked into a nursery, not the chamber of a woman.

That did not explain why he'd suddenly felt uncomfortable when he realized he had her trapped on her bed. He'd merely meant to intimidate her, but when he'd looked down at that sheet of tawny hair spread on the coverlet and the fast rise and fall of her chest, he'd felt more like a lecher.

Even worse, he hadn't managed to force her to divulge her means of escape for the attempted elopement. Ewan really didn't need her to confirm what he suspected, though it would have made informing the duke that the tree outside her window had to be cut down a bit easier. As it was, the duke was surprisingly amenable to all of Ewan's recommendations—from bolting the door to the servants' stairs to removing the tree limbs that had grown toward Lady Lorraine's window—and did not even balk when Ewan suggested he be given a room in the town house.

"Certainly," the duke said, making note of it on the paper before him. At least Ewan assumed that was what the man had written. "There will undoubtedly be nights when it is best to have you here. These balls early in the Season do tend to last until sunrise."

Ewan was less worried about staying out past his bedtime than he was about what Francis would do when he realized Ewan was protecting the woman Francis had targeted for his latest scheme, but Ewan saw no reason to alarm the duke.

"Will you join us for dinner tonight?"

"You will eat dinner in?"

"We have no plans for tonight. Gladstone," the duke called, and the library door opened immediately, revealing a small man in a dark coat.

"Yes, Your Grace?"

"My schedule."

"Yes, Your Grace." He withdrew a paper from his coat and slid small round glasses on his long nose. He consulted the paper before looking nervously at Ewan. "You declined invitations to the Althorpe dinner party and the Buckingham's fete—"

The duke waved a hand. "Just the acceptances, Gladstone."

"Of course, Your Grace. Tomorrow night you have tickets to the opera. I believe Handel's *Oreste* is playing. The duchess, Lady Lorraine, and Lord Neville will be attending with you."

"Add Mr. Ewan Mostyn to the list," the duke instructed. "Mr. Mostyn, this is Gladstone, my secretary. Gladstone, this is Lady Lorraine's new... bodyguard, shall we say?"

Ewan nodded.

Gladstone scribbled vigorously on the paper he held in shaking hands. "Pleased to make your acquaintance, Mr. Mostyn," he said with a brief glance up. "And should I add Mr. Mostyn as a fourth to your party for the Regent's ball on Thursday?"

"I think that would be best. Mr. Mostyn?"

Ewan wanted to groan. The opera and the Prince Regent. He'd rather walk unarmed into battle. He'd rather have the enemy pull his toenails out. But neither of those sacrifices would make Francis suffer.

If screeching sopranos and tolerating Prinny for a few hours were what it took to thwart Francis's plans, then Ewan would do it.

By the time Ewan had left the Ridlington's town house, dusk was settling over the already gloomy streets of London. Ewan pushed through the fog and shadows until he reached the Draven Club.

Porter opened the door, his silver hair shining in the lamplight. The Master of the House took Ewan's coat and hat. "Mr. Mostyn, would you like dinner?"

For once, Ewan's thoughts were not on food.

"Who is here?" he asked.

"Mr. Wraxall and Mr. Beaumont are in the card room. Lord Phineas is in the reading room. You just missed the Lieutenant Colonel."

Damn, Ewan thought. He would have liked to see Draven. He started away, and Porter followed. Ewan waved a hand, dismissing the Master of the House. Ewan knew the club as well as he knew any home where he'd ever lived, and he didn't want the trouble of waiting for Porter to open doors right now.

In the card room, Neil and Rafe looked up from their game as Ewan entered. Beaumont resembled a fallen angel with his tousled hair and fine features. Neil, dark and brooding, sat straight and tall, still looking very much the leader he had always been. Beaumont smiled, which told Ewan all he needed to know regarding the card game. Rafe was winning.

Wraxall turned over another card, swore, and tossed his cards on the table. Beaumont pulled the small tower of coins to the little pile he'd already amassed. No one played for high stakes at the Draven

Club, and most of the coins before Beaumont were shillings and six pence.

"Come try your hand, Protector," Wraxall ordered. "I've been soundly thrashed."

"I'll wager you two shillings he didn't come to play cards," Beaumont said, tapping his fingers on his chin thoughtfully. "He came to ask us about the Lady Lorraine."

Ewan had been about to take a seat at the table, but he paused and frowned at Rafe. Was there a woman in London the Earl of Haddington's son did not know?

"I see by your expression I am correct. And before you rip my head off," Beaumont said, holding up a hand, "I don't know her personally. Her name came up when I was making inquiries after the duke." He looked at Neil. "And before you ask for a report, she's reputed to be well-liked by other ladies and is said to be lively and vivacious."

Neil put his hands up as though attempting to ward her off. In the meantime, Rafe closed his eyes and pressed a finger to his temple. "What are you doing?" Neil asked.

"Trying to imagine the Protector entertaining this lively and vivacious chit. I can't manage it."

"I don't have to entertain her. The duke wants me to act as her bodyguard." Ewan took a seat at the table.

"Too bad. I would have liked to have seen it," Beaumont said, lifting the deck of cards and shuffling them deftly between his hands. His fingers moved quickly, cards disappearing and reappearing as though he were a magician. "I would not have connected the two of you at all, if I hadn't heard she was smitten with Francis Mostyn."

"Your arse of a cousin?" Wraxall asked.

Ewan gave a curt nod. Even the thought of his cousin was enough to make his jaw tense and his blood thrum in his veins.

"She needs more than a bodyguard." Wraxall sipped from the glass at his elbow. "She needs taste."

"Why doesn't the duke just forbid the marriage?" Beaumont asked.

"He did. She tried to elope."

"She sounds like trouble," Wraxall declared.

"She sounds interesting," Beaumont argued. "The elopement was foiled?"

Ewan wished it were that simple. But he knew his cousin too well. He could have told the lady even before the assignation that Francis would not show. "Francis told her he changed his mind about the elopement. He claims he wants the duke's blessing."

"More likely he wants the duke's daughter's dowry," Wraxall added.

As usual, Neil had hit the mark dead center.

"You're to protect the lady from another elopement attempt by your cousin?" Beaumont asked.

"And from any other fortune hunters. I understand her dowry is substantial enough to attract attention."

"And how does she feel about her new bodyguard?" Beaumont smiled.

Ewan didn't answer questions everyone knew the answer to.

"Don't tell me you have to escort her to balls and garden parties," Wraxall said, ever practical.

So Ewan didn't tell him.

"Is she at least attractive?" Beaumont asked.

Ewan rubbed at the building tension between his brows.

"What *does* she look like?" Beaumont asked. "Brunette? Blond? Redhead?"

"A female," Ewan said.

Beaumont waved an arm as though washing his hands of Ewan.

"What's your first engagement?" Wraxall leaned back and crossed his arms over his chest.

"The opera."

Wraxall groaned, but Beaumont leaned forward. "Which one?"

When the other two men just stared at him, Beaumont shrugged. "I enjoy the opera."

"You enjoy opera *singers*," Wraxall corrected. "There's a difference."

Beaumont ignored him. "You'll have to wear a cravat and pumps. You *do* own a cravat?"

Ewan cringed. "I own one." After all, he was a son of the Earl of Pembroke. His gaze narrowed on Beaumont. "How do you stay awake? I can't ever understand them."

"That's because most of them aren't in English," Beaumont answered.

Ewan hadn't known that, and he felt his neck grow warm. He'd thought opera was one more area in which he was a dimwit. And now, of course, he'd proven he was a numbskull because he hadn't even known the singers didn't sing in English. He should remember to keep his mouth shut. But neither

Wraxall nor Beaumont made a disparaging comment. These two knew his shortcomings, but they never made light of them.

"In any case," Wraxall said to break Ewan's embarrassed silence, "you won't be watching the opera. Your mission is to be on your guard, keeping an eye on the duke's daughter at all times. This is a good assignment for you, Mostyn," Wraxall declared. "You've been bashing heads at Langley's too long."

"I like bashing heads."

"Maybe you will have the chance to bash your cousin's," Beaumont pointed out.

Ewan could only hope.

Four

WHAT EXACTLY HAD HE MEANT? *YOU ARE MINE.* LORRIE hadn't been able to keep the phrase out of her mind the entire day. Had the Viking meant she was his responsibility? She certainly didn't belong to him. She wasn't his wife—thank God—or his sister or any other relation. And then Lorrie started to wonder if the Viking had a wife. Was he married? Did he have children?

If it hadn't rained all day, she might have taken Welly out and turned her mind to other concerns. Instead, she'd been stuck inside with nothing but her needlework and her mother's gossip, which Lorrie had heard last week, to keep her occupied.

She'd almost jumped for joy when her mother had sent her to change for the opera. Lorrie didn't care for the opera, especially as Francis never attended, but at this point she was desperate for any diversion.

While Nell pulled and twisted Lorrie's hair into the latest French style, Lorrie stared at her reflection in the mirror. Francis had said she was beautiful. Lorrie had been flattered, though she'd known it was hyperbole. She was not beautiful. She had pleasing features but nothing that would cause anyone to stop and stare in a crowded room.

Now, Francis was quite handsome. Ladies routinely turned their heads when he passed. Francis was a skilled dancer and a witty conversationalist as well. The Viking, on the other hand, Lorrie imagined ladies turned their heads when he passed, but it was probably out of awe and not admiration. She didn't know if the man danced, but his cousin had him beat hands down when it came to conversation.

Still, her new bodyguard managed to say quite a lot without ever having to utter a word. Lorrie stared at her brows in the mirror and attempted to raise only one. Both rose, so she held one in place and raised the other. Now she simply looked ridiculous.

"My lady?" Nell asked.

Lorrie dropped her hands. "How is your sister, Nell?" she asked quickly.

Nell smiled. "It won't be long now. The baby should be here before the end of summer. My sister and her husband are hoping for a boy, but I would love a little niece to spoil."

"So would I, but neither of my brothers seem very intent on marrying."

Nell made a sound of assent. "They are still young. Lord Neville arrived just before I came up, my lady, and Mr. Mostyn was right behind him."

Lorrie had a thousand questions at that moment—how had the Viking looked, had he spoken, did Nell know if he was married…

Instead, she said, "Good. Then we shan't have to wait on either of them."

"All the maids are quite aflutter with talk of Mr. Mostyn," Nell said, pulling a curl out of the coiffure so it framed Lorrie's face.

For some reason the maids' infatuation with her new bodyguard irritated Lorrie. "Really? The man has as much charm as a mule."

"But he's a great deal more attractive, my lady." The maid secured a small diamond pin in Lorrie's hair, which glinted softly off the candlelight.

"Don't tell me you are smitten with him too."

Nell shook her head. "I think I would die of fright if the man spoke to me. He will make a good body-guard, my lady."

That was what she'd been afraid of. With the Viking watching her every movement, she and Francis would never have any time alone, and she'd been hoping to sneak away and steal a kiss at Prinny's ball tomorrow night.

Lorrie rose. "I suppose I should go down." She pulled on her gloves and fastened a silver cuff on one wrist. She studied her reflection in the cheval mirror and supposed she would do. The gold silk dress had a modest neckline, but it was rounded enough to show her shoulders. Nell was a wonder with hair, and she'd artfully arranged Lorrie's hair into a cascade off to one side. A long, solitary curl tickled her exposed skin. The fact that Nell was able to cajole Lorrie's hair into curling at all made her invaluable. Lorrie's stick-straight hair proved rather recalcitrant when anyone other than Nell took curling tongs to it.

On the way down the stairs, she bit her lips to give them color, then smiled when she spotted Neville at the bottom of the steps. He stood tall and straight, his light brown hair waving back from his forehead.

"There you are," he said, barely glancing at her. "Maybe you can tell me why there's a man I do not know accompanying us to the opera. Father sequestered himself with the man, and Mama shushed me."

Lorrie sighed. "Father has hired him to keep us safe."

Neville's brows rose high on his already high forehead. "Us safe? You mean *you* safe from that arse Francis Mostyn."

Lorrie's smile died. She remembered why she had been happy when Neville had left for school and then found his own accommodations in London. She'd never liked Neville much. Charles, her eldest brother, was far less annoying, but he was quite involved in politics and rarely at home.

"As Francis will soon be my betrothed, I would appreciate it if you did not disparage him."

"Father will never agree to you marrying that arse."

If they'd been a few years younger, she would have punched him. Although he was three years her senior, as children she could always best him. She'd make him call "surrender," and if he wouldn't, she'd hold him down until he cried. Now she was not so certain she could hold him down. He was taller than her and at least three stones heavier. She might still be able to make him cry if she punched him in the belly.

"Mr. Mostyn is *not* an arse, and Father *will* agree to allow me to marry him."

"When hell freezes over."

"When he realizes Francis is the only man who will ever make me happy."

"Until you find another man who will"—he raised his voice to mock her and fluttered his hands—"make you happy."

Lorrie folded her arms. "There *is* no other man. There is no man better than Francis."

"My hound is better." Neville glanced at the closed library door again. "That man is your bodyguard, you say? He looks familiar."

"He is Francis Mostyn's cousin."

Neville snapped his fingers. "That's it then. He's one of Draven's Survivors."

"And what, my dear, is Draven's Survivors?" the duchess asked, gliding down the stairs. She adjusted a red and burnt-orange Turkey shawl as she walked, and Lorrie assumed she'd had to go back up to her chamber to fetch it. Thus far the spring of 1816 did not feel very spring-like at all.

The Duchess of Ridlington had married young and borne all of her children in the span of five years. She was not yet in her middle forties and looked to Lorrie as though she were still in her twenties. She had dark brown hair and hazel eyes, a small nose, and a petite form. Lorrie had been taller than her mother when she turned twelve. And though Lorrie was only average in height, she always felt like a giant compared to the duchess.

As usual, when in the presence of their mother, Neville became obnoxiously charming. He bowed over her hand and kissed her glove. "You look beautiful, Mama."

She did, Lorrie thought. Her mother had chosen an apple-green dress that would have looked too young on any other matron of three and forty, but it looked perfect on the Duchess of Ridlington.

"Thank you."

Neville cleared his throat. "Draven's Survivors was the sobriquet of a group of thirty men chosen for some of the most dangerous missions in the war against Napoleon. The men were all educated and known to have special skills. Most, if not all, came from the nobility. Younger sons, like me," he said, puffing his chest out slightly.

Lorrie wanted to roll her eyes. The closest Neville had been to a battle was on a chessboard.

The duchess tapped her fan on her cheek. "I've heard of them. And this Mr. Mostyn, what was his special skill?"

"I believe they called him the Protector. He looks like the man a soldier would want at his back in battle."

Lorrie could not argue with that.

"Well then." The duchess turned her gaze on her daughter. "You should be in capable hands, Lorraine."

"I am not in need of a bodyguard," Lorrie said stiffly. "Francis agreed to wait until we had Father's blessing." Dratted man.

The duchess sighed. "*Really*, dear." That was as much as the duchess had said when Lorrie's failed elopement had been discovered. It was not so much that the duchess, who was a rather neglectful mother, cared that her daughter had attempted to elope, it was more that she was disappointed in either her choice of husband or the poor elopement planning. Lorrie was not certain which.

If she had to guess, it was the poor planning. Francis

might not be wealthy or titled, but he was handsome and dashing. Her mother had a weakness for handsome, dashing men. As she'd produced an heir, a spare, and a daughter to carry on the family name, the duke turned a blind eye to his duchess's little liaisons.

The library door opened and the duke, dressed in his best dark coat and starched white cravat, emerged. He was followed by the Viking—only he did not look so much like a Viking tonight. Lorrie had seen him in a coat and snug breeches before, but there was something about the flowing white cravat that made him look like a lion with a collar about his neck. If the desired effect was to lessen the Viking's dangerous edge, the cravat did not achieve its aim. Instead, the Viking appeared fiercer and as though he might tear the neckcloth from his throat at any moment.

In fact, Lorrie found herself hard-pressed to look away from the man and his simple but precisely tied cravat. She'd thought him handsome before, if in a feral sort of way, but looking at him now her body warmed and her chest tingled in a manner she could not quite explain.

Even Neville seemed taken aback when the Viking stood across from him in the vestibule. The duke made the introductions, and Neville spluttered and stammered his greetings. Still, everyone smiled and pretended it was normal to have a Viking in clothing that would have made Beau Brummell proud accompanying them to the opera. Lorrie had already been introduced and was required to say very little. She was thankful for the respite, especially since the carriage had seemed far too small with the Viking seated across from her. The lamps provided a cozy glow inside the conveyance, and she knew Mostyn was not looking at her. Still, she felt his presence keenly, and the warmth she'd felt in the vestibule clung to her so that she had to lay aside her wrap and resort to fanning herself, even though the night was unseasonably cool.

Finally, they arrived at the opera, and the party made their way to the duke's box. Not long after, a throng of her mother's admirers came to call, and her father excused himself—probably to call on his own paramour. Neville put the opera glasses to use, scanning the crowd, while Lorrie waved to a few of her acquaintances and spoke briefly with several men who came to the box to call on her.

During the carriage ride she had reminded herself of all of Francis's wonderful qualities and of the brutal way his cousin, the Viking, had treated her beloved when they were children. She would tolerate her bodyguard, but she would not like him. She would not feel *warm* when she looked at him. That sort of sensation was reserved for her Mr. Mostyn. And with her love for the *other* Mr. Mostyn firmly entrenched in her mind, she was able to give only the briefest attention to the men who came to her father's box to court her. None were as handsome or exciting as Francis. It did not hurt her intended's cause that she felt strange speaking in front of the Viking. She might have flirted with a few of the men, just for fun, but how was she to flirt with the Viking watching her?

Finally, the opera began, and Lorrie turned her attention to the stage. Even though she knew Francis would not be in attendance, she surveyed the other boxes and the floor just in case. By the end of the first hour, she was impossibly bored, and excused herself to go to the ladies' retiring room. She'd no sooner ducked through the box's curtains than the Viking stepped out after her.

She wheeled around, and her heart jumped into her throat. Why, the man might as well roar like the lion he resembled. How her fingers itched to remove that cravat so she might place him back in the *feral* category and firmly take him out of the *dangerously handsome* category. Since she could not remove the cravat, or the man himself, she spoke a bit too sharply. "What is wrong?"

He shook his head. Of course the man did not speak to her.

"Then why leave the box?" she persisted.

"Where you go, I go," he said.

That was her fault. She should have expected it. "I am only going to the ladies' retiring room, and you will not be welcomed there. You might as well wait for me here."

Another shake of his head.

"Fine." She set off with him walking a few respectable steps behind her. She had nothing to hide, so she did not mind him accompanying her—well, not very much—but what would happen when she did not desire his company? The Viking would make any rendezvous with Francis even more difficult. And Lorrie was determined to steal at least one kiss from her intended at the prince's ball tomorrow night.

Most of the opera's patrons were still in their seats, so the corridors of the theater were all but empty. She did pass one or two other ladies, and she could not help but note how their faces lit with interest upon seeing the Viking. One even turned to watch him walk away.

Lorrie made use of the ladies' retiring room, and when she emerged again, the Viking was not waiting for her. She should have been pleased that he was not as vigilant as she'd feared, but Lorrie was actually rather indignant. What sort of bodyguard did not even wait for the woman he was supposed to be protecting?

She peered right and left, and when she did not see him, she headed back to the Ridlington box, taking her time as she had no desire to return to the opera quickly. The Viking met her just outside the box, seeming to step out of nowhere. Lorrie couldn't help scowling at him, both because she was startled and because his appearance caused that unwanted flash of heat again. "Where did you go?"

He raised one brow, making it look easy.

"I thought you were supposed to protect me," she said, keeping her voice low so the patrons in the boxes behind the curtains would not overhear. "But when I came out, you were gone."

"Miss me?" he asked. Lorrie could not be certain, but she thought he was almost smiling.

"No! But if you insist on skulking about, I want to know where you are doing so."

The Viking didn't speak again, and Lorrie supposed she had said her piece and should now return to her seat. But that would mean attending to the opera again. "Where did you go?" she asked, her tone placating.

"To look at the rain. It hasn't let up."

Lorrie frowned. "Are the streets still passable?"

He nodded. "You will be safe on the return home, but if the rain does not slacken, I may suggest to your father we leave early."

"Oh, that would be no hardship," Lorrie said. "I hate the opera."

He stared at her.

"Don't tell me you love it?"

He shook his head. "Hate it."

Lorrie smiled. "Good. I like you much better for admitting that. Charles, my eldest brother, pretends he adores the opera, but he is always engaged whenever we have tickets."

"I don't pretend," the Viking said.

"That's an...admirable quality," she said, though the statement flustered her. She did not know anyone who did not pretend. Everyone wore masks, and some people she knew wore more than one. She wasn't certain if she should respect the Viking more for eschewing pretense or consider him a complete simpleton.

She really should return to the box now. They had conversed enough, and she had been absent too long. Instead, she said, "If you don't like the opera, what do you like?"

"Food," he said immediately.

Lorrie laughed. "I've never met a man who didn't." This might be a weakness she could exploit. "Are you hungry?"

"Always."

"They have light fare for sale downstairs," she told him. "If you go now, you will be ahead of everyone at intermission."

He shook his head and indicated her father's box.

"I will go inside and suffer the opera while you are away. I promise not to leave my seat until you return."

He shook his head again.

"Mr. Mostyn, this is not a ploy to trick you." Not yet at any rate. "I promise. You see?" She parted the outer curtains. "I am returning right now."

She let the curtains drop behind her, then parted the inner curtains and took her seat. "Where is Mostyn?" her father asked, leaning over to whisper in her ear.

Lorrie waited a moment, expecting the man to enter at any moment, but either he trusted her more than he'd indicated or he really was hungry.

"I believe he's patrolling," she said, when the Viking didn't reappear.

Sometime before the intermission Mostyn did return. Lorrie didn't know exactly when he stepped into the box, but at some point her back prickled and she looked over her shoulder and saw him watching her. Warmth crept up her spine. As much as she might argue that she did not need a protector, she felt a strange sense of comfort when he was nearby.

He stayed by her side during the intermission, when she was surrounded by admirers. She was not so vain as to believe the men were at all interested in her. It was her substantial dowry that drew them. With Mostyn keeping guard over her, only the most desperate paid her any homage. The Viking scowled so fiercely at every man who deigned enter his lair that when Neville ducked back in, her brother looked ready to turn back around again.

Finally, the opera ended, and Lorrie tried hard not

to rub her eyes and give away that she had dozed through the last half hour. Her mind still foggy, she followed her mother and father out of the box and into the lobby. Outside, the rain still fell steadily, and the line of carriages was longer than usual. The press of theatergoers in the lobby was stifling, and once again, Lorrie was glad to have the Viking at her side. She could appreciate him more if she did not look at him too closely. Better to think of him as a sort of sentry—a suit of armor that followed her about.

"Lorraine, come stand outside with me," the duchess ordered. "I cannot breathe in this crush."

"Yes, Mama." Lorrie followed her mother outside, standing beside columns that supported a stone canopy sheltering those outside from the rain. It did not provide any heat, and the rain had brought a bracing chill with it. In her thin silk dress and summer wrap, Lorrie shivered. The Viking had followed them out, but he seemed impervious to the weather.

"Mr. Mostyn, is that our barouche?" the duchess asked, pointing to a black conveyance that looked very much like every other carriage.

He stared and frowned, apparently unable to tell in the dark. "One moment," he said, moving closer to the line of carriages.

Lorrie wrapped her arms around her middle to try and keep warm.

"Hey, watch where you step!" a man barked angrily to her right.

"I'll bloody well step where I want," was the answer.

"Lorraine, move closer to me," her mother ordered, but it was too late.

The men behind her exchanged punches and stumbled drunkenly into the street. Unfortunately, Lorrie had been swept along with them. She tripped over her skirts and fell backward into an ice-cold, muddy puddle. The shock of the cold water snatched the last bit of sleepy warmth from her mind, and she struggled to rise. Unfortunately, her skirts had tangled about her ankles and the rain was falling hard enough to obscure her vision. Her gloves made untangling the wet material of dress and cloak all the more difficult. A moment later, she let out a small scream when the men who had fallen to the ground beside her all but rolled over her, their fists flying and jabbing. With a renewed sense of urgency she ripped at the sodden fabric clinging to her legs and gained her feet. But the men—impervious to her struggles or even her presence, it seemed—rolled over like boulders and knocked her off balance again. Like a set of pins in a game of skittles, she toppled over, but this time she didn't tumble into the puddle. The arms that caught her felt as hard and unyielding as the ground, but they swept her up not down.

Lorrie blinked the water out of her eyes and looked into the Viking's face as he lifted her away from the two fighting men. His jaw was as tight as a drum, his blue eyes filled with ice. His touch was gentle, though. He carried her as one might carry a young child, and she felt as though she weighed little more than a child. As his heat seeped into her chilled body, she had the strangest urge to close her eyes and lay her head on his chest. Initially, she hadn't been frightened by the dueling men. She'd been annoyed that she'd been inadvertently involved. But the second time their antics felled her, panic had crept in. A carriage might run her over or one of the men might accidentally punch her or kick her in the head with a flailing foot. Both were so inebriated they didn't even seem aware of her.

But now, in the Viking's arms, all panic and fear subsided. His warm body held hers gently, shielding her from the worst of the rain and the prying eyes of spectators. She could hear them exclaiming about the duke's daughter, and though she probably should have made it known she was uninjured, she did not want everyone gaping at the state of her dress and the mess that she knew was her hair and her face.

Nor did she wish to pull her nose from the sweet smell of pine and spruce that seemed to cling to the Viking. If she could block out the noise of the city, she could almost imagine she were in the peaceful countryside, under the stars.

And then a carriage door opened, and she was placed gently inside. "What the hell happened?" her father demanded, taking her by the arms. Lorrie squinted at the light from the carriage lamp.

Her brother was beside the duchess and her father sat across from them, his face white with concern.

"I told you," her mother said. "Two idiots began a brawl and Lorraine was caught in the middle. Thank God Mostyn was there."

"He should have been at her side all along, and this never would have happened," the duke answered, then banged his cane on the roof of the carriage. Then he withdrew his greatcoat and dropped it over Lorrie's shivering form.

At the signal for the coachman to depart, Lorrie pulled away from her father and looked about the barouche. "Where is Mr. Mostyn?" He was not inside with the rest of the party, and she couldn't describe why, but she felt his loss keenly.

"How should I know?" her father answered. "He shoved you inside, slammed the door, and disappeared."

"I know," Neville said, pointing through the slit he'd made in the curtains. "He just hauled both of those men up off the ground and knocked them senseless."

"Oh Lord!" her mother cried. "The man is a barbarian." She turned to her husband, pointing. "What sort of man have you employed?"

But the Duke of Ridlington's expression conveyed anything but apology. "Exactly the sort we need."

∾৯

Charles Caldwell, the Duke of Ridlington, stood at the door joining his chamber to his wife's and stared. He'd stood here many nights over the years before retreating to his large, empty bed. He could not remember when or why the rift between Susan and him had begun, only that it had grown larger and larger over the years.

But these last few months, watching his daughter fall in love with the wrong man had brought memories of his youth and instant infatuation with Lady Susan. At the time, it had seemed the perfect match, but lately he had begun to wonder if he'd made a mistake. Perhaps his father should have prevented him from marrying Susan, as he sought to prevent Lorrie from marrying Francis Mostyn.

Or perhaps it was not he who had made a mistake, but Susan. Charles hadn't tried to make amends when they first began to drift apart, when their conversations had become shorter and curter, when she'd sent him from her room with complaints of a megrim.

Perhaps if he hadn't sought solace in another woman's arms, she would not have sought out her own lovers. But his pride had been hurt, first by her rejection and then by her adultery.

He should have put his foot down at her first infidelity. Instead, he'd allowed his anger and jealousy to burn until he could barely look at her. He'd been too full of pride to let her know she'd hurt him. Too aware of his own failings as a husband to blame her.

Perhaps if he'd done any or all of these things, he would not be standing on the other side of her door alone, as usual.

They had been wed more than a quarter of a century, and though he had not loved her on the day of the wedding, he'd fallen in love with her before the end of their honeymoon. He had thought she had come to love him too. Those early years had been full of nights spent dancing until dawn followed by long, lazy days tangled naked in bed. Then came the birth of their children, three perfect little babies they had both loved more than they'd ever expected.

But something had happened as the children grew into youths. Susan had been tired and distant. He had been preoccupied. There were fewer nights of dancing until dawn and no more days romping in bed. One night he woke in his mistress's bed and wondered what the hell he was doing.

He didn't love his mistress. He didn't even *like* her. She couldn't replace Susan. None of his paramours could, and that night he had decided it was past time he tried filling the hole she had left in his heart and made an effort to win Susan back.

Thus, the last few months standing before their adjoining door.

What a coward he was. What a bloody coward.

He closed his eyes and leaned his head on the door, calling to mind the image of Susan in the green gown she'd worn to the opera tonight. She'd looked radiant, as she always did. Her small, lush form was barely contained by the gown's rounded neckline and straight skirts.

And then when Lorrie had been injured in that ridiculous commotion, Susan had gone into the rain after their daughter before Mostyn had stepped in. Charles could not quite forget the way Susan's skirts had clung to her legs when she'd climbed in the carriage.

He wanted her back. He wanted her body, but more than that, he wanted her heart.

And if he couldn't muster the courage to take what he wanted now, he didn't deserve her. Before he could turn and walk away, he knocked on the door and pushed down on the latch.

To his surprise, the door opened. He had expected it to be locked, though he never called on her and there was no reason for her to lock it. So when the door opened, he all but stumbled inside the pretty chamber done in greens and golds. Sitting at her dressing table, her maid brushing her long dark hair, Susan looked up, hazel eyes cool.

If she was surprised to see him, she did not show it. "Alice, leave us, please."

"Yes, Your Grace." The woman who had been Susan's lady's maid for more than a dozen years gave a quick curtsy and all but ran from the room. This might very well have been the first time the servant had seen the duke enter the duchess's bedchamber.

When the door closed and they were alone, Susan lifted her brush and pulled it through her hair again. "I assume you came to ask about Lorrie. I had Nell give her a warm bath and put her to bed. She is fine. Very little rankles that girl."

Charles nodded. "She is much like her mother."

Susan set the brush on the dressing table, turning to face him. She wore a white robe over a thin nightgown. He could not see the nightgown, but the V of the robe showed a generous amount of cleavage. Her breasts were still high and ripe, and he wondered if her skin would still smell faintly of roses.

"What do you want, Charles? Surely you have not come to claim your conjugal rights."

She was nothing if not direct, and he was actually rather thankful for the opening. "And if I have?"

"I will tell you to go back to your bed."

"Because your lover would object."

"I have no lover at present. Wouldn't your mistress object?"

"I have no mistress."

"I see." She rose with all the grace of a dancer, though she had the body of a goddess. "Am I to fill the gap until you find another light-skirt?"

Charles curled his fingers, anger seeping through

him. How dare she act as though this rift were his fault? She was as guilty of infidelity as he. But if he allowed his anger to get the better of him, he might never have another chance to speak to her like this.

He took a breath, tried to calm himself. "The truth is, Susan, I don't want another mistress." He swallowed the lump in his throat and his pride with it.

She stared at him, uncomprehending.

"I don't want any woman…other than you."

She did not speak for a long, long moment. "Those are lovely words, but I think they come a few years too late. Go back to your room, Charles. You're not welcome in my bed any longer."

"I don't want to take you to bed."

When she lifted her brows, he spread his hands. "What I mean is, my purpose tonight was not to take you to bed. At the moment, all I want is to regain your affection." He had hoped for some reaction from her, but she only stared at him with those cool hazel eyes. "I *will* fight for you, Susan."

And he would fire the first salvo now. He took half a dozen steps until he was within arms' reach of her, then he took her hand in his. Her skin was soft and supple and slightly moist from the cream she put on it before bed.

He bent his head to kiss her knuckles, then at the last moment, turned her hand and placed a kiss in her palm. The scent of roses wafted up to him, and he closed his eyes and allowed himself to be surrounded by it.

Then slowly, ever so slowly, his lips drifted upward until they caressed the skin at her wrist, where he felt her pulse flutter.

She snatched her hand away, and when he looked up at her, her face was impassive. "Goodnight, Duke."

He bowed and left the room. Closing the door, he leaned against it and smiled. She might pretend she had been unaffected, but he had felt her pulse jump. He knew he could still fire her blood.

Now he just had to make her love him again.

❧

Ewan stopped at Langley's to change his clothing before returning to the Duke of Ridlington's town house. He had brought clothing and a few other necessities to the duke's establishment, but he had no desire to arrive mud-streaked and soaking wet.

By the time the Ridlington's butler opened the door to him, it appeared most of the house was asleep. He saw no sign of the duchess or Lady Lorraine. The duke, wearing a banyan, emerged from his library, glass of amber liquid in his hand. "I wondered when you would reappear. What the hell happened tonight?"

Ewan held his head up. "I failed you, Your Grace. It won't happen again."

"Failed me? You pulled my daughter from the middle of two numbskulls so drunk they failed to notice the lady in their path. And then you went back and took them to task. I trust you didn't kill the poor bastards."

Ewan shook his head. The men were alive and whole, though the pain of their recovery might make them wish they were dead for a day or so.

"That's not failure," the duke explained. "Why didn't you ride home in my coach?"

Ewan looked at his clean clothing. "I was wet."

The duke laughed, and Ewan's head jerked up. He was wary of laughter. It usually indicated he'd said something wrong. Again.

"We were all wet," Ridlington explained without malice. "Next time, get in the bloody coach."

Ewan nodded.

"You'll sleep here tonight."

"Yes," Ewan said, though the duke hadn't exactly asked a question.

"Good. We'll have plenty to break your fast. You know where your room is?"

"I can find it."

"Then I'll see you in the morning."

Ewan was left alone in the library. The house was quiet, and Ewan could only assume everyone had gone to bed. He was in no hurry. Sleep did not come easily to him, and when it did finally overtake him, it was not restful. The Survivors didn't discuss the nightmares often, but even a lackwit like Ewan noticed the shadows under his friends' eyes and the way many of them stayed at the club late into the night to avoid their beds.

A man did not see the things he and his friends had seen and rest easily. There had been thirty of them at the beginning; there remained only the twelve of them now. Ewan remembered each of the deaths. He'd been the muscle, the brute force that went in before the other men with more sophisticated skills. And so he'd been there when men were shot or stabbed or blown to pieces. Ewan had fully expected to share the same fate. There was nothing special about him. No reason he should be alive when so many of his friends were dead. It had been sheer luck and sheer waste.

While his dead friends were mourned by their parents and siblings, no one cared whether he lived or died. He was an imbecile, an embarrassment to the family. The Earl of Pembroke would rather not be reminded he had a dullard for a son. He had two perfectly normal sons, and if the third were to die on the Continent, he would not be missed.

As it was, Ewan came back from war and resigned his commission, which was inconvenient for everyone.

Ewan stood before one of the duke's shelves, staring at the long line of book spines. His father had a library, but Ewan had never been left alone in it. He'd never once been offered a book from the Pembroke library to read. And he'd never asked.

Ewan could read a few of the titles. Not all of the letters insisted on jumping off the spines when he looked at them. The words were not supposed to do that. His brothers and cousins had thought he was trying to be funny when he had mentioned that words and letters sometimes jumped around when he tried to read them. Ewan had never mentioned it again, but the laughter still echoed in his memory.

Something was wrong with his mind. He'd realized it that day, and he hadn't been much older than five or six. He'd known it already because he'd had trouble with nursery rhymes and learning the alphabet. But that was the day he'd known he was different from everyone else. The day he'd realized he was stupid.

Dumb.

A lackwit.

It wasn't the last time he'd felt like an idiot. His tutor had seemed to take perverse pleasure in forcing Ewan to read aloud, an onerous chore for him and anyone listening. His cousin Francis, who was closest to him in age, had sniggered and taunted him every time Ewan said *top* instead of *pot* or *loin* instead of *lion*.

Eventually, Ewan did everything he could to avoid his lessons. He argued his head ached too much to go to the schoolroom, and it was not an exaggeration. His head did pound after he tried to make sense of words jumbled on a page. And yet, as he ran a hand along the spines of the books, he wished he could read them. So many men and women seemed to enjoy the act of reading. He'd watched his friends at the Draven Club reading the paper or a book and envied them the knowledge they had. Ewan knew no stories but those he'd been told, knew no news but what he heard from others.

And here in this room were thousands upon thousands of stories, not to mention books about other places and people. And Ewan would never know any of the information because every page looked like someone had shaken it up and moved the lines of text around.

But he'd found a place in the world, despite being a dimwit. As the boys grew older, Francis had stopped laughing when Ewan had confused letters or sounds. Ewan had made him stop laughing. Francis might be able to read anything put before him, but he didn't have Ewan's height, strength, or brawn. The last time Francis had teased Ewan, Ewan had waited for him after class, picked him up, and thrown him halfway across the lawn.

After that, Francis had resorted to meaner and sneakier methods of making Ewan's life miserable. The abuse had gone beyond typical boyish pranks. Francis had managed to turn the boys' tutor against Ewan, which had resulted in beatings and extra reading and writing assignments—none of which Ewan had any hope of completing. When his brothers and cousins had gone to Eton, Ewan had followed for a year and then been sent home in disgrace. His father told him openly he was an embarrassment to the family name and honor. From then on, he'd done his best to ignore Ewan.

Only Ewan's mother, the Countess of Pembroke, had spent any time with him or seemed to love him. She'd encouraged his facility with numbers. He could do almost any calculation in his head. She'd also helped him purchase a commission in the army. As a third son, and not one well-equipped for the clergy, the army was the most logical place for him.

But his mother had never possessed a robust constitution, and she'd died before Ewan had been able to accept his commission. Without his mother in residence, Ewan had no reason ever to return to Pembroke Manor.

And now here he was in his father's world again—in Francis's world. During the war, Ewan had long hours of walking and waiting to think about his cousin's behavior. Ewan had been a convenient outlet for Francis's disappointment at his station in life. Not only had Francis not been born the son of the earl, his father was a notorious gambler who relied on his brother, Ewan's father, to free him from financial scrapes.

Francis had taken out his frustrations at his unhappy and uncertain childhood on the easiest target—Ewan Mostyn. No one would have stood for taunting or teasing of the heir to the marquessate, and Ewan's second oldest brother was both handsome and intelligent. But Ewan had been big and dumb and slow, and Francis had seemed to dislike him from the first time the two boys—just toddlers—had met.

That was all in the past now. Ewan wouldn't have wasted his time seeking his cousin to exact revenge, but neither was he averse to placing obstacles in his cousin's path to happiness. If Francis wanted Lady Lorraine, Ewan would happily thwart him. But that wasn't the only reason he'd taken this position. Ewan knew Francis better than anyone else, and Francis didn't love anyone but himself. He'd somehow managed to convince Lady Lorraine he loved her, but Ewan suspected what Francis really loved was the lady's dowry. And the only thing Francis loved more than himself was blunt.

Ewan didn't know Lady Lorraine very well yet. His impressions thus far were that she seemed to have a knack for finding trouble, and she was willful in the way daughters of dukes—and earls, for that matter— tended to be.

She had no love for opera, which meant she was not a complete loss. She was also quite pretty in a way that tended to distract him. Women did not usually distract him. Women usually annoyed him with all their games and chattering. But he hadn't found himself annoyed when he'd lifted Lady Lorraine into his arms and carried her away from the brawling men.

He'd liked the feel of her in his arms. She was soft and fragrant and warm. He'd looked down at her pale face and wanted to kiss her until the color flooded her cheeks again.

And that made her dangerous. Men might call him an idiot, but Ewan was no fool. He knew kissing Lady Lorraine was out of bounds. He was to keep her safe, nothing more. He needn't touch her or even look at her more than absolutely necessary.

He'd already looked at her far more than he was obliged. The gold dress she'd worn tonight had flattered curves he hadn't noticed before, and she had all that long, dark hair. He didn't dare to look at her eyes except when she was gazing the other way. Her eyes were far too perceptive and their shade of green was one of the loveliest he'd seen. He remembered a field in the French countryside where he and others from Draven's troop had camped one night when they'd gone ahead of the others. The spring morning had dawned golden, casting the green field in a muted light. That was the color of Lady Lorraine's eyes—a verdant field dipped in palest gold.

Ewan could never have her. She was like a pastry in a display case. He could look but not touch. Boys who couldn't read their primers weren't given pastries, and men who were lackwit former soldiers did not aspire to possess a duke's daughter.

But what he *could* do was ensure she remained out of his cousin's reach as well. Because Ewan would rather go to hell and back before he ever allowed Francis to get his hands on her.

Five

THE NEXT MORNING, WHEN EWAN ARRIVED AT HIS club, he found a summons from his father waiting for him. Porter handed it to him when he arrived, and Ewan walked into the vestibule to find his former commander staring up at the shield and sword.

"I'll leave you two alone," Porter said, making a discreet exit.

Neil glanced over his shoulder as Ewan walked past the suit of armor and the broadswords hung on the wall to stand beside him. For a time, the two stared at the shield and those eighteen fleur-de-lis carved into the flanks and base. Peter had been the sixteenth man of the troop to die, and Ewan focused his gaze on that sixteenth mark, trying to remember the man and not his fiery death.

"It should have been me," Neil said softly, so quietly Ewan had to strain to hear him. "I shouldn't be standing here. Bryce or Guy or Peter—or, hell, any of them should be here rather than me."

Ewan didn't argue. They'd all felt that way at one time or another. Ewan had often wondered why he'd lived and others hadn't, but Neil seemed tormented by his own survival. "I know what you'll say," Neil said, his gaze back on the shield and sword. "All of us feel that way, but for me it's different. It should have been me. I'm a bastard. I was unwanted and have no legitimate place. I should have died."

"No," Ewan said simply. "You kept us all alive."

It was true. If they'd lost Neil, they'd have lost their leader and their heart. Ewan doubted any of the men would have come back alive if Neil hadn't.

"Besides, I had to keep you alive," Ewan said, thinking to make light of the situation and thereby erase some of the shadows from Neil's eyes. "We couldn't have the only virgin in the group dying before he bedded a woman."

As Ewan had wanted, Neil turned and scowled at him. "I've bedded women. I just haven't performed one act."

"It made for a good rally cry. *Protect the virgin!*"

Neil glared at him. "Say it again, and I'll break your nose. It wasn't amusing then, and it's not now."

Ewan had liked it better than the one that had replaced it, a phrase about dancing with the devil.

To Ewan's relief, Neil moved toward the stairs. "Did you come to taunt me or did you have another reason?"

Ewan pulled the missive from his coat and thrust it into Neil's hands. Still striding up the stairs, Neil took the missive and broke Pembroke's seal. He scanned the contents. "Your father wants to see you immediately at his town house."

"Why?" Ewan asked, pausing at the top of the stair, hands on his hips.

Neil looked back at the paper. "He doesn't say." They continued into the reading room. "This is dated yesterday, so I imagine he's grown quite impatient." Neil headed for a grouping of chairs and sat heavily. Ewan followed but didn't have time to take his ease.

"You will simply have to tell him you were at the opera last night," Rafe Beaumont said, reading the missive over Neil's shoulder and then sliding into the chair beside Wraxall. "Quite the hero you were too— or so I heard. I want all the details."

Ewan scowled. He was no hero. He'd pulled Lady Lorraine up off the street, where she wouldn't have been in the first place if he'd been doing his duty.

"Will you go?" Neil asked.

Ewan grunted, the sound indecisive. He had no desire whatsoever to see his father. For the past two decades the man had behaved as though Ewan did not exist. Ewan saw no reason that should change now. On the other hand, the few times his father had acknowledged him were times the earl had needed Ewan's assistance—when an overly enthusiastic suitor would not accept that Lady Henrietta did not return his affections and when one of the servants, upset at having been let go without references, went about destroying one of the parlors in a drunken rage.

Little as he cared for his father, he did feel some loyalty toward his family and his name. If the earl had called for him, the matter was most likely urgent.

"You might join Jasper in a game of billiards," Rafe offered. "I've already lost five pounds to the man, but perhaps you'll fare better. And then you can tell me about your feats of valor last night."

Ewan held his hand out to Neil, who gave him the missive. "I have other business."

"Want company? Want to tell me about last night?" Rafe asked.

"No." Ewan turned and strode back out of the club. He hailed a hackney and directed the jarvey to take him to Pembroke House in Mayfair.

The house looked much as it had the last time Ewan had been here, several years before. Rectangular and white with a black wrought iron fence surrounding it and flowers in the boxes at the windowsills, the London home of the Earl of Pembroke looked warm and welcoming.

Ewan knew the truth.

He opened the gate, walked up the four steps to the door, and stared at the knocker. He did not want to do this. He did not want to go inside. Standing here, he felt every bit the miserable boy he had once been. And that boy had wakened every morning with a knot of loathing in his belly because he'd known he was a disappointment. His life had been one of looking in from the outside. He'd stood on the fringes while, knowingly or not, his parents had spent what little time they had for their children lavishing attention on his brothers and sister.

At some point Ewan must have known it was futile to try. No matter how many pictures he drew or how clean his fingernails or how straight the part in his hair, his father always found some fault with him. Ewan forgot he was a dolt and opened his mouth, saying the wrong thing; or he didn't say enough; or he knocked over a vase, breaking yet another of his mother's expensive Sevres porcelain pieces. His father would call him a "clumsy oaf" and banish him to a corner where Ewan could see but not be part of the family gathering.

Silent tears would run down Ewan's cheeks as he had to face, once again, the reality that his father would never love him. The earl would never sit him on his knee as he did Henrietta. His father would never put his arm around his shoulders as he did William and Michael and Francis.

Francis, who was not even his son, but who everyone knew the earl wished had been his son. What Pembroke wouldn't have given to trade Ewan for Francis.

Ewan didn't have any more tears left, didn't have any more hope. All he had was pain and fury, and that he tamped down before he rapped the knocker forcefully. The past was over. Ewan was no longer that boy. He was a man now, and he did not need his father or the man's love.

A man Ewan didn't recognize opened the door. He was dressed as a butler and in his late forties or early fifties with thinning brown hair and small brown eyes. He looked up at Ewan with some concern. "May I help you?"

"The earl. Now."

"Do you have an appointment?"

Ewan shoved the paper with his father's summons at the man. The butler looked at it, then back at Ewan. His brows rose. "Oh, I see. Oh." He looked from the paper to Ewan and back again.

Ewan wanted this meeting over, wanted the memory of the cowed little boy banished once again to the far recesses of his mind. "Move aside or I'll move you."

The butler's small eyes widened. "If you will wait here"—he opened the door to admit Ewan into the house—"I will tell his lordship you are here."

Ewan stepped into the house. "Where is he?"

"No, no!" The butler actually pointed a finger at Ewan. "Wait here."

Ewan waited the five seconds it took to perceive where the butler was headed, and then he overtook him and barged into the library without knocking. He no longer stood on the outside, waiting to be allowed in.

His father looked up from his desk. "What is the meaning of this?"

"Good day, my lord," Ewan said with mock courtesy. The room was much the same as Ewan remembered it. The earl's desk was French in style and overly ornate. His father kept it polished and free of clutter. Books lined the shelves on one wall. There were not as many in the earl's collection as that of the Duke of Ridlington, but it was a fortune in books nonetheless. Soft Turkey rugs in shades of blue and green covered the floor and matching curtains had been swathed back from the narrow windows that afforded a view of the barren garden. Wherever the flowers in the boxes out front had come from, it had not been the earl's garden, which appeared to be suffering the effects of the cold spring.

"My lord!" The butler raced into the library. "I do apologize. This man refused to wait."

The earl raised a hand. "Never mind, Simms. Ewan never did have any manners. Leave us."

"Yes, my lord." The butler gave Ewan a disgusted look and closed the door behind him.

Only then did Ewan notice Francis seated in the chair near the fire. Francis rose and smoothed his perfectly fitted coat. He wore the latest fashion, his burgundy waistcoat making a stark contrast to his gray trousers and coat. His riding boots were highly polished and his cravat stiffly starched. Ewan had no difficulty understanding why Lady Lorraine was in love with the man. Beside him, Ewan felt like an uncouth oaf. His hand itched to touch his bare neck, but he forced it to remain at his side.

"Cousin," he said, his tone barely civil.

"Don't remind me," Francis drawled. Ewan clenched a fist. He wanted nothing more than to break that perfect nose of Francis's and ruin his white cravat with the flow of blood. Francis stepped back, and the earl rose.

"Ewan, Francis and I called you here for a reason," the earl said, rising from his pretty desk.

Francis and I? Ewan cut a look at his cousin, who was still keeping his distance. Ewan should have suspected his cousin had something to do with this. Like his father, Francis had more failings than one could count. Chief among these was the propensity to look for the easiest path to make his fortune. That was undoubtedly why his cousin courted Lady Lorraine—or rather her dowry—at present. But what other mischief had his prodigal cousin found?

Ewan folded his arms across his chest and waited for the explanation. He supposed his father would have liked to speak of the weather or the price of corn before coming to his true purpose, but Ewan had little patience for such niceties.

"I suppose there is no way to cushion this news," the earl began, "so I will put it bluntly. We are ruined."

Ewan merely raised a brow.

The earl sank back into his chair, looking older than Ewan could remember him. His once-blond hair was now mostly white, and he had deep lines furrowed in his brow and at his mouth. "A bad investment," the earl continued. "Diamonds in Brazil, you see."

Ewan didn't see. He had a few investments of his own—he had always been good with numbers. His investments were generally on a smaller scale—a share in Langley's, another in Gentleman Jackson's, a few others.

Francis joined his father behind the desk, standing at his right hand. Ewan gritted his teeth at the picture they made. It should have been him at his father's right hand, but his father had struck him with that hand far more than he had ever welcomed him.

"He doesn't understand, my lord," Francis said with a sneer. "We shall have to explain it in very *simple* terms. Are you listening, Ewan? You must use your brain box for a moment, little as it is."

Ewan liked to imagine the arc the blood would make when his fist plowed into Francis's face.

"Just tell him," the earl said, his voice impatient.

"I suppose I must take full responsibility," Francis began. The earl laid a hand on Francis's arm. Ewan's jaw ached from the tension.

"It is not your fault. You mustn't blame yourself."

Francis nodded, as though these words had been repeated time and again. "A man came to me several years ago looking for investors to finance a mine in South America. They'd found diamonds nearby and had good reason to believe they would find more if they only excavated in the right place."

"Francis brought the man to me," the earl said. "And we went over everything very carefully—the surveyors' reports, the schemes for the building of the mine. I even had the diamonds the man brought with him as proof examined. All seemed quite legitimate."

"But it wasn't," Ewan said.

"At first the delays seemed reasonable." The earl rubbed the back of his neck. "Illness, a contagious disease, warfare among the natives. But finally I grew suspicious and sent a man to investigate." The earl's voice faltered.

"The findings were what you might expect," Francis said. "There was no mine. No diamonds had ever been found in that area. It was, in fact, rather boggy and unsuited to the deposit of such gems. Your father had been swindled."

"I was not the only one. Over twenty other men from all over the Continent and the United States were also taken in."

Ewan stared at his father, unblinking. He failed to see how the fact that other men were duped made his father's blunder any less disturbing. "How much did you lose?" Ewan asked finally when neither of the other men seemed inclined to elaborate.

The earl sighed. "I used your sister's dowry to finance the mine, and when de los Santos—that was his name—asked for more, because of the delays, you see, I mortgaged the estate in Yorkshire."

Ewan almost laughed. "So all of this is to tell me I will no longer receive an allowance." The Yorkshire estate had been their mother's and was the only property the earl owned that was not entailed. He'd used the rents from it to pay a small allowance to Michael and Ewan and to buy Ewan's commission and grant Michael the living of a curacy.

"No," Francis snapped. "That is not the reason for this meeting. Your father and I wish for you to find this Miguel de los Santos and recover the earl's money."

Ewan did laugh then. "And how would I find the man? I'm no investigator."

"But you have friends who might help. Lord Jasper is renowned for his tracking ability."

"Jasper is a bounty hunter. He's paid for his work, and you have just admitted you are ruined. I may be a dolt, but even I know it is wise to diversify investments."

"Oh, shut up!" Francis hissed.

The earl raised his hand. "I have not told your brothers about this yet or informed your sister she has no dowry. William is at Pembroke Manor, and Henrietta has gone with him. Michael is, of course, serving his parishioners. I would appreciate it if we kept this between us for the moment."

"Fine."

"I would also appreciate it if you would *consider* looking into the matter of Mr. de los Santos for us."

Ewan almost shook his head and then thought better of it. It was folly, he knew, to attempt to win his father's affections by aiding him in resolving this crisis, but if he did not help, then Michael and

Henrietta would suffer. He had never been close to them, but they had never been cruel. And though Ewan would not involve Lord Jasper in this matter—there was no point as this de los Santos had undoubtedly already spent the money he'd swindled—Ewan might be able to find some way to help his father recover. After all, what he lacked in reading ability, he made up for in mathematics.

And who was he fooling? He was still that sad little boy who only wanted his father to be proud of him.

"I will consider it," Ewan said. "Give me all the documents related to the investment."

"*Why?*" Francis asked. "It's not as though you can read them."

Ewan looked at his father. Either the earl wanted his help or not.

The earl nodded. "I will have them sent to you at your lodgings."

"Actually," Ewan said, "I have new lodgings."

"Oh?"

"Send them to me at the residence of the Duke of Ridlington." And without taking his leave, he strode out the door.

Behind him he heard Francis swear. "What the devil do you mean by this, Ewan? You'd better bloody well stay away from Lady Lorraine! I'll damn well—"

Ewan closed the library door and made his way to the front door. He heard the library door open behind him and turned, expecting Francis. He was disappointed, as he would have loved to blacken his cousin's eyes. It was the earl.

"What is this about Ridlington?" the earl asked.

"Are you trying to interfere in Francis's suit with Lady Lorraine?"

Ewan rubbed the bridge of his nose. Francis. Always goddamn Francis. Finally he looked his father in the eye. "I may be a lackwit, but *I* am your son. What did I do to make you hate me so much?"

"Do not be ridiculous." The earl looked away, nose in the air. "I don't hate you."

"You don't care enough to hate me." He had been ridiculed as much as he would tolerate today. Ewan turned his back on his father, opened the door, and strode outside. He could still hear Francis's irate voice on the walk. The visit had not been a complete loss after all.

❧

Carlton House was hot and stuffy. The Regent never did understand the value of moderation, and his guest list, like his taste in everything else, ran to excess. Lorrie would have been the first to admit that excess could be quite impressive. The Regent had certainly aimed to impress tonight.

After entering through the portico of massive Corinthian columns, one passed an army of footmen lining the path to the foyer. Unlike most London residences, one did not enter Carlton House on the ground floor. The foyer was located on the main floor, and from there one was led—or pushed, depending on the size of the crowd—into a two-story entrance hall lit from the top by gleaming gold chandeliers so heavily embellished one feared they might collapse under the weight of their beauty. The chandeliers shone down on more columns—these constructed of yellow marble. Lorrie thought the columns in the entrance hall were Ionic, but they might have been Doric. She could never remember the difference and could only identify Corinthian columns because they had the ornamentation at the top.

Entering in this manner allowed the visitor to be appropriately awed by the main staircase, which sloped gently on either side and was quite wide enough to allow three people to pass undisturbed. Lorrie knew from past visits the throne room, music room, drawing room, and dining rooms were on this floor. Each was more impressive than the last, her favorite being the golden drawing room. Never had she seen so much gilded paneling, molding, or ornamentation. Even the columns in the drawing room—Corinthian again— were gold. All of the furnishings were draped in deep crimson, and the combination of the gold and crimson gave the room the feel of cheap opulence—rather the way a brothel might look, Lorrie surmised, never having been to a brothel.

The ball tonight was to be held in the conservatory, which was in the west end of the property. Lorrie lifted the train of her ball gown and descended the staircase as gracefully as possible, trailing her father and mother and one step behind her brother, who she really thought should have taken her arm. Mr. Mostyn followed, hands clasped behind his back, looking neither up nor down, nor left or right. If he was impressed by the show of marble, crystal, and gilded glory, he did not show it.

After the heat of the house itself, Lorrie was

relieved to step into the cool night air before entering the Gothic conservatory. It had been constructed of cast iron and from the outside reminded her of an old church—all spires and soaring peaks. Inside one could not help but marvel at the walls of translucent colored glass, which threw a rainbow of color on the black and white marble floors.

The room was as long as it had been rumored to be. Lorrie had seen pictures of the structure, since it had been the site of a much-discussed fete five years before where over two thousand people had dined at a table with a stream of water running its length. The room was much grander than the cartoons made it seem, with more of the ornate gilded columns so prevalent throughout the house, and lovely gold and scarlet chandeliers hanging in the archways between the columns.

The throng of people gaping at all the golden splendor made navigation through the crowds nearly impossible. She'd been at the ball almost three-quarters of an hour, and she still hadn't spotted Francis. She knew he would be here. He'd sent her a note several days ago asking her to meet with him at the ball. If only he'd been more specific about *where* he wanted to meet her.

To make matters worse, everywhere she turned, she met with the Viking's cold gaze. They hadn't had a chance to speak since the opera the night before, and though she'd been grateful for his assistance then, she wished he would find someone else to follow now. He was wearing another dratted cravat—this one as simple as the other but no less enticing—and she felt as though she were a lion tamer pulling a beast about on an invisible leash.

She had firmly refused to feel any sort of heat or tingles when she looked at him. Those were all reserved for Francis, whom she was determined to kiss tonight. Consequently, she had avoided looking too directly at the Viking. While that plan seemed to have worked quite well, she could not prevent him from looking at her. She could feel his gaze on her body, and her body took delight in vexing her with its response.

She did not know why he insisted on watching her so closely. Any number of ladies stopped to ogle him openly, their smiles beneath their fluttering fans full of invitation. He might have had his pick. She would have been flattered at his single-minded attention to her if she thought it was out of real interest and not simply a matter of duty.

Finally, she could bear the heat of the Viking's gaze and the crush of bodies no more, and she stepped out of the conservatory, which had been situated on the manicured lawns of a park dotted with large trees. Hundreds of sconces lined the building and the adjacent lawn, leading out toward a path flanked by numerous topiaries some said the prince had commissioned for this ball in particular. She had not been outside long enough to lift her face to the cool breeze before a long shadow overtook her own.

Lorrie turned. "Mr. Mostyn, why am I not surprised to see you?"

The Viking leaned back against a spiky column and crossed his arms, apparently content to stand there as long as she did. She hadn't anticipated the effect the sight of his powerful body cased in the glow of fire from the sconces would have on her resolutions. Her traitorous gaze could not cease its perusal of him, and her chest felt tight and itchy with something uncomfortable—something she could not quite define.

His face was in shadows, which only made the hard planes and rigid lines of it more foreboding. His light blue eyes appeared even more ethereal, like those of a wolf intent on its prey. Was she the prey? And if she were, did she mind?

Dressed in an ebony coat and a dark waistcoat threaded with silver, Ewan Mostyn looked very much the Norse version of the Byronic hero. She had a momentary flash of the grim look on his face when he'd carried her through the rain, and she remembered the heat of him when he'd held her. She shivered, telling herself it was from the cold night and not the desire to step into Ewan Mostyn's arms again.

This lie required she ignore the fact that she was perspiring slightly, dampness having formed at her temples the longer she looked at him.

"I know my father asked you to keep me safe, but you needn't follow me every single moment." She sounded like a shrew, even to her ears. "I might point out that my very own mother, my most devoted chaperone, does not keep me *this* close at hand."

"She should."

Lorrie would have argued if she didn't agree. Her mother had always been a lazy chaperone, which was how Lorrie had met Francis in the first place. The Duchess of Ridlington was too interested in her own affairs to pay much attention to those of her daughter. As that fact would not serve her purpose at all, she chose to ignore it.

"As you can see, I am perfectly well and safe here. I want a breath of fresh air before the dancing begins." What she did not add was that she could not seem to catch her breath when he was near. Oh, where was Francis? Lorrie wanted to see him, to remember that it was he she loved and only him she wanted.

"It has begun."

Lorrie furrowed her brow, confused until she realized he meant the dancing had begun. Had she really been searching for Francis that long? She cocked her head toward the conservatory and heard the strains of the violin and the lower notes of the cello floating over the hum of people speaking. The Viking was correct. Lorrie had promised the first dance to the son of a duke, and now she would have to apologize for missing it. She wouldn't have cared who she offended if her search had resulted in finding Francis, but now she had missed the dance and failed to find her—what was he? A lover?

Not really. He'd only kissed her two or three times and those were mere pecks.

Her intended husband? Well, that was what *she* intended. One look at the Viking reminded her that her father had other ideas.

Lorrie decided to change tactics. "I never had a chance to thank you for your help last night. I doubt those men even noticed me. They smelled as if they'd drunk half the gin in Seven Dials."

It might have been a trick of the flickering firelight

behind him, but she thought his mouth curved upward slightly. "I don't require your thanks."

"I'm certain you don't, but that won't stop me from offering it. I did need your assistance last night. There's no danger at the prince's ball." She made a shooing gesture. "You needn't stay at my side."

The Viking did not move, and finally—hallelujah—the prickly uncomfortable feeling she felt when she looked at him was replaced by a prickly feeling with which she was more familiar and labeled *annoyance*.

Lorrie pursed her lips. "If I walk back inside, you will follow me, won't you?"

He nodded.

"Why? Is it because my father is paying you? I won't tell him if you enjoy yourself away from me."

It hardly seemed possible, but the Viking's face turned even stonier.

"Have I said something wrong?" Lorrie asked. "Was it that I mentioned money? I know that's horribly gauche."

"I gave my word," the Viking said.

Lorrie frowned, trying to understand the reference. "Oh. You mean, you follow me not because of the money but because you gave your word."

A slight nod from her bodyguard.

Well, what was she supposed to do with that? She could hardly tell the man to forego his principles and leave her be. But if she didn't, she would never have any time alone with Francis. She'd simply have to find another way to elude the Viking.

"My father won't mind if you enjoy yourself a little, tiny bit." A new idea came to her. "Perhaps when I dance, you could dance as well." Then she could slip away while he twirled his partner in a waltz. Except, it was rather difficult to imagine the Viking dancing or twirling anyone.

"I don't dance."

"Of course you don't." Her shoulders felt heavy enough to sag. "And I imagine you never enjoy yourself either."

"Balls are not enjoyable," he said.

"I don't disagree with you on that point."

The expression on his face flickered with surprise, and she smiled, pleased she had put him off his guard for once. "You think because I am on the Marriage Mart I love the opera and balls and all the rest? I suppose I enjoyed it all the first time I attended. I was a debutante last year, and it was all great fun for a few weeks. But now I'd rather be home in the country, spending time with my friends. I miss my friends, daughters of the country gentry."

Francis had told her when they married he would buy property in Bedfordshire, and then she would always be close to her childhood friends and her family. How she missed the village schoolchildren she would visit daily when she was at Beauchamp Priory, her father's estate, named after a baron who had built Bedford Castle not far from what had once been the monastery and then renovated into the Duke of Ridlington's residence.

In the meantime, it was quite obvious that Francis was not on the terrace. Could he be waiting for her in the park? It was possible, but she didn't want to venture into the unlit lawn with the Viking on her heels. There was nothing to do but return to the ballroom and make her apologies to the son of the duke. She really must try and remember his name... Lord...Something...

"Come on then," she said to the Viking, and he followed her inside.

And then a wonderful thing happened. It was the sort of occurrence Lorrie would never have been able to plan or even anticipate. And it gave her exactly the opportunity she had been searching for.

As Lorrie made her way back to the section of the conservatory set aside for dancing, the Viking so close he would have tread on her train had it been a tad longer, none other than the Prince Regent stepped into their path. Prinny had taken little notice of her on past visits, and she had not expected him to pay her any attention now. Startled, she dropped into a low curtsy. The prince nodded at her. "Lady Lorraine, how good of you to come. I saw your mother a few moments ago. Delightful woman."

Lorrie smiled, uncertain how to respond to the comment. Her mother was exactly the sort the prince seemed to prefer, as his mistresses were generally older, experienced women. "Thank you," she said simply. She might have babbled on about the house or the ball. Lorrie could not stand conversational silences, but the prince's gaze slid past her and up to her companion.

"You are one of Draven's men," the prince said. "Draven's Survivors they call you, what?"

The Viking appeared as surprised as anyone by the prince's notice, and he gave a stiff bow. "Yes, Your Highness."

The prince seemed to expect more, but Lorrie knew the Viking well enough by now to anticipate he would not use any more words than strictly required.

"I want to thank you for your service." The prince moved closer, and Lorrie was forced to step aside else she would be crowded out by the regent's considerable girth. She moved behind the prince, not minding one whit that she was to be left out of the conversation. The Viking tried to keep his eye on her, but he was obliged to pay mind to the future king. "You are Kensington's son—no, Pembroke's."

"Yes, Your Highness."

Lorrie stepped back again, back and into the crowd that always swarmed about the regent.

"Beaumont told me the most harrowing tale of when your group was ambushed in Lyon. Were you there?"

"I was, but—"

Another tiny step back and the crowd swallowed Lorrie whole.

"And what was your role?" the prince asked, excitement making his voice rise in pitch. "How did you and the others escape?"

Lorrie ducked and squeezed through the throng while the Viking gave what she knew would be a curt reply. But he would not be rid of the regent so easily or quickly, and that meant this was her chance to find Francis. Once again reminded that the dancing had begun, she started for the dance floor and had almost reached it when a man stepped into her path.

"Francis!" she said, all her breath whooshing out as soon as she recognized him. His golden hair was tousled and curled about his forehead and cheeks, his face smooth and cleanly shaven and just slightly rounded as though the last of his youth had not yet been honed away. His cravat was full and intricately tied, his coat tight over well-shaped shoulders and a lean back. She had remembered him as taller, and when she looked at him now she was startled to find they were of a very similar height. He had always seemed so much *more*. Now she realized there was probably less than two stones difference in their weight, and whereas before he'd seemed a head taller than she, he was at most only an inch taller. She doubted Francis would be able to lift her and carry her away from two brawling idiots outside the theater.

Lorrie bit the inside of her cheek and reminded herself that she did not need her husband to carry her about nor did she require him to be tall. All she required was his love.

"Francis," she breathed. He caught her gloved hand and brought it to his lips, his light brown eyes never leaving her face and a wicked smile on his mouth.

"My darling, my lady. I have been waiting for a chance to have you all to myself."

Lorrie's heart fluttered at the way his gaze slid from her eyes to her lips and back again. "You must have heard that my father hired a bodyguard."

"Oh, I heard." He straightened but did not release her hand. "Interesting choice. Do you know who he is?"

"I do." She nodded, her heart swelling with sympathy for his pain. "I'm sorry. I am certain seeing him must pain you."

"Indescribably. And it's made all the worse seeing him so close to you."

"He is something of a bulldog. He takes his duty to protect me quite seriously, I'm afraid. I could not manage to evade him."

"Yes." Francis took her hand and led her toward a door leading back out to the lawns. "He is rather simple. One gives him an order, and he follows it. I suppose that is why he was such a good soldier. If my cousin was ordered to fetch, he would fetch."

Lorrie considered arguing. After all, as the Viking had just explained, he followed her out of duty, not mindless adherence to orders, but she did not want to argue with Francis, especially not about a man who had caused him so much pain in the past.

"Let's not speak of him," she said, shivering as the cold air cut through the thin silk of her dress.

"No, let's not," Francis said, drawing her further away from the conservatory. "Let's speak of more pleasant topics. Have I told you how much I missed you?"

Six

THE NEXT TIME EWAN SAW RAFE HE WOULD GIVE HIM a black eye. Whatever had possessed Beaumont to tell the prince regent so many damned tales about the exploits of Draven's Survivors? About half of them were mostly true and the other half were truly fiction. Each had a kernel of fact—a location where the men had encountered trouble or a strategy they had used to outwit the frogs—but Ewan could hardly spend all night untangling Rafe's embellishments.

As it was, he was uninteresting enough that the regent finally sought other amusements, but it took a good half hour for the prince to tire of Ewan's one word answers. In all that time, Ewan barely kept his tone or his manner civil. Where the hell had Lady Lorraine gone? With a victorious smile, she'd melted away into the fawning sycophants that comprised the regent's entourage. Ewan had been powerless to stop her, and now he'd been separated from her quite long enough for any number of men, not the least of which was his cousin, to abduct, harass, or ruin her.

Ewan looked for her among the dancers first. That

was where she should have been. She had promised dances to no less than a flock of men, and Ewan had anticipated standing about the entire night, watching her twirl and flutter her lashes.

He stood on the side of the dance floor and studied the dancers, looking for her. He'd barely been there a moment before a man stepped in front of him. With a growl, Ewan glared at him.

"You are Ewan Mostyn, are you not?" the man asked, his face breaking into a smile that showed his crooked teeth. He had dark hair, a long nose, and small eyes.

Ewan inclined his head.

"Lord Basil Dottinger." The man bowed. "We were at school together."

Ewan merely stared at him. He'd gone to school when he was seven. He'd been there only a year before he was sent home. The excuse had been fighting, but all the boys fought at school. Everyone knew the real reason Ewan was expelled: he was unteachable.

"Do you remember me? We sat at the same table for meals."

Ewan shook his head.

"Well, you wouldn't. You didn't stay long. Did your parents enroll you in another school?"

"No," Ewan said. Heat prickled the back of his neck. The old humiliation washed over him again. This was why he avoided social engagements. He would never measure up to what the son of an earl should be. He was a dolt and a failure at so many things that came easily to other boys. And now he must stand here and have it thrown in his face. And he couldn't even punch the man because the bloody Prince Regent would scream and faint at the sight of blood.

"Why not?" Lord Basil asked, but Ewan did not miss the sly smile on his lips. He knew why not. They all did.

"Go away." Ewan turned his attention back to the dance floor and ignored Lord Basil. After a few more seemingly innocent questions that received no response, the man did go away. He retreated to a spot within earshot of Ewan and made jests to his friends at Ewan's expense.

"Was he as much a dolt as you remember?"

"He can barely string two words together."

"Poor fellow. I heard his father disowned him."

"He's only here tonight because the Duke of Ridlington paid Prinny to receive him."

Ewan stiffened. That wasn't true, was it? He felt his breath grow short, and the heat that burned his neck washed over his face. He wanted to storm out or to turn and fling each man through one of the windows. As he could do neither, he took a deep breath and balled all the pain into a tight knot.

Control. Restraint. Those traits had kept him alive in the war. This was just a different sort of battle.

Ewan forced his attention back to the dance floor. He could not waste his time with these petty men and their small worlds. Who the devil cared if they whispered about him or if Ridlington paid the Regent to receive him? He was here for a purpose, and at the moment, he couldn't find her.

Lady Lorraine was not on the dance floor, and he

was obliged to seek her elsewhere. He tried the area set aside as the supper room and that for cards with no luck. If she'd had any sort of compassion at all, she would have taken up residence in the supper room, where all sorts of delicacies had been laid out to refresh famished guests before the actual meal commenced sometime in the middle of the night or wee hours of the morning. But Ewan had only enough time to snatch a biscuit and a glass of champagne, which he downed like water, before he had to search elsewhere.

And the elsewhere was obviously to be one of three locations—the lawns, the house itself, or the ladies' retiring room. Heaven help her if she had allowed Francis or any other man to take her to the back of the house. If the chit got herself ruined on his watch, he would throttle her.

Ewan couldn't search the ladies' retiring room by himself, so he opted to begin searching the lawns. He stepped out onto the terrace where he'd last spoken with her, walked its length quickly, and swore when he did not spot her. She was in the damn house, and now he would have to murder whichever man had led her there.

He'd turned to do just that when the breeze carried the sound of a light, tinkling laugh his way.

Ewan turned back and peered out into the dark shadows cast by trees whose branches blew gently in the wind. The night was cold, and the prince had obviously thought the guests would prefer to stay close to the warmth of the conservatory and the myriad entertainments therein because, other than the sconces lining the building and the path back to the house, he had not ordered any other means of light for the lawn or park. Consequently, Ewan could see nothing but tree trunks, the stubby shadows of bushes, and the vague outline of topiaries a little further away. Surely, Lady Lorraine would not have ventured into the gloomy, cold night. She had been wearing a flimsy white dress that bared her neck and enough of her bosom to force him to look away before he looked closer. The sleeves had been little puffs and her gold wrap was so insubstantial that he wondered why she bothered with it at all.

The laughter he'd heard might have come from any woman who had sought privacy with her lover in the shadows, but Ewan had to be certain it was not his charge. He would rather apologize to the couple for interrupting their tryst than to the Duke of Ridlington for losing his daughter.

Ewan started in the direction of the laugh, and though he'd never been a great tracker, he'd spent more than enough time navigating through dark and dangerous landscape that he had little trouble locating the couple. The two were murmuring together quietly. He heard first the man's voice and then the woman's. Ewan crept closer, the topiary shielding his approach. If this was not Lady Lorraine, then he could retreat without being seen.

"Darling, I know you are impatient, but we will have our whole lives together. A few more months is not much to wait."

Ewan's heart sank into his belly. He knew that voice. Ewan felt six again, and he had the urge to shrink down as small as he could make himself and pray with all his might that no one would notice him behind the bush trimmed to look like a swan.

"But why should we wait?" the woman asked. "I told you. I don't care about the money."

The sound of Lady Lorraine's voice, quick and light as a song, was like a snowball in Ewan's face. He straightened his shoulders and rose to his full height. He would kill Francis and then make Lady Lorraine wish he'd murdered her.

"Darling, we must live on something—"

"I can find work," she protested. "I can take in washing or bake pies to sell. Any sacrifice would be worth it if I could be with you."

Ewan had been moving forward and now he rounded the main body of the swan topiary and saw Lady Lorraine put her hands on Francis's shoulders. For a moment, the sight of his old nemesis paralyzed Ewan. His body sought to betray him, and his feet would not move forward. Consequently, he had time to note that Francis did not take the liberty any other man in his position would have and put his arms around the woman before him.

"Kiss me," she said, looking up at Francis with adoring eyes the bastard did not deserve in the least. "I could wait forever if you would but kiss me."

It was perhaps the silliest speech Ewan had ever heard. It was the sort of thing he expected one of Beaumont's women to say, and yet despite the melodrama of the sentiment, at that moment Ewan hated Francis more than he ever had when his cousin had been his daily tormentor.

His loathing was so strong and so incomprehensible

that Ewan regained control of his body and stepped out from behind the topiary.

Francis saw him first, and he stiffened and stepped back, putting a respectable distance between himself and Lady Lorraine. His expression was wary and, to Ewan's satisfaction, frightened. The lady spun around as well, but her face showed no fear, only annoyance. She gave a long sigh. "Mr. Mostyn, I believe you know your cousin, Mr. Mostyn."

"Ewan." Francis looked him up and down. "We seem to keep meeting. Run along now. Lady Lorraine and I were having a private word."

Ewan held out his hand to Lady Lorraine. "Come."

"I see your vocabulary remains much the same," Francis remarked. "As I'm certain you will use your simple grunts and growls to inform His Grace about this meeting, be sure to mention that I did nothing improper."

"More's the pity," Lady Lorraine muttered. "At least the lecture and scolding would have been worth it."

Ewan had the urge to laugh. Instead, he beckoned her with his outstretched hand. She did not take it. "I am not a dog, Mr. Mostyn. You needn't crook your finger at me."

Francis bowed. "I see I am no longer needed. My lady, sleep well tonight. I will see you…soon." With what Ewan perceived was to be a meaningful look, Francis marched in the direction of Carlton House.

Since the lady seemed to have such an objection to them, Ewan folded his arms across his chest. He waited for her to speak. He felt he should say something, but he was not certain what that something should be. He had supposed Francis to be taking advantage of the lady, while it appeared she was the one intent on ruination. Francis was no paragon of honor and virtue, and Ewan would have liked little more than to beat the man to a pulp. But he could not fault his cousin for the scene he'd witnessed tonight.

"You won't tell my father, will you?" Lady Lorraine finally broke the silence.

Ewan let out a breath of surprised air—half laugh, half incredulity.

The lady grasped his forearm. "If you do, it will not only doom me, but it will reflect badly on you as well."

Ewan inclined his head, acknowledging the point. He'd made mistakes before, and he always took his punishment like a man. He was not much of a gentleman, but he had retained enough of his upbringing to know that one did not lie or cheat to avoid trouble. One faced the consequences of his mistakes with head held high. "Then so be it."

She gaped at him. "You do not even care? You will be dismissed."

Ewan blew out a breath. He did care. He cared very much, much more than he wanted to admit to.

Her hand on his forearm tightened, and he looked down at her. The damned chit was shivering with cold. Ewan was impervious to all but the coldest temperatures, but she looked almost blue. "Very well. Tell him. Nothing happened anyway."

"Not for your lack of trying. I should tell your father you don't need a bodyguard. You need to be locked in a convent."

Now her eyes narrowed, and she released his arm

as though it were filth she could not bear to touch any longer. "So now I am to be censured by you?"

He frowned at her. "Why not me?"

"Are you married?"

The question took him off guard. Conversations with women generally had the effect of unsettling him. He could never predict where their maze-like minds might wander. Conversations with men began at point A and ended at point B. Women often meandered to C then R and back to L before coming to the point.

"It is a simple question, Mr. Mostyn. Are you married?"

He shook his head.

"I didn't think so. Are you a virgin?"

Ewan gaped at her. The question was so wildly inappropriate that, in his opinion, she had abandoned the points of the alphabet all together.

She waved a hand. "Yes, I know I am not supposed to ask you that, but humor me. I am making a point. Just answer yes or no."

He shook his head, as he did not trust his voice at the moment.

"Of course you are not. And yet no one thinks anything of the fact that you have bedded a woman who is not your wife. If I had to guess, with those eyes and those shoulders and chest"—she looked him up and down, and he actually felt himself heat at her frank perusal—"I imagine you have bedded more than your share of women."

Ewan's head was spinning at the rapidity of her speech, but what he did understand was that she had just complimented him. She admired his body, and the thought of her eyes on him caused him to have to take a breath. His chest felt tight, and he lifted his hand to loosen the goddamn cravat before he remembered where he was.

"Of course," she went on, "it is seen as perfectly natural for a man to want to kiss a woman, touch her, undress her, take her to bed, and—"

Ewan cleared his throat, not only because the already inappropriate conversation had descended beyond the pale, but because her description of the intimacies between men and women made him think of doing those things with her. And now the woman had not only fired his blood but stirred his rod. If she continued in this vein, his state of growing arousal would be evident to both of them.

"My point," she said—and thank God she was finally reaching it—"is that it is considered natural for men to want these things, but when a woman wants them, then we should be locked away." She gestured wildly with her hand, losing hold of her wrap so it slid to the ground and trailed after her as she paced. "What is so wrong with wanting a man to kiss me?" She gave Ewan a direct look, challenging him to give her an answer.

He opened his mouth to reply, but she did not wait. Which was for the best, as he did not know what he would have answered.

"I love Francis Mostyn. Is it unnatural for me to want to express my love with a token of affection?"

"Kisses lead to further improprieties," Ewan said. As soon as the words were out of his mouth, he wanted to turn and see if his father stood behind him and had voiced them. It was exactly the sort of lecture the earl would have given to Ewan's sister.

"I am prepared for that," Lady Lorraine argued, turning and pacing the other way. "I want to marry Mr. Mostyn. I will make whatever sacrifice is required."

"Washing and baking," he said, recalling her speech earlier.

She stopped pacing and glanced at him. "You heard that then? Yes. As I said, I could earn money by taking in washing or baking pies to sell."

The woman had no idea what she was talking about. "Have you ever laundered a garment?" Ewan asked.

"I…" She scowled at him. "It cannot be too difficult to learn."

"It is hard work," he said. He had never washed any of his own clothing until he'd entered the army, and while the work did not tax him physically, there was an art to it. "The soap roughens your hands and burns your skin, and the fabric grows heavy when wet so that scrubbing it requires some strength. Then it must be rinsed and wrung out and hung to dry."

She put her hands on her hips. "I understand the process."

"Have you ever looked at a washer woman?"

"Yes, of course."

Ewan stared at her. He was a nobleman as much as she was a lady by birth. The nobility was not raised to look at the servants but rather to look through them.

"I have looked at them," she insisted.

"What did her arms look like?"

Lady Lorraine's brow creased as though she were deep in thought.

Ewan rarely interrupted, but she looked more chilled by the moment, and he wanted to finish the conversation and bring her inside. "Her arms were large and muscled and probably quite red and chafed. *If* you lasted in that work for a week, your delicate white arms would be ruined." He looked at the patch of exposed skin between her gloves and her excuse for a sleeve.

She looked down at it as well. And then she looked back up, her glittering eyes brimming with determination. "Then I will bake pies instead."

Ewan sighed. "Have you ever baked a pie?"

She looked at him as though she wished lightning might strike him dead. "Listen, Mr. Mostyn, I do not see why my abilities are any of your concern. And don't think I don't know why you want to thwart any chance I have of eloping with Francis."

He'd never supposed she did not know why he wanted to stop her. Her father had hired him for that precise purpose. "Your father—"

"No! That's not why. It's because you hate your cousin."

Ewan stared at her. How had she known that?

"You tormented him as a boy, and now you see an opportunity to continue the abuse."

Ewan was frequently speechless, but he'd never been made so purely by shock. Was that the story Francis had told her? Perhaps that was what his bastard cousin had told everyone. It would have garnered him sympathy, and Francis thrived on sympathy. Ewan could hardly fault her for believing it of him before they had met, but how could she think that of him now?

Ridiculous. Of course she would think such horrors

of him. She didn't know him at all. She didn't even know the man she claimed to love. Ewan wanted to pity her, but he was far too angry.

"I love Francis," she was saying, "and I won't allow—"

"You don't love him," Ewan said with more vehemence than he'd intended. That little knot of fury he'd balled up unraveled slightly. She stepped back, clearly surprised as well. "You don't know the first thing about my cousin or me or, for that matter, love." He didn't know why he'd added that last bit. He didn't know anything about love either.

"And you do?" she challenged, clearly not afraid of him.

"I don't claim to know about love," he said honestly, "but I know my cousin, and he is not the innocent you think him to be. He is conning you, my lady—an easy task, as you can be taken in for a kiss."

"That's not true."

He advanced on her, but she did not move away. She merely scowled at him.

"You think my cousin loves you? He loves your dowry."

"How dare you!"

"And if you were ever kissed by another man or two—kissed soundly and thoroughly—maybe you'd see that Francis Mostyn is not the paragon you seem to think."

He put his hands on her upper arms, and even through his gloves he could feel the coolness of her skin.

"And who will kiss me? You?"

He heard the note of hope in her voice. There was anger too, but he'd heard the hope. She *wanted* him to kiss her. Well, better him than the next man she encountered, who might be a rake or worse. He would give her what she seemed to want so desperately, and then she would see that there was a world of men beyond Francis Mostyn.

And what lies he told himself. He *wanted* to kiss her and had been looking for the excuse.

Ewan slid his hands to her back, gliding one down until he pressed the small of her back. He exerted a minimum of pressure to pull her closer and into his arms. She felt so small against him, and she trembled with cold. He wrapped his arm around her tiny waist, anchoring her to him, then lifted his other hand and brought it to her face. His palm caressed her cheek, then he pushed his fingers into her hair and allowed his thumb to trail along that cheek. How he wished he wasn't wearing his gloves. He imagined her cheek felt like velvet and her hair like spun gold.

And then he did not have to imagine any longer because he put his lips where his thumb had been and traced the path. As he'd thought, her skin was as soft as a flower petal and as delicate too. He hadn't expected the scent of her to waft past his nose and snare him. She smelled of vanilla and sweet cream and something else uniquely her that made him hungry for far more than food.

His lips skated to her ear so he could bury his nose in her hair. The scent was pink and light and womanly, a fragrance he now knew was hers alone. He pressed a kiss to her ear and felt her shiver, not from cold this time. "Enough kissing?" he asked.

"No," she said, her voice low and husky but ever

so definitive. He almost laughed again. He had known that would not be enough for her. Nothing would be enough until he plundered her body and left her limp and exhausted with pleasure.

His cock, hard now and at attention, approved heartily of that plan, but Ewan had grasped for his lauded control. At a young age, he'd learned to harness his strength and control it, and his desires were under those same taut reins. He would kiss her. Nothing more.

He pulled back slightly to look in her eyes. It was too dark to discern the color, though he knew it well, but he wanted to see the look in them. As he'd expected, there was no fear, only wide-eyed curiosity and the barest hint of heavy lids, indicating the beginnings of arousal.

Ewan traced a thumb over her lips, parting them slightly, and then pressed his mouth to hers.

Seven

LORRIE WAS IN A STATE OF ACUTE SHOCK. HER ENTIRE body quivered, and she knew it was no longer from the cold. The man holding her against him was as hot as a furnace. He was almost too hot, and she felt a single bead of perspiration trickling down her back. She did not know why she quivered except that she was giddy with anticipation. The Viking was kissing her. She hadn't known she wanted him to kiss her until he'd pulled her against him, and then she did not know how she had ever wanted anything else.

Even before his lips drove her to madness with their slow, tickling path to her ear, she knew this would be no chaste, perfunctory kiss like those Francis had given her. The Viking was not civilized. He would not kiss her like a gentleman, an assumption he proved when he growled in her ear. The heat that shot into her body at the warmth of his breath on that tender flesh had made her knees buckle. Her belly had soared and dipped and then coiled tightly as if waiting for something.

And then he'd pulled back and looked at her with

those icy blue eyes. Except they had not looked icy at all. They'd been the blue of a lake or of the sky on a perfect summer day. His large, rough thumb scraped over her lips, and the gesture itself felt so incredibly wanton that when he kissed her, it almost felt sweet.

But that was just the initial press of his lips on hers. She'd been kissed like this before—lips upon lips, mouths locked in a fleeting embrace.

Then his lips moved. He kissed one side of her mouth and then the other. Her head reeled and she felt dizzy until he took her bottom lip between his teeth and nipped. Lorrie opened her eyes—eyes she hadn't even realized she'd closed—and gasped. What sort of man bit her? But she could not begin to object because he'd taken advantage of her open mouth to slant his mouth over hers.

His *open* mouth.

Lorrie stiffened, uncertain what she should do next. Keep her mouth open? Close it?

That was when his tongue moved inside and slid across the roof of her mouth. Her heart thudded heavily in her chest and she tightened her hands on his coat both to hold herself upright—though his hand remained firmly on her back—and to keep him from stopping. She did not ever want him to stop. His tongue tangled with hers, and spikes of pleasure zinged through her body.

This was indeed the most wanton thing she had ever done, and she never wanted it to end. The Viking—my God, she was kissing the Viking— plundered her mouth. There was no other word to describe what he did. He kissed her so deeply she could scarce remember to breathe. Her head felt fuzzy and too heavy for her shoulders, while at the same time she was aware of a growing ache between her legs. The more he slid in and out of her mouth, the more he toyed with her tongue, the more the ache grew and spread. She felt it in her belly and her breasts, which grew swollen and tender. Her nipples had hardened into points that chafed against her stays.

She wanted to throw her head back and allow him to do what he would with her, as long as he never stopped kissing her.

And then suddenly there was that nip on her lower lip again, and sharp focus returned. He'd pulled back, and she opened her eyes and stared at him.

"Enough?" he asked.

She should say yes. It was more than enough. It was too much. Instead, she shook her head. "More."

He looked at her as one might look at a child who had eaten four biscuits and asked for yet another. Her lungs tightened with fear that he would cease kissing her. That he would end the magic that was this moment and she would be thrust back into reality. That she would never kiss him again after tonight. And that would be the greatest injustice of all.

"Kiss me back," he said in his usual gruff way.

Joy surged through her. He would not deny her! And yet she had no idea how to comply with his demand. "I don't know how to kiss like this," she confessed. "I've never—"

He silenced her by tracing his tongue along her

upper lip, an action that made her catch her breath. Then he pulled back and raised one brow in what seemed to be a challenge.

"Oh, you want me to do what you do," she said.

He didn't answer, not that she'd expected one, and she rose on tiptoe to run her tongue along his upper lip. At the moment before she touched his mouth, she felt rather foolish. She had never licked anyone before, but as soon as their flesh met, she forgot all about foolishness. She learned the shape of his lip with her tongue—first his thin upper lip, then the fleshier lower lip. He was clean-shaven, but the first hints of stubble tickled her tongue. She closed her mouth over his lower lip, sucking on it gently and then biting it sharply as he'd done to her.

Suddenly, she felt herself lifted off the ground, his hands digging into her buttocks and pulling her against his hard chest—but no, that was not his chest. That was—his mouth crashed down on hers and if she had thought she had been senseless before, she lost all capacity for thought now.

Her ears rang with the sound of blood rushing to her thudding heart, she did not know if her eyes were open or closed. All she knew was his mouth on hers, his body pressed to hers. All she knew was that in that instant, she was his completely.

And then she was not.

He set her down roughly, and she stumbled, hands stretched out, fingers groping wildly until she caught the back of a bench.

"Bloody fucking hell."

It was the Viking's voice, but she didn't know

where he was. She couldn't seem to reach him. She needed to touch him again, to kiss him again. She felt bereft without his hands on her. She looked over her shoulder. "Mr. Mostyn."

His hand was rough on her arm. "Sit." He guided her to the bench's seat and pushed her down. The iron bench felt cold under her thin silk dress, especially when compared to the tropical splendor that had been the Viking's body. Lorrie closed her eyes and the world ceased spinning for a moment.

Finally, she opened her eyes again and looked up. The Viking stood beside the bench, his gaze on Carlton House, just visible beyond the topiaries.

"What happened?" she asked.

He gazed down at her, then back at the house.

"I mean, I know you kissed me, but I don't understand. I didn't know kisses could be like that." Since he didn't respond, she filled the silence. "It did not even feel like a kiss. It felt…"

He glanced down at her again.

"More intimate." She met his gaze.

"Let's go."

"Why?"

His look darkened, and she waved the storm clouds away. "I know why you want to return, but what I mean is, why did you kiss me?"

"A mistake," he said. "Come." This time he pulled her to her feet, moving back to make certain their bodies did not come into contact.

"No, I won't go until you answer my question. It may have been a mistake, but *why* did you do it? Was it really just to prove Francis's kisses are much like pressing one's lips to a trout, because you proved that well enough."

The Viking's lips twitched, possibly with humor.

"You could have proven that with half as much effort."

"Later," he said and nodded toward the conservatory.

"Oh, no." She took a step away from him. "If I can't persuade you to discuss the matter now, I certainly won't be able to coax anything from you later. Why do you have such an aversion to speaking?"

"Why do *you* have such an aversion to silence?"

She smiled because she had forced him to speak. "Because I want answers, and if I don't ask, no one tells me. Half the time they don't tell me anyway."

"Once again you will be disappointed."

"No, I won't. I'm not returning to the ball until you answer me." Which would hopefully be soon as she was beginning to shiver again.

He folded his arms across his chest—a chest, which she now knew, was quite hard and every bit as muscled as it appeared. But the gesture she took as an indication he thought her threat little more than a bluff.

"I mean it," she said. "You cannot make me go in."

"Really."

Lorrie moved back again, prepared to put the bench between them. "What would you do? Fling me over your shoulder and carry me in like I was a square of carpet?"

He nodded sagely as though he rather liked that idea.

She scooted behind the bench. "Wouldn't it

be easier and less likely to cause scandal if you just answered my question?"

He sighed. "Why I kissed you."

"Yes. Why you kissed me so...so intimately."

"I wanted you." He held out his hand. "Now, let's go."

Lorrie stared at him, her fingers gripping the back of the bench so she would not fall backward. "You *wanted* me? What does that mean? You wanted to kiss me?"

"Yes." His brows lowered as he moved toward the bench. Lorrie scooted further away.

"And when you were kissing me, you wanted to keep kissing me because...because you *liked* kissing me."

He didn't give her any indication she was correct, but he didn't deny her words either.

"I liked kissing you as well," she admitted.

"I know."

Arrogant man. She would ignore that remark. "I wanted to do more than kiss you."

"No." He nodded his head in the direction of the ball. "Inside."

"That is what you meant, isn't it? You desired me. You wanted me in your bed." Her cheeks burst into flame. She did not have to see her reflection to know her face must have been as red as a beet. She was glad of the darkness in the garden.

"I answered your questions. Don't make me chase you."

But Lorrie was hardly listening. The Viking had wanted to bed her. Surely there had been other men who had considered her in this light. She had two older brothers, so she knew something of the minds of men. But the Viking was the first man who had ever acted on the desire. And if she was not mistaken, his feelings had not been entirely welcome. She remembered all had seemed somewhat…if not proper then contained until she had bitten his lip. That was when his control had seemed to break. She wondered what would happen if she did it again.

Unfortunately, her musings doomed her because the Viking took advantage of her distraction to move quickly. He rounded the bench, caught hold of her about the waist, and tucked her under his arm as though she were a parcel.

"Put me down!" she gasped. She punched his stomach, but that only had the effect of making her own hand hurt. "I will walk on my own."

"Too late."

Good grief but this was mortifying. If anyone should happen to see her, she would probably die of humiliation.

Finally, they reached the lighted area outside the conservatory, and he set her down. She swatted at him, then made a point of straightening her dress and her hair. "Oh drat. I must have dropped my wrap." She started back for the topiary, but the Viking caught her arm. "I will send a servant to fetch it. You go inside."

"Stop ordering me about." But she didn't argue further because his suggestion was actually quite sensible, and now that she could hear the music from the ball again, she remembered she really should have been dancing.

"Lorraine."

She spun around to find her mother standing on

the terrace. Lorrie had no idea how much the duchess had seen, whether she had just emerged or if she'd watched the Viking carry her back to the house.

"Coming, Mama. I needed a bit of air."

The duchess's gaze roved over the Viking and then she scanned Lorrie from head to foot. Lorrie had no idea how she looked. She hoped she did not appear as thoroughly debauched as she felt. "I am sure you did, but you are wanted in the ballroom. Hurry along now."

Lorrie lifted her skirts, climbed the terrace steps, and followed her mother into the house. If she had the urge to look back at the topiaries where she'd had her first real kiss or the man who had given it to her, she behaved like the duke's daughter she was and kept her eyes forward.

❧

The woman was as annoying as the snipers Napoleon had employed during the war. The men had always seemed to appear out of nowhere, on top of some building Draven's men needed to access, at the worst possible time. Nash could usually pick them off, but the most stubborn of them had to be left to Ewan, who would have to go around the building, sneak up to the roof, and dispose of the men without having his own head shot off.

Lady Lorraine was only slightly less aggravating and that was only because he did not have to go to the trouble of breaking her neck or throwing her off a building, although there had been several instances in their brief acquaintance when he had considered doing one or both.

Now he merely wanted to break the neck of the man she danced with. He was a thin fellow. Ewan estimated the boy probably weighed as much as Ewan's left arm. If the lad needed to shave more than once a fortnight, Ewan would have been surprised. But he had the dark, brooding looks Byron had made so popular. This son of a viscount or pasha or whatever the hell he was had long, dark hair that curled about his face, sad eyes that reminded Ewan of a pug his mother had once owned, and stark cheekbones that were in want of a good meal.

As the pug-eyed boy twirled Lady Lorraine about, making her laugh and sending her looks of puppy-like adoration, Ewan imagined wrapping his hand—it would only take one—around the lad's neck and snapping it in two.

"You wore that same look on your face when we were trapped in that tavern in Strasbourg," said a voice at his right arm. Ewan glanced over and was not at all surprised to find Rafe Beaumont standing beside him. Beaumont was a model of style and elegance, and Prinny had come to value Rafe's opinion on matters of fashion after the famous falling out between the prince and Brummell.

"You remember my expression?" Ewan said without any formal greeting, for none was needed between the two men who were far closer in some ways than even brothers.

"Perfectly."

"I remember you had your head up a trollop's skirt."

Beaumont grinned. "I remember her too. My persuasive tactics succeeded in convincing her to show us the cellar where her father hid his best wines and tobaccos. If we hadn't hidden there, we would never have taken the soldiers by surprise after they stormed the building."

Ewan did not point out that all the hiding spot had done was given them a slight advantage before the attack. He had still fought his way out with a ferocity that would have made a berserker proud.

"Is that your charge?" Beaumont asked, nodding to Lady Lorraine, still firmly entrenched in the pug's arms.

Ewan folded his arms over his chest and gave a quick nod of assent.

"She's pretty, although she smiles rather too much."

Ewan had noticed how often she smiled at the man she danced with as well. He had supposed it was out of sympathy for the ugly lad's attempts to amuse her. But just because she smiled too much for Ewan's liking did not mean Beaumont should comment upon it.

Rafe held up a hand in defense. "Pray don't look at *me* like that. I'd like to keep all my limbs in working order, if you don't mind." His gaze narrowed. "Is it because I remarked that she smiles too much? It was not a criticism, Ewan. I was merely surprised because daughters of dukes are usually so proper and haughty. She does not strike me as fitting that description."

Ewan's thoughts flashed back to the garden and the way she'd nipped his lip. Proper and haughty did not begin to describe Lady Lorraine. No proper lady would have nipped him so. And no gentleman would have reacted as he had, giving in to the sudden rush of desire that had him moments away from claiming her virtue. Ewan couldn't remember the last time he'd felt so out of control with need for a woman. In fact, he didn't think he'd ever felt that way before.

Control. Restraint. Those were the words of the day.

"But I forget how loyal you are," Beaumont drawled. "It is one of your best qualities, and since I have benefitted from it more than once, I am ever appreciative of it. Therefore, what I should say is that Lady Lorraine is all things perfect and wonderful and lovely."

Ewan clenched his fists.

"Now what have I said?" Rafe demanded, and this time he did take a step back to what Ewan assumed he considered a safe distance.

It wasn't. Ewan could have reached his throat easily.

"You cannot imagine *I* have designs on her," Rafe said. "Hell's teeth, man, I have enough trouble with the fairer sex. I needn't add to my miseries with the daughter of the Duke of Ridlington. Francis Mostyn, little bastard that he is, is the man you want to throttle."

"I caught them in the park."

Rafe's eyes bulged. "What? That arse had lured her into the park? For what purpose?"

"I am not certain it was Francis who lured the lady."

"I don't follow… *Oh*, I see what you mean. Well then, you have your work cut out for you, don't you? Neil did say the lady was trouble. Since she is your trouble, you will have to be on your guard. Fortunately, you excel at such tasks."

Ewan made a noncommittal sound. The reel or jig or whatever the hell it was she'd danced had ended and now she was on the arm of another man. This was one was a bit older and hadn't yet looked away from her bosom.

"You may breathe easier now, my friend," Rafe said, slapping him lightly on the shoulder. "Your cousin has departed. I saw him waiting for his carriage just as mine arrived."

That news did allow Ewan to relax slightly. At least he would not have to worry his charge would arrange any further clandestine meetings with Francis, and as she thought herself in love with him, she would probably resist the overly enthusiastic attentions of every other gentleman as well.

Still, he intended to keep her in his sights the rest of the evening. Until she was behind the locked doors of her father's house, he would not take his gaze off of her. Even then he could not relax. He still did not know if she had used the door or climbed down the tree when she'd tried to elope. Ewan didn't think any plans to elope had been made tonight. The conversation he'd heard seemed to indicate otherwise, but that did not mean plans would not be made in the future. Lady Lorraine seemed to possess a talent for having her way, and if he hadn't been able to resist her, he doubted his idiot cousin would.

"All of this talking has parched my throat," Beaumont said, backing away. "I'd better find refreshment."

Footmen circled the room with silver trays of champagne, but before Ewan could snatch one for his friend, he noticed the voluptuous woman making her way toward them. She moved like a lioness stalking her prey, and Rafe—the prey—would not wait to be caught. "I'll see you at the club," he said and dove into the crush of guests. Ewan, being one of the taller men in the room, could see him move expertly through the throngs, but Rafe would be quite obscured from the lioness's vision.

Ewan glanced back at the dancing, observing his charge with arms folded across his chest. Once or twice in the course of the night, the forms dictated that she stand near his side of the room, and she always glared at him.

Finally, at about two in the morning, supper was announced. Ewan neatly stepped in front of the man who'd been about to escort her into supper, and took her arm himself.

"Well, that was rude," she remarked, giving her former dance partner an apologetic smile over her shoulder. "He is supposed to escort me to supper after the dance."

"No," Ewan said.

"Yes, he is. And I know you know this because you are the son of an earl, but for some reason you are acting more like a cross gargoyle. How am I or any of the other guests supposed to dance with any gaiety while you glower at us from your corner?"

So that was the reason she'd glared at him whenever she'd danced by. He liked the way she talked, liked listening to her voice, even when it was filled with rebuke. He deposited her in a chair beside her mother and then went to fill a plate for her.

"Mr. *Mostyn!*" she hissed as he walked away.

Undoubtedly she was not pleased to be seated beside her mother and the other matrons at her mother's table. She would have preferred to flirt at a table filled with men or to gossip with some of the other young ladies. Ewan wanted her out of the way of any such trouble.

He joined the line of other men filling plates for their ladies. Lady Lorraine was correct that he had not behaved properly in taking her away from her last dance partner. A gentleman asked for the supper dance in order to be the one who escorted the lady to dinner and then claimed her attentions for the duration. Since Ewan had whisked her away, he would have to fill a plate for her. He didn't know what she liked, so he filled the plate with a bit of everything. One plate was not quite large enough for all the bounty the regent had bestowed upon his guests, so he filled two.

A pity he was working tonight because he would have liked to taste some of the fare, but he did not eat while he was on duty.

He brought the plates back to Lady Lorraine and sat them in front of her. The lady gaped at him. "Surely, you do not expect me to eat all of this!" She gestured to the food piled so high it all but reached her chin.

"I didn't know what you liked," he said.

"How very thoughtful of you, Mr. Mostyn," the duchess remarked. "And since your father has taken up residence in the card room, I will share your bounty, Lorrie."

"The card room?" said a voice Ewan recognized as the duke's. "I merely stopped in to say hello." The duke pulled a chair beside his duchess, who stared at him openmouthed.

"I would not leave my duchess to dine alone." He took her hand and kissed it. The duchess snatched it back, but the duke seemed unperturbed. He sat beside her and eyed Lady Lorraine's plate.

"Here you are." Lady Lorraine pushed a plate toward her parents.

His task complete, and both parents present to chaperone her, Ewan shoved a chair up against the wall near Lady Lorraine and sat, watching her. Two or three times she turned round and looked at him. She even looked as though she might speak—though she always looked like she might speak—but then she was pulled back into the conversation at her mother's table. Ewan did note that she hardly ate anything, though she did drink two glasses of champagne.

And then the dancing commenced again and her next partner came to claim her, and Ewan followed them back into the ballroom.

He returned to his corner and resumed what she had referred to as his cross gargoyle stance while she did some complicated turns with a young man who, from his tanned complexion, looked to have just returned from the Indies.

"While His Grace generally shows quite a bit of sense and sound judgment," a woman remarked beside him, "I will admit to doubting the wisdom of hiring you to protect our daughter."

Ewan looked down at the duchess whom he half feared he would step on and squash if he did not keep her in his sights when she was near. She continued to watch her daughter. Her gaze was assessing and critical, but far less calculating than that of the other mothers in the room.

"I am happy to say that I was wrong to doubt. You have done your duty with admirable…thoroughness."

Ewan waited. He did not pretend to have Rafe's

understanding of women or his friend's charm, but he
knew enough of them to know the duchess had not
yet said what she intended. When she did not speak,
merely watched her daughter dance, he realized he
would have to speak.

"But," he said.

"Yes, but…" The duchess craned her neck to catch
the eye of a man across the room. She smiled and then
her look turned serious again. "You need only dis-
suade Mr. Mostyn from making any sorts of advances
toward my daughter. You needn't scare off every
other potential suitor. We would like her to marry at
some point, you see."

Ewan understood the point of this ball and the rest of
the Season very well indeed. Although he'd never been
part of the London social whirl, he understood how
vital it was for great families to meet other great families so they might marry their sons and daughters and
remain great families. The Duke of Ridlington would
want to marry Lady Lorraine to one of these men she
danced with, but Ewan could not picture her saddled to
the pug or the lecher or even this East India man.

"You would not want to scare off all of her prospects, would you?" the duchess asked.

Ewan rather thought that if he scared them off so
easily, they should not have been prospects at all.

"Or perhaps you do wish to scare them away." The
duchess opened her fan and began to waft it in front of
her face. "But that would serve no purpose, as Lorrie
must marry, and we intend for her to marry well." For
the first time during the conversation, she looked at
him directly, her hazel eyes clear and flat.

Ewan might be a blockhead, but he understood her meaning well enough. The duke and duchess had higher hopes for their daughter than the third son of an earl. And Ewan was not even a favored third son. His father had all but disowned him, although Ewan doubted he cared so much about him to go to the trouble of officially disowning him. And of course, soon the news would emerge that the Earl of Pembroke had been swindled and his fortune—all that was not tied up in land—was gone.

The duchess's expression was not unkind. She was simply stating a fact, and doing so as politely as possible. He was not good enough for her daughter, and if he had forgotten that, well, she would remind him.

He had not forgotten. Not even in the park. He was a dolt—a big lumbering brute—and his place was here in the corner of the ballroom, not in the center of it. He wasn't good enough. He had never been good enough.

Ewan inclined his head toward the duchess, ceding her the point, though he must clench his jaw to do it.

"Then we are in agreement," she said, smiling. Her smile was rather like her daughter's, and he could almost picture what she might have looked like when she'd been a carefree girl dancing the night away. "And whatever happened in the park"—the fan fluttered in front of her face—"will not be mentioned again." She held up her hand before he might protest. "I do not know what happened, but I do know my daughter. I have no objection to kissing. Every woman should be kissed senseless at least once in her life, but knowing my daughter's passionate nature, once is more than enough outside the bounds of matrimony. And so, whether that kiss came from you or another man is irrelevant to me so long as it does not occur again."

He sucked in a long breath, feeling appropriately chastised. "Yes, Your Grace."

"Good." She smiled again and snatched two glasses of champagne from a passing footman. To Ewan's surprise, she handed them to him. "Drink these. They won't have any effect on you. I suppose you would have to drink several bottles to feel the effect, but at least you will have something to do with your arms other than display those impressive muscles."

Leaving him with the champagne glasses, she fluttered away, across the room to the man she'd been smiling at. Ewan downed both glasses of champagne in quick succession. He would never understand women. No wonder the duke sought refuge in the card room. Ewan would have liked to go to the Draven Club and stay a week.

Instead, he grabbed two more glasses of champagne and held them stiffly at his sides, while he attempted to watch Lady Lorraine without looking quite as menacing.

Since the duchess did not return to chastise him, he thought he'd succeeded admirably well until about four in the morning. He was not weary in the least, although his stomach had been steadily complaining for the last hour, but the more he watched Lady Lorraine, the more he could see fatigue had overtaken her. Her smile was forced, her face pale, and her eyes a bit too large for her face.

When the clock struck four, Ewan did what he thought any bodyguard ought, which was to down the glasses of champagne he'd held for the last two hours and march across the dance floor to take the lady's arm. The couples parted for him without comment, and he reached her easily.

Her back had been to him, and she hadn't seen him coming. Her partner had, however, and instead of bowing, as the next form dictated, he darted behind the lady to his right.

Coward.

Lady Lorraine turned then, but it was too late. Ewan took her arm and swept her away.

"What on earth are you doing?" she asked, struggling in vain to free herself from his grip.

"Taking you home." He pointed to a footman who ran over. "The Duke of Ridlington's carriage."

"Yes, my lord."

"I'm not a lord."

"Yes, sir." The man scurried away.

Ewan pointed to another footman, who turned pale but made haste to reach Ewan's side. "The Duke and Duchess of Ridlington."

"What about them, sir?"

Ewan stared at him. The man shrank back. "Sir?"

"I believe he wants you to fetch them," Lady Lorraine said. While the servant made his escape, the lady finally wriggled free of Ewan's hold. Or rather, he allowed her to free herself. "Why are you frightening the servants? And why fetch my parents? The ball is not yet over."

"It is over for you."

She went on as though he hadn't spoken. "Not to mention you have made a spectacle of me. And of yourself, for that matter."

Ewan raised a brow at her.

"How do you do that? Never mind, I understand what you are not saying. You don't think I care if I'm made a spectacle of, but you are wrong. I do care. And now you raise the other brow, but you've somehow managed to lower the first one. So you are capable of raising both, then?"

Ewan did not think this question required an answer. He spotted the footman he had sent to call the carriage and directed the lady toward the path leading back to Carlton House and the portico, which, with its hexagonal design, was rather too overdone for his taste.

"In any case," she continued, "I do care because whenever a spectacle is made, I must hear about it from my father, and I don't think I can express to you how much I dislike those sorts of conversations with my father."

As though he'd known he was being spoken of, the duke himself appeared. "What is wrong?" he asked, his gaze focused first on his daughter and then, when she appeared unharmed, on Ewan.

"I called for the carriage, Your Grace."

The duke looked in the direction of the conservatory, where music could still be heard. "Why? Is the ball over?"

"I assure you," the lady said, "I had nothing to do with this or with any spectacles that may or may not have been made."

"Spectacles?" her father said, his voice rising in volume.

"I was dancing a country reel," Lady Lorraine said. "Nothing more."

"The lady is tired," Ewan said. "I think it prudent she go home to bed."

The duke stared at him and then looked at his daughter. For her part, the lady appeared utterly speechless.

"Are you tired, Lorrie?" the duke asked.

"I...don't know," she stammered.

"What do you mean you don't know?" her father demanded.

"It's just that no one has ever asked me that. Well, apart from my nanny, but that was when I rather small. So I don't really know how to answer."

"What rubbish. Either you are tired or not."

"She is," Ewan said. "Shall I escort her home?"

"I'll go with you," the duke announced, signaling to the footman to hand him his greatcoat and walking stick. "I'm losing at cards anyway."

While Lady Lorraine was assisted into her pelisse, the other footman returned. "Sir, I couldn't locate Her Grace. Shall I search again?"

The duke harrumphed and shook his head. "No. We go on without her. Her Grace is quite capable of finding her own way home. When she returns to the ball, inform her we have already departed."

"Yes, Your Grace."

"Well then," he said to Ewan. "Lead on."

He led them to the carriage and assisted them in himself. Once inside the dark vehicle, Ewan closed his eyes, relishing the quiet. His ears still rang from the music and the din of voices. He had never appreciated silence so much, except perhaps after a battle.

Beside him, the duke stared out the window, no

doubt wondering where his wayward wife had gone. Or perhaps he was used to her disappearances and his thoughts tended in a different direction. Across from him, Lady Lorraine was in shadow and unusually quiet. Ewan knew that could not bode well.

It wasn't until they arrived at the duke's residence that the men discovered the lady had fallen asleep.

"By Jove," the duke whispered. "She must be exhausted. She hasn't fallen asleep in the carriage since she was about five. Bellweather," he said to the butler. "Have a footman carry her—"

"I'll do it," Ewan interrupted. As far as he could see, there was no reason to rouse more of the staff when he was perfectly capable of carrying her to bed. She weighed next to nothing.

"Very well. Make certain Nell is waiting for her," the duke instructed his butler.

"Yes, Your Grace."

Carefully, Ewan lifted the warm, limp form of Lady Lorraine and maneuvered her out of the carriage. He tried not to jostle her too much, and perhaps that was why he held her a bit too tightly.

In any case, she did not seem to mind. She curled against him, her face pressed to his dark waistcoat and her hair spilling over his arm.

In the flickering light of the vestibule, Ewan could see her more clearly now. The color had come back into her cheeks and her dark lashes lay against the roses and cream skin. Rafe had said she was pretty, and though Ewan did not have an extensive vocabulary, even he knew *pretty* did not begin to describe her. *Beautiful* might do, but even that seemed too trite.

He walked up the stairs with her and turned toward her bedchamber. There her maid opened the door and motioned him to lie her on the bed. Ewan did so, placing her down gently. But when he tried to remove his hands from under her, they did not seem to want to leave her soft, pliant form. In fact, he had the urge to pull her close again, to bend down and push the wayward tresses from her forehead, to climb in bed beside her.

Which was ridiculous because her bed was far too small for two and would probably collapse if they both occupied it. And this sort of thinking only proved he was every bit the idiot Francis always said he was, because the size of her bed was not the most compelling reason he had to release her.

He pulled his hands away rather more roughly than he'd intended.

"Thank you, sir," her maid said. "Good night, sir."

Ewan backed out of the room. *Good night.* It was already bloody morning, and he'd spent better nights in Russia in the middle of winter.

He should resign this position and return to Langley's. Francis wasn't worth the tedium of hours in a ballroom, and Ewan didn't care about the money. He should just make a clean break from Ridlington and his daughter now.

But he knew he wouldn't.

Eight

HE WAS THERE WHEN SHE STEPPED INTO HER bedchamber. Susan didn't have to see her husband. She could feel his presence, and the duke radiated anger. Without turning, she took a deep breath and quietly closed her door. Outside the inky sky was streaked with gray as dawn crept like a specter over the fog-shrouded city. Not even the servants had been awake when she'd used her key to open the town house door. The footman seated in the vestibule had snored softly in his chair. Susan had tiptoed past so as not to disturb the poor boy's slumber.

"You are up early," she said calmly, her voice betraying none of the fluttering in her belly at her husband's presence in her bedchamber. Twice in a week. That was unheard of. She turned and her breath caught.

"I haven't gone to bed and you know it," he said, not bothering to rise from the chair beside her bed. His long legs stretched out before him, making him appear deceptively relaxed. His cravat was undone, his waistcoat unbuttoned, and his shirt open at the throat.

In the hand resting on the armchair, he held a snifter of what she thought was brandy, though the amber liquid looked untouched. His dark hair, streaked with silver, was uncharacteristically disheveled, as though he'd run his hands through it over and over again. Susan's fingers itched to smooth the thick locks back into place, though it had been years since she'd touched him so intimately.

"That makes two of us." She loosed the ties of the dark mantle she wore and removed it with a bit of a flourish, laying it on the longue at the foot of her bed. She felt an uncomfortable prickle on the back of her neck at his nearness to her.

At his nearness to her bed.

Too late she wished she had kept the mantle in place. Underneath she wore a dress of black organza with cotton warp and silk weft. The heavily embroidered hem was of gold silk and metal in the shape of flowers and curlicues. Now she wished the dress was more substantial. She adored the lightweight organza but would have felt more protected in wool—she glanced at her fuming husband—or perhaps a suit of armor.

"Where have you been?" he demanded.

The prickle of awareness burned hotter, turning to annoyance.

"I beg your pardon." She cut him a look from under her lashes. "But I do not have to answer to you."

He began to rise, then seemed to think better of it.

"You left Lorrie unchaperoned. We could not find you when she was ready to depart." His tone held a note of accusation, but she was not fooled. He knew their daughter was in capable hands.

"She was hardly unchaperoned." She crossed to her dressing table and began to remove her heavy gold necklace and earbobs. "Mr. Mostyn played the part of the hawk quite well."

Charles rose and moved to stand behind her. Sitting in his presence had been a mistake. Now she was at a disadvantage. She might have risen, but he placed his large warm hands on her shoulders. Instead of relaxing her, his touch made her tense, her breathing quickened.

"He is a man and not a relation," the duke said, his voice so low she had to strain. "He is her protector, not a chaperone."

"Well, he was protecting her very well tonight out in the park," Susan said, then winced. She hadn't meant to speak of her suspicions about what had transpired outside the conservatory. But Charles's hands on her were making it difficult for her to think. She'd missed his touch, so tender and patient. She hadn't known how much she missed his hands on her until now, when he was touching her again. "But you needn't worry," she added hastily. "I spoke to him."

"I see. You think he is attracted to Lorraine?" In the mirror, his green eyes, so much like his daughter's, met hers.

"I think he kissed her."

"Interesting." The duke reached up and slid a hairpin from Susan's coiffure. She watched as a section fell down around her shoulders, the silky tresses making her shiver. Charles reached for another.

"Do you want him to kiss her? He's not one of the men we agreed upon. Not one of the men we placed on the list." Another section of hair fell, tickling her bare shoulders. Charles's gaze was hot as it held hers.

"That was your list." He gathered the fallen hair, slid his hand through it, smoothing it.

"You agreed to it." She could barely keep the tremor out of her voice, could barely keep her body from shivering. She wanted to tell him to stop, but he had every right to touch her this way. She was his wife. And truth be told, she rather liked it. It had been some time since a man had touched her, despite what the gossipmongers of the *ton* speculated. She had missed a man's touch, her husband's touch.

"I still agree to the list, but if the Protector takes Lorrie's mind off that idiot Francis Mostyn, I am all for it. Besides"—he bent and placed his lips on her bare shoulder—"a kiss is harmless, is it not?"

Oh, this was no harmless kiss. Her entire body seemed to come alive, a fire of awareness shooting through her. "Yes," she breathed.

He moved his mouth up, kissing her neck. Susan closed her eyes.

"Where were you?" the duke asked.

Susan opened her eyes, met his glittering green ones in the mirror. She could lie. She could rouse his jealousy, tell him she was with a lover. She could hurt him, as she had in the past. Hurt him in recompense for all the times he'd hurt her. Yes, he had begun to pursue her, as promised. He'd had flowers sent on her breakfast tray this morning, sought her out in the parlor as she went through correspondence, and then joined her for dinner at the prince's ball. Yes, he had pursued her, but that did not mean he would continue to do so. Who was to say he would not grow tired of her again?

She opened her mouth, the lie on her tongue, and then shook her head. She was too weary to lie tonight. Weary from the ball and weary of the wall they'd erected between them. She could lower hers, just a little, tonight.

"I left the conservatory with Lady Thorpe and Lady Lindsey. Lady Lindsey's youngest son has just left for the West Indies." Charles's lips grazed her ear and she dug her nails into her skirts because she wanted to wrap her arms around him and hold him there. "I can't remember where exactly, but Prinny has an extensive map collection in the library. He offered her use of it."

"And so you were in the library with Prinny?" The lips on her ear nipped.

She gasped at the rush of arousal that flooded through her. "N-no. A footman brought us."

Charles pulled back. "And you spent the entire evening in the library with Lady Lindsey and Lady Thorpe?"

"Why not? We had wine, books, friends." She could see by the way his mouth tightened that he didn't believe her. She hadn't thought she would care, but she did. Some small part of her wanted him to trust her again. "I suppose that's not as exciting as sneaking away for a tryst with a lover." She shrugged. "I'll oblige next time."

His hand landed roughly on her shoulder, and he spun her around so quickly she almost toppled over. He caught her by the arms and pulled her up. "No, you will not. Next time I will not allow you out of my sight."

She stared at him, hardly knowing her husband. How many years had it been since she'd seen so much passion in him—so much passion for her?

"What has come over you?" she asked.

His hands slid down her arms, protectively but sensually as well. "I told you. I intend to win back your affections."

"And how long will that resolution last? Until you find new prey?"

He leaned close, so close she thought he might kiss her. "I believe the vow I made was *until death do us part*. I plan to keep it." He did try and kiss her then. He bent to take her mouth, and she almost allowed it.

Susan braced a hand on his chest. "And I should trust you?"

He gave her a long look. "We will have to learn to trust each other."

‰

Lorrie hiked up her skirts and placed one leg over the window ledge. "Don't look down," she told herself. That was easier said than done. She reached for the tree whose branches brushed against the windowpane and woke her with their tapping on stormy nights. The tree limb was wide enough that she might crawl or scoot on it without any fear that it would break. But that would require releasing the window and grabbing the tree.

"Dratted Viking," she muttered to herself as she attempted to muster the courage.

She'd spent the past seven days trying to escape the Viking with absolutely no success whatsoever. She woke in the morning thinking of the kiss they'd shared. She went to sleep cursing him because despite the fact that she and Francis had attended more than half a dozen of the same events over the past week—two musicales, three dinner parties, a ball, and a garden party—they had not been able to do more than nod at each other. Every time Francis approached her or she passed near to him, the Viking stepped between them and whisked her away.

He was very good at whisking, that Viking. Somehow he managed to snake his arm through hers and ferry her away without making it look as though she were being dragged unwillingly.

Which she was. Mostly. And she had wanted to protest each and every time he acted so impertinently, but she quite forgot her objections when he was close to her. This led to difficulty falling asleep. She felt horribly guilty for the way her body betrayed her when the Viking was near. If she had really loved Francis, would she keep wishing his cousin would kiss her again?

Lorrie felt certain if Francis would simply kiss her again—*really* kiss her—she would not think quite so much about the Viking. And if Francis were to bed her, she would not think about the Viking at all.

That meant she needed to marry sooner rather than later. She could not wait until Francis saw reason. And the more they were apart, the more unlikely Francis was to see things her way. She could blame that on the Viking as well!

She would certainly blame him if she fell to her death climbing out the window. Lorrie took a deep breath and closed her hands around the tree limb. Behind her, Wellington yipped. Lorrie twisted her head around and glared at the puppy. "Shh! No!"

Welly yipped again and laid his paws on the windowsill, clawing and tugging at her skirts. Normally, she would have found this invitation to play irresistible, but at the moment, she wished she had sent the dog to sleep in the kitchen as she had before he had been mostly housebroken. The Viking seemed to have ears like an owl. He was bound to hear Welly's barks. He seemed to hear everything, including her whispered curses about him.

Her only hope was the Viking had not chosen to sleep at the town house tonight. He didn't always sleep under her father's roof. The family had returned home relatively early tonight, and she had gone straight to bed. Hopefully the Viking had seen no reason to remain in Berkeley Square.

Lorrie shushed the dog again, then eased her way off the window and onto the tree limb. Her heart pounded almost painfully in her chest until she was firmly planted on the tree branch. Now she only had to climb down the tree.

Fortunately, her brothers had often climbed the tree when they'd been younger, and they'd nailed small pieces of wood to the trunk to give them a better foothold. The makeshift steps hadn't been used in years, but Lorrie had surreptitiously tested the strength of the bottommost one this afternoon. It had been as sturdy as ever.

She scooted along the branch, moving closer to the trunk and avoiding looking down. Her only regret was she did not possess a pair of trousers. The skirts tended to tangle in her legs and about her ankles. She'd elected to go without petticoats in order to lessen the material that might entrap her, but the dress was still cumbersome.

Not to mention it was a cold night, and she was already shivering. She still had to make it halfway across London in order to reach Francis's lodging and speak to him. She had coin and planned to hire a hackney to transport her—she was not so foolish as to attempt to walk across London by herself in the dark of night—but she had no hopes that the hackney would be any warmer than she was right now. If only she had thought to drop a cloak at the bottom of the tree...

Lorrie finally reached the trunk. With wobbly legs, she stood and carefully placed her feet. Now she would have to step down, backward, and find the foothold. She had spotted it in the day. It was a good three feet down. She could not see it at all in the dark of night.

Gripping the trunk until the bark dug into her flesh, she eased one foot down, feeling blindly for the piece of wood. She didn't find it. She lowered herself more and moved her foot all around the trunk. Finally, she touched the foothold, and just as she did, her hands slipped. For a moment, her world went dark as she panicked, but then she caught hold of the trunk again and hugged the tree fiercely.

Lorrie laid her forehead on the trunk, momentarily

debating whether Francis—whether any man—was worth this. Unfortunately, she'd come too far now to go back. It would be easier to go down than back across.

Still holding the tree trunk, Lorrie placed her right foot beside her left on the little piece of wood. Then she began the arduous task of finding the next rung. And so it went. Little by little, she climbed down the tree until she had gone far enough that she felt safe in glancing down.

Immediately, she wished she hadn't.

Standing below the tree, arms crossed and brows creased into a V, was the Viking. With a little squeal, Lorrie began climbing back up the tree, but the dratted giant reached up and grasped her about the waist, hauling her down into the garden beside him.

"What the hell are you doing?" he asked, his voice so low it was more of a growl.

She pushed against him until he set her on her feet, but he didn't release her arm.

"You really shouldn't use such language in the presence of a lady."

"Ladies do not climb trees."

"Quite right," she said. "I will just return to bed then—" She tried to walk away, but he yanked her back. None too gently either.

He'd lit a lamp in the house, and the light spilled from the French doors of the parlor on the first floor and into the garden. She wished she didn't have such a clear view of his expression. The throbbing vein in his neck seemed to indicate he was furious.

"You want an explanation," she said with a sigh.

He nodded.

"Would you believe I was sleepwalking?"

"No."

"How about midnight gardening?"

He didn't even bother to respond.

"You won't mention this to my father, will you?"

"Yes."

"Traitor," she muttered, knowing he'd heard. "How did you know?" she asked. "Welly's barking?"

His careful expression revealed nothing. He would have made a good spy. If captured, he would have revealed none of his secrets.

"It's all your fault, you know," she said, finally.

His brow arched upward.

"If you would have allowed me to speak to Francis at the garden party—"

"Out of the question," he interrupted.

"You see!" She pointed a finger at him. "You left me no other choice. I had to see him."

"Not on my watch."

Lorrie could have argued further. It was in her nature to argue, but she could not see the point of it. "Fine. If you would release me, I will go to bed."

"Not yet," he said.

Lorrie's heart jumped with anticipation. Perhaps he would want to kiss her first.

But, no! She could not allow that. Even though she really, really wanted to kiss him again. Strange that she could hate him so and still want him to press his lips to hers.

"I want your assurance this will not happen again."

"I'm sorry. I cannot give it. I will marry Francis, and I will find a way to see him again. You will have to find another way to torture him."

The look that crossed the Viking's face actually made Lorrie cringe. His light eyes darkened with anger, and his cheeks reddened. The grip on her arm did not tighten, though, and she could only imagine the amount of control it took to leash that sort of fury.

"That is what you believe of me?" he asked. "That I tortured Francis when we were children."

Lorrie didn't particularly want to answer the question—not with him glaring at her so. "What else am I to believe? Francis told me all about it," she whispered.

"I see."

"What do you see?" she asked.

He shook his head as though he would not waste the effort it took to answer.

"Are you saying—or rather *not* saying—that you did not bully and torment Francis when you were children?"

"I did not." The simple way he said it, the ring of truth in his voice, confused her. He gave her no particulars, offered no protests. He humbly denied the charge. He made it hard to argue and, she had to admit, difficult not to believe him.

"Then why did he say you did?"

"Ask him."

Lorrie saw her chance and jumped. "Very well, I will. Release me, and I will go and ask him at once."

The Viking shook his head and pulled her back toward him. Lorrie was growing colder by the moment, and she rather wished she might step a tiny bit closer to the Viking to share his warmth. She still remembered how warm he'd been in the prince's garden. Tonight he wore only breeches and shirt-sleeves, but he did not appear cold in the least.

She supposed she could demand to return inside now, and he would probably allow it, but she wasn't quite ready to part from him. "Putting aside the matter of whether or not you bullied Francis, why do you hate him? And do not say you don't. I can tell that you do. Anyone who saw the way you looked at him would know you want to kill him."

"Why do you love him?" the Viking asked.

Lorrie wasn't prepared for the question. "I..." But why *did* she love Francis? He was handsome and charming, but were those reasons to love him? "You cannot do that," she said, pointing an accusatory finger at him. "You cannot answer a question with a question."

"Apparently, you cannot answer the question at all."

Lorrie had the urge to stomp her foot. Instead, she glared at the Viking. "I do love him. He is kind and considerate and respectful. He has never tried to take advantage of me. He loves me."

And how pathetic did that sound? She loved him because he loved her? Was she so starved for love and affection?

The answer echoed in her mind: *Yes!*

All her life her mother had practically ignored her while her father had lectured her. Her brothers had been away at school or consumed with their own affairs. Welly was the only creature who ever appeared genuinely pleased to see her, who wanted to cuddle and snuggle with her.

"Is it so wrong to want affection?" she asked no one in particular, freeing herself from the Viking's grip and pacing about a square of the garden. "Is it so wrong to want to be loved and held and kissed and—and ravished?"

"Ravished?" The word came out so low it was barely audible.

Lorrie ceased pacing and glanced at the Viking. She'd forgotten he was there for a moment. But then, what did it matter? It was not as though he were a gentleman who would be shocked at her admission. "Just because I am a woman does not mean I don't have desires. I want to be kissed and touched, like you touched me at the prince's ball."

The Viking shook his head, as though he would rather she hadn't mentioned the incident. Well, she *had* to mention it. She couldn't seem to forget it. "I know it is sinful to want such things when I'm a maiden, but if you would only allow me to leave the garden, I will go to Francis and persuade him to elope. Then even the church will sanction all my wicked feelings."

"No."

Lorrie did stomp her foot then, and she wished she could lift the rock under her foot and hurl it at his head. "*You* kiss me then."

"No." The Viking's tone was firm and unwavering.

"Well, that seems monstrously unfair. Next I suppose you will tell me I should behave as a lady ought, control my desires, and go meekly to bed."

He began to nod.

"I don't wish to behave as a lady ought! I am so very, very weary of behaving as I ought. I am exhausted by pretending I have no needs and wants of my own. And if my parents have their way, I will be locked away forever, the wife of some man I do not love. Think of that. Decades deprived of affection and love and the touch of the man I desire."

The Viking had not moved. If Lorrie hadn't known better, she would have thought him a statue.

"Why did you kiss me at Carlton House?" she demanded petulantly. "Was it just to give me a taste of what I cannot have? Perhaps you enjoy watching me throw myself at you. Well, it won't happen again. I will go back to my room tonight, but I will find a way to see Francis. I am determined. And when I have made up my mind to do a thing, no one stands in my way."

❧

Ewan followed her to her room, leaving plenty of distance between them. He made sure she was safely inside with the door locked behind her before he ventured back to the garden to stare up at the tree. The offending branch would have to be cut. His heart had all but seized when he'd seen her creep onto it. Of course, it might have been the view of her trim ankles, but Ewan was not usually a man rendered immobile by the sight of a lady's ankle.

He'd order the tree branch trimmed and then he would only have to keep watch on the doors. Fortunately, the dog tended to bark and scamper about when his mistress was awake. Ewan had trained himself to listen for the dog and thus always knew when Lady Lorraine was active in her room.

It was sheer coincidence he was here tonight. His

room at the town house was comfortable, but he'd taken to sleeping at Langley's when he was not out with the Ridlingtons until the wee hours. His charge had not been too much trouble of late, and he had thought it was safe to let down his guard.

Only then he'd remembered the time in Belgium when he and Wraxall had been watching an armory with the intent of breaking in and stealing weapons and ammunition. The entire group had been low on supplies and, without any means of replenishing them, they'd been forced to scavenge and steal when their coin had run out. Ewan and Neil had watched the armory for a day and a night without being spotted—or so they'd thought. Neil had noted the comings and goings and formulated a plan of attack. He and Ewan had sat on the roof of the building over-looking the armory, eating stolen bread and apples, and waiting until night fell so that they might return to the other men under cover of darkness and explain the plan. He and Neil had let their guard down, and it had almost killed them.

While they'd been lounging about, watching the sunset, soldiers from the armory had ascended the steps of the building and burst onto the roof, rifles firing. Ewan and Neil had taken cover behind a chimney and attempted to shoot their way out. But, of course, the reason they'd been watching the armory—or sup-posed to be watching the armory—was that they'd been low on ammunition. They'd run out long before the French soldiers had. Then Neil had been hit in the arm and a shot grazed Ewan's side, and the two had decided they had better run. They'd gone down the chimney—mercifully no fire had been burning in it—and made it out.

Ewan still had nightmares about that escape. He would have rather been shot than stuck in that chimney again. Several times his shoulders had caught, and he'd thought he might die in the brick tomb. But Neil had pulled him free, and that was just one of the reasons Ewan owed Neil.

The team had returned and stormed the armory. They'd lost a man, but they'd killed a lot more of Napoleon's soldiers and replenished their stores of weapons and food. Ewan had learned a valuable lesson. Never let your guard down.

Lady Lorraine wasn't quite as dangerous as the soldiers at the armory but she was every bit as wily, and Ewan didn't intend to be stuffed in a chimney ever again. He'd cut the branch down himself if he had to.

She might be determined, but so was he. If it came to a test of wills, Ewan had no doubt he could best her.

He wandered back inside and slumped in a chair in his bedchamber. He liked the chamber better in the dark than the light. The room had been done in blue and gold, and while it was very regal, it made him uncomfortable.

Lady Lorraine made him equally uncomfortable. She'd asked why he'd kissed her at Carlton House, and it was a fair question. Why the hell had he kissed her? He'd asked himself that a thousand times. At the time he'd told himself it was to prove to her that Francis was not the only man who could kiss her and evoke a response.

But he hadn't been prepared for his own response.

Apparently, hers had been equally as charged. Ewan wouldn't have said she'd thrown herself at him, but it had taken more willpower than it should have to resist kissing her when she'd all but demanded it of him. He'd grown uncomfortably hard when she'd begun talking about her needs and desires. Ewan had never considered that women might have the same urges men had. He'd never taken an unwilling woman to his bed, and he did not consider himself a selfish lover, but he had never thought about why the women wanted to go to his bed.

Lady Lorraine had mentioned feeling deprived of touch and affection. But those feelings weren't as wicked as she might think. He'd been similarly deprived and had learned to shove those needs down deep. Her response was to marry Francis Mostyn. But Ewan had no illusions that his cousin was in love with Lady Lorraine. He wanted her dowry, and once he had it, he would discard his wife like a browning apple core.

But even if Ewan had been able to express these thoughts in words, he had no right to mention them. He had no proof Francis would treat her badly. Given enough time, she might forget Francis. Her father certainly counted on her meeting another man who turned her head. Her mother made every effort to throw eligible men—young and old—in her path.

But in that way Lady Lorraine reminded him of himself. She was loyal to a fault. She thought herself in love with Francis, and she would not consider other men.

Ewan was trained to look for chinks in his

opponent's armor. When a man tended to shift to the right before throwing a punch, Ewan hit him on the left. If a man liked to jab low with a dagger, Ewan jumped on a table and made him jab high.

Throw off your opponent had been as much his mantra as *Control and restraint.*

And the kiss he'd given Lady Lorraine had thrown her off and challenged his control. Chagrined as he was to admit it, he was the chink in the lady's armor.

Ewan had never considered himself a man of honor. He left concerns about honor and duty to Wraxall. Ewan had no qualms about fighting dirty. But he was no rake. He didn't take advantage of women. He didn't seduce innocents or pretend a night of passion was anything more than a physical release. As he'd told Lady Lorraine, he didn't pretend.

But what was the more honorable course of action in this case? Use the lady's desire for him against her or allow her to be duped by his arse of a cousin?

Ewan didn't have the answer, but he was certain of one thing. Something must be done about Francis Mostyn.

The next morning Ewan realized it was already too late.

Nine

BREAKFAST WAS USUALLY A TEDIOUS AFFAIR. LORRIE and whichever of her brothers were home—today that was neither—ate in silence while the duke read the *Times*. Her mother breakfasted in bed and rarely showed herself until well after noon. This morning Lorrie pushed eggs about on her plate while she contemplated the large pile of correspondence to which she must reply followed by the hours she must spend dressing in order to look presentable for whichever ball she need attend tonight.

She was about to close her eyes and attempt to nap until she could be excused when the dining room door opened and the Viking strode in. Every single one of Lorrie's senses came alive then, much to her annoyance. She certainly did not want to notice how his trousers clung to his muscled thighs or how broad his shoulders appeared even in a coat that was somewhat less than fashionable. But then the Viking did not care about fashion, else he would have worn a cravat and breeches instead of leaving his neck bare and donning trousers.

His icy blue eyes rested on her for a moment before he nodded to her father.

The duke lowered his paper. "Good morning, Mostyn. I wondered when you would finally join us for breakfast."

The Viking made a sound and proceeded to fill a plate with three servings of every dish on the sideboard. Lorrie tried not to watch him and instead concentrated on her own barely touched food. But she couldn't help but gape at the mountain of food he set at the place directly across from her. He lowered himself into the chair with more grace than she would have expected. When Bellweather inquired as to whether he might like coffee or tea, the Viking answered, "Yes."

The duke laid his paper on the table. "Lorrie," he said. She sighed, wishing he would return to ignoring her.

"What do you have planned for today?"

The Viking raised his eyes from his plate to glance at her. She tried not to blush, but she remembered all too well the fool she had made of herself the night before. She'd all but thrown herself at him in the garden.

"I have letters to write and then must prepare for the Godfreys' ball, Papa."

"Good. I always say one must never neglect one's correspondence."

Lorrie gave him a tight smile.

"And you, Mr. Mostyn," the duke said, turning to look at the Viking who had managed to eat almost half of his breakfast already. "What are your plans?"

Lorrie expected the man to give a one-word answer,

but instead he set his fork on his plate. "There's a tree in the garden that must be cut down."

Lorrie's eyes widened, but she bit her lips before she could say something she would regret later.

"You wish to trim the trees?" the duke said slowly.

"Not personally."

"I see. We might hire men to do the work, but the gardener has not recommended any such action."

"I was in the garden last night. One of the tree limbs brushes against Lady Lorraine's window. The tree must be removed."

It was the first time she'd heard her name on his lips, and it almost surprised her that he knew it.

"A storm might break the glass."

"It might." Her father cut a look at her, and Lorrie looked back at her eggs, now cold and congealing.

"Speak to the gardener. He will know whom to hire for the job. I trust you will accompany us to the Godfreys tonight."

The Viking nodded and returned to his breakfast. He ate efficiently, managing to consume vast quantities without shoveling the food in his mouth. In very little time he rose to fill his plate again.

The duke lifted his paper, and Lorrie opened her mouth to beg to be excused when one of the footmen entered carrying a silver salver with a white letter on top. Lorrie expected Caleb to bring the letter to her father. Parliament was in session, and he received dozens of letters each week, but instead the footman stood beside the Viking's chair. The Viking, having filled his plate again, returned to his seat, giving the man barely a glance before he began to eat again.

"A letter came for you, sir," the footman said, lowering the tray.

The Viking gave the servant a look of incredulity, then laid down his fork and took the letter. Lorrie made no pretense of watching the entire exchange. She suspected her father peered over the top of his paper as well. She wouldn't have been so intrigued except that, despite having attended a dozen events with him, she had never seen the Viking so much as speak to another man or a woman without having to do so out of politeness. The man truly did not appear to have any friends or even acquaintances, at least not among the *ton*.

And so when he received a letter, she could not help but be curious. She craned her neck to read the envelope and caught not only Mr. Mostyn's name—the Honorable Ewan Mostyn—but the name of the sender—the Earl of Pembroke.

The Viking's father had sent him a letter. She watched as he lifted the letter from the tray, and stared at it, his brow furrowed as though it was some sort of foreign object. Then his gaze met hers and he tucked the letter into his coat pocket. She hadn't expected him to read it aloud, but she felt a sense of disappointment nonetheless.

Finally, the Viking went back to his food, and her father pretended he had never taken his eyes from the paper, and Lorrie was able to take her leave. She collected Welly and went directly to the parlor in the front of the house, whose window faced the park in Berkley Square and which was usually filled with sun this time of year. As the day was cloudy and overcast, she had to light a candle in order to write. She'd spent perhaps an hour or so in that manner, Welly drowsing at her feet and her pen steadily scratching along on the vellum, when her candle sputtered out. She hadn't taken the time to trim the wick, and it had doubled over into the wax. She searched the desk for another and finding none rose to seek out the housekeeper and ask her for another candle or perhaps a lamp.

Lorrie hadn't closed the parlor door all the way and pulled it open without making a sound. Consequently, the Viking must not have heard her step into the vestibule for he stood there, letter in hand, his lips working silently. Something about the way he stared at the letter and moved his mouth reminded her of the few times she had gone to the village school to judge the students' oration or to listen as they recited Shakespearean sonnets. Such was the life of a duke's daughter while in the country. But those had been children just learning to read, and the Viking was a grown man.

Suddenly he looked up at her, and for an instant she saw what seemed to be embarrassment cross his face.

"Can't you read it?" she asked without even thinking.

"What the devil do you care?" he said, with rather more heat than she had anticipated.

Her defenses were immediately engaged. "I don't. I thought you had a tree to cut down."

"I do."

Lorrie settled her hands on her hips. "That's not necessary, you know. That tree has been there for as long as the family has owned the house. If you—" She became aware of a maid dusting nearby. "Alice, could you ask Mrs. Davies to bring me a lamp? I need more light in the parlor."

"Yes, my lady." The maid curtsied and started away. Lorrie didn't believe for a moment she would rush to find the housekeeper if she thought there was something more interesting to be heard in the vestibule. Lorrie beckoned the Viking to join her in the parlor.

He shook his head, and she scowled at him. "For the sake of the tree, I must ask you to listen to what I have to say. You may stand on one side of the room, and I will stand on the other." She lowered her voice to a hiss. "I won't throw myself at you, I promise."

Now he had the good sense to look about him, and whatever he saw must have convinced him speaking to her in private was worth a few moments of his time. He joined her in the parlor, and this time she did close the door. She held up a hand to stave off any protest he might make. "This way we won't be overheard." She took up her position beside the desk, while he stood nearer the fire. "As I was saying, there's no need to cut the tree down. I find I have rather a strong attachment to that tree. If I promise not to use it to sneak out again, will you spare it?"

"No."

Lorrie heaved a great sigh. Speaking to the man was like trying to coax her straight hair into the curls so fashionable at present—an onerous chore. "Why not?"

He stared past her, looking out the window.

"You don't trust me, is that it? I am giving you my word."

"I would feel better if all sources of temptation were removed."

"If you think me that bad, then perhaps you should remove yourself. I am embarrassed at my demands on you last night." Her cheeks heated as she spoke, but she kept her shoulders back and her back straight. "And yet I am able to resist throwing myself at you this morning."

His eyes grew wary as though he half expected her to pounce at any moment.

Oh, but the man vexed her. "Dare I hope your father has some urgent news that requires you to return home?"

He started, appearing shocked at her words.

"Your father." She gestured to the letter he still held in his hands. "When Caleb delivered it, I saw it had come from the Earl of Pembroke."

The Viking looked down at it again, his eyes squinting.

"Didn't you read it?" she asked.

His gaze came up quickly, the ice so sharp it might have sliced through her.

"I'm not stupid."

Lorrie blinked in surprise. "Of course not. You're the least stupid man I know, which I find rather annoying, by the way. I cannot seem to manage to maneuver around you. Still, it is early days. I may yet discover a way. Why would you believe I think you are stupid?"

He looked down at the letter and then back at her.

Something prickled at the back of her neck, something she had not considered before. But she could not seem to forget the way his lips had moved when he'd looked at the letter. Before he'd known he was being observed.

"You can read, can't you?"

"Excuse me." He started for the door. Lorrie remained rooted in place. Illiteracy was nothing new to her. Most of the poor and the lower classes could not read or write. Half of the servants her father employed were probably illiterate. But of course the Viking could read. He was no poor farmer or chimney sweep. He was the son of an earl who would have been given every advantage in life.

But if he could read, why hadn't he answered her question?

"You can't, can you?" she said as he reached for the door latch. "That's why you were surprised when I mentioned your father. You didn't know the letter was from him."

He lifted the latch without looking at her, apparently unwilling to either confirm or deny her suppositions. A moment later, he was gone, and Lorrie was annoyed enough to want to put him from her mind completely.

And that was exactly what she intended to do until she found herself squinting in the gloomy light—drat that Alice!—at the escritoire as she drew a picture on a slip of foolscap.

❧

Ewan had supervised the tree trimming himself. He'd intended to have the men remove the tree closest to the town house, but for some reason he was unwilling to consider too deeply, he only removed the branch closest to the window of the duke's daughter. She would have to be daft to attempt to use any of the other branches to make a descent. Not that she wasn't daft. Most women were daft. But he had reason to hope she was only mostly daft, not completely daft.

It was late by the time the men finished and Ewan was able to venture into the kitchens and eat two bowls of soup and three sandwiches. The family would dine at the ball, but it was anyone's guess as to when supper would be served. It was bad enough he must endure the torture of a neckcloth, but he would not do so on an empty stomach.

Since he had no desire to revisit the conversation Lady Lorraine had begun earlier, he paid little attention to her when the family departed—this time her older brother Charles was with them. The Marquess of Perrin seemed to like to hear himself talk, so there was even less opportunity for his sister to speak to Ewan.

Now he understood how it was she could talk so much. She must have learned it from her brother. Undoubtedly, if she hadn't learned to speak up and make herself heard, no one would have noticed her at all.

Ewan was almost hopeful Lady Lorraine had forgotten all about the conversation in the parlor as well. He stood in a corner, watching her dance with the same men she danced with at every ball. They were mostly harmless, and only one or two required his full attention. He'd made a sweep of the house during the first set and had not seen his cousin anywhere. Now he surveyed the room continually to make certain the man did not appear.

It was almost midnight when Ewan realized Lady Lorraine was standing before him. "Thank you, Lord Drake," she said with a polite smile. "Mr. Mostyn will escort me in to supper."

Her partner bowed and moved away, throwing a look of disappointment over his shoulder. Ewan was surprised the bell had been rung for dinner. He hadn't even heard it, and that was unusual.

And as Lady Lorraine had made clear at the first ball they'd attended, she did not want Ewan to escort her anywhere. Ewan was rightly suspicious of this change.

"Shall we go in?" she asked, looping her arm through his. Ewan looked down at her white-gloved arm, so stark against the dark blue of his sleeve.

"No."

She gave him a less than polite smile. "Someone must escort me, and as you are the only unaccompanied man here at the moment, I fear it must be you."

She was correct, not that Ewan gave a damn about the rules of Society. But he'd taken this position and there was unpleasantness associated with every occupation. He led her toward the supper room.

"What was wrong with him?" he asked.

"Not a thing. He tells the most amusing stories about his time in the Americas. Pray seat me next to him so he might regale me through dinner."

Ewan thought she should have allowed the man to regale her on the walk to the supper room. He didn't like being this close to her. He could detect her scent of vanilla and cream even when surrounded by a hundred others.

They reached the supper room, and Ewan searched for the man with whom she'd been dancing. It took a moment for him to locate the lord. He looked very much like every other man she ever danced with. While he scanned the room, he felt her hand reach into his coat. If they hadn't been in full view of the entire room, he would have caught the offending hand in his and demanded to know if she was attempting to pick his pocket.

"What the devil are you about?" he asked, jaw clenched.

"You will see. Open it when you have a moment alone."

Then, apparently spotting the man she wanted, she released his arm and made her way to Lord Drake's table.

Ewan did not move for a long moment, even though he knew he was blocking the door. Finally, he stepped aside and reached inside his coat. He could feel the slip of paper inside the pocket. What scheme had she concocted now? Did she mean to force him to admit he could not read? As he'd said, he was not stupid. He would ask one of the servants to read it for him or conveniently lose the missive.

He should drop it in the fire right away, but instead he left the supper room and withdrew the letter. No words were written on the front. It was merely folded over once and unsealed. He flipped it open and stared not at words but at a drawing. Ewan could only assume she had drawn the illustration. On the left side of the paper were two figures. One was clearly a woman.

She wore a dress and her hair was in a coiffure on top of her head. The other was a man. No, the other was him. No other man would have been drawn so tall and muscular, his cheekbones so stark and his hair so short. Did that mean the woman was Lady Lorraine?

To the right of the figures was an arrow and on the opposite side of the arrow was a shelf of books, beneath which was a desk and two chairs.

Ewan understood what she wanted immediately. She wanted him to meet her in her father's library. She hadn't indicated when this meeting was to occur, but knowing the lady as he did, he could only assume it was to take place after the household had gone to sleep.

What the devil did she have planned now?

Ewan didn't intend to find out. When they'd arrived home from the ball, he'd gone to his room, tore off the offending neckcloth, and drank down a glass of wine. Meeting her in the library was a bad idea. A child would have known that much. It was one thing to kiss her by the topiaries at the Carlton House conservatory and quite another to do such a thing under her father's roof.

And even if Ewan went to the library with every intention of *not* kissing her, he was aware she tempted him in that regard more than any other woman he had ever encountered.

But very possibly this meeting was not about kisses at all. She hadn't forgotten the conversation in the parlor, and he wanted to continue it even less than he wanted to kiss her.

And so he would not go.

And if he didn't go, what would she do then? Come to his room? Draw him even more pictures? What would her father think if he knew she slipped him secret illustrations asking for private meetings? Ewan would then be forced to admit to yet another person he could not read, not to mention explain why Lady Lorraine wanted to meet with him in private.

Ewan drank another glass of wine, knowing it would take an entire bottle before he felt any of its effects, and wishing he had time to drink the whole bottle. Instead, he listened for signs that the household had gone to sleep and then descended silently to the library.

He wasn't surprised to find Lady Lorraine there waiting for him. He did take a step back when he realized she was wearing a dressing gown, not the dress she'd worn to the ball. And her hair was a straight sheet of coffee down her back. She seemed to understand his reaction immediately.

"I had to allow Nell to undress me else she would know something was amiss," the lady explained, moving around her father's desk. The fire in the hearth was low, but the light was enough that he could see her expression. "I cannot do it myself, so I had no excuse for sending her away. Did anyone see you?"

"No."

"You looked at my drawing? Oh, but of course you did or you would not have known to come here. And now you are probably wondering what it is I want and worried I mean to pounce on you. I assure you I do not."

"Get to the point," he said. The dressing gown

was thick cotton, and for that he was grateful. He could detect no glimpse of what she wore underneath, and the collar was higher than any of the gowns she seemed to own. But seeing her with her hair down bothered him. Looking at her now, he experienced the same feeling he had just before an ambush. Did she mean to tempt him with that hair? He could not help but stare at it and wonder if it could possibly be as soft as it appeared.

"Very well," she said with a huff. "I want to help you."

"I don't need help. Good night."

"You need help reading," she returned. "I am a good teacher. Well, I am not exactly a teacher, but I have spent some time in the church's school in Bedford, and I seemed to be able to impart some knowledge."

"The point," he demanded.

"I can teach you to read."

Ewan didn't see any reason to pretend he could read. It would only make her talk longer. "No, you can't."

"Why not?"

He shook his head. He did not want to discuss this with her. With anyone.

"Won't you even let me try?"

"No." He turned to go, but she moved quickly to catch his arm. He shook her off. If anyone came in, he did not want to be discovered touching her. He took two steps back and felt the door against his spine. Trapped, that's what he was. By a mere girl half his size.

"Did you have someone read the letter your

father sent yet? I thought not. At least let me read that to you."

"Why?"

She huffed out an exasperated sigh. "I already told you. I want to help."

"If I allow you to read the letter, then our meeting is over. You go to your bed, and I go to mine."

"But—"

"Not negotiable."

She rolled her eyes. "Fine." She stuck her hand out, and he withdrew the letter still residing in his coat. He placed it in her hand, and she broke the seal. She scanned the words with an ease and quickness Ewan envied.

And then her green eyes met his. "Oh dear."

Ten

"WHAT DOES 'OH DEAR' MEAN?" HE ASKED.

Lorrie cringed. She had not meant to say that aloud. "It means this is the sort of letter my father would write to me."

"That bad?"

She gave him a wan smile. "It's not good, at any rate." She laid the letter on her father's desk, where she had lit a candle. Using her finger to help him follow along, she read:

"To Mr. Mostyn."

There she looked up. "I think it always a bad sign when a parent does not use a child's Christian name."

The Viking showed no reaction to her observation. Lorrie cleared her throat.

"I send you no regards and dispense with any and all pleasantries. I write on behalf of your cousin, my nephew, Francis Mostyn."

The Viking muttered something under his breath that sounded very much like "The bastard." Lorrie pretended she had not heard.

"Francis informs me that he has, for some time, had strong feelings for a certain lady of unsurpassed beauty, grace, and elegance."

She paused. "Do you think he means me?"

The Viking gave her a long stare, and she looked back at the letter. "Ah, yes, here we were: 'a lady of unsurpassed beauty, grace, and elegance.'"

"You read that already."

"Did I?" She gave him her best innocent look, the one that had worked with her parents for at least the first seven or eight years of her life.

"The lady has assured your cousin she returns his affections, and Francis tells me he has made certain promises to this lady. Much to your cousin's dismay—and I must confess, mine as well—he reports that you, sir, have attempted to—"

She glanced up at the Viking, who was watching her, not looking at her finger on the paper. "Go on," he said in a tone of voice she could not quite decipher.

"—have attempted to steal the lady's affections and prevent your cousin from seeing the lady in social settings. Furthermore, Francis accuses you of intercepting letters he has written to the lady so she will believe his affections for her have waned."

"Is that true?"

"No."

"I didn't think so." He hadn't even been able to read the letter directed to him. How would he have known which letters arrived at the house directed to her?

But her father knew.

"Is that all?" the Viking asked.

"Er...no."

"What else?"

She looked down at the vellum.

"With regard to the other matter we spoke of recently, it has been over a sennight since I sent and you took receipt of the accounts we discussed and in that time I have had no communication from you as regards Mr. de los Santos—"

She looked up at him. "Is that correct? The name is smudged."

"That's enough." The Viking took the paper. "I know the rest."

"What accounts does he mean?"

"I agreed to look into a financial matter for my father. But apparently that is of less concern than your affections."

"I must admit I am surprised your father has taken an interest in my little love affair."

The Viking raised an eyebrow.

"Surely Francis would not have asked him to write to you. He is his own man, after all."

The look he gave her was full of pity. Lorrie

straightened her back. "You imply Francis...*tattled* to your father?"

"I wasn't implying it."

"But Francis would never behave so childishly."

The Viking lifted the letter and threw it in the fire. "Then why does my father believe I have attempted to steal your affections? Everyone knows I've been hired to protect you from unwise elopements"—she made a face at him—"and abduction plots."

"But your father chooses to listen to Francis rather than believe your interest in me is purely professional."

"He always has."

"And I suppose now you will tell me that Francis bullied you when you were children, not the other way round."

One corner of his mouth rose as though he were the instructor and his pupil had just stumbled upon the answer to a difficult lesson. His mouth looked softer when he gave that half smile, almost kissable.

"But the idea is there." She pointed to her head. "Lodged in my brain box."

"Believe what you want, my lady. I don't give a damn." He started for the door, ending their meeting and conversation as he'd stated he would do when the letter was read.

"I don't believe you," she said. "What people think of you matters more than you want to admit. Just this morning you told me you were not stupid."

He spun around and crossed the room in two steps. If Lorrie hadn't been so surprised at the quick movement, she would have dashed for the door. The expression on the Viking's face was pure rage.

Paralyzed by the crackle of danger surrounding him, she didn't resist when he backed her up against the desk, placing one hand on either side of her waist. "I am not stupid."

"And Francis said you were," she whispered, her voice refusing to cooperate and leave her some semblance of pride. He'd bent low to look her in the eye, and she couldn't help but notice his eyes were pretty this close. They looked warmer.

"Francis said a lot of things, most of them no more true than what my so-called father vomited up in that letter."

"Oh." She saw how it had been then. She could picture the Viking's childhood quite clearly now. He'd been a smaller version of himself, but still taller than the other boys and probably awkward in his skin. If he'd had trouble reading, the other children might have teased him. Had he fought back? Possibly, but he was bigger than the other boys and probably punished for what he saw as defending himself and what others might see as an unfair advantage.

But the worst of it was that his own father hadn't believed him. He'd taken the side of his nephew over that of his son. It would not be a difficult choice. The Viking could be stubborn and terse and so silent it might seem sullen. Francis was charming and amiable and quick to smile or make a room full of people laugh.

"All of this happened when you were but children. Surely you and Francis have put all of that behind you." She knew it wasn't true even as she spoke the words. In her mind, she'd wanted to protect Francis by assuming his complaints to his uncle had been taken out of context or were made out of frustration because he was denied access to her.

But this was nothing more than flattery. The same self-flattery that made her believe the Viking had desired her that night in the prince's gardens. He'd kissed her because he wanted her to forget Francis. He'd taken this position with her family for revenge.

"I won't be put in the middle of this," she said.

"You seem to think you are the center of the universe."

Lorrie pushed back on his chest to no avail. "Are you saying I am conceited?"

"No. I'm saying you think you're the center of the universe."

"Mr. Mostyn—"

"My quarrel with my cousin has nothing to do with you. You are that piece on the chessboard. He's using you."

"The piece—a pawn?" Her cheeks flamed hot. "I am not a pawn, sir."

"You were even before I met you. He wants your dowry, so he makes you believe you are in love with him and, worse yet, that he loves you. Now he uses you to turn my father further against me."

She huffed out a breath. "I think you quite capable of turning people against you all by yourself."

He smiled slightly, and she found she liked it when he smiled. His lips looked so much more kissable when he did that.

But she did not want to kiss him.

Very well—that was a lie. Still, she *would not*

kiss him again. And then she was speaking without thinking again. "Did you kiss me to exact revenge on your cousin?"

"No."

"I don't believe you."

"I don't pretend, and I don't lie. I kissed you because someone had to show you Francis Mostyn is not the only man in the world."

"I know that—"

"And because I wanted to."

"You..." Her throat had gone dry. "You wanted to?"

His hands moved in so his fingers brushed against the material of her night robe. "I don't do anything I don't want to do."

"And right now?" She swallowed. "What do you want to do?"

"This."

❧

He yanked her against him and tilted her chin up with one hand. Even as his mouth lowered to meet hers, he knew this was a mistake. He was under her father's roof. He might not be much of a gentleman, but he liked to think he had his own code of honor. Debauching virgin daughters under their fathers' roofs was well out of the bounds of his code.

Even knowing this, he didn't stop. He'd wanted to kiss her again since the first dance of the evening. He'd watched her dance at least four dozen dances with half as many partners, and it had been all part of the position.

Until tonight.

Tonight he had hated the men dancing with her. He'd wanted to rip their hands from her shoulder or her arm, tear their heads from their bodies, and smash the men's faces into the first blunt object he encountered. He'd tamped the urge down, but all the frustration of inaction had built up. And now the foolish chit had put herself within his reach. How long could a man resist this sort of temptation?

He was no longer content to stand on the outside and look in.

His lips met hers, and the sensation was even better than it had been the first time. He'd thought he'd imagined the punch of arousal in his gut and the dimming of the world around them. But it was happening again. He wanted her so badly it hurt, and he could hardly remember where he was or why he must not take her.

He was not a man of subtlety, and he did not tease her lips open. He took what he wanted, claiming her mouth as though it was a prize on the battlefield. If she'd only fought him or resisted, even slightly, he would have stopped. For all his size and strength, he was no brute.

"Yes," she moaned against his mouth. "This. This."

Ewan tore his lips from hers, his breath coming in heavy pants. "You should run."

She blinked eyes so dark green they reminded him of the deepest recesses of a forest glen. "Why?" Her arms wrapped around his shoulders, and he could feel her small, slim body press against him. He forced his hands to stay at her waist. He might have broken her in two with one quick movement.

"The things I'm thinking right now should scare you."

Her eyes widened, but not with fear. "Tell me."

"Goddamn it!" He tried to move away from her, but she held on to his neck, and he didn't have the will to remove her hands.

"You might as well call me Lorrie."

"No. This is your father's house. We cannot do this."

"Do what?"

He held his hands out to indicate their embrace. "This."

"What if we weren't here—"

"You are a duke's daughter."

"What if I wasn't?" Her hands slid up his neck to tangle in his shorn hair. "What if I was a trollop? What would you do to me?"

He shook his head. "That's a dangerous conversation."

"Would you toss up my skirts?"

"Yes." He'd tear every stitch of clothing off her.

"Would you touch me?"

"Yes."

"Where?"

Everywhere. "Go to bed."

"Would you push me back on the desk and stand between my parted legs?"

"No."

"No?" The disappointment practically dripped from her lips. What the hell sort of virgin was she to speak so shamelessly?

"Why not?" she demanded.

"Because I'd rather take you from behind."

"Behind?" Her brow furrowed in that way he could not seem to cease finding adorable.

"Like this." He spun her around and cupped a hand around her neck. He shoved her none too gently toward the desk and pushed her down until her round bottom was level with his cock. This would scare her back to sense. He pressed his hard member against that soft flesh and leaned close to her ear. "Is this what you want?"

"Yes. Oh yes." She wriggled her bottom against him.

That was the wrong answer and the wrong action. He clenched his hands to stop them from sliding under her nightgown and touching the ripe flesh he knew would be waiting.

He pushed harder against her, making sure she felt his length. "Last chance to run to your chamber."

"I'll stay right here. Take me."

Ewan released her and with a curse turned away. He slammed a hand against the marble of the fireplace, letting the pain wash over him until he could think of something besides his aching arousal. Why the hell did she have to be so perfectly wanton?

"Why did you stop?" she asked. The roaring in his ears and the throbbing of his hand made her sound miles away. "Did I say something wrong? I'm too forward."

"You are too forbidden."

She waved a hand. "Everything is forbidden. The long list of *do nots* makes me weary."

"This is at the top of the list."

"Of course it is. Anything enjoyable is always forbidden."

"If we were discovered—"

She held up a hand. "I know. I would be ruined. My family would be disgraced. It would be the scandal of the year. Well, not the year, but the Season. Someone else is bound to do something worse before the end of 1816. I know all of this, and yet"—she looked up at him—"I still want to kiss you."

He held out a hand to keep her at bay. "No."

She blinked at him. "I won't attack you. I'm not that desperate...yet," she murmured. "But I won't promise not to try and see Francis again. I don't want to be ruined—I mean, I do want that, but that's in theory. In fact, I am really quite opposed to ruin and scandal and—"

"Is this a long speech?"

She sighed. "I must marry, and sooner rather than later. Before I do something I regret."

"You will not elope with Francis."

"And the fact that I love him?"

"You don't love him." He'd expected her to argue, but she seemed to accept the statement. Had she finally realized she did not love the man or had she given up trying to convince Ewan that she did?

"I won't elope with him."

He heard the condition even before she spoke.

"But I want something from you in return."

"No."

She shook her head at him in exasperation. "You haven't even heard what it is."

"No."

"I want to teach you to read," she said as though he hadn't spoken at all.

"No."

"We meet here every other night or so—"

"No."

"—and I will teach you to read. In the meantime, you will be able to keep an eye on me and be certain I do not attempt to elope."

"No."

Her hands settled on her hips. "That is a perfectly reasonable plan. Why do you reject it? Is it because we have no chaperone? I'll bring Welly. He can chaperone us."

"No."

"I will sit on this side of the desk." She pointed to her father's chair. "And you will sit on this side. Nothing can happen when we're separated by a desk. If anyone walks in, we'll say we met by accident and are reading. It will look perfectly innocent because it will *be* innocent."

"No."

"Stop saying no. It's a perfectly good plan. Don't you want to be able to read the next letter your father sends you? You can't like being ignorant."

He didn't like it at all, but she couldn't help him.

"Then why won't you allow me to try?"

"Others have tried. I cannot read. I'm too—"

She stepped close, cutting him off. "Don't say stupid. You are not that. I will figure out a way to help you. I'm amazingly resourceful, you know. Have you noticed that yet?"

He thought it better not to comment.

"And I'm tenacious. We won't give up. Mr. Mostyn, you are really doing me a favor. I need something to focus on besides the banality of what to wear for this ball or that, and if I don't have anything to keep me occupied, then I will only begin planning my elopement. You may have cut the tree limb, but there are other ways I could make my escape. For example—"

"No examples." Dear God. He would kiss her just to make her stop talking. "Fine."

He started for the door. She was right on his heels. "Fine? Does that mean yes?"

"Yes."

"Yes, I will tutor you or yes to something else I said? I confess I can't remember everything I said. Did I ask another question?"

Ewan turned around and did the only thing he could think of—other than kissing her into silence. He put his hand over her mouth. "Teach me to read."

She mumbled something under his hand.

He frowned for a moment. "Yes, tomorrow night. After the...whatever it is we must attend tomorrow night."

She mumbled something else, but Ewan, who had gagged his fair share of the enemy, had no trouble understanding. "Fine. An hour after they go to bed, though. Take no chances."

Another mumble. He sighed. "Fine." She might as well bring the damn dog. She had more chance of teaching the dog to read than she did Ewan learning anything.

But she'd see that tomorrow night.

Eleven

THE FETE SEEMED INTERMINABLE. LORRIE GENERALLY enjoyed balls and musicales and routs and the theater—as long as it was not opera—but tonight she could think of nothing but returning home and seeing the Viking again.

Alone.

Oh, she'd promised not to attack him, and she would not, but just the thought of being with him made the skin all along her spine tingle with anticipation. She glanced over her shoulder and caught him looking at her. He was always looking at her. That was his job, but she rather liked finding his cool blue gaze on her right now. In fact, she liked it so much, she blew him a kiss.

The line between his brows deepened, and he gave her what she liked to think of as his warning look. And then a dark-haired lady—Lorrie had noticed quite a few ladies had been brave enough to approach him lately—touched his arm, and he was obliged to look down at her. The lady was at least ten years older than Lorrie, but no less lovely, and it did not take a bluestocking to deduce what she talked to the Viking about.

His service with Lieutenant Colonel Draven. The Viking was more than a former soldier. He was a war hero. Now that Society had become used to seeing him about, stories about him had begun to circulate. He'd once killed a dozen men with his bare hands. He'd carried Lord Jasper out of a burning building and ten miles to safety, all the while pursued by enemy soldiers. He'd been shot three times and had removed the balls and sewn himself up without so much as a whimper.

Ewan Mostyn was a veritable Goliath to Napoleon's scared Israelites.

It was no wonder the ladies sought him out. He was handsome—in that dangerous sort of way—and eligible and a hero. But Lorrie did not have to like it.

"I've been waiting all evening for an opportunity to speak to you."

Lorrie glanced over her shoulder, and Francis stood before her.

"Francis!" She was genuinely pleased to see him, but she was also aware of a vague sense of annoyance that she could no longer see the Viking and the lady commanding his attention.

"Shall we take a turn about the room?" Francis asked, offering his arm.

Lorrie stared at his arm, hesitating. And then with a shake of her head at her own foolishness, she slid her gloved hand into the crook of Francis's arm. What was wrong with her? This was what she had been waiting for—the chance to speak to her intended alone.

"How have you been?" Francis asked as he led her along the wall, away from the Viking. He walked with his head held high, his gaze moving from one corner to another as they walked.

"Very well, and you?"

He paused in his perusal of the room to glance directly at her. "Horrible. I pine for you every minute we are apart."

"Oh." Lorrie's mouth suddenly felt too dry. Why hadn't she thought to say something similar? Now Francis would think she hadn't missed him at all.

"I've missed you too," she said quickly. "I tried to write to you, but my father must have threatened the servants with dismissal if they delivered any more letters for me. I had hoped you might write."

"Oh, but I did," he said, his gaze flitting about the room again. "I wrote you a dozen letters, at least. You didn't receive them?"

"No. My father must have intercepted them." Except that her father was often away at his club or the Lords when mail arrived. Lorrie frequently leafed through the letters and invitations before anyone else. Her father might have intercepted some correspondence, but a dozen letters? It did not seem possible.

"Your father or my damned cousin." Francis peered over his shoulder at the Viking. Lorrie looked as well. He was still in conversation with the dark-haired woman. Well, he was not talking, but he was listening as she spoke.

"He hasn't let you out of his sight. I'm certain he'd like to thwart our marriage so he might have you."

Lorrie almost laughed, until she realized Francis was

in earnest. "Darling, Mr. Mostyn has no designs on me, I assure you." Exactly the opposite, unfortunately. "He is merely doing his duty, the one my father hired him to perform."

"The son of an earl, hiring out his services like a common tradesman. It's embarrassing to the family. And surely he can keep you safe without filching my letters."

Lorrie opened her mouth to argue that the Viking couldn't be taking Francis's letters to her because he couldn't read well enough to know to whom the letters were directed. But she closed her mouth again. The Viking had not instructed her to keep it secret that he could not read, but she felt as though she was entrusted with a confidence she should not share. But surely Francis knew or at least suspected his cousin was illiterate. If the two had spent their boyhoods together and had been taught in the same schoolrooms until Francis was sent away to school, then wouldn't Francis know his cousin couldn't read?

It hadn't taken Lorrie very long to puzzle it out. And if Francis knew this, had he merely forgotten, or did he think making the Viking a villain in her eyes was to his advantage? For the first time, Lorrie wondered if perhaps Francis had not been altogether truthful with her. He always claimed to write her letters, but she did not receive half so many as he supposedly sent. He'd told her his cousin was a bully as well. But the letter the Earl of Pembroke had sent on his nephew's behalf was more in the spirit of bullying that she had ever seen from the Viking.

"You don't like your cousin, do you?" Lorrie

asked. A few weeks before she would have immediately turned the conversation to elopement, but now it was a topic she was not so eager to broach.

"Why would I? He's a big brute, dumb as an ox. When we were children, his favorite pastime was using his fists on my siblings and me. He didn't think we were good enough to live under the roof of the Earl of Pembroke."

Lorrie's gaze darted to the Viking, but he was no longer standing in his corner. She wondered if the brunette had lured him outside. "That does not sound like the Mr. Mostyn I know," Lorrie said.

"Yes, well, he's a good pretender," Francis said.

Lorrie lapsed into silence as they continued their circuit. Francis was lying. She wasn't sure where the truth ended and the lies began—it was very possible that the Viking had beat Francis when they were children—but she knew the man well enough now to know that he didn't care a fig about being the son of an earl.

He also didn't pretend.

But perhaps Francis did.

"I couldn't bear to wait another day for an opportunity to speak to you," Francis said, finally turning to face her and give her his full attention.

"We are fortunate an opportunity arose."

"Not fortunate. I paid that woman to distract my cousin."

Lorrie felt her jaw drop. "You what?"

"I paid her. She's the sister of my landlord, and I told her if she kept the big brute distracted for a half hour I'd take her to a *ton* fete and pay her two pounds."

Lorrie supposed there was nothing illegal about what Francis had done. Neither was the woman a tart from the nearest corner, but the very idea that he had paid a woman to lure the Viking away bothered her.

"You must have been quite desperate to speak to me," she said, her voice faint.

"I didn't know if you had received my letters." Francis's eyes scanned the room again. "And I want to be certain you know how much I still love and admire you."

Lorrie watched his face as he spoke. The words might have meant more to her if he had looked at her as he said them.

Finally, his gaze flicked down to her. "Do I still hold your affections, my darling Lorrie?"

"Of course," she said as though by rote. "You know I want nothing more than to be with you, as husband and wife."

Francis's mouth tightened as though he had heard this refrain one too many times. Lorrie's chest felt tight. Was the Viking correct? Did Francis only want her money?

"I want that too." But his eyes were on the other people in the room again. "But we must wait for your father's blessing."

"No."

Francis's gaze snapped back to her with a satisfying intensity. "I beg your pardon?"

"No," she said again. The Viking spoke simply and directly all the time, and it seemed effective.

"I must say, my lady, this new behavior of yours is quite unbecoming."

Lorrie couldn't care less. If Francis really wanted

to marry her, he would have to take the becoming with the unbecoming. And he would have to prove he really did want to marry her—not her money. "I don't want to wait for my father's blessing," she said.

Francis gave her a patronizing smile, as though she were a child. "It is hard to wait, darling, but I'm afraid we have no other choice."

"Of course we do. We can elope."

He sighed. "Not this again."

Lorrie clenched her fists. "I'm terribly sorry I annoy you with my constant demands for you to marry me. Perhaps I should cease making them."

Francis seemed to realize he had done something wrong. "I don't understand what is wrong with you. This is a side of you I haven't seen before, and I must say I don't care for it much. Is it the influence of my cousin?"

"The only thing your cousin has done is point out that you only want to marry me for my dowry. A statement I begin to believe."

"That's not true. I love you."

Lorrie raised her brows. "Prove it."

"How am I supposed to prove it? Eloping and causing a scandal and pain to both of our families will not prove anything except that I can behave rashly. I love you enough to wait for you."

"Do you love me enough to go to my father and beg for my hand?"

"The duke agreed to consider my proposal."

"Because *I* begged and cried. Perhaps it is time the duke heard from you again. This time with more passion."

"You want me to beg for your hand?"

"Yes."

"Like some sort of dog?"

"Like a man in love."

Francis merely stared at her.

"Unless you aren't in love."

"Good question," came the voice to her right. The Viking stepped forward and Francis stepped back.

"You." Francis pointed a finger at his cousin. "Stay away from me."

"Stay away from Lady Lorraine. The next time you pay a woman to command my attention, choose a lady with more personality than a brick."

"*You* think to criticize her for dullness?"

"I'd criticize you, but then I'd receive another scolding from my father. You should run and tattle to him now, like you did when we were children."

"I had to protect myself."

"I fear you hit your head one time too many when you were a child. You suffer from delusions."

Lorrie covered her mouth to stifle a laugh. Francis was not fooled. "And you? You do not defend me?"

Lorrie shrugged. "I will fight for you when you fight for me." She glanced up and up at the Viking. "I'm feeling rather parched. Would you escort me to the refreshments?"

The Viking offered his arm as though he had escorted a thousand women in this manner. She put her arm through it and left Francis in her wake.

⸎

Ewan did not know why he should feel so on edge. It wasn't nerves exactly. He knew what those felt like.

He'd experienced the anxiety mixed with anticipation often enough under Draven's command. The troop had been given the impossible missions. They were not expected to succeed, much less live. Ewan hadn't expected to live, and he had a sense of peace and resignation about dying for King and country.

But his body still feared death. Thus, the nerves.

He hadn't felt them in some time now. Not since he'd been back in London long enough to believe the end of the war wasn't merely a dream from which he'd wake. It really was over. He was safe. He had no reason for anxiety.

Until tonight.

He'd escorted Lady Lorraine to the refreshment table and handed her a cup of lemon water. He would have rather drunk piss than the weak broth, but his mother had always said "*Suum cuique,*" which was a fancy way of saying "To each his own."

Before the lady had finished her cup and departed, she'd whispered, "Meet me tonight in the library."

Now Ewan stood at the door of his bedchamber—the Duke of Ridlington's chamber, really, for it was the duke's house—and listened to the silence of the house. It had been silent for more than three quarters of an hour, and Lady Lorraine was probably waiting for him.

And he hadn't yet joined her because of the nerves. He didn't fear he'd lose control and take her on the desk as he'd imagined ever since he'd pushed her down and enjoyed the sight of her rounded bottom wriggling in the air. He could control his impulses.

He didn't fear death. If the duke discovered them

and thought the worst, well, dying in a duel would be a far better death than many he had faced.

He feared the words on the page.

When he'd returned from the war, Ewan had confidence enough to stand up when called stupid. If he'd been stupid, he wouldn't have survived the war. No one without courage and cunning had survived. And he'd had plenty of both. He was not a stupid man.

The trouble seemed to be the boy still inside him. That boy was not convinced. That boy still felt stupid. That boy still wondered if perhaps the man hadn't fooled everyone, including himself.

Trying to read again would prove how stupid he was once and for all. And perhaps Ewan did not want to face the ugly truth.

And perhaps he was a bloody coward.

He lifted the file of papers he had been trying unsuccessfully to make sense of, pulled the door open, and stalked to the library. The door there was already ajar, and Lady Lorraine looked up when he entered. She sat behind her father's desk, looking quite small and feminine in her white dressing gown with its high neck. The dog was in her arms, sleeping peacefully with his chin on one paw. She'd lit a lamp and set it on the desk, and shadows flickered over the books' spines.

"I was beginning to wonder if you would come."

"We should do this another night. It's late." *Coward.*

"It's only a little after two. This might be the earliest we are home for several more nights."

"You must be tired." *Yellow-bellied coward.*

"No. Are you?"

He wanted to say yes, but exactly how afraid was he? It was words on a page, not a man with a musket. Act like a man, he told himself. "No." Abruptly, he sat in the chair opposite her, his papers on the desk. The little fur ball raised his head, then went back to snoring softly.

Lady Lorraine gestured to several books she'd laid out on the desk. "I found these primers in my—"

"What did you and my cousin speak of tonight?" he asked. He was obviously desperate if he was, one, initiating conversation and, two, discussing his cousin.

"I think you heard the most salient part of the conversation," she said.

"You want him to prove he loves you."

She frowned at him as though confused by his sudden chattiness. "I suppose some of what you said made me think. Perhaps I've been too trusting." Her gaze lowered to the books on the desk, and she laid a hand on one.

"Go on," Ewan said before she could open the book. "What else did you discuss?"

She took a breath and sat back in her chair. "I don't wish to speak of it. Nothing untoward, I assure you. But he said…several of his comments made me…if not suspicious, curious."

He nodded as though to encourage her to keep talking. The bloody woman was always talking and talking. Why did she have to choose tonight to act close-lipped?

"Mr. Mostyn, are you trying to avoid our purpose here?"

"No." *Liar.*

"Then why don't we begin? I have this primer I used when I first learned to read."

Ewan recognized the book. He'd had the same book. For years he'd struggled with it, never able to move to the next level.

"Not that one," he said, his hands growing damp. He rubbed them on his trousers.

"Why not?" she asked.

He stood, and the dog jumped up with a sleepy yip of alarm. "This was a mistake. I have to go to bed."

"What?"

She might have said more, but he was out of the room and on his way into the vestibule before he heard the click of the puppy's nails on the floor behind him.

"Wait!" she hissed, her voice sounding far too loud in the cavernous vestibule. "Mr. Mostyn!"

He swung around, finger to his lips.

"I am trying to be quiet," she whispered. "Come back into the library and explain to me."

"Go to bed." He started for the stairs again.

"If you go to your room, I will only follow you." Her voice was low but not a whisper. He could hear the threat in the tone of her voice.

Bloody woman. She'd do it too, and as bad as being discovered in the library together might be, being discovered together in his bedchamber was worse. He could lock the door, but then she might resort to waking the entire house by pounding on it.

Or she might do worse.

His thoughts flashed back to her descent from the tree outside her window. And damn him to hell if he hadn't left his father's account books in the library. He had to go back to retrieve them. Ewan marched back to the library and took his seat like an errant schoolboy. When she sat across from him, he pointed to the books, lifted one at random—not the dreaded book of his childhood—and handed it to her. "Teach me."

"Shouldn't we discuss what just occurred?"

He lifted one brow. Now that she had him here, she wanted to delay? He would never understand women.

"You are right." She opened the book to the first page. "Let us begin with the alphabet."

He raised his opposite brow.

"I know." She held up a hand. "This might be too basic, but it is the way the teachers I have observed always begin with the lit—with the new readers." She pointed to the open page filled with letters. Ewan kept his gaze on her face.

"You see, every letter has a sound. You can use the sound to help you read new words. *A* has the sounds *ah* and *ay*. *B* has a *buh* sound. *C* can sound hard or soft—"

"I know the alphabet and the letter sounds. I can read. I…" What to say without saying too much? She might not want to laugh, but if he told her the letters moved, then she might smile or think he was funning her. "I have trouble," he said finally.

"Very well. Then why don't we start with the first page of text and see where the trouble lies." She turned several pages until she reached a page with large letters printed on it. She slid the book toward Ewan, and he pulled it close, hunching over it.

He sat in a chair across from her—large, high-backed, and softly upholstered. He put his thick finger on the page to hold it down, and possibly to hold the words in place as well. The letters blurred and then came into focus.

"The." He moved his finger to the next word. This one was more difficult. First the word seemed to begin with a T but then the C came into focus. He could make no sense of it and his head started to pound. He guessed. "Tac." Next word. "Sat."

"Wait."

At her correction, Ewan wanted to hurl the book across the room. He hated this already. He felt big and stupid, as he always had.

She'd risen from her chair and moved to peer over his shoulder. Her small, delicate finger tapped the word he'd had so much difficulty with. "This word is 'cat,' not 'tac.' You see, it begins with the letter C."

Ewan didn't see that at all. Sometimes it began with a C and sometimes a T and sometimes he didn't know what the hell it began with.

"You're doing well," she said, and he looked at her as though she was daft. He was doing as poorly as ever. His childhood tutor would have smacked his hands with the book by now.

"Begin again."

He sighed deeply. "The cat sat." He knew that part. Now the next word. He tapped it with his finger. "No." He shook his head. "On." He looked up at her for confirmation. She smiled and nodded.

"Good."

Ewan shoved the book aside. "This is pointless. I can't do it."

Lorrie pulled the book back in front of him. "But you are doing it. You must have a little patience. It takes time."

"I am nine and twenty, my lady." Ewan stood. "A child reads better than I do. You are wasting your time."

"It is my time to waste."

"Waste it on someone else." He might have walked away from her, but he paused at the hard glint that came into her eyes. He didn't think he'd like what she had to say next.

"You would give up? This easily? I did not think you such a coward."

Ewan moved toward her, checking himself before he might put his hands around her neck.

"If you were a man, you'd be on your arse right now."

"It wouldn't be any less true if a man said it than when I say it. You are afraid to try."

Ewan moved toward her until he had her backed against her father's desk. "You have no idea what I have seen and what I have done. I am not af-f-f—" Abruptly, Ewan closed his mouth. He hadn't had trouble speaking since he was a young child.

"I wondered if you had stuttered as a child."

How the hell had she known that?

"Is that why you are so laconic?"

Ewan didn't answer, not trusting his tongue. His throat felt as though someone had wound a rope around it, his tongue sat like a limp trout in his mouth.

"You aren't the only one who has this problem,

you know. When I am in Bedfordshire, I like to go to the village school and help the teacher. He has too many students to focus on any one or two, and the girls are always ignored in favor of the boys. A few years ago, there was a boy who had a stutter and also what Mr. Fletcher said he thought of as some sort of word blindness."

Ewan tried to swallow past the tightness in his throat. *Word blindness.* He had never heard the phrase before, but as soon as she uttered it, he felt strangely relieved. Somewhere inside him the boy he had been raised his dejected head. Ewan had not known he was lost, but with two words, he had been found.

"I worked with the boy for months, and we had made progress, but then he had to help on his father's farm, and I had to come to Town. The next time I saw him, he was doing better, but I cannot help but think how far he might have come if we had not been interrupted at such a crucial time."

Her green eyes had been fixed on his chest, not really seeing him, but with a faraway look. Now they sharpened and met his gaze. "If you will allow me, perhaps I can help you as well. If nothing else, it is worth a try."

For a moment, he began to hope. Perhaps there was a chance his future did not have to mirror his past. He could stop standing on the outside. He could finally be part of the world everyone else inhabited—a world that, to him, was full of jumbled letters and confusion.

But he'd tried before and failed, and he had vowed never to allow himself to hope again. He had been disappointed for the last time. He did not need it proven, yet again, what a stupid brute of a man he was. He would risk life and limb for this woman because he was duty-bound to do so. What was more, he'd come to care for her, and he would have done it even if no one had paid him.

But Ewan would not risk his pride.

No woman, no *experiment*, was worth the tattered remains of the little vanity he had left.

Twelve

LORRIE HADN'T EXPECTED THE VIKING TO WALK AWAY. She'd hoped to challenge him, raise his fighting spirit, but instead he'd pushed away from her and strode out the door.

She'd stood in the office and wanted to call him back—and not only because she hated to lose. She hated to lose him. Finally, Lorrie looked down at the papers on the edge of her father's desk. The Viking had carried them into the room and left them, probably by accident. She opened the folder that contained them and scanned the contents—account books, bills of sale, mortgage papers. All of it seemed to pertain to the Earl of Pembroke. On another sheet was a long list of numbers, many of them scratched out. Was this the Viking's writing? Were these his attempt to work out the financial matter he had mentioned? But surely he would need to be able to read these papers to understand the problem. Lorrie didn't know how long she had stood in the library, looking through the papers, but finally, Welly whined and Lorrie had realized the Viking wouldn't be back.

Back in her own room—after a quick stop in the garden so Welly could sniff every flower, insect, rock, and *finally* empty his bladder—Lorrie lay in bed unable to sleep. When had she begun to look forward to seeing the Viking every day? When had the mere fact of him leaving a room made the world dim? She had thought teaching him to read would give her the time with him she craved—and perhaps result in a few more of those forbidden but wonderful kisses. Now she'd driven him further away.

"Unfortunate," she said to herself. In his little bed near hers, Welly's head popped up at the sound of her voice. "Because perhaps I really might be of some help to him."

It didn't surprise her when the Viking was absent from breakfast the next day or when he chose to meet the family at the theater—the god-awful opera again—instead of riding in their coach. It didn't surprise her when the Viking spent a week making every effort to avoid being alone with her. He was with her all the time, but always out of earshot or behind one of the half dozen or so of her fawning suitors. Lorrie was beginning to wonder if she'd ever have a chance to speak to him privately again. She'd inquired about him very indirectly on several occasions and managed to piece together half a dozen facts—the most salient of these was that he had served as the muscle inside a gaming hell called Langley's in St. James's.

Lorrie could only assume he must have had lodgings at the hell because he did not appear to own a flat, and he had to sleep somewhere when he was not sleeping in her father's town house, and that was all too common an occurrence now. Her other option was the club the Viking and the other men of Draven's troop frequented. But she thought she might have even less luck gaining entry into the club than into the hell.

She had only begun to scheme a way to pay him a visit at the club when one night, after appearing to completely ignore her at a ball, he made a point of handing her into the coach. A perfectly capable footman stood by, and so Lorrie had turned her head in surprise.

"The library," he'd whispered. And then he was gone.

She half believed she'd imagined the whispered request. She'd wanted so badly to see him that it seemed impossible her wish was finally coming to fruition. That night she'd barely paid any attention as Nell had undressed her and helped her don her nightclothes. All Lorrie cared about was the interminable amount of time before the rest of the household went to bed and she was once again alone with the Viking.

Finally, the house was silent, and she padded downstairs on bare feet. She had slippers, but she could only find one, and from the lowered ears and drooped-head posture Welly had been giving her, she could guess where the other had gone.

Lorrie pushed the library door open and stepped inside, surprised to see the Viking seated at her father's desk with his back to the door. He made the large furnishing seem so small. Indeed, the entire room, with its high ceilings and shelves of books soaring upward, was dwarfed by his presence.

And when he turned to look at her with those cool blue eyes, she caught her breath.

I'm in love with him.

The thought had come from nowhere, and she immediately pushed it away. Ridiculous. She was in love with Francis. Charming and handsome Francis… who she had not thought about in days.

"Close the door," he said.

His low voice, little more than a rumble, awakened butterflies in her belly, and she was glad to turn away and have something to occupy her hands, which had begun to tremble.

When she turned back, he pointed to the desk. The folder with Pembroke's papers were before him. Lorrie frowned, uncertainly. "You want me to teach you how to read?"

"No. I told you. It's pointless. No offence, my lady, but better tutors than you have tried and failed. My father spared no expense, and although none of them ever called what I have word blindness, they all said the same thing in the end. I will never read."

Lorrie swallowed, feeling miserable. She had wanted to help so badly. "That isn't true," she said finally. "It might be slow and difficult, but I believe you can learn."

He waved a hand. "I don't have time for slow and difficult at the moment. I need your help."

"My help?" She pressed a hand to her heart.

He wet his lips as though the act of speaking was a novelty. "I recently visited my father at his town house. Your intended was there."

"Francis?"

He made a sound of agreement. "They had called

for me to tell me…" He paused and cupped the back of his neck as though it ached. "They wanted to inform me…" He rose and paced behind the desk.

She'd forgotten how much he seemed to dominate a room when he stood. Even a comfortably sized room like her father's library seemed cramped when he moved about in it. It was as though everything that was not him or part of him shrank in comparison.

He paced, seeming to struggle with finding the words he wanted. "The problem seems to be that my father is ruined." He nodded as though to say, *There. I have said it.*

Lorrie sank into the chair across from him. "What do you mean 'ruined'?"

"He has been swindled out of all the money he has not tied up in entailments. There is no dowry for my sister, no more for my brother Michael's living, and no allowance for me. What's more, he's mortgaged the property that came to him through my mother, and now he will lose that as well. I know it's considered rude to discuss money—"

She waved her hand. "But in times like this you cannot keep quiet. I promise you, I think no less of you or your family. It has happened to many great families."

He nodded, seeming slightly less ill at ease now. How mortifying for him to have to reveal his father's personal failure. And yet, he had trusted her with the information. "You said you need my help?"

"I told my father I would look at his accounts and try and find a solution. There is probably not a solution, but I have always been good with numbers."

She nodded eagerly. She had seen the lists of

numbers he'd made the other night. "That is very good of you. And what of your brothers? Are they also looking for a solution?"

He shook his head. "My father hasn't told them yet."

"Why not?"

He sighed. "He only told me because he wants me to find the man who swindled him and beat him until he gives my father back his money."

"Oh."

He sat. "I demanded the accounts instead, but my father has no faith I will find a solution. I confess, I do not know what possessed me to ask for these files. My father is right. I'm an idiot. I can't read the first—"

She stood and slammed her hand on the desk. "You are *not* an idiot."

He looked up at her, mouth slightly quirked at her outburst.

"You have word blindness. That does not make you an idiot. Not only that, but you are smart enough to ask for help. *My* help."

"At the moment I'm not certain how smart that makes me."

She narrowed her eyes. "Very smart, because I am a very helpful person."

"You've helped others in similar situations, have you?"

"Not exactly, but I like the idea of helping others. I'm not very good with numbers, I'm afraid." She gave him a sad shrug of her shoulders. She had so wanted to be of assistance too.

"I don't need your help with numbers. I need you to read these documents to me."

"Oh!" She sat straight. "That I can do. When shall we begin?"

"Now." He slid one over to her, and she cleared her throat and began reading.

It did not take her very long before she had the general idea of what had happened and who had been behind it. After the sixth or seventh document pertaining to a diamond mine in Brazil, she looked over at the Viking, who had been carefully listening to her, occasionally writing numbers down, but mostly frowning.

"I know very little about South America, mines, or investments, but after reading these documents, I cannot believe your father would have continued to give this Miguel de los Santos any funds. It is as though your father investigated the scheme and then willfully ignored the warnings of those he asked for advice."

"It does seem that this early advice was not heeded."

"I don't understand why not. If something looks too good to be true, it probably is."

He steepled his hands. "Go on."

"This smacks of desperation. I don't mean to criticize your father, but it seems as though he was taking an awful risk."

"You aren't criticizing my father."

She frowned. "I don't understand."

"I told you I met with my father and my cousin Francis. My father did not read any of this until too late. He trusted all of it with the man who orchestrated the investment."

She shook her head. "Surely you do not mean Francis."

Ewan said nothing, not that she had expected him to.

"Are you saying your father is ruined because Francis…" There was no other way to say it. "Francis was greedy and did not heed the warnings?"

He met her gaze directly.

"No." She held her hands up as though pushing the information away. "I don't believe this. I cannot."

"Then by all means, read on."

She did, and it was even worse than she had thought.

❧

By five in the morning, when the first sounds of the servants rising could be heard, Ewan had listened to Lady Lorraine read almost half the contents of the file. Her demeanor had grown increasingly dispirited over the course of the night, as though the weight of his father's troubles weighed on her as well.

Or perhaps it was coming to know her intended's true self that weighed her down. He did not want to be pleased at her disappointment, but he could not quite keep some of the pleasure from making its way to the surface.

Despite his fatigue, he was almost smiling.

"The servants are rising," he said, interrupting her reading of the mortgage document on the property in Yorkshire.

"Is it that late?" she asked, stretching.

Ewan quickly looked away. The way she'd arched her back made his breath catch. He was already tired and his defenses weakened by the long night of work and study. He didn't trust himself with her if his thoughts turned from facts and figures toward more carnal pleasures. Thank God the servants were a danger and he would have to leave her.

"I'll go to my room first. You follow in about ten minutes."

He placed his hands on the desk and pushed up, pausing when she covered his hand with hers. "Thank you," she said.

"For?"

"For trusting me with this information. For asking me to help you."

He still could not have said why he'd done it. But when he'd finally given up all hope of ever understanding any of the documents his father had given him, when he'd resigned himself to failing his family once again, he'd thought of her.

She might have looked down her nose at him. She might have complained at the tedium of the work or the long hours. But she'd done none of that, and somehow he'd known he could trust her. For a man who trusted no one save the others of Draven's troop—men who had saved his life—trusting a woman was a new experience. Ewan still did not quite have his footing.

He looked down at her bare hand, still covering his. She had small, stubby fingers with blunt nails. He'd noticed them before when she'd thumbed through the file and the papers within. They weren't the elegant hands a lady might wish for. They were hands that were accustomed to doing more than playing the pianoforte or embroidering fripperies. He liked her all the more for those unfashionable hands.

He drew his hand away before he lost the will to move away from her at all. "Good night."

"Shall we continue tomorrow—I mean, tonight?" she asked.

"If you don't mind." And suddenly he felt shy. What if she did mind? What if she told him she would rather spend her time in some other fashion? He could hardly blame her, and yet, she must have some idea what this meant to him. He gave her a long look. "It's your decision."

"Are you giving up?" she asked.

"No!" He spoke more loudly than he'd intended, especially since he was almost certain he had heard the scullery maid about, lighting the fires. "Never," he whispered.

"Then I am not giving up either. We will find a solution. And I will see you here tonight."

They met the next night and the next, and each night he came away feeling less alone and more as though he were part of a team. He'd been part of a fighting team, so he knew what that felt like. But he had never been part of any other team. He'd never really had any friends growing up. He rather liked the feeling of having an ally and a confidante, of feeling like he was part of something, not the one looking on. At the same time, he knew it could not last. He knew she would grow tired of wanting to help him, tired of tedious legal documents, tired of not sleeping. Then he would be alone again. He had to guard his heart against that possibility.

On the third night, the cold, dreary weather turned rainy and the duchess refused to attend a scheduled dinner party in Richmond. "The drive is too long and the weather too foreboding," she said. "My head has been aching since I rose this morning, and I have no doubt I will suffer a megrim by this afternoon. Dreadful weather. I fear summer may elude us completely this year."

The family had been in the drawing room, Ewan standing by a window, watching people huddle under useless umbrellas in the deluge.

"Shall Papa and I go alone then?" Lady Lorraine had asked. And then almost as though she had sensed his gaze on her, she added, "And Mr. Mostyn, of course."

The duke shook his head. "Your mother is right. This is no sort of weather for a drive to Richmond. We will send our regrets. We could all use a night in. But I must insist we all stay *in*," he said, looking pointedly at his wife. The duke, like the rest of the *ton*, must have heard the rumors that the duchess had taken a new lover. Lorrie had noticed she wore a new diamond and emerald ring, said to be a token of love from her paramour.

But the duchess waved a hand and settled into her chair, looking quite content to stay in. "Bellweather," she said to the butler standing near the door. "Tell Cook I shall have a small meal in my room at dinner."

"I'll join you," the duke said. Lorrie glanced at her mother, but to her surprise, the duchess didn't argue.

"Yes, Your Grace. Two for dinner, then?" the butler asked.

The duke looked at Ewan. "Do you plan to dine here tonight, Mr. Mostyn?"

Ewan didn't mind the duke, but he detested the effort it took to maintain unimportant conversations through several courses. "No."

Lady Lorraine sighed, and Ewan wondered if she

was pleased he would be away or whether she would miss him.

And why the devil did he care? She would be tucked in at home all night. He could dine at the Draven Club and sleep in his own bed at Langley's. They both needed a break from all the financial papers and account books tonight at any rate. They could come at it again with fresh eyes the next night.

He would not miss ledgers or letters or the survey reports on the flora and fauna of South America his father's investigator, apparently an amateur explorer, had compiled. He would not miss *her*.

And as though to prove it to himself, Ewan made a point of ignoring Lady Lorraine for the next hour and taking only the briefest leave of her when he set out in a light drizzle for the Draven Club.

The dining room was empty. Ewan didn't mind. He was relieved at the quiet and the solitude. For once he could spend an evening without Lady Lorraine prattling on.

Porter came to offer him refreshment, and Ewan asked for wine and whatever the cook had prepared.

"Very good, sir. Mr. Wraxall and Mr. Beaumont are in the reading room."

Ewan hadn't come to the club for company, and he intended to eat alone and then find a quiet corner to be alone. But after an hour of brooding, he had checked the clock on the mantel in the empty card room three times. He realized he was waiting for the hour to grow late enough that he might meet Lady Lorraine in the library.

Why couldn't he put her from his mind?

Beaumont and Wraxall would make him forget.

Ewan joined them in the reading room, where they were drinking port and laughing over an old war story. It was one Ewan knew well.

"And when that frog came around the corner and saw Duncan running for him like a raving lunatic, the look on his face made me laugh so hard, I almost forgot to grab him," Neil said. He smiled as he spoke, and Ewan realized it had been months since he'd seen Neil give a genuine smile.

"And then the frog says, '*Mon Dieu!*'" Beaumont said, raising his voice and affecting a French accent. "And Duncan says—"

Ewan stepped forward. "I'm no god. I'm the devil who will send you to hell."

Neil and Rafe turned to look at him, Rafe frowning at having his thunder stolen.

"Give over." Ewan sat at their table. "You've told that story a hundred times."

"Because I tell it well," Rafe argued, while Neil poured Ewan a glass of port he didn't particularly want. "You have to do the accents—the frog's French and Duncan's Scots brogue."

"And the accents make it more amusing? I notice you never tell the part about how that frog died."

The other two men's smiles faded. They must have remembered that Ewan had run him through with his own bayonet, a boy too young to grow a beard.

"You're right," Neil said, putting a hand on Ewan's shoulder. "That story has grown stale." He lifted his glass and gestured with it. "I still say Beaumont should have gone into the theater."

"And make my father even prouder?"

Even Ewan had to smile at the quip. Beaumont's parent, the Earl of Haddington, was not averse to making his disappointment in his son known.

"What brings you here?" Neil asked Ewan. "No balls tonight? No operas?"

"Dinner party in Richmond, but the duchess did not want to brave the weather."

"She's wiser than her choice of bed partners would lead one to believe," Beaumont said. "Viscount Worthington? The man is nothing short of a lecher."

"Unlike you, a pillar of morality," Neil said.

"I have my standards," Rafe said, sipping his port. "Low as they may be."

"A night off and you choose to spend it with us," Neil said. "You must be desperate." He had shadows beneath his eyes, and Ewan wondered when he had last had a full night's sleep.

"I wanted a decent meal. I can't pronounce half of what Ridlington's French cook prepares."

"So you are here in spite of us," Rafe said. "I'm actually glad to see you. I heard some interesting news the other day."

Ewan set his glass on the table. "About my cousin?"

"Hell no. 'Interesting' and 'news' do not fit in the same sentence with 'Francis Mostyn.' This came from a couple of Bow Street Runners."

"I told you not to cuckold any more husbands," Neil said.

Rafe gave his friend a bland stare. "I was dining at an establishment the Runners tend to frequent."

"Which means he was hiding from an irate husband," Ewan said.

Rafe glared at him. "So now you play the court jester too? I liked you better when you didn't speak."

"It's because he uses his words so...economically," Neil said, "that when he does say something amusing it surprises all of us."

"Then let's hope he amuses us all on your account, Wraxall," Rafe said. "As I was saying, I overheard two Bow Street Runners discussing a rash of abductions."

"That's nothing new," Neil said, but Ewan didn't dismiss it so quickly. He felt his shoulders tense as they had right before the signal to attack came.

"This is new. Apparently, several heiresses have been the targets of abductions and ransoms. Two women have been taken so far, both returned unharmed after the blunt was paid."

"Why haven't I heard about this?" Ewan asked.

"The families kept it quiet. They didn't want to ruin the girls' chances at making a good match."

Ewan should have expected as much. Nothing was sacred to the upper classes save the Marriage Mart.

"You are protecting a lady with a rather large fortune. Perhaps the only threat isn't from cousin Francis," Neil said.

Perhaps it wasn't. He'd be even more vigilant the next time the family went out. And he'd mention this news to the duke when he returned to the family's town house in the morning.

"How is your bastard of a cousin anyway?" Rafe asked.

"Still an arse," Ewan said.

The other men, accustomed to Ewan's long pauses, refrained from asking what Francis had done this time.

"He has my father convinced I am trying to steal the lady away from him. My father wrote me a long letter expressing his displeasure."

"That sounds like Francis," Neil said.

"Well?" Rafe asked.

"Well what?" Ewan drank more port.

"*Are* you trying to steal the lady's affections?"

"No."

"He says too quickly." Beaumont smiled like the cat with a bird feather dangling from its mouth.

"It was a firm answer." Ewan looked to Neil for support.

Neil shrugged. "It was rather quick, and I hear the lady is pretty."

"But not clever," Rafe added.

Ewan glared at him. "The hell you say."

"Hold now, Protector." Rafe held his hands up. "I only mean she is not so clever if she thinks she's in love with Francis Mostyn."

"Women do fall out of love," Neil said, watching Ewan closely. Perhaps too closely. "And back in again. They're illogical creatures."

"One thing is for certain," Rafe said, pouring more port. "If she falls for Ewan, it's not because of his charm."

"Not all women want charm."

"As you and I know, Protector." Neil tipped his glass to Ewan's.

Rafe steepled his fingers. "If I remember correctly, there was a barmaid in Vienna who didn't look twice at me and couldn't keep her hands off Mostyn."

Ewan remembered her well enough—a buxom

blond who'd made certain he knew she was his for the night, if only he wanted her. "We had a mission."

"If that made a difference to most of the men, then my job would have been a lot easier," Neil said.

"I take missions seriously."

"As well you should," Neil said.

Rafe shook his head. "Just remember there's life after the mission is complete. You can't work all the time."

For the sake of Lady Lorraine's virtue, Ewan hoped that he could.

Thirteen

"I MISSED YOU," LORRIE SAID AS SOON AS THE VIKING stepped into the library. She'd attended a rout with him tonight, and though he'd always been within reach, between the games and the conversations about this poet or that novel, she hadn't been able to speak to him alone. Finally, six hours later, she could say the one thing she'd wanted.

The Viking took the seat opposite her, across from the desk. He wore the same clothes he had to the rout, sans cravat and with his coat draped negligently over his arm. Now he dumped that coat on the chair. She should probably worry that she had grown used to seeing him in this state of undress, but privately she liked the informality.

"I'm sure you didn't miss me at all." She hadn't expected him to claim to miss her too, but some response might have been polite. She busied herself stacking the papers he'd brought with him. "You probably had better things to do than listen to me read contracts and reports, although the surveyors' report on the estate in Yorkshire was rather well written. I'd like to see the house one day. It sounds very pretty."

"My father can't pay the mortgage, so it soon won't be ours."

"Yes, well." The papers were straight, and she had run out of ways to occupy herself. Lorrie chanced a look at the Viking. "We had a very quiet evening last night. My father and I played chess. I'm horrible at chess because I talk myself through every move and then my opponent discovers my strategy—if I even have a strategy, that is. I suppose you occupied yourself doing the things war heroes do when they aren't guarding silly girls like me. Invaded a small country or saved an old woman from a burning building."

"I went to my club."

Lorrie dropped the pen she'd been about to trim. "You have a club?"

He made a sound of assent.

"Like Boodles or White's?"

"No. The Draven Club."

"Oh, that one. Yes, I hadn't thought of it as a club, I suppose." She sat and leaned her hand on her chin. "And what do you do there? Gamble and tell old war stories?"

"We have an excellent cook."

She laughed. "Of course you do. You would not go otherwise. Did you have an enjoyable evening?" She was certain he did, and she didn't want to hear how much he'd enjoyed himself away from her. "I really don't know why I should have missed you so much." She stared at the fire, speaking almost to herself. That was easy to do since he was such a good listener. She cleared her throat and met his clear gaze. "I went to bed early and then I couldn't sleep, which meant I had time to think about your family's predicament. There must be some solution, some way to save the family. Your brothers are not married. What if one of them married an heiress?"

"Are you volunteering?"

"No." Her hands began to straighten the papers again. "If I'm not to marry Francis, I suppose I would rather go home to Beauchamp Priory. I miss my friends and my work at the school."

"You like it," he said.

"The school? I suppose I do, though it can be quite drafty in the winter, and I do wish the chairs were a bit larger."

"I mean you like teaching," he said after she had closed her mouth.

"Oh. I don't know. I suppose—"

He made a slashing gesture with his hand. "You do. Why did you decide to help that boy?"

"Martin?" Being a creature of abrupt changes in subject, she never minded them. "Oh, well, the village teacher didn't seem to have any extra time for him, and his father is a farmer, so I knew Martin would have to help with the harvest and might not ever come back to school if he didn't show any progress—"

"Lorraine."

She stilled. No one called her Lorraine without "Lady" before it. Her friends and family had always called her Lorrie. "You used my Christian name."

He nodded. "It seemed the best way to make you stop talking. And here"—he gestured to the library— "it doesn't seem necessary to use titles."

Not that she ever used a title with him. She always thought of him as the Viking. "Then I should call you Ewan?"

He gave her that half smile she liked so much, one that said the idea pleased him. "Why did you go to help at the school?"

"Oh, I see." She had to think back to what had motivated her to go to the school that first time. "I suppose I wanted something to do. Something besides paying calls and embroidering handkerchiefs. My grandmother was alive then, and she would always tell me that a noble family, such as ours, had a responsibility to its tenants and indeed to the county and the country itself. She was a great benefactress of the hospital, but I have never been very good at a sickbed."

"Really?"

She narrowed her eyes. "I do believe you are teasing me…Ewan." The name felt quite delicious on her tongue, soft and lazy—very much unlike the man himself.

"I suppose originally I intended to see what I might do for the school—sew lace curtains for the window or some such thing—but after I made the curtains and spent more time there, it became clear what the students really needed was more attention. Well, I had all of this education from my governesses over the years, and the children seemed to like me, so I began to spend more and more time there when I was in the country. After a while, I went every day, and when Mr. Fletcher worked with the upper-level students, I worked with the lower-level ones, and then we would trade places."

"Do you miss it here in London?"

"Sometimes, but I like the social whirl too. When I'm in the country, I sometimes miss London. One grows tired of dining with the same eight families all year. And then at the close of the Season, one is tired of all the great to-do and happy to return to the quiet of the country."

"And my cousin is able to support the continuation of this lifestyle?"

She frowned. Who was he… "Oh, you mean Francis." She felt her cheeks heat. What was wrong with her? She loved Francis. How could she forget about him even for an instant?

"I have told him I don't really care about all of that. I just want to be with him, but he wants to please me, of course. That is why we will have to wait and marry with my father's blessing and the dowry."

"I wouldn't wait." He sat back, crossing his arms over his chest.

Lorrie became momentarily distracted by the way the muscles of his arms seemed to swell under the thin linen. "You wouldn't?" she said absently.

"If you were mine, I wouldn't wait a day."

Lorrie blinked and looked away from his biceps. "If I were…yours?"

"If a woman loved me as you love Francis, and I loved her in return, I wouldn't wait for permission. I take what I want."

"You take it." Her voice sounded rather faint. She actually felt rather faint, or at least strangely dizzy. She cleared her throat. "But a woman—a bride—is not a city under siege or a new saber one wishes to acquire. You cannot simply take a woman."

"Don't you want to be taken?"

Oh, yes, she did. But Lorrie wasn't even certain what they were discussing any longer.

"By my cousin, I mean. Don't you want him to take you to wife?"

"I…" She should say yes. To do any less would be disloyal to Francis, but she had seen some rather unflattering aspects of Francis just lately. Honestly, she didn't know what she wanted anymore. "I don't know."

His expression never changed. "Then what do you want?"

Her head had begun to spin. "For a man who doesn't speak very much, you certainly have a lot of questions tonight."

"Questions you avoid answering."

"Perhaps it's your turn to answer a question."

He raised one shoulder as though he had nothing at all to hide.

"Very well, then." What did she want to know about him? Correction—what did she want to know that she could ask him here and now? "Why don't you like to wear neckcloths?"

His brows came together, and he gingerly raised a hand to his exposed neck. "Have you ever worn a cravat?"

"No."

"They're deuced uncomfortable."

"And you think my corset and the hairpins poking me all day *are* comfortable?"

"I have no idea. But I feel as though I can't breathe or swallow in this." He lifted the strip of linen, which looked quite limp. "Do you want to see how it feels?"

"Very well. You won't ask to borrow my corset later, will you?"

"Absolutely not."

"Good." She held her hand out for the linen. "I had an uncle who—" She stopped speaking when she noticed he was coming toward her. "What are you doing?"

"I will tie it on you. You've never tied one before, and you won't know how."

"Oh."

"Stand."

She did, and he stood before her, looping the neckcloth around her exposed throat. She was level with his chest, and she stared at the row of buttons that led from the middle of his chest to his neck. The first was undone, revealing a patch of skin. She had the strangest desire to taste that skin. She wanted to taste him. She could smell his scent, the light aroma of forest and wild lands on his hands and the shirt near her face. Or perhaps the scent lingered on the cloth he tied about her neck.

He tightened it and began to tug it and loop it.

"Your uncle liked to dress in women's underthings?" he asked evenly.

"What? Oh." Her face felt hot, and she did not think the heat came solely from the inappropriate topic of conversation. "I cannot be certain, but once, I overheard my aunt and my mother speaking. My aunt complained that Teddy—that is my uncle—stretched all her chemises and corsets, and she didn't understand why he wouldn't buy them in his own size if he insisted on wearing them." She glanced up at his face, but his gaze was on her throat. "Does that shock you? It shocked me."

"Nothing shocks me anymore. Your uncle sounds harmless."

"I suppose he is." She swallowed as Ewan adjusted the cravat a last time.

He stepped back to admire his efforts. "I'm not as proficient as some."

She touched the material, seeing the elaborate style of it with her fingers. "It's not so bad. I imagine you become used to it."

"I don't. The longer I wear one, the tighter it feels. I imagine hands closing on my throat and squeezing until I cannot breathe."

The neckcloth seemed to grow tighter with his words. He reached toward her neck, and she half feared he would draw the material tighter, but instead he yanked it loose.

"A memory from your days in the army?"

"One of the few times I thought I would fail in my task. In Draven's troop, if you failed, you were dead. The missions left no room for error." As he spoke, he unwound the cloth from her neck. "One of the enemy caught me unaware and choked me until I was unconscious. He must have thought I was dead and left me. When I awoke it was to Beaumont's pretty face and a bucket of cold water."

"That sounds rather unpleasant."

"Not as unpleasant as death."

He pulled the cloth away from her throat, slowly, far more slowly than was necessary, and the teasing material made gooseflesh appear on her arms.

"And that is why you do not wear a cravat," she whispered.

His hand replaced the material of the cravat, sliding up her neck and then down to finger the lace at the top of her night rail. Lorrie held her breath, feeling the warmth of his fingers so close to the flesh of her breast.

"Any more questions?"

"Why do you hate Francis so?" she said, without thinking. Who could think with a man like him so close?

Immediately, she wished she hadn't asked him. All the warmth fled from his eyes, and she felt as though a bucket of ice water had been thrown over her.

His hand dropped away from her. "That is in the past."

"I don't think so." She should stop talking now. He obviously did not wish to speak of this, but her mouth often moved without the consent of her brain. "He seems to bear you quite a lot of animosity, and I do believe the feeling is mutual."

He leaned back against her father's desk, his thighs resting on the edge. "You wouldn't believe me, even if I told you."

"It is hard to know what to believe when I only have one side of the story."

He gave her a long, assessing look. He'd seemed to open up to her the past few evenings. He'd spoken more, been silent less, even offered answers containing more than yes or no. Lorrie did not need to be told she was beginning to see a side of him few ever did. And so many foolish people considered him a dumb brute. They didn't know he could make sharp retorts or witty observations or clever ripostes. In short, they didn't know him at all, and the truth was, neither did she.

But she wanted to know him.

The silence had gone on for several moments, and she couldn't stop herself from breaking it. "Perhaps you think that because your father always believed Francis, that everyone else will too. But I've always known you to be truthful. Give me a chance."

His hands, which had been resting on the edge of the desk, lifted and fell again as though in indecision. "There are a hundred reasons I hate my cousin, all of them small and petty. It's the whole of them together, more than one incident, that makes me hate him."

He didn't trust her. She could see the wariness in his eyes, the way his lids lowered and his pale lashes veiled those ice-blue depths.

"Tell me one reason you hate him. Give me one incident. I know about the letter he had your father send and his role in this swindle." She ticked off her fingers. "You need only give me ninety-eight more examples for me to understand as well as you."

He barked out a low laugh. "You should have been a general. You are relentless."

She straightened her shoulders. "My governess always told my parents my persistence would be an asset when I grew older."

He looked dubious. "I will tell you one incident."

She nodded eagerly, backing up until she sat in her father's chair. She had known he would never tell her eight incidents, much less ninety-eight, but this was something. "Go on."

He closed his eyes, the image of defeat. "I used to carve wood figures."

༺༻

Her expression of eager anticipation turned to one of skepticism. "Wood figures? I thought this was a tale of your childhood with Francis."

"If you want me to tell it, you shall have to stop speaking for a moment."

She closed her lips and pretended to lock them. Ordinarily, such a gesture would annoy him, but just like everything else she did, he found it slightly adorable. She had a way of worming under his skin until he told her things he had not intended. He hadn't wanted to share his father's predicament with her, but he had anyway. He hadn't meant to tell her how much he desired her, but he'd confided that as well. She was the first person he had ever met to whom he genuinely enjoyed speaking.

Correction: She was the only person he'd ever met to whom he enjoyed speaking.

"As I said, I used to carve wooden figures. I'm good with my hands." He glanced down at his hands, trying not to think about how good he'd been at using them to cut off the life of enemy soldiers. "When I was a boy, I carved about seventy-five or a hundred soldiers out of wood." He had carved eighty-three, but she did not need to know the exact number.

"Goodness. Just the soldiers or the horses and cannons too?"

"Mainly infantry, but some cavalry and cannons as well." It had taken him hours to carve the figures over several years. Not that the time to complete the task had mattered. He was alone most of the time after he'd been sent home from school. Occasionally his father would hire a new tutor who made an effort for several weeks to teach him, but the men all gave up eventually. And so he'd had time to carve. He'd made each soldier unique, giving him a name and a facial expression as well as specific hair color and eye color. He'd even made up a history for each soldier, devising previous battles and heroic acts for his little men.

He'd known each of their names and ranks, and he loved nothing more than ordering them in various lines where he could pretend they were marching or moving into battle formations. It had been his only source of pleasure as a child, since he could not read and had no playmates.

"My brothers and Francis had been home from school on a break." He hardly remembered which one now. But the other children rarely invited him to play with them, and as they were all older than he, they teased him for still playing with toys. "And I had left my soldiers in the garden when we'd been called in for a meal. The little men had been in formation, and I'd planned a great battle for them. It was one of the few times I hadn't wanted to leave what I was doing and eat."

"Oh dear. Something happened to the soldiers, didn't it?" she asked, her expression filled with concern.

"I was inside longer than anticipated because Francis or one of my brothers had broken a lamp and blamed me, and my father had taken me to task for it." That was what his father had called it when he took a birch to Ewan's back and shoulders. "By the time I returned, the figures were completely destroyed."

"What do you mean?" she asked, sitting forward.

Ewan swallowed. It still angered him, all of these years later. "Francis had destroyed all of them."

"How?"

Ewan tensed his jaw. "Deliberately and thoroughly."

He could still see the devastation now, though he saw it with his child's eyes and through the blur of tears. That day had been one of the few times Ewan had cried as a child. He'd stared at the scattered remains of his soldiers, all of them so painstakingly carved and a sound like that of a wounded bird had broken from his lips. He knew it was silly, but he felt as though his friends had been murdered. Charles and George and Stephen and Timothy—their small faces and the expressions he'd given them—smashed into bits of wood. He'd tried to gather them, as a mother hen does her chicks, but there was no saving them. Every single one of his precious soldiers was destroyed. Not even one had survived the massacre.

And then he'd heard a low chuckling and turned to see Francis standing behind a tree, a croquet mallet in his hand. And Ewan knew. Francis had done this.

Without thinking, he'd attacked, easily wrestling Francis to the ground and taking the mallet from his hands. Ewan had then begun to pound Francis, just as his cousin had pounded his little figures into wood pulp.

It wasn't long before Ewan's older brothers pulled him off and one of the groundskeepers intervened and all the boys were dragged before the Earl of

Pembroke, who stared down at them with undisguised disgust. "What is the meaning of this?" he'd boomed, his gaze coming to rest on Ewan.

Ewan wanted to answer, but the words lodged in his throat.

"He attacked me, Uncle," Francis said. "I had done nothing! I swear."

The earl looked at his heir, and William had nodded agreement. "It's true, my lord. The attack did seem unprovoked."

"It was n-n-not!" Ewan had bellowed, unable to hold his tongue. He'd held out the remains of his little men, now little more than bits of wood covered with dirt and grass. "L-l-l-ook what he did." He pointed to Francis. "He d-d-destroyed my soldiers!"

"Did not!" Francis said. "I was with William and Michael after lunch!"

The earl looked at his sons. "Is that true?"

William looked at Francis, then down again. "Yes, sir. But he was not with us the entire time."

The earl looked at Francis. "So there was opportunity. Very well, Francis; did you destroy Ewan's soldiers?"

"No, sir."

"He lies!"

"None of that!" the earl said to Ewan. "He says he did not destroy them. Do you have proof that he did?"

Ewan had stared at his father, then his brothers. Everyone knew Francis did it. Why would no one take his side? "N-n-n—"

"Say it already!" his father demanded.

Ewan closed his eyes. "He was laughing and he had the croquet mallet—"

"Then it's your word against his, and I'll have you know, Ewan, we don't accuse men of crimes without some sort of proof. That's slander."

"He did it." Ewan had felt his lip tremble and known he was very close to tears. "I know he d-d-d—"

"That's enough," the earl had said. "Go to your room and dry your tears. Don't come out until you can behave more like a man. You're too old to play with toys anyway."

Ewan had stared, dumbfounded. *He* was being punished? *His* creations had been destroyed, and yet he was the one whose liberty was being taken away?

He'd turned on his heel and marched to the door, but when he'd stepped outside, he'd paused and looked back. Inside, the earl knelt, hand on his nephew's shoulder, and spoke quietly to Francis. In the scene was all the warmth and fatherly affection Ewan had never known.

But he knew one thing—his father did not love him like he loved Francis.

Lady Lorraine stood and put her hand over his, bringing him back to the present. "I'm sorry."

He waited for her to offer excuses for his cousin's behavior—he was jealous or boys will be boys—but she said nothing more. She squeezed his hand.

Then she moved closer and put her arms around him, her warm body pressing against his in a gesture of comfort.

"And you say there are ninety-eight more stories like this?" she murmured against his shoulder.

He nodded.

Her fingers fluttered over his back. "I'm so, so sorry."

She stood, holding him for a long time—or so it seemed to him. Finally, he brought his arms up and held her back. Strange that such a small thing should ease some of the bitterness the memory had churned in him, but then he'd had precious few embraces in his life and fewer still designed to give comfort.

When she finally pulled away, he couldn't quite allow her to go. She might have meant only to comfort him, but after several minutes of the feel of her in his arms, other thoughts had come to mind.

She looked up at him, her breath hitching in her throat in a way that made her breasts rise deliciously over the lace at the bodice of her night rail.

"Will you kiss me now?" she whispered.

He swallowed because kissing her was the most innocent of actions he could imagine at the moment. He allowed his hand to slide up her back and then around to cup her face. He raised her chin until her eyes—such lovely green eyes—met his. All of her feelings—her desire, her eagerness, her uncertainty—were written plainly on her features. "You like when I kiss you," he said.

"You know I do."

"I like it too." He looked down at her lips, and she closed her eyes.

And then opened them again when he didn't move to put his mouth on her.

"We are in your father's house and in his library. I won't kiss you here. I won't kiss you at all. That's not why we're here."

"It could be."

He gave her a long look. "What would Francis say?"

She opened her mouth, but she didn't speak. Confusion flickered in her eyes, and that spoke more than any words she might utter. She still cared for his cousin and yet she had her doubts about him as well. Her affection was torn, which had not been the reason he'd told her the story, but which served his purposes at any rate.

"You are correct." She stepped away, out of his grasp. "We should read the documents you brought. We still do not have a solution to your father's predicament."

He nodded and went to the chair across the desk. She sat too, and he was certain she read, but he didn't hear a word of it.

Fourteen

Ewan strolled through the Dewhursts' ball, keeping a few feet behind Lady Lorraine. The fourth Baron Dewhurst was one of the most fashionable men in London, despite his American wife, and the *ton* had turned out to marvel at the ballroom, which had been draped with silks and covered with Turkey rugs in order to give the impression of an eastern sheik's palace. The dance floor remained bare, of course, but surely even those brave enough to partake in the still relatively scandalous waltz could imagine they were in Arabia since the scent of flowers permeated. Ewan had no knowledge of what sorts of flowers adorned the pots and baskets hanging from the columns—he could identify roses and daisies—but he thought he recognized blue and white flowers that resembled pictures of lotus plants he'd seen in childhood books.

Lady Lorraine was not allowed to dance the waltz, and she took the opportunity to step out of the warm ballroom and into the supper room, where she sampled Turkish coffee and several other eastern delicacies Ewan did not recognize, but which he sampled as well.

Except for turnips, Ewan had never met a food he did not like, and these dishes were spicy and exotic. As a general rule, he did not eat when he was working, but one glance at Lady Lorraine showed her deep in conversation with another young woman, both ladies sipping their rich coffee.

Ewan tasted a creamy yellow concoction, a spicy red sauce he ascertained he should dip the flat bread into, and finally a thick green stew-like dish where he was pleased to find potatoes hidden. The sweets were even more tempting. Dates and figs, milk and rice topped with nuts, and some sort of pastry filled with custard and dripping with sweet syrup.

By the time Ewan had managed to clean his hands of the sugar, the waltz had ended. Lady Lorraine was no longer in the supper room. It annoyed him that she hadn't fetched him before leaving, but he supposed she had returned to the ballroom for her next dance.

He was wrong.

He'd had her recite the names of her partners for the evening, and he'd memorized the list. It was the same group of men she always danced with—an assortment of heirs to marquessates, dukedoms, or great fortunes. Ewan found her partner in the ballroom, a man a little older than Ewan who would inherit an earldom.

"Mr. Mostyn," Viscount Whatshisname—who was number four on the dance card—said as he bowed to Ewan. "Have you seen Lady Lorraine?"

Ewan gritted his teeth. "I will find her."

"I thought I saw her enter the supper room. Shall I search there?"

Ewan shrugged. The viscount could do what he liked, but Ewan had a feeling he knew exactly where the lady had gone.

As he did for all balls they attended, Ewan required the duke's secretary to provide a guest list the day of the event. The secretary grumbled about this additional task and the delicacy of requesting such information, but he managed it. Gladstone then recited the names of the guests—sometimes to Ewan alone and sometimes to both Ewan and the duke— before the ball.

Francis Mostyn had been on the Dewhursts' list.

His cousin had waited until Ewan was distracted by the food in the supper room and then whisked Lady Lorraine away. Ewan couldn't even be angry at Francis. It was Ewan's own weakness he cursed.

Turning away from the viscount without another word, Ewan ducked behind one of the silk drapes and peered out the long windows of the ballroom. The lawns were unlit and the night was cold enough that it felt more like late autumn than late spring. Ewan doubted Francis had led the duke's daughter outside, and he hoped Lorraine was not foolish enough to assent to go outside if it was suggested.

That meant she was inside the house, a large town house with dozens of rooms. Except Ewan had noted the footmen stationed about the house when he'd first come in. Clearly the Dewhursts wanted no scandals at their ball, no ladies being ruined in the library.

Ewan made his way out of the ballroom, ignored

the supper room, and passed the library. A footman stood guard there. "Did anyone enter?" he asked.

"No, sir. This room is closed."

Ewan looked about the busy vestibule with men and women coming and going, shedding wraps while others pulled pelisses on to stave off the chill. "What is that door?" he asked, pointing to another beside the dining room. It probably connected to the dining room, but Ewan had been so focused on the food, he hadn't noticed it.

"A parlor, sir."

"Is it closed?"

"No, sir. Lord Dewhurst asked that it remain open to accommodate any older guests who might need to rest later in the evening or linger over drinks after dinner."

Which meant it was probably empty at the moment. Ewan started for the door, then thought better of it. He cut through the supper room, steadfastly ignoring that sticky sweet dessert, and spotted the door to the parlor immediately. It was closed, and he put his hand on the latch and silently opened it.

One look inside confirmed his suspicions. The room was empty but for a single couple standing near the mantel. The lady wore a bluish green gown with gold along the hem and ornamenting the sleeves. The color turned her eyes blue-green and the gold leaves in her dark hair made it look even richer. He knew the dress and the lady. Lorraine stood in the arms of his cousin. Francis had both hands planted on her back, and he kissed Lorraine quite passionately.

For her part, the lady returned the affections.

Pain speared through Ewan so fiercely he all

but expected a knife to protrude from his lungs. Betrayal—he knew that feeling well—but mixed along with it was also another feeling, jealousy. He knew that one as well, had come to associate it with Francis Mostyn.

Ewan had the impulse to stand in the doorway and roar. Was this how the lady repaid him for spilling out his heart the night before? Why not just rip it out and stomp on it? It might have hurt less.

But he also had the strange impulse to close the door, not to intrude on this private moment. Of course, he'd been paid to intrude, paid to stop just this sort of behavior. If she'd been kissing another man— Viscount Whatshisname, for example—Ewan would have had an easier time looking the other way. After all, the Duke and Duchess of Ridlington wanted their daughter to consider the men on her dance card.

Ewan wouldn't have liked looking away. He would have wanted to rip her out of any man's arms and then smash that man into little more than pink pulp.

Ewan wanted to do the same to Francis. And he had license to knock Francis about a bit, and it would give him temporary satisfaction. But Ewan saw the way Lorraine's fingers closed on Francis's coat, the way her breath hitched, and her body melted into his. All her uncertainty about marrying Francis from the night before seemed to have fled.

Had nothing they'd shared in Ridlington's library mattered to her? Had nothing Ewan had said, the pain he'd allowed her to see, the embrace afterward—had none of that mattered? Ewan clenched his jaw and pushed the anger and the hurt down. He could not allow it to matter. His job was to prevent an elopement, whether the lady loved his cousin or did not, whether she eventually married him or did not, was no concern of his.

He was the man her father paid to guard her. Nothing more.

Ewan had never stood, undecided, for so long. He always acted quickly and boldly. Leave others to strategize and plan and second-guess. But he must have remained in the doorway long enough for Lorraine to sense him. She broke the kiss, and her gaze flicked directly to Ewan. In her eyes he saw a dozen emotions—embarrassment, surprise, shame, defiance—and something else that looked very much like regret.

Francis was turned slightly, and he did not see Ewan. Ewan closed the door before his cousin could spot him. A moment later, the door opened again and Lorraine stepped into the supper room. Her cheeks were flushed and her lips red from the other man's kiss. She wouldn't quite meet Ewan's eyes.

"I should return to the ball," she said, speaking rapidly. "I just needed a bit of air." Ewan could only assume this statement was made for the benefit of the others in the room because she certainly hadn't been breathing fresh air with her face pressed against Francis's.

"The viscount was looking for you," Ewan said, his voice hard and cold.

"Oh, Viscount Knoxwood. Of course!" That being all the excuse she needed, she escaped back into the ballroom. Ewan followed—he always followed—and stood in a corner, watching the dancers smile and flirt and exchange meaningful looks. Others frowned or hissed scathing retorts. Some looked shy with hope or wretched with disappointment. Men and women falling in love or out of it.

The music played on. The dancers danced on. Ewan stood on the outside, watching.

⅋

Charles found his wife on the Dewhursts' terrace, braving the unseasonably cool temperatures in only a thin emerald-green silk gown. He liked her in green. It complemented her eyes, which was his favorite feature of hers.

One of them, at any rate.

He wondered if she wore green so often because she knew he liked her in it or if that was more wishful thinking. Her hands rested lightly on the balustrade, and over the gloves, she wore the diamond-and-emerald ring he'd given her. He hadn't even been certain she'd accept it, and every time he saw it on her finger, his heart clenched with hope.

Let the *ton* gossip about her new lover. Charles knew the truth about the gift.

He stepped behind her and slid his arms about her waist. She stiffened and would have elbowed him in the breadbox, but he leaned down and whispered in her ear. "I wondered where you had gone."

"Charles." She relaxed, but not as much as he would have liked. When would she lower her guard with him? When would she believe he was sincere in his pursuit of her?

"Shall I give you my coat? Your skin is like one of Gunther's ices."

"I'm fine. I was overheated and needed the air."

He turned her to face him, noting her flushed cheeks. "Are you well? Shall I take you home? Mostyn can escort Lorrie."

She gave him a wry look. "Escort her to the library, you mean. I still don't think we should allow them to continue to meet there."

He agreed. The two of them, alone, in the dark of night was completely inappropriate. With any other man, he would have believed the worst, but he knew enough of Mostyn now to believe nothing untoward had happened or would happen between the two of them. Not under his roof, at any rate.

And with Mostyn and his daughter so preoccupied with what he assumed was their own budding love affair, he had the time and privacy to pursue his own love.

"Lorrie has not mentioned Francis Mostyn in a week or more. Pembroke's son is a good distraction for her," he said.

"I suppose we can trust him—to a point."

"That is true of all men. Women too."

Through the terrace doors, the strains of violin and cello wafted out. Charles took Susan's hand and guided her into a waltz. She laughed as he turned her, then pulled her close. She was warm, the weight of her breasts against his chest familiar and tantalizing all at once.

"Stop," she said between laughter. "Someone might see us."

"A man dancing with his wife," he said, turning her again. He wanted her dizzy—as dizzy as he felt with love for her. "How unfashionable. Imagine the scandal if you were found with me rather than Worthington."

She stiffened. "I don't know the origin of that rumor. As though I would allow that lecher to touch me."

He glided with her, feeling her body relax again. "I am glad to hear it. I do like this dance. Why did they not have the waltz when I courted you?"

"We had our own share of risqué songs and dances."

She looked so beautiful in the golden light shining through the windows of the town house. She might have been the same girl he'd first asked to dance all those years before. "Do you remember the first time I asked you to dance?"

Her brows rose. "Of course. Do you?"

He nodded. "You wore a green gown with a yellow…what do you call them? Panel or opening or cutaway? The dresses were wider then so I had no sense of what lovely legs you had, but the bodice was low enough that I could hardly breathe."

"I remember I was laced so tightly *I* could hardly breathe."

"One dance and I knew I wanted you for my wife."

Her eyes registered surprise. "You mean you knew you wanted me out of the dress."

"I was not so randy that I would have married you just to take you to bed. You were the first young woman I met who could make me laugh, who talked to me as if I were a man not solely the heir to a dukedom, who I could see myself growing old with."

"Charles…" She looked away and stopped dancing.

He placed a finger under her chin and brought her gaze back to his. "I still feel that way, Susan. I have sent you gifts, written you love poems—"

"Bad love poems." But she smiled.

"What more can I do? I want to be your husband again. I want one more chance."

She looked down.

"What are you afraid of?"

"You," she murmured. "You broke my heart once, and I know I broke yours as well. I don't want to hurt you again. *I* don't want to be hurt again."

He bent and met her gaze. "I will not hurt you again. I promise. I am older. Wiser."

"I'm not ready."

He felt as though he were a fish, flayed for her pleasure, all of his guts spilled out before her. And still it wasn't enough. But if she needed time, he had that in droves.

He stepped back. "Then I shall wait."

Her brows lowered. "For how long?"

"Forever."

She winced. "I never knew you were such a romantic. Poetry, flowery words—"

"Then here are more flowery words for you. I love you, Susan." He held a hand up. "No, do not say anything. I expect no response. I want you to know my feelings while you consider your own. Now, Your Grace, may I escort you back to the ball?"

She took his arm. "You may."

Fifteen

"I MUST GO, NELL," LORRIE SAID FOR THE THIRD TIME that morning. "With or without you."

"It's not safe, my lady," Nell answered, wringing her hands.

"Yes, all of those men trying to abduct me for my fortune. That is why I will not go alone. You can protect me."

"Oh, my lady." More wringing of hands and pleading from Nell's blue eyes, now slightly ringed with red. "Can't you go tomorrow?"

Nell had been granted a full day off the following day. Her sister had given birth the day before, and Nell had asked for and been granted time to see her new nephew.

"No. I want to go today. Look." She dumped her sewing basket over—which delighted Welly, who grabbed a bit of yarn and ran off with it—and lifted two veils from under the scraps of fabric and unfinished embroidery. "We will wear these. No one will recognize us."

"But what if someone does, my lady? This isn't at all proper."

"It's not as if we will be in St. James's at night. It's only slightly forbidden to women during the day."

Nell made another plea for her mistress to reconsider, but Lorrie had already tucked the veils under her pelisse. She had to see Ewan Mostyn, and nothing Nell said would convince her otherwise.

Two nights ago, at the conclusion of the Dewhursts' ball, Ewan had put her in the carriage with her parents, informed the party he would see them the following day, and closed the door. After the musicale last night he'd done the same thing. Her parents had not remarked on it. Why should they care if the hired help chose to sleep God knew where as long as he was present when required?

The problem was that Ewan had chosen to sleep at the duke's town house so many other nights. They'd spent hours together in the predawn, huddled close while she read to him.

And now he made those meetings impossible, and she must meet with him because she had finally solved his father's problem. She knew how to save Pembroke, and she couldn't even tell Ewan because he wouldn't see her.

And it was her fault. Lorrie didn't think it any coincidence that Ewan had chosen to avoid her after he'd caught her in Francis's arms. He'd seen her with Francis before, at the prince's ball, and the look on his face that night had been impatient and angry.

But at the Dewhursts' ball Ewan had looked more hurt than angry. And it was her fault he felt betrayed.

She had to tell him there was no reason to be hurt. She didn't care about Francis. But more importantly, she had to tell him her plan to save Pembroke.

"We'll tell my mother we are going out shopping," Lorrie told Nell, who seemed finally to have resigned herself to her fate and put a shawl around her shoulders.

"What if she wants to come, my lady?"

"She won't. She has charitable meetings all day—if that's what you want to call afternoon liaisons with her lover. She won't want us along when she sneaks off to see him."

"Oh dear." Nell pressed her hands to her cheeks, which were bright red, almost as red as her hair. "I don't think you should say such things, my lady."

Lorrie shrugged. "What other explanation is there? No one can be that charitable. You needn't pretend the staff never gossips about such matters."

"Of course I must pretend, my lady. Just as I'll pretend today that I don't know you plan to see a man in his private rooms."

Lorrie flashed her maid a warning look. "Nothing untoward will happen. I only need to speak with him for a minute or two. You can wait downstairs, and I will return so quickly you'll hardly know I was gone."

"But a gambling hell, my lady!" Nell's hands went to her cheeks again. "That's the devil's work."

Lorrie tried very hard not to roll her eyes. "Then do not gamble. I won't ask you to throw the dice, only wait a few minutes while I speak to Mr. Mostyn. Come on."

Lorrie found her mother in the drawing room and informed her of the plan to go shopping, taking Nell along, of course. Her mother suggested she also bring a footman to carry the packages, but Lorrie said she only planned to look, not buy more than a hat or a book, and Nell could certainly manage those. Then because her mother looked as though she might insist on the footman, Lorrie suggested the duchess come with them. To her surprise, her mother almost looked regretful to decline. Lorrie began to wonder if perhaps her mother really was spending afternoons attending meetings for hospitals and orphanages, and if the duchess might not wish to go out with her daughter for a bit of shopping instead.

Before her mother could insist on a footman, Lorrie took Nell's arm and hurried her outside. The day was cool and cloudy, but it was not so cold they could not walk to St. James's Street. Nell walked a step or two behind Lorrie, but Lorrie could hear the maid clearly enough when she spoke.

"I don't suppose this meeting has anything to do with the time you and Mr. M spend in the library together every night."

Lorrie stopped, and Nell plowed into her.

"You know about that?"

Nell gave her an innocent smile. "I am good at pretending."

"I'm helping Mr...M with an estate issue," Lorrie said, hoping he would not mind if she revealed a little of his private affairs. "That's all. Nothing sordid about reading documents and land surveys."

"Nothing sordid at all, my lady."

Lorrie began to walk again.

"Is that what you will be doing at Langley's, my lady? Reading land surveys?"

Lorrie didn't answer. When they neared St. James's Street, Lorrie ducked into a small shop selling soaps and perfumes. She pretended to browse. Before leaving, she donned her veil and made Nell do the same.

The rest of the walk was made in what seemed like twilight. Through the dark netting, everything looked shadowy and sinister. By the time she reached Langley's she was shaking with fright.

She told herself to stop acting like a child. What was the worst that could happen? Her identity would be discovered? That would make her life difficult for a little while, but her life wouldn't be in any danger.

Lorrie stood before the door and studied it. The hell looked closed. It was barely noon, and as most of the *ton* was only just rising at this hour, there was no need for an establishment catering to the upper classes to open its doors this early.

And since the doors were closed, how to gain access?

"Have you reconsidered, my lady?" Nell asked.

"No." Lorrie took a breath, telling herself she had *not* reconsidered. "Should I knock?"

"I think it might be better if we go in. Harder to kick someone out than refuse entrance."

That was true enough. Nell seemed to have resigned herself to this outing and apparently wanted it over and done.

Lorrie reached for the door and pushed it open. She was immediately assaulted by the odors of tobacco, spirits, and leather. These masculine scents were familiar to her, having lived with a father and three brothers.

She entered a small hallway, lined with hooks for coats and hats. At the end of the short hallway was another closed door, this one dark, polished mahogany. Lorrie pushed past the empty hooks and opened the door. It swung in, and she stared at a large room with a high ceiling. The floors were carpeted in deep crimson, like the red and black damask of the walls, and green baize tables, some with chairs and some without, were scattered throughout the room. Mirrors lined the room, above paneled walls. Beautiful gold and crystal chandeliers hung throughout the room and must have made it glitter with light when the candles were lit.

At present the room was shadowed as only a few lamps sat here and there and two maids swept floors and dusted tables. Lorrie took a cautious step inside. "It doesn't *look* like a den of iniquity," she whispered to Nell.

"Looks can be deceiving, my lady."

"Excuse me," Lorrie called to one of the maids, who looked up from her sweeping and eyed the two women in the door with suspicion. "Could you tell me where I might find Mr. Mostyn?"

The servant put her hand on her waist. "And who wants him?"

Lorrie looked back at Nell, wondering what response she was to make to this impertinence. Unfortunately, Nell's face was as shrouded as her own.

"A friend," Lorrie said finally. "I don't mean him any harm."

The servant with her hand on her waist harrumphed. "We're closed right now. You'll have to come back later."

Lorrie's spirits sank. She couldn't return later. Later the street would be full of young bucks who might accost her or, worse, recognize her. Later she would be at some affair or another, and there would be no opportunity to speak to Ewan.

"Ignore her," said the other maid, lowering her duster. "Mr. Mostyn will be either in the kitchen or in his room. I haven't seen him come out this morning, so my guess is in his room. Second floor. His name is on the door."

"Why did you tell them that?" the first maid asked, spinning on the other.

The dusting maid shrugged. "There's no harm in it, Meg." She went back to her work, while the one named Meg gave them both cool stares.

Lorrie leaned close to Nell. "I will knock on the door to his room. You stay here."

Nell blew out a breath that fluttered the veil. No doubt she did not wish to spend any more time with the unfriendly Meg than she had to.

"I'll be right back."

She hoped.

Lorrie lifted her skirts and ascended the gently curving stairway. At the top, a hallway circled the room, serving as a balcony. Guests could stand all along the edge and watch the gambling below.

Lorrie started around the hall, stopping to peer at the name placards on each. She was acutely aware she was being watched from below and also aware that she was doing what no proper lady should do—visiting a man alone in his rooms.

Finally, she stopped before a room with *Mr. Mostyn* written in elegant script on a small card in the little gold cardholder. Lorrie stood and listened for a moment but heard nothing on the other side. Lifting her hand, she tapped quietly on the door.

No sound.

She tapped again, this time louder. Finally, she heard what sounded like a curse and then a thump. The door did not open, and Lorrie began to wonder if perhaps coming here unannounced was the wisest course of action. What if Ewan was not alone? What if he'd been staying in his rooms here because he had a paramour?

She was about to turn and rush back down the stairs when the door swung open and the man himself stood before her. Lorrie forgot why she had come, forgot her own name. She simply stared at the expanse of bare muscled chest on display, her eyes unable to comprehend that this was a man and not a statue. He was too perfectly formed.

Gradually, her gaze moved up to his broad, square shoulders—shoulders that looked as though they had been sculpted from marble. Then there was the neck she was familiar with, followed by the square jaw, glinting with pale blond whiskers, the almost straight nose that had been broken at least once and probably more, and the piercing blue eyes that looked so much like a cloudless summer day she could all but feel the breeze.

"Mr. Mostyn." She gave a trembling curtsy.

He didn't move, and she realized he might not know who she was. She lifted her veil, and he blew out a long breath. "What do *you* want?"

What did she want? Something… "I wanted to speak with you a moment. May I come in?"

"No." He moved to close the door, but she shoved her shoulder against it. This would not in the least have prevented him from closing it, but it made him pause. "Go home."

"Well," she huffed, straining against the door. "I see you have forgotten your manners."

"*My* manners? You come to my room. Uninvited. You, a lady. In a gaming hell. In St. James's. And you speak to me of manners?"

That was quite a speech for a man of few words. She must have angered him more than she anticipated. "I will be on my way as soon as we speak."

"Speak."

He made no attempt at deference, didn't call her *my lady* or *Lady Lorraine* as he always did at her father's house or when they were out in Society. This was his territory, and she held no power here. She might very well regret what she was about to say, but she hadn't come all this way not to risk something.

"May we speak inside your chamber? I don't wish an audience." She glanced over her shoulder. The maids and Nell were probably too far away to hear them, but they could see them easily enough. In fact, all three women were looking up.

And then she remembered her earlier fears. "Unless, that is, you are not alone?"

"I'm alone. All the more reason for you to stay outside."

Lorrie waved her hand. "I'm not concerned. You are such a gentleman."

He gave a low laugh that seemed to reverberate through her. "No, I am not." But he stepped aside, giving her the first view of his private chamber. She stepped forward, keenly aware that he wore only a pair of charcoal trousers. Keeping her gaze forward, she noted the spartan white walls, the unembellished furnishings, the lack of any clutter or personal items anywhere. The bed was the only piece in the room worth noting. It alone spoke of comfort as the mattress was thick and the coverlet plush. At the moment, the sheets were mussed as though he had just woken.

He moved to the window and pushed one side of a gray curtain open, allowing more light inside. But the light revealed nothing new in the room. It might have been anyone's room as it was completely impersonal.

"You are inside. Talk."

He crossed his arms over his chest, making the muscles bunch. Lorrie tried to think of what she had wanted to say, but since she had seen his bare chest, she couldn't seem to remember anything.

"Might you put on a shirt?" she asked.

"My room."

That wasn't exactly an answer, but she deduced that he would not don a shirt. He must not have minded standing in front of her half naked. Lorrie looked away, hoping seeing something other than the half-naked sculpture before her would help her concentrate.

But, of course, her gaze landed on the bed. Did he bring women here and take them to that bed? It was not a large bed. A woman would have to press herself close to him if sharing it.

"It is rather warm in here," she said, feeling stifled all of a sudden. "Do you mind if I removed my pelisse?" She drew off her gloves and undid the fastenings, then laid both gloves and wrap on the bed. Next, she unpinned her veil and dropped it beside them.

"Take anything else off, and I won't be held responsible."

Lorrie's eyes snapped to his face. Nothing had changed in it, but when she looked very closely it appeared his jaw might have tensed, slightly. She was sorely tempted to remove another item of clothing—a boot perhaps—just to see what he would do. To catch a glimpse of Ewan Mostyn acting irresponsibly. But she was too much of a coward. And she'd remembered why she'd come.

"You haven't been to the library," she said.

He looked at her, arms still crossed, jaw tightening as though he was clenching it and releasing.

"What about your father's predicament?"

"I was hired to protect you. On my own time, I needn't entertain you."

That was a slap in the face. Had he really thought that was how she saw him? As entertainment? "I wanted to help you."

"Why?" His eyes narrowed.

"Because I know you want to help your father, and it would make your life better if some of what happened in the past was made right."

"You don't care about my life."

Lorrie stared at him. "Yes, I do."

"No. I am a diversion for you. Like a flower show or a home for ruined women is for other upper-class women. I give you something to do until you can either gain your father's permission to marry my cousin or until you find a way to elope with him. And if there's the chance I might kiss you, that adds the element of danger. I don't blame you for seeking out a thrill here and there. Your life must be tedious if all you ever do is look pretty and chat about the weather."

Lorrie stared at him for a long, long moment. She hadn't expected him to speak to her so. She hadn't expected him to say such awful things.

"And that is what you think of me?" she whispered when she could speak past the lump in her throat. "That I use people—that I used you—to stave off boredom?"

He met her gaze, his eyes very blue in their intensity.

She looked away, unfortunately toward the bed. Seeing her discarded clothing, she snatched it up again. "I came here to be honest with you, and before I leave I'll say what I came to." She struggled to position one of her gloves so she might pull it over her shaking fingers. "If I am brutally honest, as you have been"— she glanced up at him—"I admit there is some truth in what you say. Perhaps reading to you did begin as a diversion." She dropped the glove and had to bend over to retrieve it. "But reading to you, spending time with you, has become all I look forward to all day and all night. I think about you all the time. That is no mere diversion." Tears stung her eyes, and she couldn't see the damn glove.

"And each time I learn something new about you, I am more and more impressed not only with your bravery, but with your intelligence and your wit."

He tilted his head as though he thought this a trick.

"Yes, wit! You can be amusing in your own way. You make me smile. I know I talk too much." She was talking too much at the moment. She couldn't seem to talk and pull her gloves on. "But you always listen to me. No one listens to me. No one cares what I have to say, but you make me feel important."

"What are you saying?"

She shook her head. "I don't know. I only know I have to say it to you because—because I saw your face at the Dewhursts'. When Francis kissed me. I saw the way you looked, and I couldn't stand knowing that I had hurt you."

He lunged toward her, and she almost scurried back. "You did not hurt me," he barked. He bent, swiped the veil she had dropped, and held it out to her.

"But your face—"

"Kiss whomever you like. It's nothing to me."

"I see." She'd ceased trying to don the gloves and now passed them from hand to hand. "I confess that was not what I was hoping to hear. You see, I realized something at the Dewhursts' ball that night. It was when Francis kissed me."

She glanced at him, but he didn't give any of his thoughts away.

"I don't love him. You were right. You told me that weeks ago, but I didn't listen. And he doesn't love me either. I don't know if he has deluded himself as I had or if he just wants my dowry, but if he loved me there would be more between us."

"More?"

She nodded, still passing the gloves from hand to hand. "He's never shared anything of himself with me. Never opened up. Never written me a letter telling me his feelings for me. Never made himself vulnerable. And when he kissed me, all of that became quite clear to me."

"If you had time to think all that, he was not doing it correctly."

Her hands stilled, the gloves clenched between them. "That was the other thing. When he kissed me, I didn't feel anything. Not like…not like when you kiss me."

There. She'd said what she'd wanted to say and what she'd feared saying as well.

Ewan didn't speak—which was nothing new—and what did she think he would say, anyway? I told you so?

He held out his hand to her, and she looked down at the gloves she clenched. Slowly, she placed them in his hand. Now he'd help her pull them on and send her on her way.

And she should be on her way. Before she said too much.

"There's more," she whispered. Oh, why did she not shut up?

He nodded at her as though he knew she had not finished. He probably thought she never finished speaking.

"I came to another realization."

"When you were kissing my cousin."

She shook her head. "Before that." She cleared her throat. It was too tight, too dry. How she wished she had a glass of water. "I'm in love with you."

His eyes widened.

Lorrie held up a hand, surprised to see it shook slightly. "Don't tell me I don't know what I'm talking about. This time I do. You see, I love you despite my every intention of *not* loving you. I know we aren't suited. You are silent, and I speak all the time. You're a younger son with no fortune or title, and I'm the daughter of a duke. You are a brave war hero, and I've never done anything of any note. But I cannot seem to help how I feel when we are together. I don't want you to come to the library because you are a diversion. I want you to come to the library because you are the only true thing in my life. Don't you see? It's everything else that's a diversion."

"Lorraine."

"I know what you will say—"

"Stubble it," he said quietly.

She closed her mouth. No one had ever told her to shut up before. She'd said too much. He would send her away and tell her father he could not work for him any longer. She'd never see him again. Perhaps she should have just taken the little bit of him he offered. She could have gone on loving him in silence.

Oh, very well. Perhaps not in silence but without telling him everything she felt.

"If you don't want me to kiss you, leave now."

Lorrie stared at him. Now she must be imagining things. But, no. He moved toward her, reached for her.

"But you said, in the library, you would not kiss me."

"I said I would not kiss you under your father's roof."

"Or at all. You said 'That's not why we're here.'"

His hands, warm and solid, landed on her shoulders. "We're not there at the moment, are we?"

She shook her head.

One of his hands slid up her neck and cupped the back of her head, the other skated down her arm to grasp her waist and pull her against him. Her bare arms went around his torso, his hot flesh making her own skin heat with desire and anticipation. Everything inside her seemed to shake and tremble and at the same time she strained toward him, needing him more than air itself.

He tilted her head back and lowered his mouth to hers slowly. Lorrie closed her eyes and clenched at his strong back, attempting to hold on before the world fell away. But there was no preparing for his kiss. The moment his lips grazed hers, she saw fireworks brighter than any she'd ever viewed at Vauxhall. There was nothing tentative about his kiss, nothing soft or sweet. He took her mouth, claiming it with an intensity that left her breathless and wanting more. His lips slanted over hers, again and again, until she could only cling to him. But there was no safety in his body. She loved the feel of his skin under hers, the way his muscles corded and bunched, the way his hot, hard flesh seemed to heat even more as she explored it.

His hand moved from her waist to her rump, cupping it and drawing her forward so she was pressed even more tightly against him. And she could feel the hard length of him where their bodies met.

He had not said he loved her, but if he did not at least want her, he would not have had this reaction. And she wondered what would happen if she met his fire with her own. It was a question she had turned about in her mind countless times for the last year or so. She'd ached for the touch of a man and then shoved the need down because women were not supposed to have such feelings and such needs, especially not unmarried virgins.

When she'd kissed Francis or the small handful of other men who had stolen moments with her, she had always felt as though she must hold herself back. She sensed there was more, and yet she could not ask for it, could not even be certain what it was. With Ewan she felt the more. She did not have to ask or content herself with chaste embraces. There was nothing at all sweet or fumbling about the way he held her or kissed her. And she kissed him back with all the passion she had always been afraid to unleash. And the more she gave in to the desire raging within her, the more she wanted.

Her hands slid down his back to pass over his taut buttocks. The growl in his throat let her know he liked her boldness, liked her touch. When his lips moved to her jaw and the sensitive skin just below, she slid her hands around and up his chest. His skin was firm, the muscles beneath honed from hard use. How different his body was from hers. She was curves and softness, while he had not an inch of extra flesh anywhere.

One hand meandered down his chest to pass over his navel and then to pause at the waistband of his trousers. The most deliciously wicked idea occurred to her, and before she could think better of it, she brought her hand down to cup his hard rod through the wool of his clothing.

He groaned.

The low sound in the back of his throat did strange

things to her body. The heat she'd felt in her cheeks and under her fingers now traveled lower to settle in her belly. She was conscious of a deep throbbing and pressed her legs together in an effort to constrain it, but that only made it worse.

Her hand slid up and down the hot length of him before he finally grasped her wrist and stopped her.

"You don't like it?" she asked.

"I do. But you make me forget that I must behave."

Lorrie looked into his eyes, which were a shade darker than the summer sky she was used to. "Oh, don't behave. I am so weary of always behaving."

"Good."

Lorrie did not know what he meant by that comment, and she didn't suppose he would elaborate, especially not when his mouth claimed hers again. When she would have touched his chest again, he slid her hands up around his neck and lifted her. A moment later, he deposited her on the bed.

Lorrie stared up at him, reminded of the time he had come in her room and she had ended up in this very same position. Now the Viking was bent over her again, and the look in his eye was far more dangerous. He would not leave her untouched this time, and she did not want him to. She wanted him to kiss her and touch her and show her exactly how badly he could behave. She would think about the consequences later, and there might well be consequences. But she wasn't afraid of them. Her quest for passion had led her to attempt to elope with Francis and to sneak into a gambling hell in St. James's Street. She couldn't turn back now.

His mouth took hers again, but this time he only stoked the need in her with his lips and his tongue before trailing kisses down her neck and parting the V of the fichu she had tucked at the last minute into the bodice of her modest day dress. He pulled the light fichu away, and then his lips were on bare flesh. The tips of her breasts hardened and pushed against the thin chemise she wore under her corset. Her breasts ached, and she wanted to arch to encourage him to touch her there.

But he seemed to have his own ideas, for his lips grazed the edge of the muslin bodice and traced it from one swell of her breast to the other. Lorrie's hands fisted in his short hair. How she wished she wore an evening dress, then it would be nothing for him to push the material down and bare her to his hands and lips.

His hands moved up from her waist, and he molded her with them, making her draw in a sharp breath and the prickle of sensation. And then before she could tear at the material separating them in frustration, he put his hands back on her waist and flipped her over. It happened so quickly, Lorrie hardly knew what had happened. One moment she was staring up at him and the next her cheek was pressed against the coverlet of his bed. The bed smelled like him, like evergreen and spruce and the indefinable scent she would always associate only with him. One of his hands cupped the back of her neck and then she felt the tug of the strings holding the dress closed.

She was both exhilarated and terrified that he loosened her bodice, untying strings and unfastening hooks and eyes. When he rolled her back over again, he had no trouble lowering the material, and then it was a simple matter to loosen the tie of her stays and push the material of stays and chemise out of the way.

No one, save Nell, had ever seen Lorrie in such a state, and she had the urge to cover herself, but it lasted only an instant. One look at his face showed he clearly liked what he saw. His eyes were half-lidded and his hands touched her with a gentle reverence.

One hand slid over her bare breast, and when he rolled one hard nipple between thumb and forefinger, she almost moaned.

When she opened her eyes again, he had a small smile on his lips. And then, his gaze locked with hers, he bent and took that hard bud into his mouth. Lorrie did moan then. She arched and moaned and pulled him closer.

His mouth on her breast was the most exquisite sensation she had ever encountered. She did not want him to ever stop what he was doing—the gentle sucking and teasing and even a quick nip. He lifted his head, and she cried out. "No. Please."

He raised a brow, and then lowered his mouth to minister to her other breast.

"Oh, thank God. Yes," she said cupping his head. "Your mouth is brilliantly wicked."

His hands slid from the heated flesh of her chest down her body, pausing at her hips and taking their time as they caressed her thighs. And then his mouth left her too, and she tried to pull him back. But his hands were full of the muslin of her dress and his gaze seemed to follow the hem as he lifted it higher. She supposed she should be embarrassed. A man was not to look upon a lady's ankles, and he had lifted the dress to her knees now. But Lorrie could only stare at Ewan's face.

He did not speak much, but he did not have to. His eyes showed his appreciation and desire. When the hem was at her waist, he licked his lips and then his gaze met hers. "Still want to misbehave?"

She nodded, at a rare loss for words.

His hands touched her knees, slid up to toy with the ties of her garters and then inched higher still. The throbbing in her belly had moved lower, to the place between her legs. It seemed to coalesce there, pumping like a small heart, making her want to squirm and press her hand there to quell the ache.

Gently, Ewan parted her legs, and Lorrie had a moment to wonder if he would deflower her. She both wanted him and feared the consequences.

And then she could think no more because he pressed one hand against her center, and one of his large, long fingers slid inside her.

She bucked against him, against the sweet invasion and the myriad of sensations it brought.

"Shh," he said, and she realized she'd been all but mewing. And then he pressed the palm of his hand up, and *that* was exactly where she needed him to touch her. The pressure was there and gone and there again as he slid in and out of her, his finger slick with her arousal. Lorrie felt she might be embarrassed by all of this later, but at the moment she was too desperate with need to think of anything but his hand and the sensations he caused.

His gaze swept over her, her cheeks, then her breasts, and whatever he saw seemed to tell him something, for he slid another finger inside her.

"Oh *yes!*" she cried, unable to stop. For now he filled her, his fingers sliding against the walls of her sex and making her hips pivot. His thumb—for that must be his thumb—parted her lips and pressed against the center of the throbbing. He massaged the small nub, circling and circling until she was panting and biting her lip to keep from screaming with need.

And then she could contain her cries no longer because the world went blindingly white. Her legs shut and she took the pleasure she needed, grinding against his hand like the wanton she had always feared was inside.

And in the midst of the ecstasy, she looked up at him, dreading the reprisal in his gaze. Instead, what she saw in his eyes was the same hot lust coursing through her, and she knew then, this was only the beginning.

Sixteen

SHE CAME HARD AND FAST AGAINST HIS HAND. HE hadn't expected her to climax so quickly or with so little effort on his part, but the first time he'd met her, dashing across St. James's after her silly puppy, he'd seen she had a passionate nature. He couldn't help but be pleased that carried over into this aspect of her personality as well.

He was far from done with her. He'd wanted her for too long, and watching her orgasm had only made him want to see more. His aching shaft reminded him it too wanted relief, but Ewan still had some standards of behavior—even if he held on to them by their very last shreds.

When she finally relaxed, her body unclenching from his fingers, he slid out of her tight, wet sheath. He splayed his hands on her bare thighs and bent to kiss her again. Her mouth was a marvel to him. The more he kissed it, the more he wanted to kiss it, the more he wanted to taste her.

He could smell her arousal now. It was on his hands, and he wanted to taste that desire too. He wanted much more than that, but he could not take what he really wanted, and so he would have to content himself with the feel of her silky skin under his fingers, the flick of her sweet tongue in his mouth, and the sound of her breathing as it once again came short and fast.

He broke the kiss and glanced at her nipples. They were hard again—thick, dark red points straining upward. He took one then the other in his mouth, and she arched her back. She had large, firm breasts, and those thick nipples made him want to sit her on top of his shaft and make her ride him while he suckled her.

Most ladies of her class would probably faint at the very idea, but Ewan had the feeling Lady Lorraine had a more adventurous spirit. It was no wonder now that she had been so eager to marry his cousin. It was bedsport she wanted, and she could not have it without marriage.

But he would not ruin her for marriage. He could give her what she wanted and leave her a virgin.

Reluctantly, he left her breasts to move lower. He would have liked to strip her bare and kiss her stomach and her hips, but his knowledge of women's clothing was somewhat limited. The more he removed, the more he would have to help her put on again. And so he knelt on the floor, pulling her round buttocks to the edge of the bed so he could push her legs wider. She didn't object, but she sat, her breasts tempting him with their pert tips.

He lowered his head, kissing the inside of her thigh near her knee. He could feel her shiver.

"Oh, that is nice," she said. Before the next twenty

minutes had passed she would think what he did much more than *nice*. Meeting her gaze, he trailed his mouth higher, closer to her sex. Her eyes widened with shock and also with pleasure. Her breasts rose and fell as her breath came quick, and he could smell her need now that he was close to her sheath.

And then it was just a matter of turning his head and teasing the pink of her sex with his lips. "Oh yes," she whispered, her hands clenching the coverlet. Without him having to ask, she spread her legs wider, and he could see the slick sheen of moisture. He touched his tongue to her center, tasting her. She was sweet and tangy, and he lapped at her eagerly. He didn't bother with gentleness now. He was not by nature a gentle man, though he could be so when he chose. But now he pushed her legs as wide as he could and lashed at her with his tongue. He traced her intimately, delving inside her to touch the heat of her, then flicking at that hard little pebble.

She fell back when he did that, catching herself on her elbows and pushing against his mouth. He gripped her hips to hold her where he wanted, then flicked at the nub until she was making those kitten-like sounds again. And then, because he did not want her to come too soon, he pulled back, teasing her lightly again.

She kept up a steady stream of gibberish, most of which he could not understand but the gist of which was she did not want him to stop. She had her hands on her breasts now, her fingers massaging the distended nipples, and Ewan had to look away or else he would have lost control completely. Instead, he focused on bringing her to the brink of pleasure and then withdrawing, back to the brink and withdrawing again.

She was cursing him before long, begging him, trembling so violently he had to hold her down.

She gasped. "Ewan, *please*."

It was his name that did it. He could have continued his sweet torture, but her use of his given name felled him. Quite suddenly, his hands closed on her hips and he yanked her body against his mouth. He sucked and kissed until she shattered against him. Her body bucked and writhed, and he lapped at her until she cried for no more.

Finally, Ewan released her, catching her boneless form before she could slide to the floor. He deposited her on the bed again and bent to kiss her bare shoulder and the curve of her breast. Her arms came around him then, and she pulled him close, holding him. She stroked his back and his hair and laid her cheek against his chest. Ewan couldn't remember the last time anyone had treated him with so much tenderness.

He wanted to wrap his arms around her as well, but they seemed rooted at his side. She pulled back slightly, her green eyes so large and dark they dominated her face. She traced his cheek with one finger, then kissed it and his temple and his eyelid. "You are so beautiful," she said.

Women had called him many things—before, during, and after lovemaking—but no one had ever called him beautiful.

"Women are beautiful," he said.

"You are beautiful in a different way—in the cut of your jaw and the width of your brow and the straightness of your nose. And your lips." She smiled a secretive smile. "I did not know your lips were to be my favorite part of you."

"You don't know all of my parts," he said.

She laughed. "See, you make me laugh with your wit."

This was not the first time she'd complimented his mind, but it was the first time Ewan realized he had said something clever. She pulled him close again, and in her arms he did not feel like the big brute. He felt cherished and loved and…as though he belonged.

Gone was the fury of a few nights ago. She didn't love Francis. She didn't want him. She wanted Ewan, had given herself to him and him alone.

"I never want to leave here," she said. "I love the feel of you against me."

He liked holding her in his arms, but he couldn't forget she was the daughter of a duke, and that duke was his employer. "You must leave here. Did you come alone?"

"No." She sat and pushed her long, dark hair out of her face. Her bodice still hung open, and Ewan longed to divest her of all her clothing and lay her naked on his bed.

"My maid is with me. I left her downstairs."

Ewan wiped a hand over his eyes. He would have chastised her for coming alone, but it was almost as bad that she'd brought a witness to her foolishness. Or perhaps he should say *their* foolishness.

"I will escort you both home. I must speak with your father."

Her hands, which had been busy tying her chemise

closed again, stilled. "Speak to my father? You mean to tell him what happened?"

He nodded.

"Here? Between us? Your mouth… You cannot tell him that!"

"I intend to offer for your hand."

"*Why?*" She all but shouted the word before jumping off his bed and straightening her skirts. She couldn't right the bodice of her gown without his help, but she managed to yank it up over her bosom.

"If word of this"—he gestured to the room—"gets out, your reputation will be ruined and your family thrown into scandal." He did up his trousers and looked about for a shirt.

"It won't get out."

"It might, and I won't allow your reputation to be tarnished." A clean shirt hung on a peg near the door, and he pulled it over his head.

She stared at him as though two heads had come through the neck hole rather than one. "So this is a matter of honor?"

"Your honor."

"My father will not agree, you know that, don't you?"

He did. He should have felt relieved knowing that he was in no real danger of being leg-shackled, but the thought seemed to bring him a twinge of pain.

"He will dismiss you and then marry me to the first man on his list of potential sons-in-law."

"He has a list?"

"I don't know." She waved a hand, pacing his room. The room was only about fifteen steps across, and he was already dizzy watching her. "But he certainly won't allow me to choose."

"And you want to marry Francis."

She stopped. "No." She looked at him, and for a moment he thought she might say she wanted to marry him. Instead, she began pacing again. "I don't know who I want to marry. Perhaps no one, but I think I should be allowed to choose or at least have some say. This is not the fourteenth century. It's 1816, for God's sake. I—"

"Lorraine."

She swung around to look at him.

"This is the last time. Do you understand?"

"You won't go to my father?"

He didn't have to. He hadn't ruined her—not completely, at any rate. She was still a virgin. But he did not think he could resist taking her, if she came to him again. Now that he knew the taste of her, knew the way she moaned when she found pleasure, knew how she looked without all of those clothes—or without some of them—he would not be able to stop. He would not want to stop.

"This is the end. No more kisses. No more meetings alone."

"But your father's estate—"

"Is not as valuable as your reputation." He'd been a fool to ever agree to those late nights in the library, but she seemed to have that effect on him. He lost what few wits he possessed when she was nearby.

"Then I must tell you now or I might not have another opportunity."

"Tell me what?" His entire body tensed. God knew what the woman would reveal next.

"I have solved the earl's financial problems."

Ewan could only stare at her.

"I know you don't believe me," she said quickly, her hands gesturing wildly as they tended to do when she was excited, "but I've had time to think, and the mortgage is only for the house, not the land."

He shook his head. "I don't follow."

"The mortgage on the land in Yorkshire. It's only for the house and the furnishings and the rents from the tenants."

"And what good is the land without the house and the rents?"

"Don't you remember the survey I read?"

She had read him numerous surveys.

"Er…"

"The man wrote there was evidence of lead and iron in the area. If his suppositions prove correct, do you know what that means?"

Ewan nodded. "It means you're a bloody genius," he said, grabbing her and lifting her triumphantly in the air. "It means we're rich!"

She laughed. "Yes!" Then she gave him a serious look. "If the minerals are found in the land. You should tell your father to have more surveyors sent immediately."

"I will. I…thank you, Lorraine. I don't know why I didn't think of it myself."

"You would have," she said. Of course she thought so. She always seemed to have faith in him. Then she looked down. "If I agree to keep my distance from you—not to come back here—then you will not resign your position?"

It took him a moment to register the change in topics.

"I will still see you at balls and the like?" She lifted her gaze, her eyes all but pleading. Why should she look at him that way? It was almost as though she cared about him.

"I won't resign, provided you promise no more elopements."

"I promise. I shall write to Francis and inform him that my affections have changed. Then he will also be free to engage his heart elsewhere."

For that's what she would do. She had to marry, and he would follow her to event after event, watching while she fell in love with another man.

"That seems the sensible thing to do."

"Really?" She blinked as though surprised. "I seem rarely to do the sensible thing."

He made a circular gesture with one finger. "I'll fasten your dress and see you and your maid home. We can tell your father we met by chance as you were returning from…"

"Bond Street."

He growled in frustration as he began to fasten the tiny hooks and eyes. His fingers were far too large for the task and he fumbled. The act took so long, he had time enough to become aware of her scent again and the heat of her body where his fingers grazed the skin of her bare shoulders.

She must have become aware of him too, for she looked over her shoulder at him, her green eyes large and dark. "Are you certain we can never meet alone again?" she murmured.

"Very certain."

"That is the sensible course of action."

He made a sound of assent. Goddamn little hooks. Were they meant to induce frustration or merely make a man mad with his own ineptitude?

"The problem is I don't feel very sensible." She sighed. "I still want to kiss you."

His hands stilled on the little hooks.

"I still want to touch you."

Women had said far more erotic phrases to him, but he'd never felt the stab of arousal in his belly the way he did hearing it from her. "No." He choked the word out.

She turned and tilted her head up to look at him. "But perhaps we might kiss—just one last time?"

He abandoned the bloody fastenings and swiped the veil and fichu from the bed, shoving them into her hands. "Put those on. You are returning home. Now." He stomped to the door. Let her maid worry about doing her back up. He couldn't play bodyguard and lady's maid.

"Fine." She stuck the veil on her head and sighed. "What about a coat?"

He'd almost forgotten. He'd all but forgotten footwear as well. The woman addled his brain. He pulled a coat on and shoved his feet into boots, then gestured her out of his chamber.

Downstairs, he waited patiently by the exit while Lady Lorraine and her maid visited the lady's retiring room. When the lady emerged, she looked all fastened up again, and the veil was perched neatly on her tidy coiffure.

Immediately, he wanted to take all the clothing off again. He stuck his hands in his pockets and followed Lady Lorraine and her maid at a distance until they were back in respectable territory. Then he escorted them to the house and upon being told he was not needed until later that night, promptly left for his club to eat and have a drink.

Several drinks.

Over the next two days, Ewan held on to his resolve, barely. It helped that Lady Lorraine did not attempt to corner him alone. It did not help that she seemed to wear the most revealing gowns she owned and tended to watch him, rather than her partner, at every ball. Ewan spent hours watching her dance and mentally undressing her. Then he'd dress her again, tell himself he must stop, and start all over again. As though she knew what he was thinking, each time their gazes met—and it seemed to be every few moments—her cheeks would color pink, and he knew exactly what she was thinking because he was thinking the same thing.

But she upheld her part of the bargain, and there were no more instances of her attempting to see Francis Mostyn alone or to communicate with him. Her mother and father were overjoyed that she had put aside what they called her childish infatuation, and even more men were introduced to her. If the evenings at Society gatherings were long, the nights were endless. He did not sleep well, if at all. His dreams were full of her.

The days he spent on his father's business. He hired surveyors to go to Yorkshire and survey the land. He gathered funds to pay them and instructed them to report back to him. He wanted proof of a solution before he brought it to his father.

Several nights later the duke informed Ewan the family would stay in for a night and he was not needed. Ewan went straight to his club, and waving away Porter's offer of dinner, ensconced himself in the reading room and demanded a bottle of brandy. He didn't particularly like brandy, but it put him to sleep and he had no intention of tossing and turning, fantasizing about Lady Lorraine.

Ewan had drunk only two glasses when Beaumont took the seat opposite him. Several of Draven's Survivors had stopped in the club, but all of them had taken one look at Ewan and walked the other way. Not Rafe Beaumont.

Rafe motioned to Porter for a glass and poured a measure of Ewan's brandy in it.

"I didn't say I wanted to share," Ewan all but growled.

"I've always said your manners are atrocious. But I will not allow you to celebrate alone."

Ewan sipped the brandy and stared at him.

"Aren't you celebrating? After all, you did it." Rafe raised his glass in a toast.

"Did what?"

"Avenged yourself on your cousin."

Ewan stared at the brandy bottle, wondering if he'd drunk more than he thought. "Never touched him."

"Yes, but the news is all over Town that Lady Lorraine returns his letters and will not see him when he calls."

Ewan hadn't heard any of this.

"He's fighting mad and blames you."

Ewan grinned at the thought of his cousin inconvenienced for once. Not that Ewan had much to do with it. He may have sped up the inevitable, but the lady had made her own decision.

Rafe sipped again. "Of course the man can't do like every other reasonable man and drink himself under the table, start a fight, and move on the next morning. He's told anyone who will listen that he only wanted the lady for her dowry. Painted her father out to be as rich as Croesus."

"We all knew that already."

"Yes, but all that talk of money is rather vulgar. I would think your father might take him in hand."

Ewan rubbed the back of his neck, feeling the tightness there building.

"At any rate, I hadn't realized the Duke of Ridlington had that much blunt. No wonder he wanted a bodyguard for her." Rafe's brandy was all but gone. "I suppose he will marry her off, and then you will be back at Langley's, knocking together heads."

"I like knocking together heads."

"And that's precisely why I wanted you in my troop," said a voice from the door of the reading room. Ewan glanced up and Rafe, whose back was to the door, turned. Both men jumped to their feet as Lieutenant Colonel Draven entered.

"Be at ease," he said, waving them back down. "I'm no longer your commanding officer, thank God."

"Join us for a drink, sir," Rafe said, pulling out the third chair at the table in invitation. *Manners*, Rafe mouthed to Ewan.

"I will." He eyed Ewan. "That is if Mr. Mostyn doesn't mind sharing."

Ewan realized he had pulled the brandy bottle close to his chest, and now he set it back on the table. "It's all yours, sir."

Draven took a seat and glanced about the room. He was not a particularly tall man, but he had a barrel chest and wild red hair and a commanding voice that Ewan had heard sent more than one prime minister scurrying. Draven was in his late forties, but he was still as fit as any of the men who had served under him. He might have been tasked with giving the orders, but he'd shown on more than one occasion that he was willing to do anything he ordered his men to do.

He poured three fingers of brandy, then leaned on the table, giving Ewan a measured look. "I've been thinking about you, Mostyn."

Ewan sat up straighter, although his back was already ramrod straight. Even if he hadn't had the utmost respect for Draven, no one slouched in the man's presence.

"I heard you have been keeping the daughter of the Duke of Ridlington safe from those with designs on her dowry." The careful way he spoke left no doubt that the lieutenant colonel, like Beaumont, had heard the rumors Francis Mostyn was spreading.

"Yes, sir."

"And what are your plans when your employment with Ridlington is at an end?"

Ewan hadn't even considered the question. "I have a position, sir."

"Throwing men out of that gambling hell."

"Langley's," Rafe supplied.

"Yes." Draven's sharp blue eyes seemed to assess Ewan. He remembered the first time he'd met the lieu-tenant colonel. The man had assessed him very much the same way, then asked him the question he asked every man before adding them to his team. *Are you afraid to die?*

Ewan had said no, of course. But it wasn't until after he'd served Draven for a few weeks that he realized death would become as natural to him as life. And that sensation—the loss of life and the way it became almost commonplace—had scared him.

"You are the son of an earl, Mostyn. You are better than the muscle in a gambling hell."

Ewan didn't think so, but he would not contradict Draven. "Yes, sir."

"Gentleman Jackson's," Draven said, his eyes narrowed as he continued to assess Ewan.

"Fine establishment," Rafe said.

Draven cut him a look. "Beaumont, everyone knows you are a lover, not a fighter."

"I can hold my own," Rafe said without animosity.

Draven nodded and looked back at Ewan. "Have you ever been to Jackson's?"

Ewan nodded.

"But not often, because you have nothing to prove. Nothing to learn either. But you have something to teach."

Ewan shook his head, uncomprehending.

"Last week I went for my lesson with Jackson. I like to keep fit. Never know when another war will spring up. With these blockheads in the Lords running things, it may be any day. In any case, he told me he has a list a mile long of men who want lessons."

"I'm not surprised," Rafe said. "He's one man, and everyone wants to train with him."

"Because he's the best," Draven said.

"Exactly."

But Draven was looking at Ewan again. "You're

the best at what you do, Mr. Mostyn. You are one of Draven's Survivors, and the fact that you survived twenty-three suicide missions is no small matter. Men would flock to you to learn pugilism and self-defense as well."

"Isn't that more Rowden's area of expertise?" Rafe asked of another member of the dozen who was known for his skill in pugilism.

"He likes fighting too much ever to teach, but you have nothing to prove," Draven said to Ewan. "Not in the ring, at any rate."

Ewan stared at the lieutenant colonel, uncertain what he was being offered. But a warm feeling had begun in his belly. He could picture himself in the boxing ring, and the image seemed...*right*.

"Think about it, Mostyn," Draven said. "If you're interested, I'll help get you started. I have friends."

Started... Ewan could only stare at the man. Did he mean to back Ewan in his own business? For a moment, elation surged through Ewan. He wanted to hold out his hand and accept immediately.

And then he remembered.

How was he to succeed in business if he agreed? He couldn't read. The first charlatan who came along would cheat him.

"Thank you, but no," Ewan said, looking away so Draven would not see the disappointment on his face.

Draven seemed unsurprised by his answer. "Think about it *more*," he said. "I won't take your answer now."

"It won't change, sir."

Draven nodded, then rose. "If it does, you know where to find me."

Seventeen

EWAN WOKE THE NEXT MORNING WITH A DULL THROB in his head. He and Beaumont had finished off the brandy and another bottle besides. Ewan didn't usually drink so much, but Draven's offer had niggled him. He'd never considered that he might own a business. Ewan hadn't thought he had any skills. But if Draven and Beaumont, who'd talked his ear off in an effort to convince Ewan Draven's advice was sound, thought knocking heads together a skill, then perhaps the idea had merit.

Later, that was. When his head didn't pound.

He rolled over and the thudding continued. Ewan pulled his pillow over his head, then realized the pounding came from outside his tortured brain box.

"Go away," he called, wincing at the lance of pain through the base of his skull.

"It's important, sir. Open the door."

"Later," Ewan muttered. He was fit company for no one.

"Sir, it's Arthur. I'm a footman with the Duke of Ridlington."

Ewan sat, making his head spin. He clenched his hands and pushed down the rising nausea as he stumbled to the door to unlock and open it. He scowled at the tall footman with curly brown hair standing at attention in the doorway.

"Here." Arthur handed Ewan a note.

Ewan glanced down at it. Even if he had been able to read, his eyes were not altogether focused enough to make out any letters.

Ewan handed the note back. "Read it."

"Me?" Arthur pointed a finger at his chest. "Uh, yes, sir." He opened the note, breaking the seal with a look so guilty he might have been pilfering jewels. Arthur cleared his throat. "It says, 'Mr. Mostyn, please come directly. There is an urgent matter we must discuss.'"

Ewan snatched the note out of the footman's hand. The pounding in his head doubled, the thuds of pain coinciding with the hammering of his heart. He scanned the letter, some of the words jumping out at him. Then he looked up at Ridlington's servant. "What happened?"

"I don't know, sir. I was sent to fetch you."

"What happened?"

"I don't—"

Ewan slammed the footman against the door none too gently. "You know something. Is it Lady Lorraine?" *Don't let it be Lorraine.*

"I don't know for certain," Arthur squeaked.

"Guess."

"I think it has something to do with her."

Ewan released the footman, who straightened his

livery coat. "Nell was frantic this morning and closed herself in Mrs. Davies's room. Then Mrs. Davies and Mr. Bellweather and Nell all scurried upstairs like the house was on fire. Only it weren't."

"Wait." Ewan shut the door and dressed hastily. He didn't bother to shave, and he was pulling on his coat when he opened the door and walked past Arthur. The footman ran after him. Knowing the footman would have come on foot, Ewan hailed a hackney and gave the jarvey Ridlington's address. It was not yet nine in the morning, but London's streets were bustling. The journey seemed interminable, and Ewan's head felt as though it would roll off his shoulders every time the conveyance bounced.

Finally, they arrived, and Ewan was out of the cab before the wheels had come to a stop. He didn't knock on the door, but shoved it open and seeing no one, yelled, "Ridlington."

The butler appeared at the top of the stairs, a frown on his face. Ewan didn't give a damn if he'd broken every rule of etiquette. He would see the duke now. "Where is His Grace?"

"In the drawing room, Mr. Mostyn." The butler started down the stairs.

Ewan held up a hand. "Stay there." He took the steps two at a time, and when he reached the top, he did not wait to be announced. He opened the drawing room doors and stepped inside.

Fear gripped his chest like an iron waistcoat when he saw the duke and duchess of Ridlington. They sat in silence, hands clasped, while their eldest son, Lord Perrin, paced the room. When Ewan entered, Lord

Perrin pointed an accusing finger at him. "Where the devil have you been?"

Ewan ignored him, looking from Lorraine's mother to her father.

The duchess raised a bejeweled hand. "Charles, do not make a scene."

Ewan's gaze locked on the duke. "Where is she?"

The duke's eyes widened with surprise. "You've heard?"

Ewan hadn't heard. He'd said the first words that popped into his mind, but he had hoped he was speaking out of fear. Now the fear became something tangible. An iron cravat clamped on his neck. He could not swallow. He could not breathe.

Lorraine was gone.

Eloped? No, she wouldn't. She'd told his cousin her affections for him had changed. Lady Lorraine might be impulsive, but he didn't think her fickle. Had she gone to St. James's again and this time met with trouble en route?

"Tell me everything you know," Ewan demanded.

"If you'd been here, you would already know," Lord Perrin sneered. "And Lorrie wouldn't be missing."

Ewan was a man with an abundance of patience, but at the moment it was fleeing him fast. He gave the duke a hard look. "If you'd like your heir to keep all of his limbs, Your Grace, you'd better make him shut his mouth."

"I'll make *you* shut your mouth." Perrin started for him, but the duke rose and the action halted his son.

"That's enough, Charles. Mr. Mostyn does not answer to you. He had no obligation to be here last night. This is not his fault."

Ewan couldn't help but feel it was. Lorraine was his responsibility. He should have stayed near. If anything had happened to Lorraine, anything at all, Ewan would kill the person responsible and then spend the rest of his short life blaming himself.

When his son retreated, the duke looked at Ewan. "Mr. Mostyn, we had a quiet night. We dined at home, as we planned, and Lady Lorraine seemed tired and retired early, perhaps half nine."

"Yes, it was half nine," the duchess said. "I remember the clock had just chimed the half hour."

The duke nodded. "Her maid helped her prepare for bed, and then Lorrie dismissed her. Nell says she went to bed. This morning when she went to wake my daughter, her chamber was empty."

A thousand thoughts tumbled through Ewan's mind. He was no detective and had no way of sorting them out. He did know Lorraine. "Where is her dog?"

"What has the bloody dog to do with anything?" Perrin asked.

Ewan whipped around and slammed his fist into the man's temple. The marquess crumpled. The duchess gasped, but Perrin didn't rise.

"Forgive me," Ewan said, feeling the vise on his throat loosen the tiniest fraction.

The duke held up both hands. "I supposed he asked for it."

Ewan thought he'd asked for much more than a blow to the head. He'd asked to have his nose broken, but Ewan didn't think the duchess would forgive blood on her carpets.

"The dog?" Ewan reminded him.

The duke's brows drew together. "I don't know. Bellweather," he said to the butler, who stood at the drawing room doors gaping at the fallen Lord Perrin. "Go fetch Lady Lorraine's maid."

"Yes, Your Grace."

Ewan paced the room while they waited. The duchess remained on the yellow chintz settee, and the duke stood beside the gold chaise longue. No one seemed too concerned about the unconscious Lord Perrin on the floor beneath the ormolu side table. Ewan stepped over the prone man and went to the windows. He parted the heavy gold drapes and peered out onto Berkley Square. He hadn't noticed the cold earlier, but now he noted the men and women passing by were bundled warmly, despite the fact it was almost summer. The wind blew leaves across the brown grass of the park, just a few yards away, and the sun was hidden behind a gray fortress of clouds.

Finally, the door opened again, and Ewan watched Nell curtsy to the duke and duchess. Her gaze flicked to the marquess on the floor, but she hastily averted her eyes.

"Thank you for coming, Nell," the duchess said. "Now that you've had a few moments to look through Lady Lorraine's room, did you notice anything out of the ordinary?"

Nell cleared her throat. "Yes, Your Grace. None of her dresses are gone. Before—" Her gaze darted to Ewan.

"You may speak in front of Mr. Mostyn, Nell," the duchess assured her.

Nell nodded. "When she tried to elope, she packed

a valise with her favorite dresses and books. This time she left everything here. Wherever she is, she's still wearing her night rail."

"What about the dog?" the duke asked. "Have you seen it?"

Nell's face blanched. "Wellington? I never thought—no, Your Grace. I don't know where the puppy is."

"Could it be hiding in her room?" the duchess asked.

"I will look right away, Your Grace."

"Thank you, Nell."

The maidservant bobbed another curtsy and hurried away.

"So she has the dog with her," Ewan said.

"How do you know that?" the duke asked.

Ewan stared at him. How did the duke not know?

"She loves that dog," the duchess said. "And it yaps all the time. Nell would have noticed if it was in Lorrie's room." The duchess pressed her hands together in her lap. "What shall we do, Mr. Mostyn? Shall we call Bow Street?"

The duke hissed. "Think of the scandal!"

"Think of our daughter."

He took a deep breath. "You're right. Scandal be damned."

"Call the Runners if you like," Ewan said. He started for the door.

"Where are you going?" the duchess asked.

"To find your daughter," Ewan answered over his shoulder as he made his way out of the room, down the stairs, and into the dreary morning.

Lorrie held Welly tightly in her arms as the cart bounced along paths she did not think could properly be termed roads. Her arms and shoulders would be black and blue with bruises from the trip.

Fear made her belly tighten until wave after wave of nausea crashed over her. She shivered despite the scratchy horse blankets covering her. But she would not be sick. The hood over her face would only ensure her situation were more miserable if she were sick on top of everything else. Her hands were not tied, but the few times she'd tried to remove the hood, a gravelly voice had stopped her.

"I wouldn't do that, milady. Not if ye want yer little dog to live."

Lorrie had wrapped her hands back around Welly and lain quietly in the dark.

She didn't know who the men were or how many had taken her. She only knew one moment she had been in the garden while Welly had his nightly constitutional and the next she'd been grabbed from behind, her head shoved into the dark hood, and carried away kicking and screaming. The men must have also scooped up Welly to keep him from barking and to use against her.

Everything she knew had been gleaned from what little she could hear and feel. She was in the back of a cart that had been used to transport produce. She knew that because it smelled like dirt and rotting cabbage. She was cold, and the breeze blew on her bare arms until they'd dropped the horse blankets over her.

Those were not overly warm, but they were better than nothing. They'd traveled through London and now must be outside the city because it was much quieter. She'd been able to hear the men's voices, thick with lower-class accents. There were at least two of them, possibly three. She'd asked what they wanted and begged to be released, but they'd only told her to shut her potato hole.

Lorrie knew what they wanted, in any event. Her money. They would either ransom her or take her to Scotland, force her to marry, and claim her dowry that way. Fears swirled around in her mind—what if her father would not pay? Would the men kill her? Would they rape her and then slit her throat? And what if Ewan had been right about Francis and she had been wrong? Could he be behind this? What if now that she'd told him she didn't want him any longer, he had taken desperate measures and hired thugs to kidnap her so he could force her to marry?

But he couldn't really force her, could he? Even in barbaric Scotland, a woman had to agree to marriage for the priest to sanction it. Didn't she? Not that it would be very difficult to force her to agree. One threat against poor Welly, and Lorrie would do whatever the men asked.

She hugged her puppy tighter, and the dog licked her hand. The small gesture calmed her, as did the refrain playing in the back of her mind.

He will come for me.

Ewan would find her. He'd rescue her. He'd completed far more difficult missions during the war. Once her father realized Lorrie was missing, he'd call for Ewan and Ewan would come for her. She didn't know how he would find her, only that he would.

The blackness she'd been staring through under the hood had grown lighter, and she realized the sun must have risen. They'd been traveling all night. Surely they would have to rest the horses. Surely they did not wish to travel in the daylight. A body-shaped lump in the back of a cart might not be noticeable in the dark, but in the light, it might draw attention.

And still the cart bounced along, rattling her teeth and forcing her to take quick breaths to hold the nausea at bay.

He will come for me.

He will come for me.

Please, God, let him come for me.

Before it was too late.

❧

Ewan went straight to his father's town house. He'd hoped to return here in triumph, but once again he stood on the stoop, feeling frightened and lost. This time it was not from fear of rejection. He didn't need his father's acceptance anymore. He'd found the one person whose opinion had mattered. How could he not have seen this before? Why hadn't he done as he'd said his cousin should—scooped her up when he'd had the chance?

Damn the rules of Society and damn his own insecurities. If he ever found her, he would never let her get away again.

He knocked on the door. This was not his house, nor would it ever be. His father had made that clear enough. This was the last time Ewan would ever grace its halls.

The same butler who had opened the door the last time Ewan had come opened it again. "Oh, you," said the man, narrowing his small brown eyes. "May I help you?"

"The earl. Now."

"Do you have an appointment?"

Ewan, who was normally a patient man, had as much as he could tolerate.

"Move aside or I'll move you."

The butler's small eyes widened. "If you will wait here"—he opened the door to admit Ewan into the house—"I will tell his lordship you are here."

Ewan stepped into the house. "We have been through this before. Tell me where he is or—"

"The library!" the butler said hastily, jumping out of the way. Ewan marched in that direction and flung the door open.

"What the devil!" The earl half rose from his desk, looking shocked and almost wide-eyed. Ewan was struck by how much older his father appeared in that moment. He was not the invincible tyrant as Ewan had always pictured him. He was just a man.

"Where is he?" Ewan demanded.

"Where is who?" his father asked, slowly sinking into his seat. "Good God, Ewan. Must you always barge in here like a cart horse who's been stung by a bee?"

Ewan crossed the room to his father's desk. It did not seem as large as it once had, and the man behind it seemed smaller as well. This man had never taken Ewan on his knee or put his arm around him or walked with him side by side. Ewan no longer needed that from him. His father couldn't hurt him anymore. Francis couldn't hurt him.

"Tell me where Francis lives."

"No."

Ewan blinked slowly, his gaze boring into the earl. He was a little, little man. Ewan could have crushed him with no more effort than it took to crush a fly.

"I won't have you abusing him."

"I won't abuse him unless he deserves it."

The earl actually drew back slightly, seeming afraid of Ewan. Good. There were enough times Ewan had been afraid of his father. It was time the tables were turned. "What is this about, Ewan? Did you find de los Santos? Did he tell you something else about Francis?"

Ewan had forgotten all about the diamond mine swindle and for a moment he was thrown off guard. "What else would he have told me?" And then Ewan knew what his father suspected. No, what his father *knew*. Francis had been part of the swindle. He'd hoped to make millions but instead Francis, the swindler, had been swindled.

Ewan couldn't stop his lip curling in disgust. "And that is the man you would rather have as a son? He has no honor, no scruples—"

"At least he's not a complete idiot," his father retorted.

"And who is the real idiot?" Ewan asked. "You are the one who has lost everything. And do you know that your idiot son has found the solution for you?" Ewan started around the desk, moving slowly but deliberately. The earl shrank back in his chair. "That's right. I'm too stupid to read Latin or Greek, but I understood the mortgage documents. You mortgaged the house and the rents in Yorkshire, not the land. That I assume was a fortunate coincidence, because I doubt you ever read the surveyor's reports. If you had, you might know that the land is full of iron and lead. I sent surveyors there myself a few days ago to be certain. You should have their findings in a sennight at most."

The earl's jaw dropped, and he was the image of complete astonishment. "But that's it," he muttered. "I never...there could be minerals...if we dig..." He looked up at Ewan. "How did you think of this?"

He hadn't thought of it, Lorraine had, and now she was the one in danger. "I've helped you, now you help me. Tell me where Francis lives."

The earl shook his head. "I know what this is about, and your cousin didn't mean it."

Ewan lowered his arms so his hands clenched the sides of the chair his father occupied. "Tell me or I will make you tell me."

"It's nothing. I've said too much."

Ewan lowered his head until his face was an inch from his father's. "Do you know what working for Draven taught me? How to make a man talk. I break a finger or a toe, your tongue still works. I break a hand, and you may cry, but you can still blubber."

"You wouldn't!" the earl hissed. "I'll ring for the butler."

Ewan blinked, bemused. "Is he stronger than he looks?"

"You wouldn't!" the earl said, voice wobbling.

Ewan leaned close. "Think about all the times you used your fists on me, *Father*. Then tell me you don't deserve a taste of what you gave me."

The earl cringed back and his lip trembled.

Ewan leaned forward, and the earl began to talk.

❧

Susan knocked on her husband's bedchamber door before she even knew what she was about. This was no time to hold on to her pride, no time to wonder whether she could really trust him, really believe he loved her this time.

She needed him. Lorrie was his daughter too, and only he could understand how she felt right now. Only he could understand her pain, her fear. He knew the same pains, the same fears.

He opened the door himself, and though she had intended to say something, she fell into his arms, weeping. He caught her and pulled her close, his coat smelling of bergamot and tobacco, familiar and soothing scents to her.

"Shh," he whispered, stroking her hair. "You don't have to be strong in front of me."

The words were what she'd needed. She'd been so strong all day, and now she felt all that resolve crumbling. "If anything has happened to her—"

"Mostyn will bring her back. He won't allow anything to happen to her."

Susan looked up at him. She wanted to believe him, needed to believe him. His green eyes met hers, filled with a calm strength that gave her strength. Her fingers closed on the lapels of his coat, holding on to him tightly.

"I'll ring for tea and a cold compress," he said.

She shook her head. "I don't need tea."

He placed a finger over her lips. "Let me take care of you, Susan."

"Yes." She wrapped her arms around him. "I don't need anything but you."

"I'm here."

"Just hold me."

He led her to the bed, gathered her in his arms, and held her.

Eighteen

SHE'D PRAYED THE TORTURE IN THE CART WOULD end—the bouncing and rattling that left her battered and bruised. When it did end, she had regretted her prayer immediately.

"He'll come for us, Welly," Lorrie whispered, holding the puppy close. Welly had managed to fall asleep, despite the new surroundings and Lorrie's palpable fear. The dog snoozed peacefully, while Lorrie stared into the gloom of the room. She'd decided it must have been the gardener's work shed at a great house once upon a time. It smelled of dried herbs and peat, and underneath all that, the sweet scent of fruit or flowers. She'd had a glimpse of a long table and windows in the large room after her captors had pulled off her hood but before they could close and lock the door. The room she occupied was smaller, three paces by two paces. At one time it might have been used to store gardening implements. Now there was nothing inside but a muddy apron. Lorrie had put it on the floor and sat, pulling her knees close to her chest.

The tiny room boasted no windows, but the small

building was old and in disrepair, and she could see sunlight through cracks in the wooden slats. Beyond the sunlight was green and more green. This might have been a gardener's work building before, but now the area around it was overgrown.

They'd traveled through the night, but it was still morning, which meant they couldn't have made it far outside London. Still, it was far enough. Lorrie didn't see how anyone would ever find her here. The thought was enough to bring fresh tears to her eyes.

She swiped them away. She wouldn't cry. It would only make her thirsty, and except for a small cup of stale water and one moment of privacy in a makeshift privy out back so she might relieve herself, her captors had given her nothing.

They hadn't even spoken to her, though she'd asked for their names and what they wanted. Their silence scared her more than anything else, but it also gave her hope. If they had planned to kill her, would they have taken the trouble to cover her eyes so she could neither see them nor their destination? Would they have been cautious about speaking in front of her? Perhaps this was all a misunderstanding or a mistake and they'd bring her home in the morning—

The lock on the door rattled, and Lorrie squeezed herself back against the wall tightly. Welly went stiff in her arms and growled low in his throat, his brown and white fur bristling. The door scraped open, and a man blocked the exit. His hat rode low on his forehead and the collar of his coat concealed the lower part of his face.

Lorrie looked down, not wanting to meet his gaze,

the fear clawing inside her like a rabid animal bent on escape. The man crouched, set a cloth on the ground, then backed up and closed the door again. The lock sliding back into place made a rusty scratching sound. Welly let out a small yip, then scrambled off her lap to nose the cloth. Lorrie grabbed it and unwrapped the contents—a slice of bread and an apple.

Her stomach rumbled with hunger she hadn't felt until now. Before she could devour all the food herself, she broke off a piece of bread and fed it to Welly, who gobbled it and then looked at her hopefully. Lorrie sighed and gave him the rest of the bread, contenting herself with the apple.

She brushed away the unshed tears that had stung her eyes since the ordeal had begun. Crying would accomplish nothing. Ewan would come for her, but what if he was too late? She had to try to escape and run for help. If this was an old work shed, surely the house it had been part of still existed. There would be a path leading to it or tenants' cottages. She just had to find it.

She reached for the door latch and lifted it. The sliding lock on the outside was probably a new feature her abductors had installed. She wanted to test it further, but if she rattled the door, her abductors would come to check on her. The little closet had no windows, and she was not quite tall enough to reach the roof, but it looked secure.

She sat again, leaned back against the wall. The wood creaked. Perhaps she could find a weak plank in the wall. If she wedged it open far enough, Welly could escape. Perhaps the little dog might fetch help.

Well, that was unlikely, but if she managed to make the hole big enough, perhaps she might be able to squeeze out.

Lorrie knelt and began to push quietly on the walls surrounding her.

✌

His cousin held court in a small coffee shop in Fleet Street. It wasn't the most fashionable part of town, but if it had been the haunt of those with titles and wealth then the nephew of an earl wouldn't have held sway.

Francis sat at a table in the middle of the room, three or four of the young men Ewan had seen with him at various functions throughout the Season seated beside him. The men talked loudly, laughed loudly, and in so doing commanded the attention of every other patron.

Ewan had tried Francis's modest flat just around the corner, but after he'd knocked loud enough to bring out the neighbors, he'd been told Mr. Mostyn was at the coffee shop.

Ewan had not been pleased to hear it. He'd known Lorraine wouldn't elope with Francis, but he'd still hoped that was the explanation for her disappearance. It was a far worse situation than he faced now— Francis entertaining a group of people and Lady Lorraine nowhere to be found.

Just where the hell was she?

His cousin hadn't seen him come in. Ewan knew how to be unobtrusive when the situation called for it. He'd slid in behind a group of men entering and moved to the side where he could stand in the shadows. There were not many shadows remaining. It was midday now, and the sun was bright in the sky. The two men seated at the table beside Ewan had taken one look at him and elected to find another coffee shop. He pulled a chair back and sat, keeping his head down and his shoulders hunched.

If he'd learned anything from Neil, it was to observe before acting. So now he would observe. He didn't see Lorrie, but that didn't mean she wouldn't make an appearance in another moment or so. In the meantime, he listened to Francis brag about his social calendar.

When he mentioned the daughter of the Duke of Ridlington, Ewan's eyes fastened on him.

"And when I marry Lady Lorraine," Francis was saying, "I'll have enough blunt to buy this shop and a dozen more. We'll travel the world together, won't we, Tommy?" He slung an arm around the man seated beside him.

Tommy smiled affably enough, but the other man at the table snorted. "You might have held the affections of the duke's daughter at one time, but I hear she returned your letters and won't dance with you at any of the balls."

Francis shrugged. "Oh, I have a feeling she will come around. I just need to play the part of Lancelot and save her from danger." He winked at a pretty girl who set glasses on a nearby table, then checked his pocket watch. "Not long now until I rescue the damsel in distress."

Ewan rose slowly, not taking any care not to be seen. He supposed he wasn't as stupid as everyone had claimed him to be because all the pieces in Lorraine's disappearance came together now.

Francis looked his way, just as Ewan stepped into the light.

"What the devil are you doing here?" he asked, a note of fear in his voice. Ewan could recognize the sound of fear—panic and dread too. He'd heard them often enough.

He crossed to Francis, batted the man called Tommy out of the way, and lifted his cousin up by the throat, then threw him across the room. Francis smashed into a table, toppling it and spraying coffee and tea all over the walls, the floor, and the patrons. A wide circle opened around Ewan as people attempted to stay out of his way. Notably, no one came to Francis's aid either.

Ewan advanced on him, and Francis scrambled back. His cheek bled from a small scrape and his always perfectly styled hair was wet with coffee and cream. "What is wrong with you?" he shouted at his cousin. "Are you mad as well as stupid?"

"I'm neither," Ewan said so low he wondered if even Francis could hear him. He stooped, lifted Francis, and pressed him against the wall. He lifted his cousin just high enough so that his toes rested on the floor. "I should kill you," he said, his voice a rumble. "You had her abducted. You paid to have her taken so you could ride in and save her."

"What the devil are you blathering about? Put me down!"

But Ewan had seen the fear in Francis's eyes—the fear and the guilt. Ewan hadn't made a mistake.

Ewan shoved him back against the wall. Francis's skull made a satisfying thunk against the wood. As much as he'd like to hurt his cousin right now, that would have to wait. Lorraine needed him. "Where is she?"

"I-I don't know what you're talking about."

Ewan slammed Francis back against the wall, the man's head thunking on the wood once again. "Where is she?"

"I told you—"

Ewan raised a brow. "If you like your head with its skull intact, I suggest you answer me now."

"I didn't hurt her," Francis said now, his voice whiny and much like it had been when they were boys and Ewan had fought back after Francis's bullying had gone too far. "They won't hurt her."

"Where. Is. She?"

"I don't know exactly, but I was to meet them at an inn in Edgware at midnight tomorrow. Then they'd take me to her and I could…" He trailed off.

Ewan dropped Francis and kicked him lightly like the rubbish he was. "Pathetic. If I ever see you near the lady again, I'll make you wish you were never born. Go crawl back to my father. He's the only one who can't see what a lily-livered coward you really are."

Ewan tossed a few coins to a man he assumed was the proprietor. He was the only man looking concerned, folding and unfolding his hands at the wreckage. Then Ewan strode out of the shop.

Ewan would find her.

But he would not do it alone.

He went directly to the Draven Club. He didn't

have any time to waste, and as soon as he arrived, Porter informed him that the Duke of Ridlington was looking for him.

"Did he send a note?" Ewan asked.

"No, sir," Porter answered. "The footman merely asked if you were within and when I informed him I had not seen you today, he asked me to tell you the duke asks you to call on him forthwith."

The duke wanted news of his progress, and Ewan could hardly blame him. But he didn't have time to indulge the father at the moment.

"Who is here?" Ewan asked. "Stratford? Lord Phineas?"

"No, sir. Mr. Wraxall is here and Lord Jasper. Would you like me to send word to the others?"

"No." He thought about asking Porter to send for Rafe and decided against it. The mission Ewan had now was not one suited to Beaumont's skills. Jasper, however, was exactly the man he needed. He'd had considerable experience as a bounty hunter, even before joining Draven's troop. He could find the men who'd taken Lorraine. Neil would lead them. Ewan was no leader, but Wraxall had no qualms about giving orders. He'd know where Jasper and Ewan should begin, and he'd know what to do when and if they encountered trouble.

"Where are Grantham and Wraxall?" he asked.

"The reading room. Shall I bring you—"

But Ewan was already striding away. He took the steps two and three at a time and was barely winded when he pushed open the heavy oak door to the reading room. Jasper sat at a table with a large book of maps spread out before him, and Neil lowered the paper to peer at Ewan from a dark chair near the fire.

"What has you looking so"—Neil furrowed his brow—"animated?"

"I need your help," Ewan said.

Neil nodded and dropped the paper, and Jasper rose. "I'll always row in your boat, Protector," Jasper promised.

He'd known they would agree, but the readiness with which they did so made his heart clench for a moment. The men of Draven's Survivors didn't ask questions of their fellows. If one of their own said he needed help, the others agreed without question.

"How can we help?" Neil asked.

"Lady Lorraine has been abducted."

"Kidnapped?" Jasper stepped forward. The scars on the side of his face appeared red and angry in the firelight. He wore his mask out in public but found no such protection from stares and ridicule necessary here at the club.

"Are you certain she hasn't simply eloped?" Neil asked, sounding as logical and levelheaded as always.

Ewan took a breath. Words had never been his allies, but he would have to speak now, speak and explain. "Her father sent for me because the lady was not in her bed this morning. Nothing had been taken from her room. Only the lady and her dog were missing. I went to my father and ascertained the location of Francis Mostyn's residence. I found him at a coffee shop nearby. He had her abducted so he could play the white knight and rescue her."

"Bloody idiot," Neil said.

"I trust you'll give him a topper once the lady is recovered," Jasper added. "I can sniff her out."

"That's why I'm here. My cousin was to meet the

men he hired at an inn in Edgware at midnight tomorrow. I want to find the men before this meeting."

"Has the duke received a ransom note?" Jasper asked.

"No."

"He might have. We should pay him a call—" But even as Neil spoke the words, Porter knocked on the door, carrying a silver salver.

"A missive from the Duke of Ridlington for you, Mr. Mostyn."

Ewan took it and broke the seal. The enclosed paper fluttered to the floor. He lifted it and cursed his inability to read. He held it out, and Neil, who was the closer of the two soldiers, took it.

He looked up at Ewan. "It's the ransom note we expected. They want twenty thousand pounds for her safe return."

Jasper whistled. "For blunt like that, they might decide to keep her. Francis doesn't have the yellow boys to cover that."

Neil continued to read the paper. "The abductors request the duke to come alone to an inn in Edgware tomorrow night at midnight. If he doesn't appear, comes with other men, or doesn't bring the blunt, they'll kill Lady Lorraine." He looked up. "And her dog."

Ewan looked down at the paper that had held the note. The words on it moved and rearranged themselves, but he finally had the gist of the brief message from Ridlington.

"He asks for my advice."

"Tell him." Neil waved a hand. "Porter! Paper and ink, please."

"Yes, Mr. Wraxall."

"I'll write to him and you sign it," Neil said. "I'll tell him to stay here. You'll go in his stead and bring her back."

"How will I find her? Francis didn't know any more than to meet them at the inn." No doubt the abductors thought to bring the duke and their employer together and see who would pay the most for the lady. If neither man would pay or anything went wrong, they would probably find it easier to kill her and be done with the scheme all together.

"Leave finding her to me," Jasper said. "I can find anyone."

"Given enough time. We have a day and a half," Ewan argued.

"Edgware isn't far outside of London, and I know the area well. We'll find her, and we'll crash the culls your cousin hired to take her."

For the first time since he'd stepped into the Duke of Ridlington's drawing room, Ewan relaxed. Jasper was the best tracker Ewan had ever known. He would find Lorraine, and when Ewan got his hands on the men who had taken her, he would kill them with his bare hands.

❧

By the time darkness fell, Lorrie had managed to loosen not one but two planks of the wall. It had been slow, tedious work, because she must do everything silently. Using her feet, she had braced herself on one side of the room and pushed against the loose planks with steady pressure. Now when she pushed one of them, the bottom gaped enough so Welly might slip through it. She hadn't allowed the puppy to escape. That would alert the men holding her when they returned.

She'd almost been caught once. She'd been pushing against the plank that was not quite as loose when she'd heard the lock slide against her door. Welly had barked a warning, but it hadn't been necessary. Lorrie had slid in front of the planks to shield her work from view.

"Get up," the man who opened the door ordered. She couldn't see his face under the coat collar and lowered hat, so she had no idea if it was the same man who had brought her the bread and apple earlier.

Lorrie rose, her heart pounding. Her knees felt weak, and she couldn't catch her breath. Had she been wrong about the men's intentions? Would they rape and kill her now?

"What do you want?" she asked, trying to keep her voice from trembling.

"Here." The man threw her a length of rope. It fell to the floor, and Lorrie stared at it. Would they tie her hands?

"Put it on the dog," her captor said. "We don't want it running away."

"Where will you take me?" Lorrie asked, bending to scoop up the rope. She saw now it had been fashioned into a sort of lead, with a loop around one end. She put the lead around Welly's neck and tightened it enough so it would not slip off.

The man moved aside. "Out." He pointed into the main room of the workhouse, which appeared empty at the moment.

"Where are you taking me?" she asked again.

"Walk or I'll make you walk."

Shivering with fear, Lorrie pulled her night robe close around her neck and held the leash in her other hand. She led Welly into the main room. The windows had been shuttered and the hearth was cold and dark, but she could see well enough to avoid bumping into the long table.

She'd expected the man to lead her, but he stood staring into the little closet. "What is that?" he asked.

Lorrie swallowed the panic. He'd seen the loose planks. She didn't know how, as they still fell flush against the foundation if she did not push on them, but something had given her efforts away.

Lorrie turned slowly to peer into the closet.

"I...I don't know what you mean."

The man pointed into the closet, but when she followed the direction of his finger, he wasn't pointing at the loose planks. He pointed at a corner where Welly had relieved himself.

"The dog needed to go out. He's still a puppy. He hasn't much control."

He looked at her—at least she thought he looked at her. It was difficult to tell with his eyes so hidden. "I suppose you want me to clean it up."

Lorrie didn't know how to answer. She'd forgotten about it in her efforts to escape. She might be a duke's daughter, but she'd spent most of her youth in the country. A little puppy pee didn't upset her.

The man jerked his head toward a corner of the room, and Lorrie realized a man in a dark cloak sat there. She hadn't been able to see him in the dark.

"Clean it up," the first ordered.

The second said nothing while the first gave her a shove. "Outside."

He opened the door to the small work shed for her, and she blinked at the bright sunlight, lifting a hand to shield her eyes from the glare. Welly barked and started forward, and Lorrie almost pitched down the two steps leading up to the door. She followed the puppy down, and he immediately lifted his leg to relieve himself.

Lorrie was aware of a growing discomfort in her own bladder, but her captor pointed to the small privy near the trees. "Hurry up. Take more than two minutes, and I'll come in and fetch you."

Lorrie hurried. She could think of little more humiliating than being interrupted while squatting in the privy. She felt better when she emerged, not only because the privy stunk, but because she could see her surroundings in the daylight. There was indeed a path leading away from the work shed. It was somewhat overgrown, but it had been worn over time and was still visible. It must lead to the big house, and surely that had not been abandoned.

She peered in the opposite direction, hoping to spot horses or a glimpse of the road they had traversed. But wherever the men kept their mounts and the cart, she could not spot them from where she stood. They were no fools, these men. No smoke poured from the chimney, no light shone from within the building. To all outward appearances, the place was abandoned.

Even if Ewan did come for her, how would he know to look here? He might walk right past it and never know she was imprisoned within. Lorrie couldn't leave her escape to chance. She had to find a way to get out. Glancing at the shed again, she focused on the rear where she'd been held. From the outside, the boards she'd loosened looked slightly askew. She hoped the men wouldn't look at them too closely. She hoped she could loosen them in time. Especially since she had no idea how much time she had left.

"Back inside," her captor ordered.

"But we just stepped out. Can't I take my dog for a walk? He needs exercise." Anything to stall or to give her more time to look around.

"Get inside or I'll make you."

Lorrie swallowed. She did not want him to make good on his threats. As slowly as possible, she made her way back toward the steps. She tried to take in as much of the landscape as possible. She would need a mental map of the place when she had to run away, and as that would most likely be under cover of darkness, the better she knew the landmarks, the more likely she would find the path and be able to follow it. She had the fleeting urge to run, but a flash of color caught her eye. A few yards away a third man stood near a tree, keeping watch.

Lorrie knew if she ran now, she would not make it far.

Once inside the gardener's shed, her captor shut the door and barred it. The other captor was back in his chair, and she wouldn't have known he'd left his spot except that Welly's accident in the closet had been cleaned up.

She went willingly back into her prison. Hoping

to discourage the men from interrupting her again, she decided to make her demands now. "May I have some water?"

Her captor shut the door in her face.

"What about more bread?"

The lock slid into place.

Very well. She would just have to be very careful and ready for guests at a moment's notice. Taking a deep breath, Lorrie sat and wedged her feet against a third plank. Closing her eyes, she began to push.

Nineteen

EWAN PRIDED HIMSELF ON HIS PATIENCE. IN A FIGHT, A hot head was almost always a liability. He knew Draven had wanted him for his brute strength, but Ewan didn't consider his strength and size alone his only skill. He knew when to hit first, when to wait for the advantage, when to allow his opponent to tire himself out with impotent punches.

Ewan possessed considerable patience.

And it had all deserted him today.

He'd seen Jasper track dozens of times. He knew one step forward often meant two steps back. In Belgium there had been a week they'd circled the same two miles repeatedly, tracking a French spy.

But Ewan hadn't cared about the French spy. He cared about Lorraine and now, on the second day of the search, the hours seemed to fly by. It was almost dusk, and Jasper still hadn't found where Lorraine was being held. In the wooded area where they tromped through damp leaves and ducked under low branches, the light faded quickly.

In front of them, Jasper held up a hand, then

dismounted. Ewan's arse was sore from sitting in the saddle all day, and he dismounted as well. But before he could follow Jasper into a cluster of trees, Neil stepped in front of him.

"Crowding him won't find her any faster."

"What if I thump him on top of the head?" Ewan asked.

Neil gave him a wry smile. "Also not helpful." He placed a hand on Ewan's shoulder. "Jasper will find her. He always finds his man—or in this case, woman."

Ewan looked at the sky, a mottled gray through the canopy of branches.

"There's still time," Neil said.

"Only a few hours, and we have no rescue plan, no visual on the prisoner's location."

"The rescue plan is my mission. I think fast. That's why you wanted me here. Jasper tracks. That's why you wanted him. Let us do our jobs."

Ewan blew out a breath of frustration. Neil was right. But that didn't stop the clawing panic scratching away inside Ewan's chest. What if she was injured? What if her captors had abused her or killed her? Yes, the note claimed she hadn't been hurt, but once the men had the money, there was nothing to stop them from running. Nothing to force them to return Lady Lorraine.

Jasper walked back to where Ewan and Neil stood. "Some cull came through here recently. I don't know if it was the rogues we're after, but the odds are strong."

Odds. Ewan scowled. He didn't want odds. He wanted Lorraine back in his arms—rather, the arms of her family.

"What's nearby?" Neil asked. "Where might they be heading?"

Jasper stared into the distance and thought about it. Ewan's hand itched to thump him—just once—on the head. Maybe he'd think a little faster. As though reading his mind, Neil gave him a narrow-eyed stare.

"There's an estate about two miles north. I forget what nob it belongs to—an earl, I think. He bled a lot of money on a canal scheme—"

"The Marquess of Wight," Neil supplied. "He invested all his money in a canal scheme in Birmingham, where he owns property with…" Neil scratched his head. "Was it limestone deposits or some mineral?"

"Iron ore, I thought," Jasper said.

Ewan growled low in his throat. Jasper gave him an odd look.

"Whatever it was," Neil said with a warning glance at Ewan, "the locals opposed the canal, and the scheme failed."

Ewan pointed in the direction Jasper had indicated he saw tracks. "Go."

Jasper and Neil ignored him.

"He's been living in Town for the last few years," Neil said. "Not enough blunt to keep up the country estate."

"Wight House."

Neil smiled. "Clever."

"If he was clever, he wouldn't have sunk all his yellow boys into a canal scheme."

"Can we discuss canals later?" Ewan demanded.

"In any case," Neil said, holding a hand up when Ewan looked like he wanted to interrupt again. "His lack of funds means Wight House has been closed up for some time."

Impatient for the conversation to cease, Ewan wandered to the patch of leaves that had so interested Jasper. He saw nothing indicating anyone had passed this way.

"A good place to plant yourself if you don't want to be found," Jasper said, coming up behind Ewan. He pointed to a broken twig. "There. See it?"

Ewan grunted. It was a broken twig. A fox or a deer or a boar might have broken it.

"And there." Jasper pointed to a bush, apparently seeing a sign Ewan didn't. "Some cull came this way. We follow the trail and see if they're still nearby."

Finally, someone was talking sense. He walked back to his horse and prepared to mount, but Neil shook his head. "Jasper says the estate is about two miles from here. Better to leave the horses. They make too much noise, and we don't want anyone to know we're coming."

Ewan took a slow breath. Neil had a point, but it would mean hobbling the horses, and that would be yet another delay.

"Since we've stopped, we should pull out the grub," Jasper suggested.

"No food."

This time Ewan caught the smile Neil and Jasper exchanged and realized he'd walked right into that one.

As Neil went about unloading the packs from the horses and securing them, he kept up a steady conversation with Jasper, who, despite Ewan's injunction, had pulled out an apple and munched on it. Ewan ignored them, taking what he'd need for the walk out of his pack.

He stood, arms crossed and booted foot tapping, as Neil took his bloody sweet time. Neil glanced at him once. "Never seen him like this. Have you?"

Jasper glanced at Ewan, and he realized they'd been discussing him.

"Can't say that I have. I thought he would throw me onto the saddle this morning."

"Your life has been in danger more than once today," Neil said. "Do you think he's that loyal to Ridlington?"

Jasper pretended to consider. Ewan rolled his eyes at the way Jasper rubbed at the stubble on his chin in mock thought. He should have thrown the man *over* his saddle this morning. Maybe he would have landed on his head and sense would have been knocked into him.

"I don't think it's the duke who has him so out of sorts," Jasper said.

"I am not out of sorts."

"Well, you're not…in sorts," Neil remarked. "Why does no one ever say 'in sorts'? Wouldn't that be the converse of out of sorts?"

"The converse would be sorted out," Jasper declared. "Out of sorts implies a cove is all muddled."

Ewan started for Jasper. "I'll muddle you if you don't bloody lead us on this invisible trail in three seconds."

"Definitely out of sorts," Jasper said, then ducked when Ewan threw a punch.

"And discombobulated," Neil remarked. "There is only one power known to man that inflicts so much disruption."

Jasper rubbed a hand on his chin again. Ewan wanted to break it. "Volcano?"

"Woman." Neil raised his brows at Ewan. "I'd wager it's not the duke Ewan is concerned about, it's the duke's daughter."

"Obviously," Ewan said. "She's the one abducted."

"And you wish to save her because…"

"I don't want her harmed. Can we walk?"

"That time in Egypt, when I was taken by Turkish soldiers." Neil threw his pack over his shoulder, which Ewan considered a good sign. "You didn't want me harmed, but no one said you threatened violence while Lord Phineas took a week to bribe half the local sheik's men."

"You aren't as pretty as Lady Lorraine," Jasper said, starting in the direction of Wight House.

Finally! Ewan wanted to scream.

"No one but Beaumont is that pretty."

Ewan rounded on Neil. "Don't insult the lady."

"Then I take it you consider her prettier than Beaumont?"

Ewan said nothing.

"Does she kiss better than Beaumont?" Neil asked.

"How the hell would I know? I never kissed Beaumont."

"But you have kissed Lady Lorraine." Jasper paused and looked over his shoulder.

Ewan didn't say a word. He knew a trap when he saw it—even if he was already snared.

"Why don't you just admit you have feelings for her?" Neil asked once they were hiking again.

"Did you do more than kiss her?" Jasper asked.

Ewan glared at him. "I *will* hit you hard enough to make your ears ring for a week."

"I'd take that as an affirmative," Neil said, then jumped out of Ewan's reach when he grasped at him.

"Exactly how serious is this?" Jasper asked. "Do you love her? Want to shackle yourself to her?"

Love. She'd said she loved him, but Ewan didn't know what that meant, what that felt like. Was the clawing sensation tearing at his gut love? Was that how it felt?

"I can't marry her. She's rich and the daughter of a duke."

"You're the son of an earl," Neil pointed out. "The legitimate son." An important distinction to Neil, who had been born on the wrong side of the blanket.

"The third son," Ewan said. "No property. No money. Nothing to offer."

"What a pile of horseshit," Jasper said. "You're a decorated war hero. You're invited everywhere—or would be if you ever moved out of Langley's hell. You're from an old and honorable family, and you don't need blunt because she has piles of it. Ridlington should be glad to have you."

"The real question," Neil said, "is do you want Ridlington? Do you want his daughter?"

Ewan was saved from replying when Jasper raised a hand. It was a signal Ewan and Neil knew meant stop. The two men halted as Japer crouched and studied the ground. This time Ewan didn't have to wonder what had caught Neil's eye. He saw the imprint of the boot clearly in the damp mud.

Jasper wiggled his fingers, indicating the men could move forward again, but Ewan knew better than to make any noise. Not that he had anything to say.

Silence suited him very well, and it would keep Neil from baiting him.

They walked a few more yards and Jasper signaled again. Ewan halted and glanced at Neil. Neil's gaze moved back and forth, searching for possible threats. The gesture had been second nature during the war, but Ewan hardly thought it necessary back at home.

"Protector," Jasper whispered and motioned to Ewan.

Moving as quietly as he could, Ewan crossed to stand beside Jasper. He pointed to the ground, not as muddy here, but soft from recent rains.

"Most of the footprints were washed away in the rain last night. This imprint is a bit deeper." He pointed to an indention in the mud that Ewan hadn't seen at first. It was smaller than the other and less well defined. "That's why it lasted. The other was a beater case—a boot, but this…I don't think so."

Ewan nodded his agreement. This was no boot print.

"It's smaller. Perhaps from a lady's slipper."

Ewan's gaze locked on Jasper's face, now difficult to see in the shadows from the fading light. Another quarter hour and it would be futile to search for footprints until the morning.

The deadline was midnight. Morning would be too late.

"It's hers," Ewan said.

Jasper looked up, then back at the print. "I can't know that, but I do know it was made within the last few days. Otherwise it would have washed away by now."

"Lead the way."

Jasper flicked his fingers at Neil, and he followed, keeping an eye on the rear. Ewan didn't know how Jasper could see to track, but he walked with confidence for another half mile at least.

"You sure you know where we're headed?" Neil asked, his voice a low rumble. "I don't relish spending the night walking in circles."

"When have I ever led you in circles?" Jasper demanded.

Neil raised his brows. "There was that time in—"

"I *knew* you would mention Lisbon," Jasper retorted. "A cove makes one mistake." Suddenly, he raised a hand, and just as Ewan sidestepped to avoid smacking into his back, Jasper gestured down. Ewan lowered to his haunches, followed by Neil. Jasper bent double and crept forward. He moved through a dense patch of foliage, and Neil looked at Ewan.

"This had better not be a diversion tactic so we don't notice he's leading us in circles," Neil said.

Ewan watched the spot where Jasper had disappeared. A moment later it rustled, and the bounty hunter emerged. He gestured for Ewan and Neil to move back a few feet with him. Under a large tree, he waved his fingers, gesturing for them to stand close. "There's a cottage through those bushes. This looks to have been a wild garden at some point, and now it's just overgrown. It was probably a gardener's cottage or workhouse, but it looks abandoned."

"Empty?" Neil asked.

"Looks to be," Jasper answered. "Except I saw a rogue standing guard on what is probably the path to Wight House. He had a rifle."

"Why would an armed man guard an empty cottage?" Neil asked.

"I wondered that myself."

Both men looked at Ewan.

"Shall we go in and find out what he's guarding?" Neil asked.

"You think she's in there?" Ewan asked.

Jasper shrugged. "Only one way to find out."

"Then we take it." Ewan looked at Neil. "What's the plan?"

❧

Inside the dark closet, Lorrie had no idea how much time had passed. She knew night approached, but she intended to wait until it settled in. Even when she'd finally loosened the last plank enough to squeeze her body through, she hadn't done so. She didn't want to go until she had the cover of darkness to shield her.

She'd whispered this plan to Welly, who had yawned without much interest. Lorrie had taken the opportunity to close her eyes and sleep. She'd slept perhaps thirty minutes when she sat, startling the puppy awake.

"Welly!" she whispered. "What if waiting is a mistake?"

Welly cocked his brown and white face and his soft brown ears lifted.

"We can't wait," she told the dog. "I'm assuming they intend to keep me here several more days, but why would they do that? The longer they have me, the more chance something goes wrong. If this is a ransom attempt"—and she was more and more certain that's exactly what the abduction had been—"we might be out of time."

Which meant she would have to make her escape now before true dark set in, because if her abductors intended to move her, that's when they would do so.

Lorrie pushed one of the loose planks forward and peered out.

"Gah!" she hissed. "It's only dusk." Her white night-clothes would shine like snow under moonlight in the waning light. If she managed to make it to the woods, she'd cover herself with leaves and mud to dull the white.

Lorrie eased the plank back into place and took a deep breath. Ten minutes. She'd wait ten more minutes. That should lengthen the shadows and turn the pewter-gray light into more of a charcoal.

Her hands shook as she began to count slowly and evenly to sixty. She'd do this ten times, and then she would gather Welly in her arms and run.

❧

"That's it," Neil said, glancing at Jasper, then Ewan. "Any questions?"

"What the hell kind of plan is that?" Jasper asked.

Neil frowned at him. "If we were at war right now, I'd have you sent to the stocks for that."

"That's why I never said it when you were my commanding officer. God knows I wanted to plenty of times."

Neil looked at Ewan. "Any questions?"

Ewan had the same question Jasper expressed. But Neil had come with him as a favor, and he didn't want to incur his friend's wrath. "Go over it again."

Neil sighed. "Jasper and I approach the building, one from the left and one from the right. We move quietly and come from far enough back that we incapacitate any guards on either flank. Jasper takes the left flank. We know there's a guard there, and he's seen him and can anticipate his location."

"Thanks," Jasper muttered.

"Once Jasper and I reach the cottage, we flank the door. If all goes well, we've been quiet enough not to alert those inside. Then you come out of cover—that's the bushes Jasper described in front of the place—and we knock on the door. When it's opened, you pound the man who opens it. Throw him aside and pound the next one. We'll cover your back and come in behind."

"And if the rogues inside *are* alerted to our presence?" Jasper asked.

"Then Ewan runs out early and starts beating the hell out of anyone in his way. Ewan and I take care of the men outside while you go in and find the lady."

"She doesn't know him," Ewan pointed out.

"She'll only be frightened for a moment, and once she sees you, she'll be relieved," Neil said.

"What if she won't leave with me?" Jasper asked.

"She's little more than a girl," Neil said by way of answer.

"You don't know her," Ewan remarked. "She's not…" What was the word? "Biddable."

Neil sighed and muttered something about chits. "Take her dog. She'll go where it goes. Get her to Ewan and he can carry her as far away as possible. We meet back at the inn in the village. We guard her tonight and take her back home at first light."

"A lot of variables in this plan," Jasper said.

"Then think on your feet." He looked at Ewan. "Don't kill anyone. This isn't France. If we can, Jasper and I will restrain the men so the constable can collect them in the morning."

"Don't let them get away," Ewan warned. Like Jasper, he worried too much about how Neil's plan could go wrong. But it was better than any he might have devised. Neil moved in front of Jasper and Ewan, taking the lead. It felt natural to follow Neil this way. Ewan found it actually calmed him. Neil's plans weren't always successful, but he'd managed to keep twelve of thirty men alive through suicide missions Ewan did not care to remember. That was enough for Ewan.

"Put on your dancing shoes, lads," Neil murmured almost by rote.

"Time to dance with the devil," Jasper answered.

The three started forward. As they neared the cottage, Neil motioned for Jasper and Ewan to get down. Being taller than the other two, Ewan caught a glimpse of the building before lowering to his knees. It looked as Jasper had described—old and in disrepair. No signs of smoke or lamplight that would indicate habitation.

The three crept forward until Ewan was in position.

"Jasper." Neil pointed to the left, then to himself and to the right. He held up five fingers, intending to count down, but he'd lowered only one finger before Jasper started in his direction.

Neil scowled. He hated when his plans weren't followed exactly. Jasper, on the other hand, liked nothing better than riling Neil by going his own way.

Or leading the men in circles, as Ewan was pretty

certain the incident near Lisbon had been intentional. The troop had lost two men in the mission just before, and no one—except Neil, it seemed—was eager to engage in the next suicidal foray.

Ewan peered through the bushes as Neil moved away. He knew the time between now and when Neil or Jasper made the first strike would seem like an eternity. His heart thudded with familiar excitement and a new sensation he recognized as fear. It wasn't like the fear he'd had in the midst of battles—the fear that a cannonball would blow his leg off or smash his skull flat like the bodies of the men whose remains littered the ground.

This fear wasn't for him. It was for Lorraine. If he died fighting for her, so be it. But if she was killed and he survived, he did not know how he could go on.

And what the hell was that feeling? Was this love? He would have died for any of the men in Draven's troop, and he'd mourned them when almost twenty of them had been killed. But he'd gone on. There had never been a question of wanting to live. But without Lady Lorraine in his life, Ewan couldn't see the point.

Something on the left side of the cottage, near where Jasper would emerge, moved. Ewan drew his shoulders down and tried to find a better view. Had Jasper already taken the guard?

Part of the wall of the cottage seemed to push out, and then a small ball of fur Ewan recognized dropped to the ground, followed by long legs clad in white.

Ewan wanted to scream at Lorraine to go back. Not now! Of all the times to make an escape attempt. Why should he be surprised she'd chosen now?

"Hey!" the guard Jasper had mentioned yelled.

Lady Lorraine tumbled out of the wall of the cottage, looking right, then left. And stumbling as though disoriented. The guard on her left started for her, and to Ewan's horror, she ran toward him. Any sane person would have run the other way. Neil's plans were shot to hell now. Without waiting for Neil and Jasper to circle around, Ewan jumped out of the bushes and raced to intercept Lorraine.

∽

"Welly!" Lorrie yelled. "Come, Welly!"

But the little dog raced, yipping with all the ferocity of a child's toy, toward the guard charging them. Lorrie could see exactly what would happen. Welly would nip at the guard's heels and the guard would kick him away and hurt the little puppy. She couldn't leave Welly alone and hurt in the woods.

The silence of the late afternoon shattered as the guard yelled at her again, Welly barked, and more shouts rang out. Lorrie didn't bother to look behind her. If the men in the house were after her, she'd rather not know how quickly she'd be apprehended.

"Welly!" she yelled again, but the little dog's fur bristled and his focus was centered on the guard who had almost reached them. Lorrie took two more steps, bent to retrieve Welly, and missed.

An arm came around her waist and lifted her off the ground and away from her puppy.

"No!" She fought her captor's hold, twisting and kicking violently. The man was like a marble statue. Her efforts were useless. She screamed one last warning to Welly, then watched in amazement as a man with dark hair falling over a face with one side horribly disfigured grabbed the guard by the back of the neck and threw him down. Welly seemed equally surprised, dancing and barking around the men as they struggled on the ground.

"Stop kicking," a voice said in her ear.

Lorrie froze. She knew that voice—that low stilted growl. She'd know it anywhere. Her Viking!

"Ewan!" She tried to crane her neck to see him, but at most she caught a glimpse of light hair. Behind him, shouts and the sound of muffled thuds punctuated the air. She couldn't see anything or do anything about the way he carried her into the woods and away from Welly. "Put me down."

"No."

"But Well—my dog. I can't leave him."

He swore under his breath, and that was his only response before he deposited her—none too gently—behind a row of shrubs. He took both of her shoulders and turned her so she could see his face. "Run."

"But—"

"I'll fetch the dog. You run." To emphasize his words, he pushed her away from him.

She stared into his blue eyes. "Promise? You won't leave Welly behind?"

Ewan nodded. Lorrie took two steps away, then three, then raced back to him. She threw her arms around him, hardly able to believe he was real.

"I knew you'd come," she said, squeezing his solid form with all her strength and the love flowing through her. "I knew you'd find me."

"Go." He pushed her away again, this time more gently. Lorrie ran.

Twenty

EWAN HADN'T EXPECTED THE EMBRACE. HE HADN'T expected the words she'd given him. She'd believed he would come for her. She had trusted in him. No one in his life, save the men of Draven's troop, had ever trusted in him or relied on him or believed he was capable of anything more than brute feats of strength.

His head felt strangely light as he turned and tromped through the overgrown garden. He almost wanted to smile.

In the midst of the clearing, Neil valiantly fought off three men who had surrounded him. On the left, Jasper dealt what looked to be a final blow to the guard he'd incapacitated. The dog—the goddamn dog—made whining noises, as if deprived of the pleasure of attacking the man himself. Neil needed his immediate assistance, and Ewan jumped into the fray, his back to Neil's.

"Just like old times," Neil said, throwing a punch.

Ewan ducked and jabbed. "Once again, I save your arse."

Neil laughed, but when the next punch landed,

Ewan lifted one of the abductors and tossed him into the man who had hit Neil. Both men went down, groaning softly. The third man, eyes wide, took a step back. Neil wiped sweat from his eyes, but Ewan wasn't even winded.

"Go ahead," he goaded the man, sticking his jaw out. But the abductor thought better of it and raced into the trees. Ewan started after him, but Neil grabbed his arm.

"We'll let the locals deal with him. Help me tie up these two."

"Three," Jasper said, hauling the guard over. "Not a bad bit of work."

But the woods were too quiet. The damn dog had stopped barking. He looked toward where Jasper and the guard had fought.

No fur ball.

"Where's the dog?"

Jasper gave him a skeptical look. "How the hell do I know?"

Ewan turned a circle, scanning the entire clearing and the side of the gardener's work shed for a bit of white and brown fur.

"I could use some help here," Neil said, knotting the rope he'd pulled from his pack. Jasper bent to help him secure the men who'd abducted Lady Lorraine.

"Where's the rum mort?" Jasper asked.

"I told her to run."

"Good. I'll track her, and we'll have her safe in no time."

"I have to find the dog."

Neil wiped his brow. "What dog?"

"*Her* dog. I promised I'd bring it back to her."

"Tell her we'll find it in the morning," Jasper said.
"No."

"It's a dog, Ewan. It will be fine outside for one
night." Neil tightened a knot on the ankles of one of
the men. "We have to find the lady, send the constable
this way, alert the magistrate, and I wouldn't mind a
drink and food."

Ewan continued searching the darkening garden for
the dog.

"It's a *dog*!" Neil said again.

"She does love that dog," one of the abductors
chimed in.

"Shut up." Jasper kicked his foot.

"I promised," Ewan said.

Neil held up both hands. "Fine. Let's find her and
take her to safety, then you search for the dog while
we deal with the law officers."

Ewan's gaze swept the area one last time before he
gave a reluctant nod. "Let's go."

❧

She couldn't run any further. Her side felt like it had a
knife plunged in it, and her feet stung from the sharp
rocks and twigs. She didn't see how her flimsy slippers were any better than bare feet, and she promised
herself the next time she took Welly out for his nightly
constitutional, she would wear boots.

Thick boots.

She leaned against a tree, lifted a foot, and rubbed
at the raw skin. It was too dark to see much, now that
night was falling, but she could feel the torn flesh.

She lowered it and reached for the other when a dark shape stepped out of the trees in front of her.

She screamed, but the sound was immediately cut off as a hand clamped over her mouth.

"Quiet," that voice she knew so well growled in her ear.

"Ewan," she said, or at least tried to say. He lifted his hand, and gestured to the man who'd stepped out of the foliage.

"Mr. Grantham." He gestured to another man she hadn't even seen beside him. "And Mr. Wraxall. Good friends of mine. You can trust them."

"You're the men who saved me," she said.

"The Protector saved you," the one Ewan had called Wraxall replied. "We just came along for the entertainment."

Lorrie looked at Ewan. "Where's Welly?"

He sighed, his face looking pained. "I don't know—"

She gasped. "He's lost? We have to look for him!" Her heart started thudding painfully in her chest again, and she tried not to imagine her poor puppy alone in the dark, scared and cold. "I'll look this way."

Before she could start searching, Ewan grabbed her arm. "I will find the dog. You go with Wraxall and Grantham. They'll take you to Edgware and find a room where you can rest."

She clutched his arm. The prospect of Ewan in the dark scared her as much as Welly, lost and alone. "No. I can't let you go alone."

Ewan gave her an impatient look. "Wraxall and Grantham have to find the law officers. Three of the four men who abducted you are tied up in the gardener's work shed. You aren't dressed for a walk through the woods. I'm the only one who can go."

As much as Lorrie worried about Welly, she couldn't allow Ewan to walk away. Anything might happen to him, and she needed him. She needed to wrap her arms around him and close her eyes and feel safe once more. She didn't know if she'd ever feel safe again, but she knew in Ewan's arms, she had a chance.

"Don't go," she whispered.

A man cleared his throat behind them. "Ewan, are you coming or not?"

Ewan's gaze flicked to the speaker and then back to her.

"Not." He removed her hand from his arm. "I promised I would bring you that dog." And he walked into the night.

❧

The inn Ewan's friends had found was clean and quiet. Lorrie had been pleasantly surprised to discover they had horses tethered nearby. They'd wrapped her in a blanket, helped her mount Ewan's horse, and taken her straight to the inn. Grantham had secured the best room, while Wraxall had hurried her in through a side door, the blanket pulled over her head like a cloak.

She'd wandered into the room, which was spartan but clean, feeling lost and disoriented. She had no luggage to unpack and put away in the bureau, no letters to write at the little table. The bed looked comfortable enough, but how could she sleep while

Ewan and Welly were both out wandering in the cold and the dark?

The dark-haired Mr. Wraxall cleared his throat. He had been kind, but he did not seem to know what to do with her. Not that she blamed him. She didn't know what to do with herself.

"I will order you supper and warm water. Is there anything else I can do for you at present?"

She shook her head. "No. You have done too much already. Thank you, Mr. Wraxall."

He inclined his head. "It was my pleasure, my lady. Grantham and I will pay a visit to the constable and the magistrate. I don't anticipate we shall be away more than an hour at most, but these things do take time. For your own protection, I ask that you stay in your room. I will check on you when I return."

"And Mr. Mostyn?" She clenched her fingers together. "Will he know where we are staying?"

"If he returns before we do"—his tone indicated he thought this unlikely—"he will have no trouble finding you. Ewan is not the dolt some people think him."

"He is no dolt at all," she said.

He gave her a small smile. "I see you know him better than most. You needn't worry, my lady. Nothing will happen to Mostyn."

"If it does, I have no one to blame but myself. I don't know why I insisted he go after Welly. I wasn't thinking straight. He shouldn't have listened to me."

"He would have gone after the dog even if you hadn't asked. He cares about you. Love has a strange effect on a man—or so I have heard."

Lorrie felt a lump rise in her throat. "Love? He hasn't

said he loves me. Not even when I…" She broke off, aware she had probably already said too much.

"Do you think he would go after anyone the way he did you?"

"It's his duty. My father—"

"The duke could hire an army if he wished. Ewan volunteered, and when he came to our club and asked Jasper and me to help, we said yes without hesitating."

"You are loyal friends," she said. "He is lucky to have you."

"We aren't so loyal that we want to traipse about in the countryside for two days. But any man who knows him can see Ewan is in love with you."

Lorrie stared at him. Too scared to believe it to be true. She was afraid to hope, afraid happiness might float within her reach and then be snatched away if Ewan's friends were wrong.

Wraxall inclined his head. "I have stayed too long. I beg you give me leave to see that the men who abducted you are taken into custody."

"Of course. I await your return, Mr. Wraxall."

He bowed and left her. Wraxall had very pretty manners to go with his pretty deep blue eyes. But she was thinking of eyes a lighter blue and a man not with raven black hair but cropped blond hair that gave him the appearance of a fierce Viking warrior.

Supper arrived and she ate as much as she could stomach. Her belly twisted with worry about Ewan and Welly. She asked the maid who brought the soap and warm water to leave the food. Ewan and his friends would be hungry. Surely one of them would appreciate the food, especially as it was nearly midnight and the cook would be in bed before long, if she wasn't already.

When the maid asked if she could lay out a clean change of clothing, Lorrie was forced to admit she hadn't anything but the clothes on her back.

"If you have an old dress you don't need anymore, I would be happy to pay for it."

"Oh, don't you worry, now," said the woman who was probably the same age as the duchess but looked ten years older. "I'll find you something, my lady. It might not be as fine as what you are used to, but it will be clean."

"Thank you." Lorrie lifted the clean towels from the chair where the maidservant had laid them. "And thank you for not asking too many questions. I know this is out of the ordinary."

"It's none of my affair, my lady. None at all." She left, walking briskly, no doubt in search of something that would fit Lorrie. Lorrie could only imagine what the woman must have thought. She had arrived in her nightclothes with two men as chaperones. Even if the maid was discreet, there was no way to keep some of the story from making its way to London. She would be quite the scandal, and depending on the way the gossipmongers spun the tale, she supposed she was ruined.

How ironic that now that she did not court scandal or ruination in order to marry Francis Mostyn, she had finally achieved it. No man but the most desperate for her fortune would have her now. And she would not have any of them. She wanted to marry for love. If she couldn't have Ewan, she wanted no one.

He found the fur ball. It was running about the gardens with its tongue lolling out of its mouth, investigating every blade of grass and leafy bush and marking his territory on all of it.

The dog must have thought the evening's drama a grand adventure. He hadn't realized he was lost, or he didn't care. And when Ewan tried to catch the little ball of fluff, he danced and ducked and darted out of Ewan's reach.

After thirty minutes of playing catch-me-if-you-can with the fuzzy demon, Ewan was hungry and thirsty. The dog probably was too. With a smile, Ewan retrieved a piece of cheese from his pack and offered the dog a small morsel. The dog snatched it and backed away. Ewan offered more and then more, slowly gaining the puppy's trust until the fur ball was close enough that he could grab it. It gave a surprised yip, but ceased struggling when Ewan fed it another piece of cheese.

Tucking the dog into his pack, he started back toward the village. He had no idea of the time, but he suspected it was close to morning. As he wasn't far from the gardener's work shed, he cut through the yard and noted Lorraine's abductors were no longer tied to the nearest tree. Hopefully that meant Neil and Jasper had been able to find the constable and see the men locked up for the foreseeable future.

It took him another hour or so to make his way back to the village. It wouldn't have taken quite that long if he hadn't made several wrong turns in the dark. Surprisingly, the puppy had fallen asleep in his pack, and the warm weight of him was calming against Ewan's side.

When he reached the village, a quick survey of the inns led him to the one he considered the fanciest. Jasper didn't care where he slept, but Neil was more particular, and he would never have brought a lady to a second-rate establishment. Ewan tried the door at The Queen's Inn, but it was locked and barred. He knocked and no one answered. He knocked again, louder this time, and heard a grumbling from inside. Expecting an irate innkeeper, Ewan blinked when Neil answered the door.

He yawned. "I wondered when you'd finally make an appearance."

"Did I keep you awake?" He gave Neil's sleep-tousled hair and half-lidded eyes a pointed look.

"No, but your lady is probably pacing a groove in the wood floors." Neil moved aside and Ewan entered the dark inn. In the public room, a lamp sat on one table and Jasper snored in a chair. Another chair beside it had probably been Neil's bed.

"Is Lady Lorraine hurt?"

Neil shook his head. "She seems fine to me. She just about burst into tears from worry about you. Said she shouldn't have asked you to go after the puppy. I told her you could take care of yourself." He glanced up at Ewan. "And that love makes men do strange things."

Ewan stilled in the act of removing his pack from his shoulder.

"Don't tell me you intend to deny it," Neil said. "Jasper and I can see it as plain as day. Rafe told everyone at the club a week ago, but we didn't believe it."

Ewan simply stared at him. What the hell had Draven's Survivors seen that Ewan himself hadn't? How could they know he was in love when he didn't even know himself?

"So?" Neil asked after the silence had gone on for some time. "Do you love her?"

"I don't know."

"What do you mean you don't know?" Jasper asked from his chair. Eyes still closed, he was obviously wide awake. "Hurry up and answer. I can't sleep with all this twitter."

Ewan spread his hands, trying to find the words he wanted. "How do you know?"

Neil gave him a horrified look. "How am I supposed to know?"

They both looked at Jasper, who had slung his legs over the chair and stood. "You're both idiots. This isn't that hard."

"So you know?" Neil asked, crossing his arms.

"I read," Jasper said. "Don't act so surprised. I've read novels, so I know the symptoms."

"The love symptoms?" Neil asked.

Ewan wished Wraxall would stubble it so Jasper could describe the signs.

"Right. When you're in love, you feel sick to your stomach."

"That's called the grippe," Neil said.

"Stubble it."

"What else?" Ewan asked. He did not feel sick to his stomach. He felt hungry, but then he was always hungry.

"Your heart beats faster when you see the lady. You think about her all the time when you're not together."

"This sounds like an awful affliction," Neil said.

"And you want to bed her. Desperately."

"I take it back," Neil said. "I've been in love several times."

Jasper ignored him. "Any of those seem familiar, Protector?"

"No." They all seemed familiar. He was starving because he hadn't been able to eat when he'd been worried about Lorraine and searching for her. He could always eat. He'd taken time out of a battle to eat during the war. His heart did thump harder and faster when he saw her. He thought about her all the time, usually about what he would do to her if he had her in bed. That was two symptoms in one.

"Where is she?" he asked.

"Best room," Neil told him. "Upstairs, left, all the way to the end."

Ewan started for the stairs.

"Do you need a chaperone?" Neil asked.

"Hell no."

❦

Ewan stood outside her door, feeling his heart thump. Hell, he hadn't even seen her yet. No nausea, but he wasn't as hungry as usual. If he'd lost his appetite, the situation must be worse than he'd thought. He raised a hand to knock on the door, then considered the time.

It was after two in the morning. She must be sleeping, and he didn't want to disturb her if she was resting. On the other hand, if she were tossing and turning with worry, he wanted to allay her fears.

He would not think about the sight of her tossing and turning in bed—her nightgown ruched up, her hair tousled around her rosy cheeks…

Ewan knocked quietly. He'd wait ten seconds and if—

The door opened, and Lorraine stood, wide-eyed and hopeful, on the other side. "You're back!" She reached for him, but Ewan grabbed her wrist and glanced behind him to ensure no other doors had opened.

She would wake the entire inn.

He quickly pulled her inside and closed the door behind him, locking it. He was glad he had not waited until morning to see her. She hadn't been sleeping. The bed was unrumpled and she wore an old green day dress that fit her a bit too snugly across her—and he had better look up at her face.

Her long straight hair fell about her shoulders and down her back, a few strands still damp. The room was full of a scent that reminded him of rain and flowers, and it clung to her as well.

"Thank God you are safe," she said, lowering her voice but not her enthusiasm. "I was so worried, and I knew if anything happened to you it would be all my fault for sending you after the silly dog."

Ewan frowned at her. Now the dog she had made him promise to fetch was silly?

She raised a hand. "Not that Welly doesn't mean everything to me, but I would rather only one of you lost and alone in the woods than both of you."

"I was not lost." He pulled the sleeping dog from his pack. "Or alone."

"Welly!"

Ewan gritted his teeth, fighting the urge to put a hand over her mouth. Did she want the entire inn to know he was in her chamber?

He handed the dog to her, and she cuddled it in her arms as though it were a baby. She buried her face in the dog's fur, and when she looked up at Ewan, tears shone in her eyes. "Thank you. You don't know how much this means to me."

Hell, if he'd known she would cry about it, he would have left the dog until morning.

She closed her eyes and rocked the dog. "How can I ever thank you?"

"No more crying."

She burst out laughing, and the dog gave a loud snort of disapproval at being disturbed. With a laugh, she gathered a blanket from the bed, placed it on the floor near the hearth, and settled the dog on it. Ewan shook his head. Leave it to her to take a perfectly good blanket and throw it on the floor.

The woman was daft, and if he kept thinking of her that way, perhaps he could forget the pain in his chest every time he looked at her. She gave the dog a last pat and stood, turning to face him.

He should go now. He'd forgotten to keep his eyes on her face, and they'd dipped to the low bodice of the dress. He'd seen her wear ball gowns cut even lower, had managed not to ogle the swells of her chest when she wore them, but that was before he'd touched the soft flesh of her breasts, kissed them with his lips. That was before he'd been alone with her in a bedchamber, before he'd thought she might be dead or injured, before he'd thought he'd never see her again.

She raised her head, her eyes a deep green in the firelight. He meant to take a step back, toward the door, but instead he took a step toward her.

"Ewan." The word came out on a strangled sob, and then she launched herself at him, running into his arms. He caught her, lifted her, buried his face in her sweet-smelling hair. She enveloped him—her arms about his neck and her legs about his waist. Her soft body, so warm and generous, pressed against him with a desperation he understood very well. Her hands pulled fervently at his hair, and he lifted his head, claiming her mouth.

He was home. He, who had never belonged, never had a place to call home, belonged here in her arms, his body pressed to hers. He slanted his mouth over hers, kissing her deeply and still unable to take his fill of her. He moved, stalking across the room until he pushed her against a wall. Now his hands were free to cup her face, pull back, and look into her eyes.

"Yes," she whispered, looking up at him.

He wasn't aware he'd asked a question.

She turned her head, her mouth grazing his palm, brushing kisses on the inside. "Yes," she said again. Her hands on his neck tugged, lowering his head so their lips could meet again in that frenzied dance of heat and lightning. "Yes," she said as her lips met his with a bruising need he knew well and could no longer keep in check.

"Yes," she said when his hands slid down, pushing

the dress off her shoulders, so his lips could plunder the skin there.

"Yes," she cried when he cupped her breasts, his thumbs circling the hard points of her nipples through the fabric.

"Oh yes," she moaned when a hand slid up her bare thigh to curve around her plump bottom.

The question of whether or not to take what she offered had been answered, but how to take it still remained. Ewan was no gentle lover. His lovemaking, if one could call it that, had always been rough and wild and a little savage, but he could hardly take a virgin up against a wall or shove her face down on the bed and lift her skirts.

If he was to be her first, he would have to do this right. Reluctantly, he slid his hand from the smooth skin of her rump and lowered her to the ground. She clung to him, her kisses fervent and distracting. She made him forget his good intentions.

For once he wished he'd listened to Rafe's talk of women more. Rafe would have known what to do, how to seduce and tease, how to be tender, how to ease her pain. He had no idea what to do. Perhaps if he—

Her hands slid from his hair to his coat, shoving it off his shoulders until it fell to the floor. He couldn't help but think of her garments falling to the floor. If he had her naked, he would forget all of the rubbish about gentleness, push her hands over her head, and thrust into her until she screamed his name in ecstasy.

He clenched his fists to ward off the image, and her hands slid down his back, leaving a hot trail of fire behind. And just as he steeled himself to that sweet torture, she pulled his tails from his trousers and ran her hands up the bare skin of his back.

He made a strangled sound, and she looked into his eyes, her own sparkling with mischief. "Yes," she whispered, sliding the linen shirt up and over his head. He allowed it, allowed her to strip him because he needed her hands on him. He didn't expect her to step back and give his chest a perusal worthy of a rake prowling a line of wallflowers. Her gaze slid from his shoulders to his pectoral muscles to his abdomen and then to the bulge in his trousers.

She licked her lips and took a shaky breath. "Oh yes," she murmured.

Ewan's control shattered. He took her wrists in one hand, pinned them to the wall above her head and ravished her mouth. She met him, kiss for kiss, thrust for thrust, nip for nip. He needed this, needed her with a desperation that terrified her. It wasn't just her body—though God knew he adored her lush body—it was the feeling he had when he held her. He didn't know what to call it. Didn't know what it was, but he felt warm inside. His chest ached, his lungs burned, his heart clenched almost painfully. And yet, there was nowhere else he wanted to be.

His hand slid to the bodice of the dress. He wanted to drown in the softness of her body, bury himself in the silky heat she offered. When he couldn't free her breasts, impatience reared a head and he tugged hard.

"No," she breathed.

He froze.

She looked up at him. "This isn't mine. Unlace it in back."

He released her hands, and she twisted around. He pressed her against the wall as his thick fingers fumbled with strings and tapes and tiny little clasps.

He thought he would never touch bare skin, would go mad with need for the feel of her, when the dress suddenly slid down, revealing a very thin chemise underneath.

And nothing else.

His breathing sped up as he realized he had no stays, no petticoats, no more layers to breach. One hand fisted around the waterfall of her hair, and he moved it away from her neck and the bare scoop of flesh at her back. He kissed her there, felt her shiver. His lips moved her to her spine, and he kissed each ridge of it until the thin fabric of her shift impeded his progress.

Her hands were splayed on the wall, her cheek turned toward him, but now she pushed away slightly, her hands going to her heart. Her back still to him, her eyes locked on his, she made a sharp movement, and the chemise went slack. She lowered her arms, and the fabric fell away. She stood before him, naked, skin burnished by the glow of the fire, an offering even a saint could not refuse.

God knew Ewan was no saint.

Twenty-one

THE COOL AIR BRUSHED HER SKIN, BUT EWAN'S GAZE was enough to heat her flesh. She could feel his eyes rake over her, making her skin tingle as he studied the hills and valleys of her back and buttocks like a general surveyed a battlefield. Lorrie wanted to be taken. She knew all the reasons she should not allow this, but now she also knew life was short. She was safe. She would return home to her father and mother, but everything might have ended so differently. She didn't want to look back on her life and know nothing but regret.

She did not want to look back on her life and wish she'd had one night with Ewan, with the man she loved. Because Lorrie knew she loved him. She'd thought she loved Francis, but that feeling had been paltry—nothing but infatuation with charm and good looks. Ewan had no carefully crafted charm, no boyish good looks, but he was true and honest and flawed. And she loved him. It was that simple. Lorrie loved him because of his flaws, not in spite of them. And fifty years from now, she would look back on this night and know that for one brief moment, she had loved and been loved in return.

He hadn't said he loved her, but Lorrie looked at him over her shoulder now and no words were necessary. He didn't need to say the words. She could see his feelings written on his face. She shivered at the predatory look in his eyes as he swept his gaze down her body. He wanted her as fervently as she wanted him.

He made a low sound, almost a growl in his throat, and then his hand was on her hip. His bare skin on hers, that place where no other man had ever touched, burned. He took her with both hands and pushed her against the wall again, the cool wood making her breasts pucker and long for the inferno of heat behind her.

His body pressed against hers, and his hands coiled in her hair, pushing it over her shoulders. His hot, wet mouth was on her neck, then her shoulder, then tracing every single vertebra down the column of her spine.

Her fingers splayed on the wall, and she dug her nails into the wood as his lips made slow progress down her back. Finally, he knelt behind her, his breath warm against the small of her back. His hands slid up and down her thighs, making her tremble with need as they crept closer to her center. His lips trailed down her bottom, kissing the curve as his hands slid up to part her legs.

She knew the pleasure he could give her now, and her body ached for it. With the gentlest pressure, she parted for him, moaning softly when his fingers tangled against her damp curls.

She knew this was wanton. She'd always imagined her deflowering would take place in a bed, in the dark, with her nightgown ruched to her waist. But this would be no hurried coupling in the shadows, and when his fingers stroked over her small, sensitive nub, she felt more vulnerable than she ever had.

"Ewan," she breathed.

He made a sound, like a low rumble of pleasure.

"Ewan, I…" She caught her breath as his fingers teased at her center, making her want to buck her hips. "I…love you."

"Yes," he said, the stubble of his jaw brushing against her rump.

That was the closest he had ever come to acknowledging his feelings for her, and her heart jumped at the same time her body convulsed. Her knees went weak, but Ewan braced her, his fingers plying her until he had wrung every last bit of pleasure from her.

This time had not been the violent climax she'd experienced in his chamber, but a long, sweet rise that left her brow damp and her body flushed.

Hands on her waist, he turned her around, pushing the back he had just claimed against the wall. His eyes seemed to drink her in as she struggled to catch her breath. One hand touched her hard nipple and she shuddered. The pink tip was sensitive, and the one finger he ran over it seemed to tug at a string inside her.

Heat flooded her body again, making her legs wobble. She put her hands on his chest, as much for support as for the pleasure of touching that hard, honed body. Then she leaned against him, rubbing her breasts over his chest, and had the satisfaction of hearing him inhale sharply. She took her time exploring his back and his chest, finally resting her hands on the fall of his trousers. They bulged with the force of his erection, with the proof of his desire for her. But when she tried to unfasten the fall, his hands caught hers.

"Not like this," he said, his voice even rougher than usual.

"Then how?" she asked. "Show me." She leaned back against the wall, expecting and hoping for another thorough inspection by his lips, but instead he swept her up in his arms. She laughed at the unexpected rush of dizziness as her feet left the floor and dangled over his arm. He walked to the bed, kissing her, then laying her down gently on top of the bedclothes. He knelt, his knee between her calves, and reached for his trousers. Then he hesitated, looking at her face uncertainly.

"What's wrong?" she asked, barely able to resist pulling him down on top of her. She wanted the feel of his body on top of hers, his hard muscles against her softness.

"Nothing. You are perfect."

She shook her head. "*You* are perfect. Look at you." She gestured to his chest. "You are like a marble statue in a museum. Touch me again. I'm cold."

He reached for her, then paused again.

Lorrie's heart caught. Dear God, please do not let him stop. She would die from needing his touch if he had changed his mind.

"Touch me, Ewan." She took his hand, placed it on her abdomen, then slid it up to the curve of her breast. His hand fisted. She shook her head. "Don't stop."

"I don't know how to go on."

Lorrie blinked. "Have you never—"

"I have, but…" He seemed to struggle for words, to search for the right words. "I never cared." He shook his head. "That sounds wrong."

Lorrie smiled, love for him rushing through her all over again. "I mean something to you," she said. "*This* means something." She gestured to him and then to herself.

He nodded.

"Show me what I mean to you."

"I don't want to hurt you."

She waved a hand. "You would never hurt me. And if there's some pain, it will be worth it to have you inside me."

He made a low groaning sound. "You make me lose control."

She smiled. "Good. Take off the rest of your clothes."

She thought he would take her then. His blue eyes flashed fire, and sharp arousal pierced her. But he seemed to rein his need in, determined to go slowly and cautiously. He put his hand on the fall of his trousers. "Don't be scared."

"I'm not a complete innocent," she said. "I *have* seen statues, you know."

He made a noncommittal sound, obviously unimpressed with her knowledge of male anatomy. And then he flicked the fall open, and he sprang free, and she understood why he'd cautioned her.

He was as large there as he was everywhere else.

He rose and removed the rest of his clothing, and though Lorrie wanted to enjoy the view of him entirely naked, she could not quite drag her gaze from his magnificent manhood. It jutted proudly from a thatch of blond hair between his legs, hair slightly darker than that on his head. His organ was thick and the skin darker than the rest of him, the tip slightly pink and slick.

She blew out a slow breath as he first knelt, then changed his mind and lay down beside her.

"You're scared." His body was inches from hers, but he didn't touch her. She wanted to roll into his warmth, but she couldn't quite find the courage to move.

"A little. You're larger than the statues."

"I'll dress."

She grabbed his shoulder before he could roll away. "No." She wrapped her arms around him, moving closer to him until her body was flush with his. His organ lay hard against her belly. The sensation was rather pleasant. "I want you, Ewan Mostyn. Just like this. There's nowhere I'd rather be, no one else I want to give myself to."

"One day you might regret—"

She put a finger over his lips. "One day you and I will laugh about this." She had to believe there was a future for them. Had to believe this night would not be the only night. She kissed him, giving herself over to hunger and need. He pulled her closer, his body fastened against hers, his knee parting her legs and sliding between them until he rubbed her at her core and she could not stop a small moan of pleasure.

His mouth turned hungry, and she went from taking to giving as he rolled on top of her, bracing his weight on his arms and pressing her legs wider. And then his hand replaced his knee and she writhed against the pressure building inside her. "Yes," she whispered. She put her arms around him and pulled him against her, closing her eyes to memorize the feel of his body on hers.

He groaned at the same time a finger slid inside her, and she clenched around him, pleasure already beginning to build. And then his finger was gone and something hotter and larger replaced it. Lorrie felt the first stirrings of a deeper need and she slid her legs up and around him.

"Yes," he said, his breath against her ear. And then he kissed her neck and her cheek and looked down at her, his gaze meeting hers. He kissed her gently, easing himself inside her. Lorrie wet her lips as her body stretched to accommodate him.

He kissed her lips softly, then looked back into her eyes. Heat flooded her where their bodies met, heat and need, but when she tried to move, he grasped her hips. "Not yet."

And then he moved again, filling her more, and she had to bite her lip at the first sting of pain. His brow creased as he watched her face, then he bent and kissed her lip, easing the tension there. Under her hands, his body felt like a tightly coiled spring, and she knew he was holding himself back for her. He was giving her time to adjust to the feel of him inside her, and the more time she had, the more the need built. She wanted to move against him, to push up and ease the ache of longing.

Seeming to sense her need, his hand stroked where their bodies joined, and when he skated over her tight bud, she gasped.

"Open for me. Yes," he said. He moved deeper inside her, stretching her more than she ever thought possible. How much more of him was there to take in? But just as worry threatened to overwhelm pleasure, his thumb circled her, and she cried out, her hips rising slightly. Pain lanced through her as she took more of him in, and stinging tears sprang to her eyes. But his lips took hers with a sweetness that cut through the pain, and then there was the pleasure again as he circled her slowly, so slowly.

"Ewan." She clutched at his back as the pleasure built, and the feel of him inside her, filling her, made that pleasure all the sweeter. And then he finally pressed against her center, and she broke apart, sobbing his name. He surged into her, and the pleasure sharpened and she was not sure where it ended and pain began. She cried out at the invasion, at the sting of penetration, then fisted her hands and gritted her teeth to hold in her cry.

"Sorry," he said. "So sorry." His voice was tight and sounded muffled through the haze of her pain.

"Does it hurt you too?" she asked, wiping away a tear that had escaped.

He shook his head.

"Oh." The pain had faded enough for her to gather her thoughts. "Then you are worried about hurting me?"

"Yes," he said through clenched teeth.

The sweet man. How could anyone ever think him a brute? He was a gentle giant. Unclenching her hands, she wrapped them around his bare back, pulling his chest against hers. "I love you, Ewan Mostyn."

He shifted to look down at her, and the movement made her grimace with pain.

"I have to say I don't know why anyone should want to couple like this. Are you certain we are doing it properly?"

He chuckled, a sound she had rarely heard from him. "It will be better for you next time."

Next time. Would there be a next time with him or was this all she would ever have with him? If this was all, she should try to make the most of it. "It's not so bad now," she said, and though she was still uncomfortable the pain was not unbearable any longer. "Are we through?"

"There's a bit more—"

"You mean that is not all of you?" she all but screeched.

He pressed his lips together, trying not to smile, she supposed. "I mean there is more to the act."

She drew back as much as she could. "What else is there?" She hadn't meant to sound wary, but she was not sure she wanted any more of this.

"I'll show you." His hands cupped her face, and he bent to kiss her. As their lips met, he moved inside her, gently thrusting deeper.

Lorrie inhaled sharply, but his hands stroked her cheeks and his lips kissed away the pain. He withdrew, and she was surprised that she missed the feel of him. And then he was inside her again, filling her, stretching her. She bit down on her lip, but the pain had faded to mere discomfort. He moved again, pushing deeply, and something inside her fluttered and wakened. She met his gaze, the blue of a moonstone, as he looked down at her. The next thrust pulsed inside her, and she could not quite stifle a moan. Ewan's brow went up.

"Better?"

"I see"—she caught her breath as he moved again—"how this might be"—if only the pain did not distract her—"pleasurable."

"Next time," he promised. "This time...I can't..."

She felt his hands tense on her cheeks, and he thrust again, this time hard enough to make her gasp. And then he threw back his head, the muscles of his neck straining, and let out a guttural groan. Poised above her as he was, his glorious body straining with pleasure, she thought he must be the most beautiful man ever to walk the earth. Instinctively, she closed her legs around him, pulled him tighter to her.

"I shouldn't." He panted. "I can't stop."

And with a roar, he thrust deeply, sending another spiral of pleasure through her.

⌦

Ewan lay beside her, cursing himself. He shouldn't have spilled his seed inside her. They weren't married. Her father was unlikely to give him permission to marry her, though Ewan could certainly force his hand.

The fact that Lady Lorraine might be carrying his child was an incentive for the duke to wed her quickly.

But would he wed her to Ewan? Certainly the man had other suitors in mind, men who would take her even though she might be ruined. Men who could overlook an indiscretion when faced with the lure of her dowry.

She made a small mewl of contentment and

snuggled closer to him. He'd pulled her into his arms, and she'd fallen instantly asleep. She must have been exhausted. Now she lay in his arms, her head on his chest, her breathing deep.

Ewan had always known Lorraine was not for him. But damn if he did not want her now with a fierceness he'd never before allowed himself to feel. As a child he had wanted toys or treats, and it had always seemed that the more he wanted something the less chance he had of receiving it. He'd learned to tamp down his wants. If he didn't desire, he wasn't disappointed.

His arms closed tightly around Lady Lorraine. He wanted her. He wanted her in his arms like this night after night. He wanted to give her the pleasure he hadn't been able to tonight, watch her come apart as he held her. How would he manage to stand by and watch her wed to another? To know another man put his hands on her, breached her tight walls, knew the sounds she made when she found release?

He'd kill the bastard.

Which left one option. He'd return her to London, then go abroad. Perhaps in Rome or Austria he would be far enough away to, if not forget her, put her out of his mind. He would find work. There were always kings and emperors looking for mercenaries to fight their battles. He could kill for profit, and imagine every man he slaughtered was Lady Lorraine's new husband.

In the meantime, he couldn't stay here tonight. They might be in Edgware, but that would not stop gossip from spreading if he were to be found in her bed in the morning. Ewan carefully extricated himself from Lorraine's arms and dressed. With a last look at her sleeping figure, he exited the room, closing the door behind him.

He'd expected the public rooms to be empty. It was still too early for any servants to be awake, but as he descended the stairs, he saw Neil's dark head bent over a cup. Without looking up, Neil said, "Join me." He pushed another cup to the place across from him.

Ewan glanced about for Jasper but the bounty hunter was not present.

"He's sleeping. No rooms available here, so he bedded down in the stable."

Ewan sat, lifted the cup, and sipped the ale. "You aren't tired?"

"Oh, I'm thoroughly done in, but someone had to make sure you weren't caught with the lady. I would have given you another half hour, then come up and dragged you out myself."

Ewan sipped the ale.

"Did you ruin her?" Neil asked.

"You knew what would happen when I went to her room."

Neil nodded. "I hoped you might exercise some restraint, but I imagine the lady was overcome with gratitude. She's in love with you."

Ewan nodded.

"You will marry her." It was not a question but an order. Wraxall's voice took on the same quality it had when they'd fought together and Neil had been his superior.

Ewan looked down at his ale.

"She was ruined before you…er, went upstairs, but at least we could all swear she was untouched. Those fiends were just after the blunt."

"Where are they?" Ewan looked up, his hand clenching the cup enough to bend the metal.

"Locked up in jail. Safe from you. The magistrate will take care of them. I imagine they'll be transported or worse, so don't get any ideas. At the moment, we have another problem—Lady Lorraine."

"Her father won't want me."

Neil waved a hand. "Doesn't seem to matter what the duke wants at this point. You've ruined her, and you will take responsibility."

Ewan nodded. He would. It was the honorable thing to do, though he could not claim to have much honor after his actions tonight. "What do I do?" he asked.

Neil frowned. "Go to His Grace and tell the truth... Well, omit a *few* details."

Ewan waved a hand. "I mean, when he says no."

Neil considered for a long moment. "Is the man that much of an arse?"

Ewan raised his brows.

"You think he'll marry her to one of those fops with an old title and not two farthings to rub together?" He studied Ewan. "That is what you anticipate. And what is your plan? Kill the groom?"

"Go abroad."

Neil slapped a hand on the table. "Run? *You?* You've never run from a fight." He held up a hand. "Don't tell me you can't win, because I've watched you overcome worse odds than this. You don't run, Protector. You fight for her."

"Why? To leg-shackle her to the muscle in a gambling hell?"

"Do you think that's all you are?"

Ewan shrugged.

"All you can be?"

Ewan raised a shoulder.

Neil stood and shook his head. "Then perhaps I was wrong. You don't deserve her."

❦

Charles ran to Susan's room, the letter crumpled in his hand. He did not knock. He merely opened the door and rushed inside. Susan's maid gave a little shriek as she pulled Susan's robe over her nude body.

Charles might have taken more time to admire the glimpse of naked flesh, but he was too happy. "Look." He held out the parchment he'd crumpled in his haste to show his wife.

"If you don't need anything more, Your Grace," the lady's maid began.

Susan waved a hand. "Thank you, Teasley."

As the maid exited the room, Susan took the paper from Charles's hand. He knew what she saw—

Your daughter is safe and unharmed and will be returned tomorrow.

Susan wobbled, and Charles caught her before her legs could give out. "She's safe," Susan said, tears filling her eyes. "He found her."

"Of course he did." Aware she wore nothing beneath the robe, Charles did not take her into his arms. He had exercised extreme control these past weeks, holding her when she wanted affection but asking no more of her than that. Now, he was not so certain he could keep his hands from stroking the bare skin beneath her robe.

She looked up at him. "She's ruined, you know. Even if we try to keep this a secret, word will get out."

"We can't force Mostyn to marry her. He didn't abduct her."

"Perhaps he will want to marry her. I do not think Lorrie would object," Susan said.

The tears in her eyes had cleared, and he could see her thoughts had moved to how they might handle this crisis. "And what of the list you made?"

She wrapped her arms around his neck, and Charles lost his breath for a moment from the shock.

"Perhaps I was wrong about the list. Perhaps title and pedigree are not the most important factors in choosing a mate."

Charles looked down at his wife, stroked her cheek. "You want her to marry for love."

"Don't you?"

"I want them both to marry for love. I won't make it easy for him."

"Good." Susan nodded her approval. "Your Grace," she whispered, pressing against him. "I have a secret."

He raised his brows.

"I married for love."

His heart felt so full he was not certain his chest could contain it. "I love you too, Susan."

"Then what are you waiting for?" She stepped back and dropped the robe to the floor. "Take me to bed."

The duke was never one to disobey a direct order from his duchess.

Twenty-two

LORRAINE HAD IMAGINED THE JOURNEY BACK TO London would be one of laughter and triumph. After all, she was free. She was safe. Ewan, the man she loved, had come for her, as she had known he would.

But silence hung over the coach the men had hired for the return journey. No one spoke. No one looked at her or at each other. Lorrie didn't expect the men to have much to say to her, but weren't they old friends? Had they had a falling out?

Ewan's silence was familiar to her, but she could not deny his refusal to look at her hurt. She did not regret giving him her virginity, but perhaps he regretted taking it? Had she talked too much during the act? Had she failed to please him? She'd woken alone, and when she'd come down after dressing, he'd only nodded at her. Did he think she would force him to marry her? That was the last thing she would do.

But why *didn't* he want her? She knew he loved her.

And if only they could speak of some of this! But they had no privacy, and Lorrie suspected that even if they had, she would have had to pry answers from

Ewan. All she could do was wait until they reached London and her father's house. Then she would see what Ewan did. Please let him declare his love and beg for her hand.

Please.

By afternoon, the coach rattled through Piccadilly, taking her back to Mayfair and home. The men had used old blankets they'd found under the seats to cover the windows so they would not be seen by those passing by. Mr. Wraxall had asked the coachman to take them to the back of the duke's town house, and Ewan had hurried her out of the coach and into the servants' quarters faster than a hare chased by a hound.

Once inside the house, Lorrie was immediately engulfed by servants, who rose from their chairs in the dining hall. One footman took Welly from her arms while Mrs. Davies embraced her. "Oh, my lady! You are home. You are safe!"

"Yes, Mrs. Davies. Thanks to Mr. Mostyn and his friends." She managed to extricate herself, and then Nell took hold of her.

"My lady! I feared I'd never see you again!"

Lorrie hugged her maid back. "I fear your days of dressing my hair are not yet at an end. No doubt it will behave as unruly as usual."

Nell wiped her eyes. "I don't mind a whit."

The sound of a man clearing his throat cut through the chatter, and Lorrie glanced over to see Bellweather in the doorway. "My lady, we are most thankful for your return, and it would be best if you went to your father and mother at once."

"Of course." Lorrie looked behind her, relieved

Ewan still stood in the dining hall, waiting for her. His face was stoic and unreadable, his blue eyes clear and steady. He nodded to her, as though urging her onward. Lorrie took a deep breath, lifted her borrowed skirts, and followed Bellweather.

As soon as she stepped into the drawing room, her mother, father, and two brothers rose and exclaimed all at once. Lorrie ran to her father and then her mother, while her two brothers patted her on the back and said, "We knew it wouldn't be so easy to be rid of you!"

Lorrie laughed and stood smiling as her mother held her at arm's length to look her over. "Are you hurt?"

"No. The men who abducted me were not kind, but they did not harm me. I do believe they simply wanted the ransom." She looked over her shoulder at Ewan. He stood against a wall, a gentle giant who looked as though he would have preferred to be anywhere else. "Mr. Mostyn and his friends from Lieutenant Colonel Draven's troop saved me. A Mr. Wraxall and a Mr. Grantham, I believe."

Ewan nodded.

"They have our thanks," the duke said.

"They must come to dinner," the duchess added. "We wish to thank them personally."

"And we will make certain you are rewarded as well, sir." The duke moved forward to shake Ewan's hand.

Ewan offered his hand but did not smile. "I don't want your blunt."

The duke clapped Ewan on the shoulder. "Then another gift. We will discuss it later."

Ewan nodded. "I'd like to meet with you in private."

The duke furrowed a brow. "Of course. The library in an hour."

Lorrie moved toward the two men. "I'd like to be present as well."

"No," the men said in unison.

Lorrie huffed. "I assume this meeting has something to do with me. I have a right to be present!"

"Now, my dear," the duchess said, moving forward. As petite as she was, she possessed a tone that brooked no argument. She took Lorrie's arm and led her from the drawing room. "You need to rest. Let the men have their little talk. Nell!" She motioned to the maid, who stood waiting outside the drawing room. "Have the footmen fetch water so Lady Lorraine might bathe. Then you must put her straight to bed."

"Yes, Your Grace." Nell bobbed and rushed to do the duchess's bidding.

The duchess led Lorrie away and toward her room. As they walked, she said, under her breath, "We have managed to keep your abduction quiet, but God knows as loyal as our servants are, someone will talk. They always do."

"And I was in the presence of men who are not relations, unchaperoned for several days," Lorrie said.

Her mother gave her a penetrating look. "Fortunately, those men did not hurt you, but that will not quell the scandal. It does not help that you are infatuated with that soldier."

Lorrie gasped, tripping over her feet on the landing leading to her bedchamber.

The duchess caught her elbow. "Did you think I didn't know? Your face has always been an open book. The men who abducted you may not have touched you, but he has."

Lorrie's face flushed scarlet. Her mother held up a hand. "Don't bother replying. You will only stammer or babble on. This is not the situation I wanted for you, but then you have never done what anyone wanted. We will marry you with haste, and please do not dare suggest Francis Mostyn."

"I would never marry him!"

"Or his cousin."

"But, Mama!"

The duchess glided to the closed door of Lorrie's bedchamber and opened it. "I have a short list, Lorrie. Very short. You will marry one of those men or you will expose us all to scandal and ridicule. Is that what you want? To see your brothers and your father humiliated? To watch as they are shot on the dueling field because they are forced to defend your honor?"

"Dueling is illegal."

Her mother sighed. "Lorrie, you are no longer a child. Cease behaving like one."

"Then cease treating me like one! I shall marry whom I like."

"Not with my blessing or that of your father. Think about that, Lorrie. And while you do, consider your future. Do you really wish to be saddled with a man who spends his nights brawling with drunkards outside a gambling hell? I thought I raised you for better than that."

"There's more to him than that," Lorrie insisted.

"I know. He also debauches young girls." And with that, her mother walked away.

Lorrie stared after her, then, sensing a movement,

spotted Nell stepping out of the shadows. "I don't mean to interrupt, my lady."

"You heard?" Lorrie asked, moving into her room. Nell followed.

"Yes. I'm sorry. I could not help it."

"And do you not think my mother the most hypocritical woman who ever walked the earth? How many lovers has she had? Three? Four?"

Nell busied herself turning down the bedclothes, as though she actually expected Lorrie to sleep. "I don't know anything about that, my lady."

"Of course you do. Everyone does. And now she thinks to lecture me on morality."

"She only wants what's best for you, my lady. May I?"

Lorrie nodded, and Nell began to unfasten the borrowed dress.

"She wants what is best for her. I love Ewan!"

"Have you told her that? Have you told His Grace?"

Lorrie bit her lip.

"Ask yourself, my lady, is love enough?"

Lorrie closed her eyes, weariness suddenly pounding down on her. "I don't know, Nell. But I have to believe it will be."

❧

Ewan entered the duke's library, keenly aware that while the dark paneled room with its shelves and shelves of books had not changed since he had first stepped into it, he had changed a great deal.

The duke looked up from his desk, a smile on his face. "Mr. Mostyn, no doubt you will feel better after a bath and a change of clothing."

Ewan nodded.

The duke gestured to his desk, littered with papers Ewan could never hope to read. "I have here details on several of my properties in the north of England. None of them are more than modestly successful, but I think with a man like you managing them, they would be bettered. In exchange for your service to my family, I'd like to gift you with one of them."

He continued speaking, but Ewan could not hear over the rushing in his ears. His own property. His own house and land. Tenants and a living. He had never hoped for so much.

And yet, he knew it would never be enough.

"Thank you, but no," Ewan said, interrupting the duke.

Ridlington scowled. "May I ask why you dismiss my offer without even hearing all of the details?"

"Because I can't be bought."

"I beg your pardon!" Ridlington stood. "I resent that accusation."

"You want to give me a property so I will go away and leave Lady Lorraine to your designs."

"I didn't say that, but I would expect you to live on the land I gift you. And the lady in question is my daughter. I do not have designs on her."

"I wish to ask for her hand in marriage."

"Good God." The duke rubbed the back of his neck as though attempting to unknot it. "The duchess warned me this would happen."

"Then you will have prepared an answer. Before you give it, let me be frank with you."

The duke raised his brows and gave Ewan a steely look. "Go on."

"It gives me no pleasure to confess that my actions toward your daughter have not been wholly honorable."

"I see." The duke went rigid, though his expression showed no surprise.

"We were alone at an inn, and I...took advantage of the situation. I take full responsibility. And now I wish to do the right thing and marry her."

"No," the duke said.

The single word was like a pistol shot booming through the room. Ewan could only stare at the duke.

"Take the land and go. You will not have my daughter."

Rage began to build inside Ewan, but he tamped it down with a fierceness borne out of long practice. "She is ruined, Your Grace. She may be carrying my child."

"The child, if there is one, will not be a bastard. She will be married posthaste." The duke sat back at his desk, evidently dismissing Ewan.

"But not to me."

"Not to you, sir. She is the daughter of a duke, the granddaughter of a duke, and a distant relation to the King. She will marry a man whose rank and position are equal to hers."

"A man who needs her dowry."

The duke looked up sharply. "That is not your concern. Now, I suggest you accept my offer of land before I withdraw it."

"No," Ewan said. "Good day, Your Grace."

The duke rose. "You are no longer welcome in this house, Mostyn."

Ewan stalked toward the door.

"Do not come back, sir."

Ewan opened the door and slammed it shut behind him. He barreled through the vestibule, his peripheral vision colored with red. He didn't see Lorraine until it was almost too late. He had to catch her shoulder else he would have knocked her over.

"I heard," she said breathlessly once she'd regained her balance. "I'm sorry, but I eavesdropped outside the library."

Of course she had. He should have expected it.

"What are we to do?" she asked, looking up at him with those green eyes that were almost too pretty to be real. She looked to him to save her, and he could not.

"I'm leaving."

"And will you take me?" she asked.

He wanted to scoop her up and carry her away. He wanted to hold her against him and kiss her until she clung to him and begged for more. He could do it too. He could carry her out of her father's house. No one could stop him. God help them if they tried, but once outside, where would he take her? To Langley's? Were they to live at a gaming hell? What kind of life would that be for her?

"No," he said. "Goodbye."

Lorrie gaped at him. "That's it?" She caught his arm, and though she was not strong enough to stall him, he paused. "That is all you have to say to me?"

"What do you want me to say?"

She shook his arm, her eyes pleading. "I don't know! I love you? I want to marry you? Please come with me?"

Ewan blew out a breath. "Fairy tales."

"They don't have to be."

"I'm no prince, my lady. I'm a former soldier and an illiterate brute. You deserve better than me."

"I don't want better than you!"

"*I* want better for you." He lifted her hand from his sleeve and bent until he could look directly into her eyes. "Goodbye."

It took great effort, but he managed to lift his leaden feet and make slow, plodding progress toward the door. The butler opened the door with a sniff, his nose in the air. Ewan stepped forward, leaving the house, but not before he heard a muffled sob and the sound of slippered feet running away.

Twenty-three

SHE THREW HERSELF ON THE BED, SOBBING UNTIL NO more tears remained. Sobbing until her head ached, her eyes stung from the tears, and her pillow was damp. When Nell came, Lorrie ordered her away. She ignored her mother's pleas for her to come to dinner, and she threw a book at the door when her father dared knock.

Welly she allowed to comfort her. The puppy licked her face and whimpered quietly before lying next to her and watching her with large brown eyes.

"He doesn't deserve me, you know," she told the dog, stroking his soft brown ears. "If he won't fight for me, he's not worth these tears."

Welly whined and pushed his nose into Lorrie's hand.

"I should forget him." She laid her cheek on the coverlet and closed her eyes. A moment later they popped open again. "No. I should give him a piece of my mind." She sat, and Welly bounced up too, his tail wagging. "He thinks he will just walk away? I won't make it so easy." She stood and bent to retrieve

her half boots. Shoving them on, she ran to her dressing room to pull a cloak over the simple day dress in
white with pink roses at the hem Nell had dressed her
in after her bath. A glance in the mirror told her she
looked a fright. Her hair was half pinned up and half
falling down, and her nose was red, her eyes swollen.
She didn't care. If she was to play the part of the
shrew, she might as well look like one.

She flung open the curtains of her window and
blinked at the tree outside. "Wretched man," she
muttered, remembering that he'd had it trimmed to
prevent her from sneaking out. She would have to
take the servants' stairs. They were busy serving the
family dinner, so she need only worry about the valets
and maids. If she was lucky, they would be occupied
ironing clothing for the morrow or repairing hems or
buttons that had come loose.

With a last pat for Welly, Lorrie crept out of her
room, down the stairs, and out into the night.

The hackney moved faster than she had anticipated,
and she arrived at the address on St. James's Street
before she had an adequate speech prepared. She'd
never been on St. James's at night, and she could not
help but gawk at the young men prowling about and
calling to the women on the street, who called right
back to them.

She pulled her hood close about her face and
hopped down when the driver opened the door.
"Here you are, miss. Are you certain this is where you
want to go?"

She pressed a few coins into his hand. "Yes, thank
you."

"Should I wait for you, miss?"

She shook her head. "No."

Taking a deep breath, she entered the club. A man almost as large as Ewan immediately stepped in front of her, blocking her way. Arms folded over his chest, he watched the men coming and going with narrowed eyes. Lorrie scooted around him, almost wishing he had tried to stop her. Stepping into the gambling hell was like entering another world.

Smoke from cheroots hovered in the air, making everything look hazy and murky. The candles from the chandeliers twinkled almost too brilliantly, illuminating the too-bright eyes of the men and the too-red cheeks of the women. A few turned to look at her as she entered, but she kept her gaze down. Laughter rose up around her, making her jump, and a man wobbled back, drink in hand, almost ramming into her. Lorrie skidded around him and headed for the stairs.

Another man, wider than he was tall, blocked her way. "This area is closed."

Lorrie hadn't expected to be stopped. She took a step back. "But I have to pass."

"No entry," the man said.

"I'm a friend of Mr. Mostyn," she said, pushing her hood back slightly so he might see her face. "Please."

The man's eyes widened, then narrowed. "Does your mother know you're here?"

Lorrie blinked. "Do you know my mother?"

"No, but if I did, she'd want me to send you back where you come from. Go home, little girl."

"I will. After I see Mr. Mostyn. Please."

The man gave her an exasperated look.

"*Please.*"

Blowing out a breath, the man glanced around. "Fine," he said, his voice low. "Go quickly before you cause us all more trouble than you're worth."

"Thank you!"

"Go!"

She hurried up the stairs, holding her skirts out of her way. Trying to keep her head down in the vain hope she wouldn't be seen, Lorrie hurried to Ewan's room. Oh, she had done it now. Her father would murder her for this outrageous behavior, and he'd have every right to do it too. She halted outside Ewan's door, took a moment to catch her breath, then rapped sharply on the thin wood.

No answer.

Lorrie rapped again. Oh Lord. What would she do if he were not here? She had not even considered that possibility. "Ewan!" she said, leaning close to the door. "Open the door."

No sound but the laughter of the people below and the rattle of dice.

"Ewan!" she said louder.

The door flung open, and Ewan stared down at her, his pale blue eyes shooting her looks laced with white-hot fire.

"Don't stand there." Lorrie looked over her shoulder. "Let me in." Not waiting for him to comply, she shouldered her way in, forcing him to take a step back. Once inside, she leaned on the door, closing it firmly.

The room was as bare as she remembered it, and Ewan was as starkly handsome as ever. His strong features—the sharp cheeks, the blunt nose, the wide eyes—were so familiar to her now that she almost did not fear the hot fury coming off him.

Almost.

Lorrie held up a hand. "Do not say anything." She shook her head. "Oh, never mind. You never say anything. But hear me out before you throw me out."

"Do I have a choice?"

She glared at him. "Now you choose to become loquacious? When *I* have something to say?"

He settled his hands on his hips, making the open V of his shirt part further and stretching the material across his chest. Looking past him, she noted his coat lay on the bed, as did a valise he seemed to be in the process of packing. "You *always* have something to say."

"Is that why you won't marry me?"

"No. I usually like hearing what you have to say."

Lorrie had to restrain herself from diving into his arms. The taut material of his shirt was making her just a little light-headed. She knew what his chest looked like under that shirt, and she needed to press her cheek to it, her lips, her teeth, once or twice or a thousand times more.

"Then why?"

"I told you already."

"Fine. Then I have come to tell you how ridiculous you are. How can you think you are not worthy of me? I've done nothing but been born to titled parents. I haven't earned a thing I've been given, whereas you are a hero and a self-made man."

He looked about the room. "I have not made much of myself."

"By whose standards? You had the courage to

thumb your nose at your father and all of Society. Can you not do it again? For me?" She pointed to the valise. "Don't run away."

"Yes."

Lorrie blinked. "Yes what?"

"If you would ever ask a question and wait for an answer, our conversations might be easier."

Lorrie caught her breath. "Are we to have more conversations then?"

He sighed. "And yet another question."

She held out both hands, forestalling him—though he was unlikely to speak again. "One question." She closed her eyes. This was the only question that mattered. "Do you love me?"

The silence seemed to drag on forever, and then she felt his warm hand take hers. She opened her eyes.

"Yes," he said softly.

Lorrie's heart hammered so hard she pitched forward. He caught her, and she pressed her cheek to his shirt, inhaling his clean scent. "Please do not go away."

"I must."

She clutched the linen beneath her cheek. "Why?"

"Because I cannot obtain a special license in London."

Lorrie stilled, then looked up and up until she met his gaze. "A special license."

He nodded.

"Then you *do* want to marry me? And you… Oh, wait. One question at a time. You *do* want to marry me?"

"Yes." His thumb stroked her cheek so lightly and so gently she felt the sting of tears.

"But you told me—"

"What I told you still stands. I'm not worthy of

you, but since you do not seem to agree, and since I took advantage of you in Edgware, I will do my duty and marry you."

Well, it wasn't romantic, but it was the best she could hope for from him. And he'd admitted he loved her. He loved her!

"I can't marry you and have you live here at Langley's."

"Oh, I don't mind! We can fix it up with some bright curtains and we'll put Welly's bed in that corner and—"

He put a finger over her lips. "I have another proposal. Draven has offered to assist me in a new venture. I will open a boxing club and give instruction in pugilism."

Lorrie's mouth dropped. She would never have thought of such an idea, but it really was the perfect role for him. She could see he thought so as well. His eyes were bright with excitement.

He nudged her chin to close her mouth, then covered her lips with his finger. "I told Draven no before because I am no businessman. But if you consent to marry me and if you will help me—"

"Of cour—"

He tapped her lips again. "If you will read contracts and legal notices and keep the books, then I will give it a go."

Lorrie nodded, and Ewan removed his finger. "I will do all of that and more, but on one condition."

He raised a brow.

"That is only my role temporarily. Because I know that you *will* read, Ewan. I'll teach you or we will find someone who knows how."

He took her hand, such love in his eyes, and she knew it was rare for others to show faith in him and hers meant all the more because of the death in his life.

"And I think Lieutenant Colonel Draven's idea is a marvelous one. You shall be on par with Gentleman Jackson in no time." She laced her hands around his neck and pulled his mouth to hers. "But even if you were a beggar, I would still love you." She kissed him lightly. "I love you no matter what, Ewan Mostyn."

He made a low sound in his throat, and she understood the sound was one of desire. His hands came around her waist, pulling her close so she fitted against him. This big, hard body would be hers. Ewan would be hers for the rest of their lives.

His mouth came down on hers, his kisses far harder than hers had been and that much more satisfying. She pressed harder against him, sliding her hands down his back and yanking his shirt out of his trousers, then pushing it up and up until he had to stop kissing her to drag it over his head.

He would have lowered his lips to hers again, but she took a step back. "I will never tire of looking at you," she said, trailing a hand down his chest and watching the muscled skin pebble with goose flesh.

"Nor I you."

She needed no further urging and untied her hat, then began to undo the fastenings of her pelisse. His gaze seemed riveted to her movements, but he said, quietly, "Perhaps we should wait until after the wedding."

Her hands stilled. He must think her a harlot to behave so. She glanced up at him. "If that is what you want…"

"Is it what you want?" he asked, voice thick.

"God no."

"Good."

And then she was in his arms again, his hands working on her clothes as deftly as his mouth teased the sensitive skin at her neck. By the time she wore only a chemise and stockings, she was breathing hard and her body felt as though it were on fire.

Ewan pulled her to the bed, swept the valise and the clothing off it with one gesture of his hand, then laid her down. Just as quickly, he tugged her up again and pulled the chemise from her.

Lorrie laughed when he tossed it carelessly behind him. She bent to untie her garters, but he took her hands. "Leave them."

Hands on her waist, he eased her into a sitting position on the bed and knelt between her legs, spreading them. Then he unfastened the fall of his trousers and that glorious male part of him sprang free. She had not imagined the size of him before. He was large and thickly veined and absolutely beautiful. She ran a hand over him, marveling at the smooth skin overlaying the hard iron of his erection.

He pushed his trousers over slim hips and tight thighs, then stood still while she explored his member. She ran her hand up and over it, sliding her hand around it, though it was almost too wide for her to close her fingers. The blond hair at its root was soft and springy, and she touched it, then delved lower to cup the sac hanging beneath.

He inhaled sharply, and she smiled up at him. "You like that." Determined to torture him more, she continued her exploring, but she had not gone far when his knee nudged her legs open farther and pressed against that intimate part of her. Now it was her turn to inhale sharply as he rocked gently against her, causing warmth to spiral into her belly.

Her hand moved faster on his rod, and he finally caught her wrist to still her. "You don't like it?" she asked.

"I won't last long if you continue." He gave her shoulder a slight push and she fell back on her elbows. He came down beside her, his mouth on hers, one hand on her belly, the other cupping her breast. His rough hands on the tight bud of her nipple sent shivers through her, and when the hand on her belly drifted down, sliding into the crease between her legs, she let out a low moan.

He continued to kiss her while his hand stroked between her legs, causing fire to race up her body as she strained for the pleasure she knew he could give her. One of his thick fingers entered her, and her hips bucked. He released her breast and cupped her cheek. She opened her eyes and found him looking down at her.

His expression was so tender, so loving her heart hitched. She loved him so much. And this—this exquisite pleasure between them—was the expression of that love. She had never loved anyone like she loved Ewan. There would never be another man for her.

He traced her cheek, holding her gaze while he slipped another finger inside her.

"*Oh yes*," she moaned. "Oh, but that feels good."

The heel of his hand pressed up, sliding over the

tight little bud there. Lorrie opened her legs wider and he nodded his approval. Then, with what seemed infinite patience, he slid his fingers in and out, brushed his hand or his thumb over her nub until she was gasping for breath. "Please. *Please*."

Nothing existed now but the two of them. Nothing and no one else mattered.

His gaze still hot on hers, he flicked his thumb over her once, then twice, and Lorrie felt the world shatter. Her entire body convulsed in pleasure, and yet she could not look away from his eyes. He was her anchor. If she dared break contact, she feared she might splinter from the spasms rocking her body.

Finally, *finally*, the room stopped spinning and the wracking pleasure ebbed. Ewan slid his fingers from her, and Lorrie could not stop a cry of loss.

"Shh," he said, moving to nudge her legs open even wider—as though she were not splayed wantonly enough. Then it was not his fingers but his large, hot member pressing against her entrance. Remembering the pain of their first mating, Lorrie clutched at the bedclothes.

~∞~

Ewan entered her slowly and by degrees. It was no easy task, as he wanted to drive into her and feel her slick walls close around him. But Ewan believed his patience would be well worth the effort. She had looked utterly beautiful when she'd climaxed a moment before. Her eyes had been so green, her cheeks so perfectly pink, her rose-tipped breasts straining upward to rub against his chest.

Now he could see fear of the pain from their first

joining in her eyes. He had penetrated her with no more than the tip of his member, allowing her time to adjust. But even as he tried to be patient, her sex clenched around him in anticipation.

Her body knew what she needed. Ewan prayed he did as well. He slid further into her tight sheath, and she clenched again. He groaned, his jaw flexing as he tightened it. Rocking against her gently, he watched as she loosed her hands of the white-knuckled grip on his coverlet. Her arms came up to caress his back. With a low growl, he pushed deeper inside her.

Now it was her turn to moan. Her hips rose to meet his, taking more of him than he'd been ready to give. "Lie still," he ordered.

"I can't," she said breathlessly. "You feel so good." Her hands kneaded his back, then slid down to grope his arse. His cock jumped, and she made a sound that almost had him losing all control.

Her hips rolled under him, and he did his best to hold her body still as he rocked inside her, giving her a little more of him, inch by inch. She shuddered beneath him, and one look at her flushed face told him she was close to climax again. God, how he wanted this woman in his bed—now, tomorrow, forever.

Her tongue darted out of her mouth to lick her kiss-swollen lips, and he could not stop himself from burying himself in her to the hilt. He closed his eyes, anger at his clumsiness warring with the pleasure of feeling her body close around his. Before he could open his eyes to beg her forgiveness, he heard her sigh and felt her hips rise to grind against him.

Little vixen.

He opened his eyes, pleasantly surprised to see her writhing not in pain but in search of more pleasure. He would give it to her, now and always. He slid out and then in again, her tight body closing around him as though it had been made for him. As he drove into her fully, she cried out in pleasure, rising to meet him. Ewan tried to move slowly, to maintain control, but the sounds she made and the way her hips pistoned against him drove him mad.

He had been afraid he would hurt her, but she was proving no delicate flower. She was taking as much as he was giving. He gave her more, thrusting hard—the way he liked it. Her breasts bounced with the movement and her fingers dug into his arse so hard it almost hurt.

"Yes," she said on a moan. "Like that."

Still holding himself back, he slid deeper than he had, angling up to press friction against her center. He knew the moment his efforts had succeeded. Her eyes widened and she rose up. He thought she might kiss him, but the vixen went for his shoulder, biting him hard before falling back and screaming loudly enough to alert the entire club to their activities.

Not that he cared. That bite was his undoing. He lost all sense of control, battering into her until he spilled his seed, hot and wet inside her. The orgasm seemed to go on and on and finally he realized it was not her shouts he should have worried about.

It was his own.

When they were both quiet, breathing heavy in each other's arms, Ewan buried his face against the sweet skin of her neck. She was more than his match, more than he could ever have hoped for.

And she deserved more than a wedding by special license.

Reluctantly, Ewan pulled away from her and sat. Her body, pink and slightly damp, beckoned him back, but he resisted. There would be time to take his fill of her after they wed, time to indulge in all the fantasies he'd dared not allow to cross his thoughts, time to take her hard and slow and so gently it left them both limp with pleasure.

"Get dressed," he said, rising.

Lorraine opened one eye. "I thought it was wonderful too."

Ewan suppressed a smile. He supposed he might also need time to develop sweet, romantic words to give her.

He pulled her up and dumped her chemise over her head. Pulling the fabric down until it covered her body, she uncovered her eyes. "Are you taking me home?"

"Yes."

"And if I don't wish to go?"

"I won't leave you here, and I plan to speak to your father."

He dragged on his trousers, well aware that her shocked silence would not last.

"I beg your pardon? Shouldn't you fetch the license first? Rather, why do we need to speak to him at all? He has already given his opinion, and I for one do not need to hear it again. Why would you speak to him?"

As usual, he did not know which question to answer first. "I will inform him," Ewan said, opting to answer her last question. "That I will marry you with or without his blessing. I'll give him a chance to see us wed properly."

She stared at him, her green eyes glittering like emeralds. Bloody hell, he hoped those were not tears making them so shiny. "You mean like in a church?"

He nodded.

"With banns and guests and attendants?"

Good God, he hadn't thought of all that, but he could not backtrack now.

"He will say no." She grabbed Ewan and hugged him. "But thank you for asking. You never do take the easy way, do you?"

Ewan supposed he didn't.

At least not intentionally, but to his surprise the duke not only agreed to see him when, after ensuring Lorraine returned safely to the house through the servants' stairs—he should have installed a permanent lock and key on those—Ewan darkened the duke's door. The butler returned from the duke's library and motioned Ewan to follow him.

Ewan was so surprised he almost wished he'd worn a cravat.

When the library door opened, the duke turned from the window, where he'd stood gazing into the small, struggling garden. He nodded at Ewan and looked back out the window. "This is by far the coldest spring I remember. Look." He pointed out the window. "The trees are still bare and the leaves brown. I have to wonder if we'll even have a summer or a single flower."

The butler closed the door behind him, and Ewan crossed his arms. He had never been one for meaningless chatter, and he had nothing to add to the topic of flowers or spring. "I want to marry your daughter."

The duke turned to face him. "I did not think you had come to discuss gardening. But I did hope you would not bring up a topic we have already put to rest." He put his hand on his desk and slid a folded paper toward Ewan. "This is your salary. Take it and we can conclude our business once and for all."

Ewan didn't even lower his gaze. "I want Lady Lorraine."

The duke's gaze remained on Ewan. "I am offering you payment for services rendered. That is all."

Ewan wanted to turn and go. He wanted to walk away, acquire the license, and ride hell for leather back to London to steal Lorraine away. But she wanted a wedding and banns and attendants.

He tried not to shudder.

"I do not need your blessing, but I would like it. The lady has already agreed. She wants announcements and guests and a church."

The duke raised a brow. "I can keep her from you."

Ewan didn't even bother giving a response. No one could keep Lorraine from him, and the duke must have known his words were empty threats.

"What do you want?" Ridlington finally asked. "Do you want a wedding with all the fanfare?"

Ewan gave him a stony stare. "I want her happiness. Nothing else matters."

The duke sighed. "So do I." He rounded the desk and slapped Ewan on the shoulder. "You don't know how pleased I am to see you and hear you say you will not give up."

Ewan narrowed his eyes. Was the duke feeling well? He did not smell of spirits.

"You are not the man I would have chosen for her, but you are the right man after all. You love her, and that makes all the difference." The duke stepped back. "You do love her, do you not?"

"Yes."

"Then love is what matters." He pointed to Ewan. "Do not let anyone tell you differently. I had to learn the hard way. Too much pride to fight for the woman I wanted and loved. I had to make sure you were smarter than I."

"I have your blessing?" Ewan asked, still uncertain.

"Yes."

The library door opened, and the Duchess of Ridlington entered, followed by Lorraine, who looked as surprised as Ewan.

"You have my blessing as well." The duchess left Lorraine at his side and crossed to stand beside her husband. Lorraine elbowed Ewan in the ribs when the duke took the duchess's hand in his.

"When would you like to have the wedding?" the duke asked.

"Tomorrow," Ewan said.

Lorraine gave him a look of exasperation. "You know it will be at least a month before all the banns may be called."

"And there is Lorrie's trousseau to think of," the duchess added.

"One month then," Ewan said. When the women looked as though they might protest he held up a hand. "No more."

"Lieutenant Colonel Draven has offered to assist Mr. Mostyn in opening a pugilism club. I believe he is eager to marry so I might be able to assist him," Lorraine explained.

"I believe that is one reason he is eager," the duke muttered. "A pugilism club is all well and good, but you needn't ask Draven for help. You will have Lorrie's dowry as well."

Lorraine gasped. "Really? Even though I am not marrying the man you chose?"

"We want your happiness, dear," the duchess said. "But we wanted to make sure this was not another passing fancy. If you love him—truly love him—so do we."

"Oh, Mama, I do! I really do."

"I see that." The duchess gave the duke a look that spoke more of love than any Ewan had ever seen. Then she tugged her husband's arm. "Let's give the two of them a few moments to discuss details." She wagged a finger at Ewan. "Just a few moments and just a discussion."

He bowed slightly.

When the door closed behind the duke and duchess, and Ewan and Lorraine were alone, Lorraine twirled into his arms. "I confess I am shocked at this reception. When I found my mother in my bedchamber, I thought she would thrash me. I cannot think what has come over the two of them." She looked into his eyes. "Do you think they've fallen in love again?"

"Probably."

She brought a hand up to his cheek and rested it lightly against the bristle. "Do you think we shall ever fall out of love?"

He took her hand and placed it on his heart. "Not so long as this is beating."

Lorraine's eyes widened. "So you *can* be romantic!"

"Only when it's what I truly feel." And before she could say more or her parents could return or the madness of wedding preparations could begin, he took her lips in a kiss designed to show her exactly how romantic he could be.

Twenty-four

NEIL COULD HAVE KILLED THE PROTECTOR. NOT ONLY did the bloody fool want to leg-shackle himself, he felt the need to drag Neil, Rafe, and Jasper into the fray as well. Why not make all the men of Draven's troop attendants and be done with it? His men had suffered through more dangerous missions, although all the weeping ladies in the church definitely ranked this task one of the top five most miserable.

Neil could see Stratford and Phineas grinning at him from the third pew. They obviously thought it amusing to see Neil and Jasper shifting uncomfortably while the vicar droned on. Rafe, for his part, stood beside Neil looking as cool as a stream in spring. But then Rafe was a master at dodging matrimony. He was probably not standing here imagining himself in Ewan's position.

Neil glanced at Ewan, who towered over his pretty bride, her small hand in his larger one. He couldn't see Ewan's face, but he could see Lady Lorraine's, and she was smiling so brightly he almost needed to shield his eyes.

Ewan had looked the same when he'd asked Neil to stand up for him. The Protector had been doubly pleased because not only would he wed the woman he loved, but he'd heard the Earl of Pembroke had thrown Francis out of Pembroke House and cut off his allowance. Neil might have had some part in making sure the earl knew of Francis Mostyn's latest transgressions.

The Protector's beaming smile caused Neil the moment of weakness that had led to his agony at present. He had not been able to refuse Ewan's request to serve as an attendant, even though he not only detested weddings, he detested pomp and ceremony. If Neil had been in Ewan's position, he would have said the vows in front of two or three witnesses and been done with it.

That would not have won Ewan much applause from his bride, and that was why Ewan had agreed to suffer through this ritual. Neil would not have left one of his men on the battlefield, and this wedding was tantamount to an offensive. Neil couldn't retreat now. God knew Ewan needed reinforcements to shore him up.

God also knew they could all be drinking at the Draven Club right now, enjoying peace and quiet and a lack of weeping, if Ewan hadn't fallen in love.

Poor man. He'd probably never have another moment's peace and quiet again. Lady Lorraine was pretty and amusing, but in one hour the chit said more than Ewan ever said in a year.

To each his own, as the saying went.

For Neil's part, he'd stick with peace and quiet. After surviving years of chaos and commotion on the battlefield, Neil relished what little peace he could carve out of life. It wasn't much: The nightmares still haunted him, as did the echoes of the men he had left behind—the ones he'd had no choice but to leave, the ones he had shoved a knife into, the ones whose blood he had felt warm on his hands as their lives drained away.

The people in the church erupted into cheers and clapping, and Neil started, his thoughts still anchored in a smoky battlefield where the mud would be stained red for years to come.

Beaumont's hand landed on his shoulder, warm and reassuring. "It's over," he said.

Neil didn't know if Rafe referred to the wedding or the memory of the battle. For Neil the war would never be over. Marriage, babies, a family—those tenets of normal life were for other men, men like Ewan.

And oh how, for one fleeting moment, Neil envied his friend.

Read on for a sneak peek at book 2
in Shana Galen's Survivors series

No Earls Allowed

Coming soon from Sourcebooks Casablanca

London, 1816

NEIL WOKE AND GULPED IN AIR. THE ACRID SMELL OF
cannon smoke burned his lungs, and the stench of
burning flesh assaulted his nostrils. His hands fisted in
the sheets on the bed, their softness reminding him he
was not lying on a battlefield beside his dead brother
but in his own bed in his own flat in London.

Without looking, he reached for the glass of gin on
the bedside table. There was always a glass of gin on
the bedside table. It wasn't a gentleman's drink, but
here, in the dark, alone with his demons, Neil didn't
want to be a gentleman. And so he bought gin for the
nights when the dreams of battle haunted him. And
when he drank the bitter brew, he tried to forget he
was the son of a marquess.

He sipped the gin and lit a lamp, taking solace in the
fact that his hands didn't shake. If he'd dreamed on, he
likely would have woken with trembling hands and a
scream echoing in his ears. For, as he'd lain beside his
dead brother on that hill in Portugal, the smoke of the

battlefield had coalesced around him, settling inside
him. Instead of stifling him, the smoke caught the
breeze and the flame of rage ignited within him. The
fire built until it seared and burned, and he'd not been
able to quench the heat until he rose and, with a roar,
stumbled after the French soldiers the dragoons hadn't
routed. Like a berserker, he'd cut every one of them
down, even as they raised hands in surrender, even as
they'd begged for quarter.

Neil had expected to be reprimanded for his behavior that day—behavior unbecoming a gentleman—but
Draven had pulled him aside and given him a promotion of sorts.

If one could call leading a suicide troop a promotion.

The flame of rage had long been extinguished, and
in its place laid a weight like a sodden mantle, bowing
his shoulders. Neil could not shed it, no matter how
hard he tried. Now he rose and pulled on trousers and
a linen shirt. He didn't bother to tuck in the shirt or
button it at the throat or sleeves. Instead, he padded to
the window and pushed the heavy curtains open. He
had a view of St. James's Street. He liked the sight of
carriages and men coming and going from gambling
hells or brothels. He liked the noise and the lights
spilling from the establishment. It drowned out the
sounds of battle that too easily plagued him in silence.

Neil stood and stared out the window for a long
time before shoving his feet into boots and shrugging
on a coat. His manservant would not arrive until later
in the morning, so Neil managed on his own with
the cravat.

He had no one to inform of his departure. He lived

alone, a necessity when one woke screaming five out of seven nights of the week. He took his walking stick as a precaution against drunkards, who might be stupid enough to accost him, and left for his club.

Twenty minutes later, Porter greeted him. "Mr. Wraxall," the older distinguished man said as he opened the door. "A pleasure to see you, sir."

Neil handed the master of the house his walking stick. "Don't you ever sleep, Porter?"

Porter raised his brows, silver to match his hair. "Don't you, sir?"

"Not unless I have to. I know it's half past three. Is anyone here?"

"Mr. Beaumont is asleep in the card room."

No doubt Rafe had retreated to the Draven Club to escape some woman. Neil might have laughed if he hadn't come to escape his own demons. Not that the club didn't have its ghosts. His gaze strayed to the shield hanging directly opposite the door where no one entering could miss it. It was a silver shield bisected by a thick, medieval sword with a pommel shaped like a fleur-de-lis. Under the grip, the cross-guard was ornamented with a skull. It would not have been particularly macabre except for the eighteen marks on the flanks and base. Each fleur-de-lis, nine on the dexter side and nine on the sinister side, stood for a member of the troop of Draven's men Neil had lost during the war. Neil often felt he carried the weight of the enormous shield on his back.

"Anyone else here?" he asked the master of the house.

"No, sir." Porter placed the walking stick in a stand,

his wooden leg thumping on the carpet. "Would you care for a drink or something to eat, sir?"

Neil wanted more gin, if only to settle his nerves, but he could have drunk himself into a stupor at his flat. He'd come here to affect civility. He'd come here because it was the closest thing to home he'd ever known. "Brandy would suit me, Porter."

Though Neil could have found it blindfolded, Porter led him up the winding staircase and into the dining room. The five round tables in the wood-paneled room were empty, their white linen tablecloths bright and clean, anticipating the next diner.

Neil chose a chair near the big hearth and settled back. The silence here didn't bother him. He could all but hear the echoes of his friends' voices—those who had survived—raised in song or laughter. He half expected to look to the side and see Ewan Mostyn, the brawny, muscled protector of the group, bent over a meal, or spot Rafe Beaumont leaning negligently against one of the walls under a sconce.

Neil never felt alone here.

Porter returned with the brandy on a silver salver. Neil had told the man a hundred times such gestures were unnecessary, but Porter believed in standards. Neil lifted the brandy, then frowned at the folded white paper that had been beneath it.

"I almost forgot, sir. This note came for you a few hours ago."

Neil lifted it and nodded to the silver-haired master of the house, who departed quite gracefully, considering he had but one leg. It didn't surprise Neil that correspondence meant for him had been sent here. He was here more than anywhere else, and anyone who knew him knew that. He broke the seal and opened the paper, recognizing the hand immediately. It was from the Marquess of Kensington. It said simply:

> *Call on me at the town house at your earliest convenience. I have need of you.*

> —Kensington

Acknowledgments

I'm so fortunate to have such a supportive group of friends and colleagues to shepherd this book toward publication. I already mentioned Sophie Jordan, who gave me the idea for this series at the RT convention in Dallas in 2015. We were sitting in our hotel room, and I told her I needed an idea for a new series, and she said, "Have you ever seen the movie *The Dirty Dozen*?" Honestly, I don't know how she thinks of these things, but as soon as she said *dozen*, I had that little spark of an idea I know will flame into something bigger.

Joanna Mackenzie and Danielle Egan-Miller fanned the flames by helping me brainstorm and by shaping the series idea into something more tangible and sophisticated. They are two of the most savvy, intelligent, and creative women I know. I'm so proud they represent me as my agents.

Deb Werksman, my editor at Sourcebooks, molded the manuscript further with her wonderful insights and suggestions. Ewan would not be the hero he is without her guidance.

My friends Tera Lynn Childs, Lily Blackwood, Nicole Flockton, Lark Howard, Sophie Jordan, and Mary Lindsey helped brainstorm titles, as they often do, for this book. Beth Sochacki, my awesome publicist, had so many wonderful ideas for the title of the book, the series, and of equal importance, presenting it to readers. Dawn Adams and I had several conversations about the cover, and I count myself lucky to work with the most talented cover artist in the industry.

My friends Susan Knight and Sarah Rosenbarker brainstormed heroes with me, and the Shananigans gave me much-needed encouragement and support.

My husband deserves special mention for doing his best to give me extra time to work when I need it and not complaining when I had to write instead of watching *The Walking Dead* with him.

Finally, thanks to Gayle Cochrane, who is a friend and my biggest supporter, and who is always ready with a fabulous idea or a word of encouragement.

About the Author

Shana Galen is a three-time RITA nominee and the bestselling author of passionate Regency romps, including the RT Reviewers' Choice award winner *The Making of a Gentleman*. *Kirkus Reviews* says of her books, "The road to happily ever after is intense, conflicted, suspenseful, and fun," and *RT Book Reviews* calls her books "lighthearted yet poignant, humorous yet touching." She taught English at the middle- and high-school level off and on for eleven years. Most of those years were spent working in Houston's inner city. Now she writes full time. She's happily married and has a daughter who is most definitely a romance heroine in the making.

Also by Shana Galen

SONS OF THE REVOLUTION

The Making of a Duchess

The Making of a Gentleman

The Rogue Pirate's Bride

LORD AND LADY SPY

Lord and Lady Spy

True Spies

The Spy Wore Blue (novella)

Love and Let Spy

JEWELS OF THE TON

When You Give a Duke a Diamond

If You Give a Rake a Ruby

Sapphires Are an Earl's Best Friend

COVENT GARDEN CUBS

Viscount of Vice (novella)

Earls Just Want to Have Fun

The Rogue You Know

I Kissed a Rogue